29/9/16

Glen Erik Hamilton is a Seattle native. His second Van Shaw novel, *Hard Cold Winter*, will be published in spring, 2016.

Further praise for *Past Crimes*:

'A debut novel from a gifted writer with a sure hand. As much fun to read as Lee Child's Jack Reacher.' J. A. Jance

'An exciting heir to the classic detective novel. A well-written modern rendition of the old-fashioned gritty noir.' *Kirkus*

'Hamilton is an author to watch.' *Booklist*

'Readers will be eager to see more of this tough, clever hero.' *Publishers Weekly* (starred review)

'Edgy and suspenseful.' *Crimespree Magazine*

'Glen Erik writes taut, hard-edged thrillers that I simply can't put down. Tight prose. Intriguing characters. Here is some fantastic storytelling you don't want to miss.' Steven James

'This is a great thriller. Glen Erik Hamilton can certainly write a story that hooks, and has created a cast of characters who, although decidedly dodgy, are human and strong. The Seattle setting is vividly portrayed, with the see⸻ ⸻ ⸻ it taking lead roles.' *R⸻*

Essex County Council

3013021176016 9

'[It] neatly bypasses the simpler label of 'thriller' and instead, through the strength of his characterisation and observation, is on a par with the very best of American contemporary fiction.' *Raven Crime Reads*

'The balance between a tight, gripping plot, with headlong narrative pace and plenty of surprise twists, and characters that are very much life-size, though highly original, is one of the most remarkable features of *Past Crimes*.' *Thriller Books Journal*

'*Past Crimes* is a blasting edge-of-the-seat ride that leaves readers breathless with excitement. Great stuff!' *Upcoming4.me*

———————————

also by Glen Erik Hamilton

HARD COLD WINTER

PAST CRIMES

GLEN ERIK HAMILTON

FABER & FABER

First published in the UK in 2015
by Faber & Faber Limited
Bloomsbury House
74–77 Great Russell Street
London WC1B 3DA
This paperback edition first published in 2016

First published in the United States in 2015
by William Morrow
an imprint of HarperCollins Publishers
195 Broadway, New York, NY 10007

Printed and bound by CPI Group (UK), Croydon CR0 4YY

All rights reserved
© Glen Erik Hamilton, 2015

The right of Glen Erik Hamilton to be identified as author of this work has been asserted
in accordance with Section 77 of the Copyright, Designs and Patents Act 1988

*This book is sold subject to the condition that it shall not, by way of trade or otherwise, be lent,
resold, hired out or otherwise circulated without the publisher's prior consent in any form of
binding or cover other than that in which it is published and without a similar condition
including this condition being imposed on the subsequent purchaser*

A CIP record for this book
is available from the British Library

ISBN 978–0–571–31459–1

FSC
www.fsc.org
MIX
Paper from
responsible sources
FSC® C101712

2 4 6 8 10 9 7 5 3 1

For Amy Leone
First, last, and all stations in between

PAST
CRIMES

CHAPTER ONE

WHEN I STEPPED OFF American Flight 9601 at Sea-Tac, I could hold the sum total of my personal possessions in my one good hand. Passport. Travel warrant. Cash and cards and my army tabs and ID, all held together with a large paper clip. My cell phone. A red rubber ball that the physical therapist at Landstuhl had given me.

And a single folded sheet of yellow notepaper. A letter from my grandfather.

> *Tar abhaile, más féidir leat.*
>
> —*Dono*

Irish Gaelic. My grandfather's English was just fine after forty years in the States. But he used the language of his childhood in County Antrim when he wanted to keep our conversations private. Which was most of the time.

Translated, the words written in the old man's bold cursive scrawl said:

Come home, if you can.

It was 0430. None of the rental-car agencies had customers waiting. I stepped up to the first counter, where a woman stood and stared blankly down at a computer screen.

"I want something with horsepower. Full-sized," I said.

"Are you a member of our Platinum Club?" She didn't lift her gaze from the screen.

I was not. I gave her my ID and driver's license and credit card. She glanced up to compare the photographs on the cards to my face and got her first look at me.

It woke her right up. Her eyes flickered to the thick, white scars that furrowed my left cheek and jawline, then up to the slimmer line that bisected my eyebrow on the same side.

I'd carried the facial scars for more than eight years, since my first rotation overseas. I was used to people's reactions. The marks on my face were nothing important, not like a lost limb or a blinded eye. But they were always the first things anyone noticed.

The rental agent was polite. Her welcoming expression slid quickly back into place.

"If . . . you'll just fill this out, please, Mr. Shaw." She passed a legal-size form across the counter and placed a pen beside it before turning her eyes away.

Come home, if you can.

Home had been anywhere the army had sent me, for the last decade. Fort Lewis, Fort Benning, Baghdad, and a dozen forward operating bases in Afghanistan. A few other side trips between rotations. Home wasn't the old house on Roy Street. Not anymore.

If Dono's letter had stopped at the comma, I would have tossed it in the trash and gone back to squeezing the cursed red rubber ball. My left hand felt strong enough. There had been two intricate surgeries to correct the recent damage to the muscles and tendons of my forearm, when I'd caught some random shrapnel a few weeks before. But the arm still ached half the time, and I had been going crazy after a month of desk duty, waiting for the doctors to clear me for a rotation back to my unit. When Dono's letter arrived, it gave me an excuse to apply for immediate leave.

Even so, I would have mentally told the old man to stick it, if it hadn't been for the last three words. *If you can.* That passed for "please" in my grandfather's way of talking. Made it an entreaty instead of a command.

If you can scared me a little, coming from that immovable son of a bitch.

The captain running the travel assignments at Landstuhl had told me that the next available flight left out of Frankfurt to New York in two hours. I didn't even pack a bag.

The rental agent took the completed form and started copying all the information into the computer. "How long will you need the car, Mr. Shaw?"

"Ten days," I said. "Maybe less."

She handed me the completed contracts and directed me to where I would take a shuttle out to the agency's garage. I reached to put the papers into the breast pocket of my ACUs before I remembered that I was wearing civilian clothes. Jeans and a T-shirt and a gray wool zip-front coat, all purchased the day before in Frankfurt while I was killing time before my first flight. Only my tan combat boots were regulation. I had considered taking the uniform with me, but it was threadbare after too many industrial washings. Instead I tore off the Velcroed-on Ranger Scroll and Third Battalion tabs and other insignia and left the jacket and trousers in storage.

I chose a new black Charger off the rental lot and made it roar up the ramp and onto Interstate 5. North, into Seattle.

Ten years had done more than just change a few freeway signs. There was a train now, a light-rail running parallel to the freeway. When I reached the southern tip of the city proper, I saw the football stadium, as shiny and colorful as a giant music box against the dark background of the skyline. It had been brand-new the last time I'd passed this spot on I-5, heading in the opposite direction to Fort Lewis and a new life.

Land and sky were turning different shades of black by the time I turned off the freeway. I drove over Capitol Hill, east toward the hesitant dawn.

Dono might be up before sunrise, waiting for me. My grandfather's schedule had always been unpredictable. Some nights he would be in a mood and stay at a bar until dawn, lost in his own thoughts. Usually he drank at the same bar he owned, the Morgen, but sometimes he picked a different watering hole. A few places knew enough to just leave the big man alone with the bottle and ask him to lock up when he left.

I parked the Charger in the first available space, halfway down the block from the house. Roy Street was steep, like every other street running east-west this side of the hill. Before I got out, I turned the wheel so that the tires were wedged against the curb on the steep grade. Habit.

I looked at my old neighborhood for the first time in over a decade. Unlike downtown, it didn't seem to have changed much. Two-story homes packed close together on small lots. Most of the cars were a few years old, but none of them showed signs of being permanent fixtures along the curb.

It was cold enough that the dew had turned to frost on the thicker lawns, and condensation formed on my lips and jaw as I walked up the hill. Damp leaves made the sidewalk slick.

I stopped at the top of the block to stare at my childhood home. The streetlamps around the house had always been weak, and their glow didn't encroach far onto Dono's property. No lights were on inside either. In the dimness, the old house loomed almost a full story above its nearest neighbors, on a lot half again as wide—a massive dark block that faced the cold and seemed to radiate it right back.

The foundation of the original house had been laid well over a century ago, when most of the eastern side of the big hill and the smaller slopes beyond had been pastureland. The years had been cruel to the house. By the time my grandfather came to own it—"bought" might not be the right word—the roof and walls sagged against the tough skeleton of the place. Dono had spent years razing and rebuilding what needed doing. The patchwork quilt of rooms he made of the once-grand home would not have pleased either a building inspector or a historical society, but since neither of those would ever be allowed inside, what was the worry? It suited Dono and his young daughter, my mother, well enough.

At least until she left him, just before I was born.

I walked up the long set of wide stone steps to the porch. The porch wrapped around the house, with the front door around the side, so that the street saw only windows with their lace curtains. After ten years away, I was ready to knock on the wide oak door and to see Donovan Shaw. I was his namesake.

The porch light was out.

The door was wide open.

My scalp prickled. The inside of the house was completely dark— and silent. The doorway made a gaping ebony rectangle in the middle of the dark blue siding.

There were no signs of forced entry. And your average B&E man couldn't beat the heavy dead bolt and strike plate that I could just make out on the door, much less whatever custom alarm system my grandfather surely had these days.

I could have beaten the lock. But then I had been Dono's protégé.

A sound from deep inside the house. A soft thump, like an old refrigerator kicking on. Or maybe a footstep.

"Dono?" I said.

No answer.

I edged inside. There was no sign anything was wrong, other than the door.

Still. Bad news and blasphemy, the old man would have said.

Three more steps until I could see into the front room. The sky outside the broad picture window had turned the color of a pale rose.

Just enough light for me to clearly see the body.

He was lying facedown, feet toward me, tall and rangy and dressed in dark brown trousers and a thick blue chambray shirt. The hair was more gray than black, different from the last time I'd seen it.

Dono.

I ran to him, and as I knelt down, there was a crash from the rear of the house. The kitchen door, slamming open. Then footsteps, running off the back porch.

But I couldn't chase after. There was blood on Dono's head. A lot of blood.

CHAPTER TWO

I HAD THE HORRIBLE FEELING of coming full circle. My last sight of Dono before I'd left Seattle, when I was eighteen, had been in the kitchen of this same house. He'd been lying on the floor then, too. His face dark with rage. I'd been aiming a gun at his heart.

But any blood Dono and I had spilled back then could be measured in drops. Not like this.

The running footsteps outside were gone.

Dono was still warm. I leaned down and put my ear near his cheek. One breath. Two. Light as a spiderweb.

"Dono!" I shouted in his face. "It's Van." No response. Not even a twitch behind the closed eyelid.

More blood was pooling on the floor under his head. My knees slipped in the wet. Then I caught the smell of singed hair and burned powder. Gunshot.

I tore off my jacket and my T-shirt, wadding up the shirt and pressing it against the oozing hole behind his left ear. His hair was sticky.

"Dono!" I shouted again. "Hang on!" With my other hand, I felt for a pulse at his carotid. It was there. Barely.

Come on, you tough old bastard. Stay with me.

I kept one hand on Dono's head and reached out with the other to my jacket. His blood was seeping through the wadded layers of T-shirt cotton. I was fumbling to unbutton the pocket and reach my cell phone when I heard a creak of wood on the porch outside.

Had the guy who ran out circled back to finish the job? I didn't have a gun. Dono and I would both be easy.

I heard many quick and muffled footsteps outside, coming toward the door. Then silence.

Cops. Had to be. Coming in quiet, until they got in position.

"Here!" I yelled. "In the front room! He's been shot!"

"Police! Who's inside?" shouted a male voice.

"Me and my grandfather," I said. "Somebody ran out the back door a minute ago."

"Come out of the house, sir. Now."

"He's bleeding out, goddamn it. I've got pressure on it."

Ten long seconds passed before silhouettes appeared at the edge of the door. Stick formation. Single file.

"Here," I said again.

"Let me see your hands," the cop in front ordered. He had a shotgun leveled at me.

I raised one red-stained hand up high. "I'll step away. But somebody has to take over, fast. His skull might be fractured."

"Do it," the cop said. I put the other hand in the air and stood up. Blood dribbled down from my palms onto my forearms and bare shoulders. "Turn around," he said. I did a one-eighty so he could see there was no weapon tucked in my jeans.

"Now back slowly toward the door," he said.

I backed up. One of the cops ran around me to kneel by Dono. His partner covered me as I edged out toward the one holding the shotgun.

They let me come all the way out onto the porch, backing up to keep some distance between us. The second cop in the line was big, maybe six-three with an extra layer of padding in the face and belly. He spun me around so that my nose was three inches from the dark blue paint. Shotgun was on the other side of the doorway, watching the entry and the hall beyond.

The big cop reached for his shoulder radio. "We're inside. Detaining one male at gunpoint. Victim down. Need rescue."

"I've got combat medical training," I said to the cop. "Let me help." I willed Dono to keep breathing.

"The officer there is an EMT. We'll take care of him. Is anybody else in the house?" he said.

"I don't know," I said. "I got here two minutes before you did. The door was open. My grandfather was on the floor. Somebody ran out the back when I came in."

And someone must have called 911, before I'd even arrived. A neighbor? Or the same guy who'd shot Dono?

"What's your name?" Shotgun said to me.

"Van Shaw. My ID is in the jacket on the floor by my grandfather."

"You live here, sir?"

"No. I flew in to Sea-Tac about an hour ago. All right if I turn around?" I wanted to see if the cop working on Dono had the wound stanched.

"Go ahead."

I edged sidewise to look through the entryway. The EMT cop had pressure on Dono's head, and with his free hand he was checking for pupil dilation.

More cops were moving around upstairs, sweeping the place. I'd cleared my share of houses and other structures. Their team knew how to do it. They moved fast and quiet, checking every room and closet and anywhere else a human might hide.

"Gun," said the partner of the guy kneeling by Dono. He was pointing at the floor of the front room. In the low light and with the rush to help my grandfather, I hadn't seen what had been there. A tumbler glass had fallen and broken near Dono's ancient leather wing-back chair. Lying behind it was a snubnose .38 revolver.

"Yours?" the big cop said to me. His name tag read OLSSEN.

"No." And whatever gun had made that hole in Dono, it wasn't as big as a .38. Maybe the revolver belonged to Dono himself. Had he been carrying it? And had he been too slow on the draw to save himself?

Two paramedics came running down the porch and past us into the house. They had a pressure bandage on Dono's skull in under a minute and a ventilator down his throat one minute after that. I was trembling slightly. A little from the cold air, mostly from adrenaline. Tiny droplets of half-dried blood quivered off the ends of my fingers.

Fight harder, Dono. You have to wake up.

Every time the EMT squeezed the bulb and forced air into Dono's lungs, I exhaled as if to push a little more life into him. The medics counted three and lifted him onto the stretcher and carried him to the door.

"Harborview?" I said. Too loud. One of them flinched.

"Yes," he said.

"Sir, I'm gonna need you to stay here," said Shotgun. R. VOH. "You said your identification is in the room there?"

We stepped inside, Voh and Olssen keeping me between them. I pointed at my jacket on the floor. Voh stepped carefully into the front room, around the spatters of blood and bloody footprints. He fished out the contents of the jacket's pockets without moving it from where it lay.

He glanced through my papers. "You're deployed overseas, Mr. Shaw? Or Sergeant Shaw?"

"Yes." On the wall of the foyer was a shallow metal panel, the size of a paperback book. Dono's house alarm. Homemade. I reached out and flipped the panel door open.

"Hey," said Olssen. "Sir, don't touch anything, all right?"

Dono had upgraded the system since I'd lived here. It was plain-looking, just flat stainless steel and a ten-digit keypad with a single light to show when it was armed. The light was off.

So maybe somebody knocks and Dono wakes up and turns off the alarm to open the door. Or maybe the shooter was here already and the alarm never got turned on because the old man never went to bed last night.

Either way, odds were damn good that Dono knew the person. Hard to imagine a stranger getting close enough to put a gun to his head at five-thirty in the morning.

Two men came in through the front door. Detective badges clipped to their belts.

The first was forty-something, with prematurely white hair. His blue suit was pressed and clean. The second detective was closer to my age, a thin guy in a brown sport coat and a shiny shirt with matching tie. He took in the scene in the front room and let out a low whistle. His partner frowned.

The white-haired cop took my identification and papers from Voh and looked at me for a moment. "I'm Detective Guerin," he said. "This is Detective Kanellis."

"Van Shaw."

"Would you excuse us for a moment, Mr. Shaw?" He motioned to Voh, who followed the two detectives out onto the porch. Before he stepped outside, the thin cop looked me up and down.

"Keep an eye on things here, Bob," he said to Olssen.

Olssen and I were left in the foyer. He shifted his feet.

"You in the war?" he said.

"Yeah."

I had been on base in Germany, fourteen hours ago. Less than a day before that, I'd made the decision to come back to Seattle.

Damn it, Dono. I'd been ready. I'd been locked and loaded to actually talk to you again. I know you, old man. That letter had not been easy for you to write.

I felt a cold breeze across my chest, coming down the hallway. The shooter must have left the back door open when he ran out. Christ. If the cops had been quicker getting here, they might have caught the fucker.

And if I'd taken a cab instead of renting a car, I might have kept Dono from getting shot entirely.

The detectives and Voh came back in, and behind them I heard more footsteps tramping along the porch. A parade of four tired-looking men in blue SPD Windbreakers and carrying tackle boxes followed. Guerin pointed, and they carefully edged into the front room. Crime-scene crew.

Guerin motioned to me. "Let's talk in the back, where it's a little quieter."

The two detectives followed me down the hallway. Voh and Olssen stayed with the techs.

Dono's kitchen was small and crowded with cabinets and appliances. There was almost no counter space, so he kept a butcher's block in the center of the tiled floor. A fat man would have trouble squeezing between it and the refrigerator. Next to the kitchen was a dining alcove with a circular pine table and three rickety wooden chairs, the same old set that had been there when I was a kid. The breeze coming through the house was stronger here, icy across my face and bare chest.

Guerin motioned to a chair. I stayed standing. Kanellis sat.

"I'm sorry about your grandfather, Mr. Shaw," Guerin said. "Or do you prefer 'Sergeant'?"

" 'Mr.' is fine."

"Okay. Tell me what happened," he said.

I recapped what I knew. From receiving Dono's letter all the way to finding him on the floor. It didn't take long. The detectives listened and nodded. Kanellis fidgeted in his seat.

"Do you know of anybody who might have wanted to hurt your grandfather? Or any arguments he might have had with anyone?" Detective Guerin said.

"No."

"The front door isn't broken open. Did anyone else have access to the house? A girlfriend, maybe?"

"I don't know." Christ, Dono might even be *married*. There wasn't any sign down here that a woman now lived in the house, but I'd only seen three rooms and the hallway.

"Do *you* have a key to the place?" Kanellis said.

"No."

One of the crime-scene guys came into the room. He said, "Excuse me," and began to put adhesive strips on my hands and wrists. Testing for gunshot residue. When he peeled the strips off, the dried blood came up with them, leaving rectangular tiger stripes of pink. I walked past

Kanellis to the kitchen sink and began to scrub my hands half raw with Dono's scouring sponge.

There was a clock with a picture of a bull on it hung over the window. Another new addition. By the little hands shaped like matador's swords, it had been forty minutes since the medics had taken Dono out.

He'd be through triage by now. The hospital would be able to tell me something.

I looked at Guerin. "I need to follow him to Harborview."

He thought about it. I knew he was going to check out my story from stem to stern and back again before he crossed me off as his primary suspect. If he ever did.

"Do you have a cell phone?" Guerin said. I gave him the number. I saw that the phone had one of my fingerprints on it, in Dono's blood, from when I'd started to dial 911.

"Who called for help?" I said.

Kanellis nodded. "A neighbor heard a gunshot. They called 911." He was careful to avoid mentioning the sex of the neighbor. Which meant it was probably a woman.

"But I didn't hear the shot," I said. "Even though I parked and walked almost halfway up the block to get to the house. So the shooting happened at least a couple of minutes before I came through the door."

Guerin considered it. "All right," he said.

I glanced at the open back door. "The guy was still inside when I came in. Why stay in the house that long? What was he doing?"

"Tossing the place?" Kanellis said. "Looking for cash? Or something to sell?"

I didn't answer. Guerin didn't either. Maybe he was thinking the same thing I was. The shooter would have to be batshit crazy if he were searching the house after shooting Dono, with the front door still wide open. Or he was one ice-veined son of a bitch.

"I'll be at Harborview," I said.

"We'll meet you there," said Guerin, "after our team is finished with the scene."

"Don't leave town," Kanellis said. His partner exhaled, almost a sigh.

The lab rats had taped off the front room. One was taking photographs, and the rest were spreading fingerprint dust on everything. I grabbed an old barn jacket from a hook in the foyer and walked out.

Out on the street, clumps of people stood around the cluster of police cruisers and unmarked vehicles. Neighbors, holding their coffees. Early-morning joggers, pausing to watch the show.

"Hey!" one of them yelled as I ran back to the Charger. "What's going on?"

I wished to hell I knew.

CHAPTER THREE

THE WORST INJURIES IN Seattle, and usually the western half of the state, headed straight for Harborview's trauma center. If Harborview couldn't help you, the next option was the morgue.

The admitting-desk receptionist told me Dono was in surgery. No, there wasn't any news of his condition. He was Patient ID 918. She said they'd let the doctors know I was there, once they came out.

The waiting room had a few dozen black-and-gray plastic chairs, arranged around low tables with stacks of donated magazines. People had pulled the chairs together to huddle in close groups, like prayer circles. Nobody was reading the magazines. There was a flat-screen monitor on the wall that told where patients were. I waited until the display cycled through to read "918—Surgery Begun."

I claimed a chair and sat. And stared at the cream-colored wall.

I'd spent a lot of time in hospitals. Twice from my own bad spins of the wheel. The first had been at Walter Reed when I was twenty years old, after my face had been redecorated. The second bought me that desk duty during the last two months, when my forearm caught a whirring piece of shrapnel right as our platoon was being lifted out of the extraction point in Kandahar.

In between those two visits, I'd logged a few hundred hours in waiting rooms, while buddies or my own men were under the knife. Sitting silently with the rest of our unit, none of us daring to tempt fate by saying it was going to be okay. Those hours were a hell of a lot worse than being in a hospital bed myself.

The very worst time, the reigning King of Bad, was the one I hardly remembered. I was six years old. I didn't know how I'd come to be there, in the ER. I stood in a room a lot like this one while people I didn't know whispered and cried around me. And then my grandfather was standing there.

I had only met him a few times. He was always a little scary. He leaned down and spoke to me, saying the same thing a few times before I got it. He was telling me that I couldn't see my mom right now. That we'd be going home for a while. His home, not the apartment Mom and I shared.

I'd asked why. When he finally answered, there was a stone solidity to his words that I knew the truth behind it, even if I couldn't understand.

"She'll be here," he had said.

And there she stayed. Even after she died and was buried and long gone, I felt she was still in the hospital, somewhere just out of sight. The six-year-old me would feel that forever.

If Dono died here, would he occupy the same corner in my mind? I didn't want to find out.

The big automated glass doors leading from the street slid open. Guerin and Kanellis came in. Kanellis spotted me first. Something was different about their vibe, just from their walk. Kanellis stood up straighter. Guerin looked grim.

"Sergeant Shaw," Guerin said, "you've been keeping things from us."

They sat in chairs on either side of me. Guerin left a seat in between us. Kanellis sat close. Guerin was carrying a blue manila folder. It was thick, maybe thirty or more pages.

Kanellis smirked. "Your grandpa is a very bad guy."

"I know Dono's got a record," I said.

Guerin opened the folder and looked at the first page.

"Your grandfather has a business license as a general contractor and electrician," he said. "He's held that for twenty-three years. And there's a stack of building permits and a number of other public records that have his name on them."

I sat, waiting for what I knew would come next. Guerin turned the pages, reading from the top of each one.

"Arrested on suspicion, armed robbery. Suspicion, breaking and entering. Conviction, armed robbery. Conviction, grand larceny." Guerin looked up at me. "He served four and a half years on McNeil Island for those last two, since it was a federal currency depository."

"Your granddaddy must have really pissed off the judge," said Kanellis. "McNeil was hard shit, back in the day."

"Before my time," I said.

Guerin turned once more to his pages. "Arrested on suspicion, burglary. Twice on that. Suspicion, aggravated assault. Suspicion, grand larceny again. And one last count, for possession of an unregistered firearm. Fourteen months in King County."

The detective showed me the top sheet on the stack. It must have been Dono's first arrest record, or at least his first in the United States. His face—young, handsome, and mocking—both front view and profile, in a mug shot over a reader board with his name and booking date in 1973 spelled out in uneven white plastic letters. The reader board said POLICE—ALLSTON MA. Sometime before Dono and my grandmother and my mother, just a toddler then, had moved across the country to Seattle.

I was fascinated. Dono hadn't kept any photos around the house. I'd never seen him as a young man before.

He looked a little like me.

Guerin raised his eyes from the page. "And speaking of guns, the pistol on the floor had your grandfather's prints on it. We also found another .38 Special upstairs, and a shotgun hanging by a strap under the coats in the kitchen. The pistols were registered to a man who passed away at age ninety-three, eight years ago."

Guerin closed the blue folder and put it on the chair next to him. "You didn't say a damn thing about any of this. Which makes me wonder if you're mixed up in his work. Maybe all the way."

It was almost nostalgic. Cops asking me what I knew about my grandfather's night work. I hadn't had to play this game since I started middle school.

"How old is the last charge on that list?" I said.

He didn't have to look. "Eighteen years."

"Right."

"Just because he hasn't been busted again, that doesn't make him clean," Kanellis said. "Clean guys don't keep guns hidden behind the laundry soap."

I said, "Dono was always a little paranoid. Guns in the house don't mean he's robbing liquor stores either."

"You must have known about his rap sheet, growing up," Guerin said. "You were living with him when he was arrested the last time."

"I was. Dono told me that bust was a case of mistaken identity." I shrugged. "I was a kid, I believed it."

Kanellis pointed a finger at me. "You went into the system then, right?" he said. "Foster care. That couldn't have been a shitload of fun."

The detectives had done some fast digging. I'd been a ward of the state for a year and a half, assigned to foster homes during Dono's trial and while he served his stretch in County.

"If you checked my record," I said, "then you also know I went into the army right after high-school graduation. I haven't been back. I don't know anything about Dono's life nowadays."

"You said you didn't know if he had any enemies now. What about back then? Any old grudges? Anybody who seemed like bad types, coming to the house?"

"He never talked about anything but his construction work," I said. "Sorry."

Guerin stared at me. Kanellis did, too, although he kept flicking his gaze back to his partner to check for approval.

"I need you to level with us," Guerin said finally. "You're not doing your grandfather any good by keeping his life a closed book. I don't think you shot him. I spoke to your company's executive officer. You've served your country well."

He leaned forward. "But it's too damn big a coincidence. Dono getting shot the same day you come back to town."

The detective was right. The same morning. Almost the same hour.

I hadn't told anyone other than Dono that I was coming. Had he?

I looked at Guerin. "If I knew anything that would help you catch this guy, I'd tell you. I want him nailed more than you do."

A slight man in fresh green hospital scrubs walked over from where he'd been talking to the receptionist at the admitting desk. He had a full beard of black hair and wore a burgundy turban that looked like an autumn leaf above the walnut color of his tired face.

"Which of you is with Mr. Shaw?" he said.

"I am," I said. Guerin opened his jacket to show his badge.

"I'm Dr. Singh, Mr. Shaw's surgeon. Mr. Shaw is coming out of the postoperative ward now. He should be placed in a room before very long."

"So he's alive?" My pulse jumped. I hadn't allowed myself the idea.

"He is. The bullet fractured his skull. It also did considerable damage to his left temporal lobe underneath. His heartbeat is steady, but his breathing still requires assistance."

"When can we talk to him?" said Kanellis.

Singh tilted his head. "That's very difficult to predict. His anesthesia will wear off in two or three more hours, but—" The doctor made an almost imperceptible shrug.

"How bad is he?" I said.

"I'll be direct. In cases of brain damage like this, consciousness is not always regained. And when it is, the patient is not often lucid."

"Did he say anything on the table?" Guerin pressed. "Anything that might identify who shot him?"

"No. I'm sorry," said Singh. "And I must ask that you not disturb him. If he wakes, we can call you immediately."

"I'll post someone here," said Guerin.

Not only to hear what Dono might say, if he woke up and started talking. The shooter might learn that the old man was still alive and try again.

Singh turned to me. "If you will excuse me, did your . . . father . . . ?"

"Grandfather."

"Oh? Your grandfather, then." Singh's surprise wasn't uncommon. Dono and I were only thirty-six years apart in age. "Did he have any sort of living will or advance directive? Something that might indicate his preference of care?"

"I don't know. I'll check with his lawyer, but I doubt it," I said.

"I see."

"You saying he might be like this for a long time?"

"Again, I am sorry. If you would like to see him, he should be prepared now."

Prepared. Like a corpse for viewing. We followed Singh to the elevators and up to a ward on the third floor, where he checked a computer screen at the front desk and led us down a long hallway. The room had two beds, but only one was occupied.

Dono lay with his upper body slightly elevated by the articulated bed. A mass of gauze and tape made a small pillow across the back of his head. Electrodes to monitor his pulse were stuck to his wrist and shoulder. IV needles in his arm, hidden by tape. The bulb of a plastic ventilator tube perched obscenely on his lips like a thick soap bubble.

"Leave me alone with him," I said. "All of you."

Guerin and Kanellis glanced at each other.

"I'm a suspect or I'm not," I said. "Either way, I'm not going to unplug him with you standing outside the door."

Guerin frowned at that, but they left, with Singh following.

I took a chair from against the wall and set it by Dono's bed. For a few minutes, I just watched him, trying to see past the medical apparatus. People at death's door are supposed to look smaller, shrunken. But the old man was as sizable as I remembered. A shot glass over six feet, and rangy. His hair had turned from salt and pepper to iron gray in the last decade and receded a little more. There were a few extra creases around the eyes. He still had the knuckled hands of a stonemason. I rested my own hand on the bedsheet. A tanned version of his paler one.

He had asked me to come back home, without any hint as to why. And I hadn't made it here in time. By ten minutes.

"Christ, Dono," I said. "One of us really fucked up."

I had lied to the cops about one thing. My grandfather hadn't straightened out when I was a kid. He'd just gotten better at his job.

Dono Shaw was a thief. He'd been a career criminal since his teens. Robberies mostly, wild cowboy shit. After that approach had earned him the sorry record that Guerin had shared with me, Dono smartened up and changed his methods.

And he had taught me. About stealing cars and forgery and security alarms. And money. How to find it, how to take it, how to hide it. At twelve I could use a thermite mini-lance well enough to beat the relocking safety on most commercial safes. By fifteen I probably knew more about police interrogation tricks than Kanellis did now. I had been hot shit.

I doubted that Dono had changed in the ten years I'd been gone. Either my grandfather had made a score recently or he was planning one soon. He didn't take vacations.

I'd lied to Guerin about Dono's work. But not about his shooting. If I knew anything that might catch the motherfucker who did it, I'd happily hand it over. The detectives had the resources to follow every lead.

But I could find other sources. Better ones. Guys who would rather cut off their own toes with a penknife than help the cops.

This was assuming that any of those old bastards would still talk to me. I'd been gone a long time.

Dono had known the shooter. I felt that in my gut. Had he been a partner?

On those infrequent occasions when Dono had worked with partners, he never double-crossed them. He thought it was bad business. So I couldn't buy that anyone had shot Dono in the back of the head because the old man had cheated him.

Which meant it had been an ambush. Were Dono and his shooter meeting to hand over somebody's share of a score? Dono's .38 had been on the floor. Had he been too slow when the shooter reached for his gun?

"You asked me to come back," I said to Dono. "I'm here. It's your turn, goddamn it."

The accordion pump of the ventilator eased up and down with a soft wheeze each time it pushed air into his slack lungs.

I stood and put the chair back against the wall. "I'll be around," I said.

Out in the hall, I saw Guerin down near the ward desk, talking on his cell phone. I turned and went the other way, a few yards to the door of the stairwell.

It was Sunday afternoon. There was only light traffic as I drove through the streets and over the hill, back toward the house. A couple of the streets had become one-way since the last time I'd seen them, and I had to backtrack once or twice. I concentrated on each step, like a student driver. Pressing the accelerator gently. Clicking the turn signals.

He might be like this for a long time? I'd said the words to Singh, and the surgeon hadn't given me an answer. Which had been answer enough.

What if this was the last of it for the old man? What if he didn't open his eyes and tell me who'd shot him?

What if I never learned why?

The curb in front of the house was empty again, and I parked the Charger and went up the stone steps to the porch. I stopped at the door. The forensic crew had attached a padlock to the jamb. They hadn't wanted to use the regular lock, in case they needed access again.

I stared at the padlock for a moment. Then I raised my boot and stomped the door above the knob. The wood cracked and bent, but the lock held. I reared back and kicked it again, harder. Splinters exploded from the jamb as the padlock and hasp flew through the swinging door.

Yellow crime-scene tape was stretched wide over the entrance to the front room. Ivory fingerprint dust was everywhere. And red across the floor, like a demon's blanket.

The rest of the room looked pretty much as I remembered it. Over-stuffed bookshelves. Lamps made of heavy brass. The same old painting of the rocky landscape of County Clare hanging above the mantel of the fireplace. The television was newer, a flat-screen plasma, but sitting on the same built-in cabinet where the old one had been. Dono's leather chair was also in the same spot. The old man spent most of his time in this room. *Had* spent.

I walked down the hall and into the kitchen. Dono had always kept his liquor in the cabinet above the refrigerator. He still did. I grabbed the first bottle I saw, Kentucky bourbon, and took a long pull from it. Then another. It helped my mood about as much as pissing on a bonfire.

I threw the bottle across the room, and it shattered against the counter. That was more like it. I snatched up one of the wooden chairs and smashed it down on the breakfast table, once, twice. Music. On the third swing, the chair fell to pieces, and I threw the fragments aside.

I was looking around for something else to break when someone knocked on the open front door.

CHAPTER FOUR

OVER THE POUNDING IN my ears, I heard another knock. A dog started barking. A big dog, from the low rumbling sound of it.

"Hey," a woman's voice called. "Everything all right in there?"

I took a couple of long, slow breaths to steady my pulse before I left the kitchen. My boots made wet bourbon footprints on the hardwood of the hall.

A woman stood in the open doorway, only half visible in the ambient light coming from the back of the house. She was old, as short and stout as a mailbox, with spiky white hair. The dog was white, too. Some sort of mutt, maybe pit bull and water buffalo.

I stopped in the hall, well away from the door and the dog. It barked again at me and shifted its muscular weight onto its front paws, straining at the leash.

"Stanley," the woman said to the dog. It stopped barking but whined and tugged to be free. I wasn't sure if it wanted to play or to eat me. The woman leaned back to hold the animal in place. In her other hand, she carried a baking tray covered in Saran Wrap.

"Help you?" I said.

"You must be the grandson," she said. "I'm Addy Proctor." She didn't sound alarmed, even though I was still wearing Dono's old barn jacket, with no shirt and bloodstained jeans. The dog growled.

"You one of Dono's neighbors, Ms. Proctor?" If she knew I was related to Dono, she must have heard it from the cops at some point this morning. She'd probably seen the whole show, complete with lights and sirens.

"Addy," she corrected. "I'm down the street, in the bright yellow house."

I remembered the place, from my walk up the block when I'd first arrived. The image stuck because of the big blue NEIGHBORHOOD WATCH sign on her lawn.

She hefted the baking tray. "I've brought you something."

I was too damn tired to entertain the local snoop. I reached over to flip on the hallway light. She wore an ivory cable-knit turtleneck sweater and black pants, with clunky slip-on black shoes. Thick black glasses with square frames. I put her age somewhere north of seventy.

"That's real nice of you, but—"

"It's no trouble," she said. "Hot-link casserole. Hope you eat meat."

"It's just that—"

"I'll pop it in the oven. Is the kitchen back here?" And she marched in, dog leading the way. I had no choice but to retreat. We made a clumsy parade, me shuffling backward and Stanley barking eagerly.

In the kitchen, shards from the bottle of bourbon covered half the tiled floor. The fumes stung my nostrils. Stanley snuffed in protest. Pieces of the broken chair were strewn around the room. The breakfast table had fresh gouges exposing raw wood beneath. A glass salt-and-pepper set had fallen off and shattered. The spilled contents soaked up the whiskey.

Addy Proctor took it all in and tugged Stanley back from the broken glass. "Redecorating?" she said.

Christ. If I let the old woman start cleaning, she'd be here all night.

I grabbed a broom from the narrow space between the fridge and the wall and began to sweep the worst of the mess out from underfoot. I'd just reached automatically for where Dono and I had always kept the brooms and mops.

"I'm not up for visitors tonight, Ms.— Addy," I said.

"No need to entertain me," she said. "I just saw you come back a few minutes ago and wanted to drop this off for you. And ask how your grandfather is doing."

Right. Of course. Give her a nugget of gossip to spread around, and she and her dog would be out the door.

"He's alive," I said. "But beyond that they don't know."

She frowned. "You don't sound hopeful."

"His surgeon had a hard time putting a positive spin on it. Nothing to do but wait."

"Damn," she said. "The doctors never are encouraging, are they? Just in case they're proven wrong. They drive you mad." She watched me dump a dustpan full of glass into the trash. "Is that what all this was about?"

"Yeah."

She nodded and looped the end of Stanley's leash around the door-knob. He whined. "Hush," Addy said. "Sit. *Sit.*" The dog did, reluctantly, and sniffed in the direction of the casserole. Addy opened the oven door and removed the plastic wrap from the tray. "Twenty minutes," she said, setting the dial.

"Thanks," I said. "I'll have some before I sack out."

"I've already done a phone tree." She straightened up. Her eyes were green and bright behind the mannish black glasses. "Nobody on the block saw anyone around your house this morning. Except me. And I only saw you, when you first arrived."

"You're the one who heard the gunshot."

"I heard something. I was out on my front porch." She grimaced. "Smoking. I can't quite seem to give up that first cigarette of the day. Sixty damn years. I wake up earlier and earlier now, and I still can't beat it." She shook her head. "I was in my robe, standing just outside my door looking at the fog, and that's when I heard the . . . well, I didn't really know it was a gun. Kind of a snapping sound. Not like on TV."

"Small caliber."

"I'll take your word for it. Guns aren't my favorite thing in this world. I wasn't even sure where the sound had come from."

"But you called the cops."

"Dono's house here was the only one with lights on. From my porch you can see up the hill and through your window, just a piece of that room." She pointed back down the hall.

"The front room."

"Yes. I looked up here toward the light and saw shadows moving around, moving quickly. And I had a very bad feeling. I told myself that if it turned out to be nothing, I'd feel like a fool, but if it were something serious, then I'd *be* a fool, and that's much worse. So I picked up the phone."

"You did right."

"Still. I wish I'd have walked out and looked. Maybe I'd have seen who did it."

I wished that, too. That Addy Proctor had rushed recklessly to the scene and gotten a glimpse of the shooter before he went out the back. But what she wanted was reassurance.

"You made the smart choice," I said. "Dono needed the paramedics more than anything else. All I had was bare hands and a T-shirt."

Addy exhaled. "Thank you. I've been kicking myself all damn day about it. That's why I've been keeping half an eye on your house today. Sometimes you have to do something. Or go nuts."

I shook my head. "I owe you one, Addy. No. I owe you two." I went to the other side of the kitchen and brought over a big red leather barstool that Dono had owned since before I was born, and I put it down so she could take a seat. "One for calling for help, fast. It saved Dono's life. And two for seeing me and telling the cops about it. Otherwise they might have me locked up for Dono's shooting right now."

I took two glasses out of the cabinet and used the sink filter to pour water for both of us. There was a loaf of Van de Kamp's wheat bread on the counter. I opened the plastic bag, balled up a slice of bread, and tossed it on the floor for Stanley. He wolfed it down in two chews.

The chair was too tall for Addy. Her chunky shoes barely touched the metal ring around the legs meant as a footrest. "Do the police have any leads?" she said.

"Not that they're sharing." I didn't think they would find anything at all, not if Guerin and Kanellis stuck to standard operating bullshit. Phone records and last known associates weren't going to cut it.

"You're Neighborhood Watch," I said. "What's the recent history around here? Any break-ins?"

"There was a burglary a couple of years ago, on the next block over. A few of the usual stereo thefts out of parked cars. Nothing like this," she said.

"I should let people know what's happened," I said. "Did Dono ever mention any friends to you? Maybe a girlfriend?"

She shook her head. "He and I only said hello on the street, that sort of thing. He was pleasant, but . . . well . . ."

I nodded understanding. Dono had always kept the neighbors at a cordial but firm distance. On those occasions when some especially sociable people moved onto the block, he would politely decline any invitations to join them for dinner or a beer until they took the hint.

We hadn't ignored them completely, of course. Dono would run a background check on their names, along with any of their family who lived in the city. He'd try to verify occupations and former addresses. Find out if any of them had arrest records. Just in case the new arrivals turned out to be cops, or were the sort of people who attracted attention from cops. The old man believed that good fences and a traceable history made for good neighbors.

I looked at Addy. What had Dono's check on her told him?

"Have you lived here long?" I said.

"I moved in three years ago. Magnus and I had owned the house forever. When he passed on . . . well, it made sense to stop renting it out and just use it myself." She pointed at my boots. "Are you in the service?"

Apparently we were trading fact for fact. "The army."

"Magnus was in the army, too. Sweden's."

"You see anybody else around here recently? Any visitors?"

She considered it, taking off her glasses and wiping them on her sweater. There was a fine web of lines on her round face.

"I did see someone. A man, and I'd seen him here before. A friend of your grandfather's?"

"When was this?"

"Most recently? Last week, I think." She shook her head. "I'm sorry. The days get blended together. I haven't been retired that long, and it's like vacation, when you suddenly realize you've lost track of what day of the week it is."

"But about a week ago. There was a man with Dono? What did he look like?"

"Yes. Out at the curb. I was driving past, I remember that now. He was kind of large. Not tall, but barrel-chested?"

"Okay. Keep going."

"Maybe your grandfather's age, sixtyish. His hair might have been lighter. Like orange or red."

A burly redhead. I knew a man like that.

"You said they were at the curb. By Dono's pickup? Or the other man's car?"

"Must have been the other fellow's. I know your grandfather's big blue truck—it wasn't that."

"Was it something like a Caddy? A soft top?"

"Yes. Yes." She widened her eyes, excited. "Damn if it wasn't. A big American gas guzzler. With black paint, I think."

Hollis Brant. He always went for those old boats, with the bench seats that gave his wide frame a little more elbow room.

So Hollis was back in Seattle now. Just like me.

"He's a friend of Dono's," I said to Addy. "I'll call him."

"I can't believe that car of his didn't come to mind right away. So few convertibles in Seattle."

I stretched. "It's been a hell of a day." How fast could I reach Hollis?

Addy took the hint and put down her half-finished water glass. "I imagine." She dropped off the high stool. "I'm very sorry about Dono. You'll let me know what I can do to help."

It wasn't a request. I had to smile. "I will."

"I'm glad you're here for him. I'll be back for the dish. Don't forget to eat." She tugged on Stanley's leash. As he passed me, he nosed my hand with his huge head, looking to get his ears scratched or maybe just hoping for another piece of bread. They went down the hallway and out the open door. After a moment I followed. I could hear Addy's shoes thunking against the pavement as she made her steady way down the hill. Odd old bird.

MY GRANDFATHER HAD MADE a few changes on the second floor. The master bath had been remodeled, and there was new carpeting in the same shade of dusty brown as before. A small TV was on the wall in his bedroom.

Wound around the lamp on the nightstand were the only two religious items I'd ever seen in the house. Both family relics. A string of rosary beads, which had belonged to Dono's late sister. And a St. Christopher medal. Dono had told me once that my grandmother, his wife, had left the medal to my mother. It found its way back to Dono again when she died.

He'd added more bookshelves, which were crowded with nonfiction books on boats and naval battles and, most of all, about pirates. Dono probably knew as much about crime in the seventeenth century as he did about the twenty-first. He had told me once, when he was drunk and rambling a little, that he'd wanted to name my mother Grace, after the Irish pirate Grace O'Malley. My grandmother had prevailed, and Mom was named Moira instead.

The biggest difference to the upstairs was in my old room, which was nearly empty now, save for a few file boxes, an old rolltop desk, and a leather couch. Not that any of it had value, sentimental or otherwise.

I went back downstairs.

The pantry had once been a boiler closet. It was large enough to lie down in, if you were short. I moved a few cans of tomato soup out of the way to allow access to the back wall. Where Dono had built one of his little tricks.

It worked on the same principle as a Chinese puzzle box. Twist a shelf support one half turn, move a bracket to the side, and presto. The drywall between the studs swung up with a gentle push against a spring hinge, revealing a foot-square hole.

There were a few things squirreled away in the small hollow. A lock-pick gun and a more basic set of picks fashioned from dental tools. False driver's licenses with Dono's photo, in three names and three states. A mismatched pair of handguns—a little .32 and a newer, meaner nine-millimeter Browning. All useful in an emergency.

Each of these, or similar items, I remembered being in Dono's hiding place the last time I'd seen it. He also used to keep cash on hand, maybe nine or ten grand in twenties and fifties. Nothing like that now. Maybe he'd switched to cash cards.

There were two sets of keys as well. The bigger set looked like its keys would fit the house and truck and other things around the place.

The second set was more unusual. Two pairs of keys. The first pair was silver and pistol-shaped, with the shaft of the key coming off the rounded head at a ninety-degree angle. Keys for an engine. Maybe a generator. The second pair was small and brass-colored. The four keys were attached to a small, rough chunk of reddish wood. Someone had drilled a hole in the wood, to thread the key chain through it. Odd. Not Dono's usual style.

There were also three cell phones, the cheap kind you could buy at any drugstore and use with a prepaid SIM card. Two were still sealed in their plastic packages. I tried turning the other one on. Its battery had a couple bars. I took the phone and pocketed both sets of keys before closing the compartment and putting the soup cans back in place.

The phone's log showed only one call, placed the day before to a Seattle number. A 206 area code, one of the old ones. There was no name assigned to the number. I checked the phone's contact list. Empty. No saved names or numbers at all. I counted myself lucky just to find the single number in the log. The Dono I knew would have made sure to wipe the log after every call. Maybe he was slipping.

I went back to the Seattle number and pressed CALL. There were two rings, and then a female voice came on the line:

"*You have reached the law offices of Ephraim Ganz. Our office hours are Monday through Friday, eight* A.M. *to five* P.M. *Pacific time. If this call is urgent or if you need to post bail, please contact Martone Bail Bonds at—*"

I hung up. Ephraim Ganz had been Dono's criminal attorney for as long as I could remember. And apparently still was. Was Dono in trouble with the cops again? Detective Guerin hadn't mentioned any recent arrests, but maybe he was keeping that little fact to himself.

What Dr. Singh had asked me earlier that day came flooding back. Did my grandfather have a living will? Christ, was that why Dono had called Ganz? Had he known that trouble was coming?

My fingers gripped the phone, as if testing the limit of strength in my healed arm. Tomorrow was Monday. Ganz's office would be open. Or I could find Hollis.

Addy Proctor had summed it up for me: *You have to do something. Or go nuts.*

I was halfway to crazy already. It was time to start pushing in the other direction.

AGE NINE

Granddad had told me that the cabin we were looking for was only fifteen minutes from the town of Gold Bar. I guess he was thinking about regular streets, because the rest of the drive took at least half an hour. It got even slower the farther we went, winding our way up into the hills. The roads changed from paving to gravel to hard-packed dirt. Granddad kept glancing at the directions he'd written down on a notepad, checking the odometer on the Cordoba's dashboard to know when to turn.

He was mad. Maybe at how long it was taking us to get there. At least a little at me. He'd told me on the hour's drive from Seattle that he was going to talk to a man about some guns. Not the sort you could buy in any shop, he'd said. I thought it was awesome. I asked a lot of questions. Granddad eventually told me to shut it.

So I read my X-Men comic books. *Tried* to read them. They had been building up to this big fight with Sabretooth for like a year, and I wanted to read it so much I'd brought the new issue along, and I never read stuff in the car. But now I couldn't think about it. I wondered who sold guns way out here in the woods.

Finally the road widened into a clearing, and we pulled up to the cabin.

It was a dump. It looked as if a gigantic crooked woodpile had been quickly covered with tree sap and olive paint all mixed together. Its roof, if it had a roof, was hidden under layers of fallen leaves and millions of pine needles.

A guy was standing in the doorway, watching us. He was a grown-up, but short, and his face had baby fat. His brown hair stuck up in tufts. The face of a taller woman appeared over his shoulder, peering at us through thick glasses. She was stout, dressed in brown overalls with a flannel shirt underneath. The man idly wiped some black grease off his fingers onto his purple Huskies sweatshirt.

"That's Hazeldine. And Becky," Granddad said, opening his door. "I'll talk with them for a few minutes, and then he and I will head out."

Granddad stepped from the car and zipped up his green parka. I stayed put, and after a moment he leaned in to look at me. "I should be back here before long," he said.

I kept my eyes on the floor of the car. "Can't I come?"

"I've answered that question enough times today." He swept an arm wide, toward the line of giant pine and scrub brush. "You do what kids are supposed to do for once. Play in the damned woods."

"There's no trails here." We'd brought my Giant mountain bike. Thinking that maybe I'd use it on an actual mountain, or at least something more than steep city streets.

Granddad's jaw tightened. "So leave it on the back of the car and use your feet."

I didn't want to play in the damned woods. Granddad read my expression and shook his head angrily. "There's no effing TV inside, and if there is, you're not going in there anyway. Take some air. And take your coat." He shut the door and walked toward the cabin.

I unlocked my bike from its rack on the back bumper and wheeled it into the forest. I left my coat in the car.

The constant shade had let moss spread over every surface, carpeting the dirt and making baseball-size clumps on the boulders. Gold Bar was at the western side of the Cascades. The first big foothills of the mountain range weren't far away. I could feel them more than I could really see them. It was gloomy.

There was no way to ride my bike more than a few yards

without having to carry it over a boulder or a fallen tree. I left it lying on the ground and spent half an hour hunting for rocks and throwing them at tree branches, seeing how far back I could get and still knock off a chunk of bark.

The branches on the pine trees were too high and too far apart to climb. I clambered up onto the tallest boulder to see if I could see anything, but the forest was thick. Just more trees, everywhere I looked. I tried two more boulders before I gave up and sat down on top of the last rock. I wished I had my coat. The damp moss made my jeans wet, and I tore up clumps of it and made a pile while listening to crows squabble over their territories.

A car horn sounded. The Cordoba's horn, I was pretty sure, returning to the cabin. But the cabin was in the other direction. Or was it? I was a little lost.

It sounded again, and I realized that the car was moving. I scrambled down from the boulder and ran toward it, so fast I nearly forgot my bike and had to double back to find it. I half pushed, half dragged it to the edge of the clearing, behind the cabin.

The Cordoba was stopped there. The driver's door was open.

I froze, just staring at the car.

Granddad's green parka had fallen half out of the open door. The parka was stained with something dark, and the fabric was split open. There were a few loose feathers scattered across the bucket seats and the floor. Like flower petals. White on the floor, turning pink where they touched the seats.

Because the driver's seat of the Cordoba was drenched with blood. It started halfway down the ivory leather upholstery, as pink smears that thickened to purple in the vertical seams. I'd never seen so much blood.

"Fuck!" Granddad. From the front of the cabin. I came out of my daze and ran.

He was seated crookedly on the second step down, leaning with one hand on the railing. His light blue T-shirt was purple at the bottom, and his pants were even wetter than mine. His face was sweaty and pale.

"Hold still, goddamn it," said the woman, Becky. She was pressing a wadded dish towel hard against Granddad's lower back with one hand and fumbling in a cardboard box with the other.

I ran over. "What happened?"

She adjusted her hand on Granddad's spine, and he hissed through clenched teeth.

"Where's Haze?" Becky said.

"He ran off into the trees," said Granddad.

"You sure?"

"He'll be all right. No one's chasing after him. I made damn well sure of that. Son of a whore, that hurts."

"What happened?" I asked again.

Becky took another folded towel out of the cardboard box and put it on top of the soaked one on Granddad's back. "I can't just tape this up," she said to him. "You're cut too deep. You need an ER."

The muscles in Granddad's forearm shook where he clutched the railing. "Not out here, I don't. I've a man in the city who can do for me. Patch it."

"That's not—" Becky began, and then sighed. "Screw it. Be an idiot. Kid, come here." I took a couple of steps closer. "Come here. Go into the house, get the paper and pen on the table. And the big bottle of water. Get."

I got. I was back in ten seconds, poised like a reporter with the pen. Becky took the bottle of water from me and unscrewed it with the same fingers. She took the towel off Granddad's wound and poured the water over it. A pink wash dribbled down the cabin steps.

Becky was looking so closely at the wound she might have been smelling it. She braced her elbow against her thigh and put pressure on it again. Sweat dripped from Granddad's chin. He was muttering something in Irish.

"Write this down," Becky said to me. "Sterile dressing. Not gauze. Get a bunch of it in the three-inch squares, or as big as they come. Two rolls of athletic tape. Saline wash. Some Neosporin. That comes in a tube, like toothpaste. And a box of Midol. You know what that is?"

"I'm not on my fucking time of the month, woman. Get codeine," Granddad said. The words seemed to come with effort.

Becky grunted. "It has to be something your boy can buy off the shelves."

Something *I* can buy? Where was I going to go?

"I can't drive," I said.

"Neither can I," Becky said. "Not anymore." She tapped her thick glasses, and it was then that I noticed a milky film over her eyes. "You'll have to take your bike. Just keep going down the hill, turn right when you hit the asphalt. There's a grocery store and drugstore about two miles on."

"Wallet," said Granddad. It was in his back pocket. The brown wool of his pants had turned black with blood.

"Go on," Becky said, and I reached into Granddad's pocket with three fingers and grabbed the leather corner of the wallet like I was grabbing a mouse by the tail. I stuffed it into my jeans.

"Fast as you can, now," said Becky. "Understand?"

As I pedaled madly down the dirt road, I glanced back. Granddad and Becky hadn't moved. Could I trust her with him?

Somehow the bike didn't crash as it pounded down the long hill. I gripped the handlebars so hard that I mashed the plastic ridges flat. The wheels bounced over every rut and rock. My teeth chattered, and I bit my tongue more than once.

When I came to the paved road, I turned right like Becky had told me and pumped the pedals as fast as if Sabretooth himself were chasing me, fangs snapping.

The drugstore was a Price 'n Save. My legs shook as I got off the bike. I'd left my Kryptonite lock back on the Cordoba's bike rack. No way I could risk someone stealing the bike. I wheeled it into the store.

I looked frantically over the rows until I found the one with the sign over it reading FIRST AID. Neosporin, okay. I cleared the shelf of dressing pads. Pain reliever was on the same row, and I found extra-strength Midol and some Advil like Granddad kept at home. Maybe he could take both. I grabbed some rolls of elastic bandage, too. It was hard to balance everything and hold the bike, and I put it all down and ran to the entrance to get a basket.

When I came back, a salesclerk in a light blue vest was standing over my bike. "You can't bring that in here," he said.

"Sorry," I said. I tossed the pile of items into the basket and picked up the bike like I was ready to leave.

He didn't move. "You gotta take that out."

"Okay." I nodded, checking Becky's list. "Can you tell me where the saline wash is?"

"It's by the contact-lens stuff. Aisle 3." The salesclerk looked up from the bike to me. He wasn't an adult, not really. Maybe not even out of high school. He had clusters of zits across his forehead and cheeks, which he'd spread cover-up makeup on. Gross.

"You all right?" he said.

I tried to slow my breathing. "Uh-huh. Yeah. I'll take this outside." I spotted a box labeled SOLIBOND PLASTER—FOR DEEP CUTS and scooped three of them into the basket.

"Somebody get hurt?"

"What? Oh. No. Nobody's hurt." I looked down at the pile in my basket. "It's a school project. We're doing first aid.

With a real fireman." I hoped that was right. Did firemen know first aid? Or was that only the guys in the ambulances?

"Oh, all right." He smiled broadly. "Here, you'll want some of these, too. And these." He took packets of antiseptic wipes and a whole box of plastic gloves off the shelves and put them in the basket without asking.

He followed me to Aisle 3 while I picked up the saline, and I nodded along with his suggestions.

"Thanks a lot," I said. "Do you have anything else?" I took Granddad's thick wallet out of my front pocket. The clerk's eyes got wide.

"You know," he said. "This is silly. We have some pro-quality first-aid kits in the back. Just like the medics use. That's what you want, not all this junk. It's a guaranteed A-plus."

"It won't cost too much?" I said.

He grinned. His teeth were crooked, the front two shoved back by the sides. "Tell you what. You give me fifty bucks and I'll call it good. My employee discount."

I smiled and nodded. We walked to the rear of the store, me still wheeling the bike, and he opened the door to the pharmacy. It was a quiet weekday afternoon. Nobody was in line to pick up a prescription.

"Hang loose," he said. "I'll go find one of the best ones." He shot me a thumbs-up, and I returned it. Before the door closed behind him, I stuck the bike tire in the gap.

I was through the door the second he was out of sight. To my left was a wall of drugs. The filled prescriptions were on the upper shelves, in plastic bins. Cabinets took up the rest of the wall. A key was left in the cabinet door, for convenience maybe. I opened it.

Rows of generic-looking plastic cylinders filled one side, slim rubber-banded stacks of foil-packet pills on the other. Everything had stick-on labels in small, plain type. I didn't

recognize any of the names. Nothing said PAIN RELIEF or AN-
ESTHETIC or THIS WILL KEEP YOUR GRANDDAD FROM DYING. I
was tempted to just start grabbing things, but I couldn't hide
much in my jeans or socks.

The salesdork couldn't be much longer. I could hear him
moving around in the back.

I was about to give up when I saw a small brown plastic
bottle with a label that said PERCOCET 0H10MG. I knew Percocet. A painkiller. Some sixth-graders at school had gotten
busted for having it in their lockers, pills stolen from their
parents. I'd thought they were stupid, keeping it where any
janitor might look.

The bottle was half full of white oval tablets. And there
were two more bottles. I took them all and tucked them
under my belt, in the elastic of my underwear.

I was collecting my change from the cashier when the
salesdork came running up, holding a huge tackle box.
"Hey," he said.

"Sorry, my mom's calling. I gotta go." I was on my bike
before the automatic door slid closed behind me. Then I
was across the parking lot and on the road and pointed east.
Standing in the saddle, pumping hard to make the bike fly,
the pills in their bottles rattling to keep time.

CHAPTER FIVE

FOUND HOLLIS BRANT'S NUMBER in Dono's address book. My call went straight to voice mail. I left a message. Hollis hadn't seen me in a dozen years. But he knew how I'd left things with Dono. It wouldn't be much of a leap for him to figure out something was very wrong, if I was in town.

At three o'clock in the morning, I was on the couch in my old room, settling into something close to sleep. My phone rang.

"Van? It's Hollis." He was almost shouting, trying to hear himself over a deep, throbbing pulse in the background. "How is he? Have they caught the fucker?"

"You know about Dono?" I said. Stupid question. I was still groggy.

"Course I know. The second I got your message, I made some calls. Now, tell me how he is, goddamn it." I got a fix on the pulsing sound. A boat's diesel engines. Not far from shore, if Hollis could get cell-phone coverage.

I shared what I knew. Hollis responded mostly with curses—at the shooter, at the doctors, at the whole damn world. I told Hollis I needed to talk to him, in person.

He grunted assent. "I'm on the water right now. You know Harbor Island?"

"Yeah."

"I should make port by six-thirty—I'm running with the current. At Malcolm Yards, on Malcolm Road. Not far off Terminal 19."

"I'll find it."

"Good. We'll get the bastard who did this, count on that. And, Van? It's good to hear your voice again, lad. Too fucking long."

I wondered who had clued Hollis in to what had happened with Dono. And why Hollis was making port at Harbor Island. He used to moor his big Chris-Craft, the *Francesca*, way out in Ballard along with half the other pleasure boats in Seattle.

There was no hope of sleep. I got up and showered. My jeans were stiff and flaking with dried blood. In Dono's closet I found trousers that fit me well enough and a tan chamois shirt that wasn't too tight. I was a little shorter than Dono, but bigger across the chest and shoulders.

I drove to the 5 Point Café on Cedar Street near the elevated monorail tracks to kill time and pound coffee while watching the night traffic drift by.

Come home, if you can.

Hollis was a smuggler. He was an occasional business partner of my grandfather, usually when a job called for getting things across the border from Canada or down the coast by boat. More than that, he was one of Dono's few friends. Or he had been, the last I knew. The old man didn't socialize a lot.

Hollis, on the other hand, picked up friends like pennies. He seemed to have a well-placed contact in shipping or customs at any Pacific port that Dono could name.

There was a good chance that whatever job Dono had been working, Hollis would be part of it. And if Dono had found himself in real trouble, Hollis would be someone he'd want on his side.

Unless he already knew that his friends couldn't help him. Maybe mending fences with me was Dono's last resort.

And a shitload of help I'd been to him.

I looked at my watch. 0500. Too early. But moving felt better than sitting. I left money on the counter and drove out to see the orange dinosaurs.

That's what I used to call the gigantic gantry cranes on Harbor

Island when I was a kid. Dinosaurs. In fact they were much bigger than any beast that had ever lived. Ten stories high at the operator's shack. Twice that if they raised their long necks. Big enough to lift multiple boxcar containers at one time off the commercial freighters. Even miles in the distance, as I came down the long avenue onto the island off the West Seattle bridge, the cranes looked like monsters, gazing at the coming dawn.

The Port of Seattle had major terminals on Harbor Island, along with docks for a hundred other companies, ranging from big to not-quite-big. A few private moorages were there as well, but the vast majority of the island was industrial—shipyards, importers, and acre after acre of massive white cylindrical petroleum tanks.

I found the right road and the right gate and parked the Charger.

Malcolm Yards looked like a small drydock operation. It was closed, the rolling gate locked with a chain looped around its posts. An eight-foot chain-link surrounded the yard, with razor-wire strands angled out over the street side. Beyond the fence, in the weak illumination thrown by a handful of floodlights, I could see a squat office building and a big, square-framed lift machine to haul boats out of the water.

The little drydock had lots of privacy on its cul-de-sac road. A nice choice for a smuggler. I guessed Hollis wasn't making port here because he liked to watch the cranes working.

The sky had turned a pale gray, not yet daylight but with enough sun bouncing off the cloud cover to make it feel like dawn could break any minute. Cars on the overpass zooming between West Seattle and the city sounded like the buzzing of bees. It was still too early for the Monday-morning rush hour.

A white Ryder moving truck drove past me and made a partial circle around the cul-de-sac. It parked on the opposite side, about a hundred feet away. Roads were very wide on Harbor Island, to allow room for commercial vehicles to maneuver. The moving van wasn't that large. A fifteen-footer, just big enough to handle a one-bedroom apartment, if you stacked it right.

There were two men in the cab of the Ryder truck. The one closer to me on the passenger side glanced at the Charger. In the half-light, he probably couldn't see me sitting inside.

The driver got out and walked up to the gate and unlocked it, letting the chain hang loose. He pulled hard on the gate, and it moved an inch. He was tall, but as thin as a marathon runner, and it took another two hard pulls before he got enough momentum going and the gate rolled slowly open. He climbed back into the Ryder truck and drove it through the entrance. They left the gate open.

As the truck's headlights shone across the yard, I saw something else. There was a man on the bow of one of the boats tied up at the Malcolm dock. The dock was fifty yards from where I was parked, but even at that distance I recognized Hollis Brant's broad, sloping shoulders and thick arms.

The Ryder van stopped halfway from the office building, a hundred feet or so from the dock. Its headlights went out, but the parking lights stayed on. The thin driver and the passenger got out. They walked toward the dock—and Hollis's boat.

So it was business. Hollis had told me to get there at six-thirty, so he could take care of whatever deal he had with the guys from the Ryder van before I showed. He must have seen me pull up early in the Charger. He'd chosen to stay put on his boat rather than come and unlock the gate.

I could take the hint.

The driver and the passenger reached the boat. There was enough light now for me to see Hollis wave them aboard. They climbed up, and the three men went down below.

A couple of minutes passed. Then the rolling door on the back end of the Ryder truck began sliding upward. A big guy ducked under the door and stepped down. He wore a leather jacket with a few too many zippers and studs on it to be for real, and motorcycle boots.

He peeked around the truck at Hollis's boat. Everything there looked quiet. He flipped his jacket up to adjust a pistol stuck in his waistband, getting it comfortable against the small of his back. Then he began walking toward the dock.

Maybe it was nothing. Maybe Hollis was expecting the third guy to join the party.

But it didn't feel like nothing.

Crap.

I started the Charger and drove it through the open gate. The Ryder truck was between me and the dock, shielding my car from view. I lined up my front tires with the side of the truck and gave the accelerator a gentle tap before putting the car in neutral. The Charger kept rolling forward at a fast walking pace as I opened the door and stepped out.

I had plenty of time to jog over to the front door of the little office building. The Charger rolled into the side of the Ryder van. It made an impressive crunching sound. I was glad I'd opted for the insurance.

There were shouts from the direction of Hollis's boat. Running footsteps pounded on the wooden planks of the dock. I poked my head around the corner of the building.

"Ah, shit!" I said, loud enough to carry. "Goddamn it!"

I might have been right about the driver being a marathon runner. He reached the two vehicles, which were now connected in a T shape, at the same time as his big friend with the motorcycle boots. Behind them I saw Hollis, stepping off his boat.

"What the fuck?" the driver said. More startled than angry.

"Goddamn it," I said again, "that fucking parking brake. I know I set that damn thing."

The passenger finally caught up with his two buddies. "What happened?" he said, puffing. His sweatshirt read CHICAGO BEARS in orange letters. The big biker just stared dully at the crash.

"This asshole," said the driver, jabbing a finger at me. "All we fucking need right now."

"Hey, I'm sorry," I said. "I swear to God I set that brake. It's a rental, see?"

"Fuck you and your piece-of-shit car," said the driver. The biker nodded. Happy to have some direction. He was my height but must have outweighed me by sixty pounds, thirty of it a rubbery layer that strained at his XXXL T-shirt. The Bears fan moved around to the other side of me. He was smaller than his partner, but not by a whole lot.

"I'm covered for that, no problem," I said, gesturing toward the Ryder van. Hollis was about twenty yards away, ambling like he had the morning to spare. I couldn't tell if he had a gun. "At least it's a rental, right? You guys work here?"

"We ought to fuck you up," said the driver.

The biker took that as a command. He reached for the gun at his waist, and I punched him in the throat, as hard as I dared without crushing his windpipe. He gagged and staggered back. The gun clattered on the asphalt, and I kicked it away under the moving truck.

The Bears fan tackled me. I got an arm in between us, and as we hit the ground the point of my elbow dug into his chest. The pain made him wince. My left forearm went numb. I grabbed him by the shoulder and bucked upward, head-butting him in the face. Blood spurted from his nose, and I twisted sharply and got free.

I rolled up onto my knees, just as a kick from one of the biker's motorcycle boots missed my skull by a hair. I upper-cutted him in the balls. He screamed. As I got to my feet, the Bears fan swung blind, and his fist glanced off the side of my head. My ear rang.

My left arm wasn't responding fast enough. I hit Bears twice in his bleeding nose with my right and kicked his legs out from under him. He went down hard. I could feel the biker coming up fast behind me. I turned, bracing for the hit, just as the biker was suddenly yanked away.

"I said knock it off, you little shits." The speaker was a wiry man in his fifties, with a bald head and a disgusted expression on his face. The biker was being restrained by one of the largest men I'd ever seen. In his grip the big biker looked like a teenager getting a hug from his father.

I knew both of them. The wiry, bald one was Jimmy Corcoran. The giant was Willard. I'd known them almost as long as I'd known Hollis, who'd finally joined the rest of us. I saw the bulge of a pistol under his blue tank top.

"Look, dude," I said to the driver in between deep breaths, "I'm just here to see about getting my boat hauled out. I didn't want trouble."

Corcoran and Willard both glanced at me, then at Hollis. Apparently it was his party.

Hollis made a show of looking at the vehicles and shrugged. "Screw it. A couple of dents. Let's just forget about it." He turned to the driver. "Forget all of it."

"Hey," said the driver. "We had a deal." His eyes kept flicking back to Willard, who loomed behind the biker like a wall. Willard had that effect on people.

Hollis smiled. It was not a friendly smile. "Which you wanted to renegotiate. Isn't that how you put it? So we're renegotiating. Here are my new terms: Fuck off."

The driver hesitated, but the Bears fan had already started moving toward the Ryder truck, holding his smashed nose. Willard took his hand off the biker's shoulder, letting him follow. The driver gave me one last glare and turned and walked to the moving truck.

They didn't wait for me to back the Charger away from where it still touched the side of the Ryder truck. They just put it in gear and pulled out with a grinding of metal against metal.

"Well," said Hollis, "wasn't that a fine start to the day?"

CHAPTER SIX

YOU OWE US," JIMMY Corcoran said to me as we sat down in the cockpit of Hollis's boat. "And not just for keeping your ass from getting stomped."

Hollis opened the sliding glass door to the cabin and went into the little galley. He spoke loudly enough for the three of us outside to hear. "The deal was going south anyway."

"I owe you for the save," I said, "but not the money. Those guys weren't planning on paying for whatever they wanted."

"Laptop computers," Hollis said.

"Hey," said Corcoran.

"Oh, stuff it, Jimmy," Hollis said, chuckling. "Van doesn't give a shit. And he may have just spared me some serious grief. Now, do you want breakfast or no?"

Willard smiled. Corcoran still looked dyspeptic.

"Shouldn't have made a deal with those idiots in the first place," Corcoran said. The face below his bald skull was heavily lined. Too many years of squinting angrily at people and gadgets. Corcoran was a tech guy. In his youth he had been a prodigy with electronics. Dono was no amateur, and neither was I for that matter. But Corcoran had the touch.

"How's Dono?" Willard said. His voice was like gravel in a cement mixer.

"I called the lads after we talked," Hollis said to me. He turned on a drip coffeemaker and came back to the cockpit as it started gurgling. "They both wanted to be here, to hear what happened straight from you."

Hollis resembled nothing more than an orangutan. Short and very wide, with strong, overlong arms. He was a little more potbellied than the last time I'd seen him, and his tight orange curls were dusted with white. He wore a sky blue tank top and baggy khaki shorts. Way too light for the morning, but the cold didn't seem to bother him.

I gave the three of them a condensed version of the past day, including the fact that Detective Guerin might be looking up Dono's known associates. That earned frowns from Corcoran and Willard.

"You know this guy Guerin?" Corcoran said to Hollis.

Hollis sighed. "Not one of mine. Jesus, boyo. What a Christly homecoming for you. Let me get a look at you." He made a show of it, examining me head to toe like I was a racehorse. "Damnation. You used to be a bulky kid. The army shaved you down a layer."

"Fifty-mile marches will do that," I said. The fight had tired me more than it should have. Too many weeks of soft time in Germany and not enough sleep in the last forty-eight hours.

"What happened to your face?" Corcoran said.

I rolled my neck, trying to get some of the tension out. "When was the last time any of you saw Dono?"

Hollis leaned against the cabin, folding his arms. "I saw him just last week. First time in a while. We met at the house and shared a drink or two."

That must have been the visit when Addy Proctor saw him. "Talking about work?" I said.

He smiled ruefully. "Talking about old-man stuff. I had a little health scare. A tumor, right here." He pointed to his right shoulder blade. "Not malignant, as it turns out, but oh, shit, did it put me on my guard. Nothing to shrivel up your balls like having your doctor ask you to come in so he can tell you news in person."

"I'm glad it's all right."

"You and me both. But your man didn't talk about his work. And it's been a year or more since he and I put any deals together. Fucking economy, you know. I got the impression that your granddad had been taking some time off for himself."

That got Corcoran's attention. "He could afford that?"

Hollis brought the coffee out on a big metal tray with crackers and cream cheese and a large hunk of smoked salmon. The coffee smelled good. He set it down on the pedestal table in the center of the cockpit. "Whether Dono could afford it or not, he was doing it. Tuck in," he said.

I wasn't hungry, but I took a big gulp of coffee before I realized that Hollis had laced it with whiskey. My nasal passages closed up. I coughed and sputtered, and Hollis laughed and nearly fell back into the cabin.

"Oh, my Jesus, kid. I am sorry. I forgot it's been forever and a day since you've broken bread with me." He wiped his eyes, and I began laughing with him, the adrenaline from the fight finally starting to ebb.

Hollis hadn't forgotten to warn me. He just knew how to lighten the mood.

"How about you?" I said to Willard and Corcoran.

"Shit," said Corcoran. "I haven't seen Dono Shaw in months."

Willard nodded. "Almost half a year for me."

"What was our last job with him?" Corcoran asked Willard. "That place out in Magnolia?" Willard nodded again, and Corcoran looked like he wanted to spit. "That was last summer. Your granddad was never much of a joiner, kid, but he'd become a fucking hermit recently."

That startled me. Not that I thought Jimmy Corcoran was Dono's favorite person, but he or Willard or both of them would meet Dono at his bar, the Morgen, for a drink from time to time. Even if there was no score to plan, they kept in touch. It was part of the same grapevine that had so effectively passed the word about Dono's shooting. Hard to imagine Dono cutting himself off from it.

I took another sip. The coffee was burned, but you could hardly tell with half the mug filled with hard alcohol. "Hollis, you already knew about Dono when I called you."

He nodded. "I got a call from Ondine Long."

"No shit?" said Willard. It took a lot to break his habitual placid expression.

"In person, no less," said Hollis. "I gathered she'd heard the news directly from the police. You know how connected she is."

I did. Ondine was a fence and a fixer. She knew people everywhere. People a hell of a lot more influential than an old smuggler like Hollis.

"She was calling just to tell you about Dono?" I said.

"She was asking me," said Hollis. "What did I know, if Dono was mixed up with any trouble. I didn't have anything to share, of course, and she told me to call her if I learned more."

Corcoran's mouth twisted an extra notch. "And you were eager to help."

"Screw off. I've done business with the woman," Hollis said.

"Did Dono have a girlfriend?" I asked.

Hollis shrugged. "Not that he mentioned. And I can usually tell when he has a woman around regular. He'd shave more. Dress a little better."

Willard shifted uncomfortably. The narrow bench seat was too small for him. Of the three of them, Willard seemed to have changed the least. His heavy brow and jaw were maybe a little more so, making his face even more doleful than it used to be, but his eyes were still quick and alert. Willard was muscle, of course, but not dumb muscle. And his huge size made him too memorable for a lot of jobs. Occasionally he worked as a driver. He was surprisingly skilled, provided he could fit behind the wheel.

"Did you say he was shot point-blank?" Willard said.

"To the back of his head," I said. "Just inside the front door. Maybe the shooter was at the door and Dono turned away. Or maybe they were both inside and Dono was leading him out. Either way—"

"You think Dono knew him. Or her," Willard said.

"Yeah."

"Well, I hope to shit you don't mean us," Corcoran said, reddening.

"Of course not, Jimmy," said Hollis.

I remembered Hollis's tendency to be the peacemaker of the group.

Dono was too flinty, too much the leader. Corcoran couldn't help being an asshole. And Willard followed whoever had a sensible plan. So it was left to Hollis to smooth the waters.

"I'm not looking at you," I said. "But if anyone knew what was happening in Dono's life, it would be you three. Some score he was working on—or had already done."

"Which might have gotten him shot," Willard said. He shook his head. "I got nothing."

"I need to get moving," Corcoran said, nudging Willard. Willard stood up and stepped out onto the side deck, which was enough to make the *Francesca* rock a little.

"Sorry again about Dono," Willard said.

"Yeah," said Corcoran, following. "Sorry."

Hollis and I watched as the two men got off the boat and walked up the dock. The morning breeze had some force to it now. Each time the wind gusted, I could hear loose sailing lines tap and clang against the aluminum masts in the marina in a dissonant melody.

"Do you think they're telling the truth?" I asked Hollis. "About not working with Dono?"

Hollis took a big swig out of his mug and refilled it from the thermos. "Willard, yes. Hard to say with Jimmy. He doesn't like people knowing his business any more than your grandfather does. But I think Dono would have mentioned it to me if they had something on. What department did you say your boy Detective Guerin worked out of?"

"H.A." Homicide/Assault, downtown.

"So they're not letting the East Precinct handle it as an aggravated," Hollis said.

"No. It's attempted murder, straight up." We both understood the implication. The cops didn't expect Dono to recover.

We sat quiet for a moment. The seagulls floated on the air over the breakwater, dipping down with renewed hope to look for small fish each time the surface water rippled in a way I couldn't perceive.

"Are you done with the army?" he said.

"Just on leave. Ten days." Down to eight now. Better get my ass in gear.

"And you decided it was time to see Dono. Good." He flexed his fingers. "Fucking arthritis. So who knew you were coming home?"

I looked at him. "You've been wondering about that, too."

"Of course I have."

"When did he tell you he'd written to me?" I said.

Hollis frowned. "Boyo, he didn't say a fucking thing to me about it."

When I was small, Hollis Brant often brought me a gift when he came to the house, a Japanese windup toy or some other exotic item from one of his friends on the freighters, as he called them. As I grew older and started to help the two men with their work, Hollis would slip me a few bucks on the sly with a wink. I knew where Dono hid some of his money and would help myself when I needed it, but I appreciated Hollis's gesture. I liked him. He might even have liked me, but eventually I realized that the toys and the money were just part of Hollis's method, being generous and building alliances as an investment for the future. I might be in a position to help him out someday. Bread on the water.

I wondered how strong the friendship between him and Dono still was, if Dono hadn't told Hollis that the prodigal grandson was on his way home.

"Dono must have told somebody I was coming," I said. "Maybe even when I was going to arrive."

"You didn't tell someone yourself? Not even your young friend—what's his name?"

It took me a second to realize whom Hollis meant. "Davey Tolan? No, I haven't talked to Davey in years."

And it hadn't even occurred to me to call Davey, during the storm of the last day. Hollis was right. A hell of a homecoming.

"I can't leave this to the cops," I said. "What they know about Dono isn't going to give them a lot of extra motivation."

"You want to . . . ah, deal with this bastard yourself?"

"Serving him to the cops on a platter will be enough."

"I'll tell you, Van, I'm surprised you're back," said Hollis. "Happy, too, don't get me wrong. But I thought you'd put Seattle behind you.

The way you and Dono parted. He hadn't even mentioned your name to me in God knows how long."

"I decided to bury the past."

"And this kind of business," he said, pointing to where the three morons had driven the Ryder van away from the crumpled Charger. "It isn't your life anymore, is that it?"

I'd done well in AIT, Advanced Individual Training, during my first months in the army. A recruiter for the Seventy-fifth Regiment came by to talk to a few of us. As part of his sales pitch, he had recited some lines from the Ranger Creed. Mentally alert, physically strong, and morally straight. It was the last bit that had made my ears prick up.

"No," I said to Hollis, "it's not my life now. But I don't give a damn what anybody else does."

He stared at me for a moment, brow still furrowed. Then he sighed. "All right, then. I won't judge you either. Some of my best friends are citizens. Or so they claim."

"Here's to profit," I said, quoting one of Hollis's own lines.

"Nah. Here's to Dono." We drank. Hollis swished the coffee through his teeth like mouthwash before swallowing.

"Your granddad," he said "He wasn't much for the light hand with you. But he did care."

"I know."

"You may still get your chance," Hollis continued. He didn't seem to have heard me. "Your man was always a quick healer. You recall the time? No, certainly not, you were very small. He had dislocated his shoulder somehow, but it didn't stop him from leading a little discussion we had with the Fitzroys. Nasty pieces of work, those lads, but we showed them something. That was a fine day." He waved a paw toward the city. "A bed in a hospital. That's no proper fate for a man." His empty coffee mug dangled from his finger. From out across the sound, the low horn of a ferry echoed.

"Showed them," he said again. And damned if he wasn't welling up, the tears starting to roll down his ruddy cheeks.

Hollis could have gotten close enough to Dono, no question. He might have had a little automatic ready. He could have put the muzzle right up against Dono's head as they walked to the door after a long night of bullshit and booze.

But even if I could fathom some motive for why Hollis might have wanted to kill his oldest friend, I couldn't see him as the shooter. Dono was still alive. Hollis would have finished the job.

I stood up and patted him on the shoulder. He nodded. I stepped out of the cockpit and down to the dock and walked away. When I looked back from the shoreline, he was still sitting there, head down and mourning one of the last of his kind.

CHAPTER SEVEN

WHEN I GOT BACK to the house, there was a folded note tucked into the doorjamb, just below the splintered holes where I'd torn out the police padlock. The note had been scrawled in blue ballpoint ink on white notepaper with the name and address of a business printed at the top: FRAZIER BROS ELECTRIC. The handwriting was so bad I had to piece together the message word by word.

> Van,
>
> *Missed catching u here. Meet me at Morgen after 6? Things sometimes suck, right?*
>
> *—Davey*

Even after I'd left town, I'd kept half an eye on Davey. Old habit. He had his whole life online, naturally. He and his high-school girl, Juliet, had gotten married. I'd seen pictures of Juliet carrying a fat and smiling baby. They all looked happy—and settled, which was a relief.

I looked at the note again. Davey had pressed so hard while writing that the letters made thin furrows in the paper, like embossing.

Screw it. As long as I was in town, I might as well tie up all my unfinished business. I could blow off some steam drinking and catching up with Davey. And I could see Dono's bar again.

I wondered if Dono's business partner, Albie Boylan—who actually ran the place—had changed it much. Not likely. The Morgen probably still had a ceiling stained the color of charcoal from decades of cigarette smoke and Albie's aluminum baseball bat taped up under the cash register, ready to keep the peace.

That was, I suddenly realized, if Dono still owned the Morgen. Maybe he had sold it off. There was too much about the old man's life now I didn't know.

I took out my keys to unlock the front door. The house keys snagged on the second set, the two smaller keys attached to the chunk of red wood. I looked at them again and remembered where I had seen keys like them before.

For outboard engines. The larger models, 250 horses or more. And the chunk of wood was to keep them from sinking if they fell in the water.

Dono had a boat.

I unlocked the door and went straight to the pantry to open up Dono's hiding place again.

Dono's personal and business files were all upstairs in his desk. I'd seen them the night before. The old man hadn't gone digital yet, and he was a meticulous record keeper. An hour going through the files could paint me a complete picture of his life as a general contractor and bar owner. But that wasn't the right paper trail to follow. There was another.

At the back of the one-foot-square hole was the small stack of Dono's fake driver's licenses. I flipped through them. Two in the same name, one for Washington State and one for California. A second name for Washington, again. And a third for West Virginia, of all places.

It was common enough for Dono to have false identification. Or at least false names, with verifiable licenses. A few thousand slipped to a DMV employee might do it.

But none of these names was the one I was looking for. John Terrence Callahan. That was the one name I knew that might have a real address attached to it. Someplace I could search. Assuming that J. T. Callahan still existed.

Convicted felons can't do a lot of things. Depending on the laws of the state in question, the felon might lose the right to vote, to hold a professional license, or to serve on a jury. A few people I knew would think earning that last restriction was worth committing a major crime. Felons have trouble getting a passport. And the law might sit up and take notice if a former convict began purchasing unusual equipment like plasma cutters or wireless alarm transmitters.

That was where J. T. Callahan came in. Like Donovan Shaw, J.T. was sixty-four years old, six foot two, and he worked in construction. He was an occasional reseller of industrial equipment and was certified in multiple services, including a federal license granted by the ATF to purchase and operate Class 1 explosives.

Not bad for a guy who'd only been walking the earth for seventeen years or so.

Dono had created Callahan shortly after he got out of County and reclaimed the house and his life. I was eleven. A little young to fathom the workings of my grandfather's mind, but I think at the start he just wanted to have a passport and a new name close at hand, if ever the time came to disappear.

Over the years Dono realized that J.T. could serve other purposes as well. Thus the Callahan identity began eking out a living and acquiring the right background. I would bet my entire meager bank account that the old man had kept up the charade.

Hollis and Willard and Corcoran were a dead end. And I didn't buy what Dono had told Hollis. Dono wasn't taking time off. Whatever my grandfather was into, he had been doing it without his old team. If I could trace Callahan's activities, I might learn what had really been going on.

The advantage of a complete false history is that it holds up under most scrutiny. The disadvantage is that the identity really exists, even if the man behind it doesn't. Even a paper life carves paths and patterns that can be followed. J. T. Callahan must have a Social Security number. He must file tax returns. He'd have at least a mailing address, somewhere.

And if I was right about the outboard keys, Callahan owned a boat, too. I'd start there.

Dono's charged cell phone was still in my pocket. I took it out and went to the call log again. Still just the one number, outgoing to Ephraim Ganz's office the day before Dono was shot. I hit SEND.

"Ganz and Quinlan," a husky female voice answered.

"Mr. Ganz, please. It's Van Shaw."

"Oh, yes. One moment, Mr. Shaw." A strong note of recognition there. Did she think I was Dono?

"Van? It's Ephraim Ganz." His voice was high-pitched, fast and aggressive. I could picture him clutching the phone. A small man with enough energy for three large ones.

"Hello, Ephraim. Long time."

"You aren't shitting me. I was just thinking, the last I saw you, you must have been . . . what, about to graduate high school?"

"You've heard about Dono?"

"Hell, yes. Cheryl caught the early Sunday news and woke me up. Terrible. I've heard about you, too, from my friends at East Precinct. That's why I told Gloria here to pull me out of meetings if you called. The cops questioned you? Why didn't you call me?"

"No need. A neighbor saw me arrive after the shooting. That cleared me."

"No need, he says. Listen, if they bring you in again, you call me. First thing. Pretend not to *sprechen sie* English if you have to."

"The detectives are more interested in Dono's action. You know anything about what he's been doing?"

Ganz paused. "I was going to ask you the same question."

"Dono and I haven't spoken since I left." I gave Ganz a quick rundown on how narrow the time was between my arrival and his shooting. "I spent the morning talking to some of Dono's old friends, which got me nowhere. I'm starting to think he was practicing to be a hermit. So it's over to you. Has Dono made a dent in your retainer recently?"

"He hasn't needed to avail himself of my services. No arrests or other trouble."

"Dono called your office on Saturday."

"Yes. Gloria said he left a message on Paul Arronow's extension, asking Paul to call him back. Paul's our associate in estate law."

"Estate? Like, for Dono's last will and testament?"

"Right."

"Then if Dono's reaching out to him, it's to make a change. Who stands to inherit?"

Ganz grunted. "It's you. You didn't know?"

"I've been gone ten years, Ephraim. Are you telling me Dono never updated his will in all that time?"

"Your mother, Moira? Dono didn't change his will when *she* left. She was going to inherit everything, up until . . . well, until you came to live with him. Then it became you. And it's stayed like that."

"Until now, maybe."

"Maybe," Ganz admitted. "But don't jump to conclusions. Maybe he was just adding something. Did he buy a new house or something else big?"

"Not that I know of."

My mother had walked out on Dono. I had, too. And Dono had still considered me his heir?

I looked at the keys attached to the piece of red driftwood.

"You have any friends at the state vehicle-license bureau?" I asked Ganz.

"Huh?"

"I need a name checked."

"Ah. I'll have someone call you."

"Good."

"And, Van? If SPD pulls you in again, you call me, understand?" I was already hanging up.

Too many lines intersecting. Dono asking me back to town. Changing his will at the same time.

Had he been planning to surprise me with that change? Dono wasn't the spiteful type. He wasn't looking to throw his house and his bar in my face, like some sort of piss-ant revenge for my leaving. There must be something else behind it.

At least one thing was clear. Not good, but clear. If Ganz was right, and my name was still on the line marked "beneficiary," then I had a bigger problem looming.

Easy to predict how the cops would assemble the puzzle pieces. Dono had his house in the city. His bar. I stood to inherit property worth somewhere north of a million, maybe two. But Dono was looking to change his will. And he wound up shot the morning I arrived.

I was about to leap back into the bull's-eye as prime suspect.

CHAPTER EIGHT

ADDY PROCTOR WAS AT the front desk of the Trauma ICU. She wore a black woolen coat long enough to almost touch her clunky shoes. From behind, her white hair looked like the crest on a cockatoo. I walked up just in time to hear the tail end of her conversation with the nurse making her sign in.

"We're all praying for him, dear," Addy said. She had a beatific smile on her face. "My nephew was a scoundrel, but the good Lord will make sure he recovers."

She looked over and saw me standing next to her, grinning.

"Aunt Addy," I said.

"Oh, Van, I'm so happy you're here." She ushered me quickly away.

"Darn good thing you're family," I said. "They wouldn't let you in otherwise."

She snorted. "Stupid rule. What if someone has nobody else to watch over them? There are plenty of old farts in my circle who'd rather have their friends than their next of kin in a time of need."

As we walked past other rooms, I saw some of the same visitors still here from the day before. There were a lot of round-the-clock vigils in Trauma.

A uniformed cop sat on a chair outside Dono's room, watching us walk toward him. I introduced myself and Aunt Addy. He nodded in recognition at my name and let us into the room.

Dono looked the same. Down to the position of his feet under the thin cotton blanket.

Addy sat in one of the chairs and set her big wicker purse beside her. I stood. We both looked at Dono. The IV tube pulsed almost imperceptibly as the drip moved through it to his arm.

"I've sat with people before," Addy said. "I like to read to them. Passes the time, at least for me. Do you think he'd mind? Would you?"

I sat down. "He liked to read."

Addy pulled a paperback in a fabric slipcover from her purse, put on a pair of tortoiseshell glasses, and began to read out loud. I couldn't see the title and didn't know the book. From the language I could tell it was old, maybe nineteenth century.

"What is that?" I asked when Addy paused to turn the page.

"Dickens," she said. *"Our Mutual Friend."*

"I didn't understand the part you read about 'Six Jolly . . .'"

" . . . 'Fellowship-Porters,'" she said. "It's the name of a pub."

I nodded. A big day for taverns. I wondered what Dono would need me to do to keep the Morgen running while he was laid up. Maybe his partner, Albie Boylan, would know.

"You read a lot of classic lit?" I asked.

"I have," Addy said. "I was a teacher, once upon a time. And a librarian. Back when the card catalogs had actual cards."

My phone rang.

"I'm calling about the name," said a high male voice in a whispering rush. "You asked our buddy to have me call you?"

Ganz's guy from the DMV. Our Mutual Friend, sure enough.

"John Terrence Callahan," I said, "or John T., or J.T."

I heard fast typing. "There're a few of those in the state. Date of birth?"

"Start with the oldest and work up."

Heavy exhale. "One in 1936 . . ."

"Too old."

"Next is 1950."

"Try that one. What are the stats on it?"

"Six foot two. Gray hair, brown eyes. Serious-looking picture. Not bad if you like silver foxes."

Dono. "Give me everything on him."

More sound of assaulting the keyboard. "Okay, he owns one car, a 2005 Lincoln." He read off the license number. A Lincoln. Callahan traveled in style.

"What's the address?"

"It's 495 East Pike, number 1701."

No building in that part of the Hill had seventeen floors. Probably a private mailbox business. So 1701 would be Dono's box number.

"He's got a boat, too," I said.

"I see that. King County, but there's no moorage location listed here. The registration address is the same as on the driver's license."

"What kind of vessel?"

"What? Oh, the boat. It's a . . ." He said each item separately, like reading off a list. "A 2006 gray fiberglass twenty-two-foot Stingray 220SX outboard gasoline pleasure sport boat. I swear I have no idea what most of that means."

"Anything else?"

"About the boat?"

"About anything at all. More vehicles, more licenses. Parking tickets, if you have them."

"I don't. Those are only on file with— Oh, you're joking. Jesus. No, there's nothing else, except that Mr. Callahan is licensed for commercial vehicles—Class C. And he's not an organ donor."

I looked at Dono's still form and the machines keeping him alive. I hung up.

"Who's Callahan?" Addy said.

"I have to go."

"I guessed that. I'll read for a while longer."

I nodded. She didn't open the paperback. We both watched Dono.

"What would he want?" she asked.

"What *I* want is to help the cops find who did this to him. And I don't want him to die while I'm away doing it."

"No clear choice," Addy said. "Maybe if I stayed for you?"

"Thanks. But the hospital knows to call me if anything changes. It's not about having someone here."

"It's about you and him."

"Yeah."

Barely a week until I had to report in at Benning. I could watch Dono every hour, and he might still be exactly like this when I left.

I got up. "Thanks for coming."

"Anytime," Addy said. I heard her start reading again before the door closed behind me.

CHAPTER NINE

THE BUILDING AT 495 East Pike was less than a mile away from Harborview. It was a large, two-story brick structure with a chiropractor on the second floor and a Mailbox Worldwide shipping franchise on the first.

It was before the lunch hour, and the Mailbox office was quiet. Between the painted words on the windows, I could see a young woman behind the counter, sealing boxes with strapping tape.

A man walked in and headed for the bank of golden-doored boxes on the side wall. I followed him inside and pretended to be listening intently to my phone while finding Box 1701, high on the right side. I watched as the man used a short silver key with a circular head to open his box. Dono had a similar silver key on the big key ring in my pocket.

When the woman carried the cardboard box into the back, I walked over to the wall and opened Box 1701 with Dono's key. It was crammed full of envelopes and postcards. A lucky spin for me that Dono hadn't picked up his mail in a while. I stuffed the stack of mail into my jacket and left. I sat in the driver's seat of the Charger to leaf through J. T. Callahan's correspondence.

Most of the stack turned out to be advertisements. Tool shops obviously liked Callahan. The more personal items included a bank statement, a couple of letters from workman's associations, and an envelope from Western Maritime.

I opened the envelope. It was a receipt correction and a letter, apologizing to Mr. Callahan for the incorrect pricing of his purchases in February and hoping that he was enjoying them to the full. I looked at the receipt. A Lowrance HD Chartplotter, a Garmin VHF radio, and other equipment. Over four grand of new electronics in all.

Which confirmed that Dono had acquired a boat, and recently. But it didn't tell me where it was.

I checked the bank statement. It was short. The balance was just under twenty thousand. There had been automated withdrawals for his mailbox, for the car insurance on the Lincoln, and for Altamont Garage, which I guessed was where he kept the Lincoln.

And one more withdrawal, for something called BLUERIDGE MOOR LLC. I took out my phone and searched for the name. There was a Blue Ridge Marina, a couple miles north of the big public piers at Shilshole Bay in Seattle.

Hot damn.

AT FIRST GLANCE THE marina didn't look like much. Just a row of six or seven short docks separated from Puget Sound by a breakwater. Maybe two hundred slips in all. But the resident vessels were upmarket, mostly oceanworthy sailboats and tall cruising yachts. I saw a lot of varnished teak and shiny brass fittings that managed to gleam even on this overcast day. It was Monday, and the docks were empty of people.

Each floating dock had its own entrance door, made of flat steel mesh with side extensions and razor wire on the top to keep the riffraff from climbing around to the ramp.

I knew from Ganz's guy at the DMV what I was looking for. A twenty-two-foot gray Stingray speedboat. All the boats near that size were parked in the slips closest to shore, because they had shallower drafts than their bigger cousins. I walked down the row of docks, looking at them. Most were white, with a few blues and blacks. Only one was gray.

The lock on the steel gate was a heavy mechanical combination type. Six punch buttons marked with letters of the alphabet, A through F. I had a pry bar from the truck under my coat, but a quick glance at the lock told me I wouldn't need it.

Four of the six buttons were shiny from repeated use. Each button can only be used once in a mechanical lock, since each corresponds to a separate tumbler inside. Four buttons, twenty-four possible combinations. When I put a little tension on the door handle and pressed gently on each button, I could tell by touch that button C was first in the sequence, because its tumbler wasn't providing as much resistance. Eight possible sequences left. By trial and error, I had the gate open in forty more seconds.

It had been a long time since I'd greased a lock with just my hands. Score one for the riffraff. I walked down the dock to the boat.

The Stingray was a sport boat, built for zipping between islands on day trips or dragging water-skiers behind it. About half of its length was the sleek bow section in front of its raked windshield. No name was painted on the stern. Nothing about the boat stood out as particularly unique. Even the gray paint was dull.

There was a buff-colored canvas cover over the entire cockpit and engine, to keep both shielded from the weather. The cover was fastened in place with hooks and elastic cord every foot or two around the edges of the hull. I unhooked the cord and pulled the canvas back until I could fold it out of the way onto the foredeck.

The engine was a monster, a black Mercury 300-horse. Dono had covered it with a rubber muffling cowl to help keep the noise from rattling his eardrums loose. There were two red five-gallon jerry jugs tied to the inside of the stern, spare fuel tanks that could be connected with a hose directly to the thirsty engine.

The whole package wasn't as fast or as flashy as a go-fast boat, the kind made famous by drug smugglers around the world. But I would lay money that the deep spearhead of its hull could manage forty knots an hour on a flat sea without straining. Add in the extra fuel tanks and the boat might have a range of a hundred miles or more.

Two short, narrow doors separated the cockpit from the cabin. They were locked. One of the little gold keys attached to the chunk of red driftwood matched.

The cabin had a single cushioned seat on each side and room forward of the seats to sleep two people on a thin sectional mattress. The mattress pieces were shaped to fit the sloping V of the boat's bow. Under the mattress was a big trapezoid area for storage. Bolted to the cabin wall, on a swing arm so it could be pulled out and seen from the cockpit, was the Chartplotter depth sounder I'd seen listed on the Western Maritime receipt mailed to J. T. Callahan.

I pulled the seat cushions and mattress pieces into the cockpit and searched the cabin.

The storage area was divided by wooden slats into sections. Most of what I found inside was normal pleasure-boat stuff. Lines and life vests and foul-weather gear.

There was a set of scuba gear. One tank and a regulator. A buoyancy-control vest and a weight belt. And a wet suit that looked like it would fit Dono. The set looked used but in good shape.

I sniffed at the wet suit. It had been rinsed clean, but rinsing never fully got the saltwater smell out. I looked closely at the tank. There was a little salt rime in the grooves of the valve handles.

I was sure the gear had been used sometime recently. A week ago, maybe. No longer than a month.

Stranger and stranger. Dono hadn't bought the speedboat just to motor around the sound, and he didn't dive for the fun of it either. At least not when I'd been with him. I wasn't even aware that he knew how.

The ivory paint on the wooden bottom of the storage space was fresher than the shade on the sides. I knocked the wood, and it echoed. I felt around the edge. On the aft side, there was a small half circle cut in the wood, just out of sight.

I put my finger in the little hole and pulled up, revealing a shallow space along the V of the hull. A bolt-action Remington 30.06 hunting rifle was secured with rubber ties on the starboard side. There was a slim stainless-steel case that I opened to find an older Beretta handgun and boxes of cartridges for it and the rifle.

The Remington and the Beretta were safety measures, just like the life jackets. If Dono had had to choose between the two, he'd have taken the guns.

I climbed out of the cabin, back into the cockpit. There were water-tight compartments along the sides of the cockpit seats. I opened them with the same key as for the cabin.

The forward compartment held the VHF radio and thick books of nautical charts. I pulled out the books. They were a set of three, covering the West Coast from southern Oregon up through Washington and the San Juan Islands and farther into British Columbia, as far north as Queen Charlotte Sound.

An idea struck me, and I turned on the VHF. The monotone voice of NOAA Weather Radio came out. NOAA was the coastal marine fore-cast, broadcasting out of Port Angeles on a continuous loop.

Like a car radio, the VHF had a row of buttons for preset channels. I hit the next button, and there was the same recorded voice again, much fainter. I listened until it identified itself as being for the Bellingham area, just an hour south of the Canadian border. The third channel gave me only garbled static.

Tucked under the VHF was a paper booklet that looked like it had come with the radio, covering basic radio protocol and a long list of channels and their uses for the Northwest coast. The frequency shown on the radio's display for the third channel matched the Weatheradio Canada broadcast out of Vancouver. The fourth, fifth, and sixth buttons were not preset, showing the end of the VHF frequency range.

North, then. Dono had taken the boat north, and not too far or he'd have needed the weather station for farther up the Canadian coast.

Fast boat. Longish range. Maybe up as far as Canada. Had Dono been smuggling something?

Smuggling wasn't his usual racket. Moving contraband was Hollis Brant's line of work. And why Dono's sudden interest in scuba? I put everything back in the storage area and locked up the cabin and the compartments.

The sun was low on the horizon. Its light bounced off the calm sound, making a glowing white rift in the wide expanse of steel-colored water on either side. Across the water was the dark green line of Bainbridge Island, and far beyond that the jagged white-gray of the Olympics. The mountains here looked different from the ones in Afghanistan. Gentler. The Afghan ranges were like cliffs, shaped into crude knife edges at the top.

I checked my watch: 1815. Davey would be at the Morgen soon.

I took Dono's key and turned it in the ignition. The big Mercury gave a high roar and then settled back into a bubbling growl. I'd drive the boat up to Hollis's slip at Shilshole and ask him to look it over. His practiced eye might spot something about the gray Stingray that I'd missed.

For a moment I was tempted to let my reunion with Davey slide. But I was coming up dry on learning what action had been keeping Dono busy lately. Finding his boat had added more questions than it had answered.

Maybe blowing off some steam would do me good. Have a beer and a laugh before I found myself head-butting a wall.

CHAPTER TEN

DONO AND ALBIE BOYLAN had bought the Morgen over thirty years ago, before I was born. Dono had the money, and Albie had a criminal record free of felony convictions, so the two men went into partnership on the bar. Real estate in Belltown was a hell of a lot cheaper back then. They secured a fifty-year lease on the first floor of an apartment building for less than it would cost to buy a condo in that same building today.

The deal was that Albie ran the place and Dono kept it afloat by laundering his stolen money through the accounts. Bars were great for that. Lots of cash changing hands.

As a kid I'd been a little scared of Albie. I remembered him being lean as a viper and about as sociable. There was never a bouncer at the entrance of the Morgen. If Albie didn't care for the look of you, he'd catch your eye and angle his head back toward the exit. And if you were stubborn or just slow on the uptake, two or three of the patrons would suddenly invite you to go elsewhere for your evening's libations.

I was surprised at how eager I was to see the bar again. I walked down the alley off Battery Street to the dark green door with no sign on it and pulled on the carved iron handle. It swung open easily, revealing the wide expanse of the main room.

The place looked like it had been waiting for me. The same square plank tables, scarred and stained, crudely arranged into rows. A long bar covered in pallid ash veneer snaked along the curve of the opposite wall, with matching pale shelves stocked with liquor and glasses standing behind.

Instead of a mirror over the bar, there was a tapestry, a crude medieval image of a woman on horseback racing through the ocean surf. It was the thing about the bar I remembered best.

When I was around ten years old and waiting for Dono to finish some deal back in the billiard room, I had screwed up my courage and asked Albie if the woman was a queen of some kind. The laughter of the men at the bar was the only answer I got.

I sat silently, fuming, until Dono came back and we left. I had sour rage all the way up to my hairline. The old man seemed cheerful enough, with an envelope of cash under his jacket and a few shots under his belt. I took advantage of his good humor and asked him about the woman. He told me that she was a pagan harlot who had slept with the devil and tried to escape the wrath of the sea.

I hadn't understood, but I didn't press for details. He might have laughed, too.

If the decor hadn't changed with the times, the clientele had made up the difference. The bar was nearly full. The crowd was mostly college-age or a little older, draped across the chairs and booths. There were also more women than I'd ever seen in the Morgen, where females had been tolerated if not encouraged in Dono's time. The bar may have adapted to survive, but I wasn't going to complain.

As I scanned the crowd, Davey Tolan stood up, grinning at me.

His brown hair was longer, and he'd added maybe a nickel to his buck-and-a-quarter frame, but the grin was exactly the same—an even mix of genuine happiness and self-mockery. Davey had been my best friend from the day we met in second grade until the night I'd left town. My only friend, by most people's definition of the word.

We hugged. "Goddamn, Van. Holy shit," he said.

"How are you, Davey?" He let go, and we stood there. His eyes moved to the scars on my face.

"Tough about Dono, man."

I nodded. "No change yet." For two days I'd done nothing but talk and think about Dono's shooting. I needed to shove the topic to the back of my mind for a while.

I motioned for Davey to sit. "How's Juliet?"

"She's great. Here." He took out his phone and started showing me pictures of his wife and baby.

Davey still dressed like a teenager. He wore a black concert T-shirt for a band I hadn't heard of, threadbare grayish jeans, and black sneakers. A leather motorcycle jacket was thrown over the back of his chair; the chair's strut poking through a tear in the shoulder. At the table nearest us, two college girls kept peeking around their laptop screens at him. Women had always cast glances Davey's way, and he was always a little oblivious, which only seemed to add to his charm.

He was telling me about baby Frances starting preschool, when he stopped short and set the phone down in midsentence. "You're a real fucker, you know that?"

I leaned back in my chair. "I pissed you off."

"I didn't let anybody even mention your name around me for like a year after you'd left." He ran his hand over his head. "I imagined all kinds of shit. Like you and Dono got into another fight, and it went too far, and he'd killed you and buried you somewhere."

I'd never given Davey the whole truth about the Shaw family line of work. But there was no way to keep Davey from knowing that Dono and I had butted heads repeatedly during those last couple of years at home. Or from sensing my grandfather's capacity for violence.

"I needed a clean break, Davey," I said.

"Every couple of days, I'd come by the house, hoping you'd turned up. I didn't trust Dono to be straight with me if I just called. Finally he showed me some papers that had been sent to the house instead of to you. That's how he found out you'd joined the army."

"And he wouldn't even have learned that without the mail screwup. That's how I wanted it."

"Just a big fuck-you to everybody, huh?"

The server came over and put down two chocolate-brown pints in front of us. "Saw's Porter," she said.

Saw's had been Dono's brew of choice when he wasn't drinking whiskey. It was the first drink Davey and I had ever stolen a taste of as kids. And it was an uncommon brand.

I raised my eyebrow at Davey. "You ordered already?"

The grin reappeared, wider than before. "Nope."

We both looked at the waitress. She was tall and in her mid-twenties, with hair the color of polished brass, cut to a length that showed off her good shoulders. Square jaw, wide cheekbones. She had on a white shirt with the sleeves rolled to her upper arms, black jeans, and a short, cream-colored bar apron. Even a little disheveled from the evening rush, she was a beauty.

"Anything else I can get you?" She was looking at me, not both of us.

"A first name," I said.

The waitress's mouth stayed serious, but there might have been amusement in her light gray eyes. "Miss," she said.

"Good to know."

She nodded and headed back to the bar. I tried not to admire her too openly as she walked away, but it took an effort. The black jeans fit very well.

I turned to Davey. "So when did you tell the waitress about this?" I tapped the glass.

His smirk was unforgivable. "I haven't said a word to the woman, I swear."

Davey was going to have his fun no matter what. To keep from giving him any more satisfaction, I took a healthy pull on the pint. It was rich and tasted a little like coffee. Perfect.

I got out the note that Davey had left on the door at the house and showed him the logo at the top. "Frazier Bros Electric. Is that where you work?"

"Yep," he said, beaming. "Union man. It's good money. Speaking of." He put two fifties down on the table. "The night's on me."

"To payday," I toasted him.

"D'you like the army?" His eyes went to my scars again.

"I like the guys in my unit. And I like the toys they let us play with," I said, grinning.

"Not married?" said Davey.

"I got close, at least once. I'm never in one place for long."

"Hell, you're here now." He pretended to scope out the room. "I'm sure one of these girls is drunk enough."

"Let me catch up to the lucky winner first." I drank another mouthful of porter.

Davey glanced over my shoulder toward the far end of the bar. "Hey, there he is."

I looked to my right. The fire exit was propped open. A young guy carrying a pony keg was working his way through the tables toward the bar. He was large enough that the keg didn't give him much trouble. He had curly black hair and sideburns and wore a blue plaid lumberjack shirt and jeans. He looked a little familiar at first, and then suddenly it clicked.

"Holy shit, Davey," I said. "It's Mike."

Davey nodded. "I do recognize my own brother. But it's early yet." He took another mouthful of beer.

Michael Tolan was Davey's younger brother and only sibling. Twenty-two or twenty-three years old now.

I got up. "Be right back."

"Take your time. I'm going outside." Davey fished a pack of American Spirits out of his jacket.

I walked over to where Mike was hooking up the keg to a tap under the bar. "Mike," I said. "It's Van Shaw."

He looked up, and his eyes widened. "Hey!" He rose, and we shook hands. He had half a foot on his older brother and a broad, solemn face. Davey looked like their mother, Evelyn, small-boned and blue-eyed. Evelyn's husband, Joe Tolan, had left the family around the time Davey and I met; I barely remembered him at all.

"How'd you end up working for Albie?" I asked.

"Albie Boylan?" he said. "Albie's dead, Van. Three or four years back. Heart attack. Dono gave me this job."

I stared at him. "I didn't know you and Dono even knew each other."

"We didn't. I was looking for someplace I could balance with my classes. Mom called Dono. You know her, the Irish network."

And Evelyn would have known that Dono would pay Mike under the table. Tax-free tuition money.

"You went into the army, right?" Mike said.

"Yeah. Just back for a few days."

"I heard about Dono," he said. "I'm sorry. You have to come by. Ma will want to see you again."

"Still the same house?" I said.

"Yep. I'm still living there, too. Davey and Juliet escaped to their own place." Mike shook his head, mock mournful. "Lucky shits."

I smiled. "Don't knock it too much. You'll probably miss the meals." Evelyn Tolan had been a good cook, I remembered. Dinner with the Tolans had always been a nice break from Dono's potatoes-and-meat served seventeen ways.

Mike picked up a case of beer and began unpacking the bottles into a fridge under the bar. "If it got me my own apartment, I'd live off cat food. Or even cats. It's good to see you, man."

"You, too."

I turned to see the blond server standing by our table and watching me and Mike. She'd traded her tray for a clipboard, and she had three shot glasses of golden whiskey already set on the table.

"A touch of Frost," she said as I sat down, quoting an advertising slogan. Galway Frost was a brand I hadn't even seen since leaving home. Hollis used to acquire crates of it.

I was about to surrender the game and ask her directly how she knew me when the clipboard in her hand gave it away. With it she didn't look like a waitress. She looked like a boss.

Albie Boylan was dead. Maybe his half of the bar hadn't defaulted to Dono. Maybe it had gone to Albie's nearest relative.

"How you been, Lucy?" I said.

She smiled. "Glad you caught up. I'm good. And it's Luce now."

"I'm sorry about Albie."

"I'm sorry about Dono." She picked up one of the shot glasses. I did the same. "To the boys at the bar," she said, and we downed the whiskey.

It took ten seconds for my throat to open up again. "When was the last time we saw each other?" I said.

"It was right here at the Morgen," she said, "in the back room. You were here with Dono. You played your Game Boy while I read magazines."

"Your memory's a hell of a lot better than mine."

"I was only pretending to read. But you ignored me."

I grinned. "Well, I was pretty stupid then. Fourteen?"

"Around that age. I was eleven." She set her shot glass down on the table. "Are you here to talk business?"

"Do we need to?"

Luce's gray eyes narrowed a fraction. "Eventually."

If Dono died, I'd inherit his half of the Morgen. Was she worried about that? Or was she more concerned about the loss of cash flow if Dono wasn't washing stolen money through the bar's registers?

Maybe it was both. No wonder Luce was giving me the charm offensive.

"He's not dead," I said.

The skin tightened around her good bone structure. "I didn't mean it that way."

"Thanks for the drink."

She stood a little taller, then turned and walked back to the bar. Her hair was a much darker blond than when we were children.

Davey passed her on his way back to the table. He pointed at the empty shot glass of whiskey in front of me. "Now you're talking."

Another server took over our table for the next round, and the rounds that followed, and it wasn't until Davey got up to take a leak that I thought to look for Luce again. She wasn't behind the bar anymore. The place had thinned out, and the remaining staff was busy cleaning up for the night. Before long they would start to throw hinting glances in our direction.

Davey came back to the table. "I think she left," I said to him.

"Who? Oh." He laughed. "Her."

"Didn't say good-bye," I said.

"Didn't she? No, I guess not. We'd remember that, wouldn't we?"

It had been a while since I'd thrown it back with such enthusiasm. Damn nurses hadn't allowed booze in the hospital at Landstuhl.

"What?" said Davey.

"What what?" I said.

"You said something about damned nurses. I don't think lovely Luce is a nurse as well as a bartender, buddy."

Hmmm. "I'm drunk, Davey. And I'm going home. You, too. Juliet will be waiting up."

"Ah, my Julie. Too fine a girl for me," he said. I was a little afraid he'd break into song. "You driving us?"

"I'm paying for our cab. We can get the cars tomorrow."

Twenty minutes later I watched sleepily as Davey clambered out of the backseat of a taxi onto the sidewalk in front of his house. The living-room lights were on. I had called it right. Juliet had a candle burning to mark the way home for her man.

"'Home is the sailor, home from the sea,'" said Davey.

"That's an epitaph, Davey," I said.

"A what?"

"It's for a gravestone." I closed my eyes.

"Oh," he said. "Crap. G'night, Van."

"Night, Davey." I gave the cabdriver careful directions, probably un-necessarily, as he drove me two miles north to my own street. I handed him a wad of bills and got out. The streetlights were weaker than ever in the night fog. I stretched my legs and took in slow drafts of the chill air until my head cleared a little. In front of me, the old house was dark.

"No candle for me," I think I said.

My keys were hiding from me. It took half a minute of fumbling in the dark before I could find the lock. I walked inside and felt for the light switch, and then there was a massive bright burst inside my head that spun me around like a doll cast aside by a toddler. The floor slipped away from under my feet, but it was only gone for an instant. The hardwood came rushing up to meet me. My world was sideways.

Someone ran past, almost tripping on my legs. I glimpsed a corona of curly white hair and a human figure in dark blue, in between the unbearably bright spots floating in front of my eyes. Another moment and even those miniature suns turned the color of midnight.

AGE TEN

Granddad was staring at me. He was impatient.

But I had to concentrate. This was *crucial*.

"I think," I said, "I'm gonna have the Boom Blast."

"That's what you told me before we sat down," said Granddad.

"I know, I know," I said. The Boom Blast had chocolate brownie and chocolate ice cream and salted peanuts. I liked all three things. The Boom Blast was what I always pictured in my head whenever somebody said the word "dessert." I hadn't had one since my last birthday. That had also been right here at Farrelly's, not in this same booth but in the one across the room. A fat kid in a green sweater was sitting in that spot tonight.

I'd been thinking about the Boom Blast all week. Although I really wished Farrelly's were just a plain old diner. It was a little stupid, with bright red vinyl booths and cartoon farm animals on the walls and everything striped like candy canes. I wouldn't have wanted to come back if it weren't for the you-know-what.

But then, on the big plastic menu with the pictures of every dish, there was something new. The Avalanche. Three kinds of ice cream *and* whipped cream *and* cherries *and* your choice of sprinkles. Gargantuan. That was what Davey would have said.

Granddad raised a hand, and one of the waiters in the candy-cane shirts hurried over. Granddad could always do that, have someone run right over to help him, without him even saying anything. It was cool.

He ordered a dish of mint chocolate chip for himself and the Boom Blast for me. For an instant I thought of changing my order—again—but I really didn't like cherries, and the Avalanche had those. Even if I picked them off, I might still taste them. Stick to the plan.

Granddad sipped his coffee. "Mrs. Stark tells me you're doing better with your spelling."

"Yeah," I said.

Like I had a choice. Mrs. Stark was a buster. Another of Davey's words. If I got behind again and failed another quiz, she'd be on the phone to Granddad in ten seconds.

"How's social studies?" said Granddad.

Uh-oh. Did he know somehow? "It's okay."

It really was, even though I hadn't done the homework last week and Mr. Smithson wouldn't let me make it up. I was doing good on all the tests this semester. I knew that my grade wasn't on a shit slope. But if Granddad learned about the homework, he'd be pissed.

Maybe even pissed enough to skip our Saturday lessons and make me do extra chores instead. When I'd been caught at the 7-Eleven instead of in class last year, he'd canceled our Saturdays for a whole month. And I really wanted some more practice on that five-pin Yale lock. I knew I could beat it.

"Mr. Smithson sent me a note," Granddad said, "asking if you and I wanted to book time with the school counselor."

I almost fell back against the bench with relief. So that was all it was.

"Did he mention your mother again?" Granddad said.

"No." And he hadn't. Not since that one time.

On the first Wednesday of the school year, Smithson had kept me after class. I was more confused than freaked. I couldn't be busted *already*, right? I waited at his small, banged-up desk at the front of the classroom.

Smithson asked the last student out to shut the door.

"I was one of your mother's teachers, you know," he had said. "A long time ago."

No shit, I'd thought. Back when my mom was my age? That had to be fifteen or sixteen years. I wondered what she'd looked like. Did Smithson know she was dead?

"She was a good student," he said. "I'm happy to have another Shaw in my class."

I nodded. Smithson was definitely old enough. The little halo of hair still on his head was the same shade of white as the dandruff flakes on his sweater. He was thin, I guess, but he had a belly that made Terry Bonder next to me whisper *"Beer here"* like the guys selling plastic cups of Budweiser at the Kingdome.

"You living with your dad now?" said Smithson.

"No," I said.

He waited for me to say more. I didn't. I hated telling people that I'd never met my dad, and that the guy *wasn't* my dad, not really.

"Do you live with your grandfather, then? Your mom's dad?"

I nodded again. Smithson nodded, too, like he'd been expecting that answer all along.

He tapped the top of his desk with his fingertips, staring at the coffee-cup stains on the wood. "When Moira—your mom—was here, she went to live with Mrs. Reynolds and her family for a couple of years. Did you know that?"

"No."

"Sharon Reynolds was one of the first-grade teachers then. She had your mom in her class." Smithson's watery brown eyes narrowed. "Your grandfather was . . . away. Is he around a little more these days?"

"Uh-huh. All the time."

Which was true. I didn't count Granddad's trips out of town, which were never more than a few days. He always made sure I was okay. I had my spare key, and he'd give me cash for food.

Smithson sighed and smiled. It wasn't a very big smile. "Well, I'm glad to hear it. That everything's cool." The word "cool" sounded totally wrong coming out of his mouth.

"Yeah."

"Moira was a very sharp kid. She would have gone far if—" He stopped.

If she hadn't had you, was what I put on the end of that.

Right then I decided I didn't like Mr. Smithson. Even if he had liked my mom.

The waiter came back and put the dishes of ice cream down in front of me and Granddad, and I forgot all about my social-studies teacher and his stupid questions. I was too busy letting the salt from the peanuts melt into the chocolate on my tongue.

When I was done—after running the long-handled spoon around the inside of the dish so that the brownie crumbs would soak up the melted ice cream and get that last bite and a half left—I looked up and caught Granddad watching the front entrance. His mint ice cream was only partly eaten, and mostly liquid.

He wasn't looking straight at the front door, of course. He was watching from the corner of his eye, only flicking his gaze in that direction every few seconds. But I could tell.

I dropped my spoon on the red vinyl bench. When I bent to pick it up, I peeked under the table.

Two Seattle cops were standing in the entrance, next to another man who wore the same striped shirt as the waiters plus a red vest. The cops were acting casual, talking with the guy in the vest, but they were watching me and Granddad. They weren't as good at hiding it as Granddad was.

I started to turn and look at the back of the restaurant, but Granddad said, "Don't." I snapped my head around. Don't look at the rear exit. Don't signal that we might go that direction.

But then a second pair of cops in their two-tone blue uniforms stepped up to the booth. And I realized that "Don't" had meant "Don't bother."

"Mr. Shaw?" one of the officers said.

Granddad nodded.

"There may be some trouble with your car, sir," the cop said. Louder than he had to for just me and Granddad to hear him. "Would you come with us?"

Everyone was staring. The fat kid's mouth was wide open. He had yellow ice-cream dribbles down the front of his green sweater.

Granddad got out of the booth without a word, and both cops took a hasty step back. I grabbed my coat and stood up, too, dodging one of the officers as he tried to put a hand on my shoulder. We all walked out of Farrelly's, all four cops and me and Granddad.

There were two more uniformed cops in the packed parking lot outside, standing by our black GMC. The passenger-side door to the truck was open. One of the cops—a woman—was sitting in the cab, rummaging through the glove box.

My face got hot. Our truck!

The cop standing next to the one in the passenger seat looked up and saw us coming and walked over. He was as tall as Granddad and much thicker. His name tag said YOUNGS. "You're Donovan Shaw," he said to Granddad.

"What's it about?" Granddad said. Not angry, not in a hurry. Cool.

"This is your truck?" said Officer Youngs. Dumb question—they must have seen the registration. Maybe he was required to ask, like a cop thing.

"I don't think I have any unpaid tickets," said Granddad. "And the tabs are up to date."

The cop who'd tried to put his hand on my shoulder came around in front of us. He was older than the other cops, and his head was shaved bald. The two of them stood a few feet apart, one on either side of Granddad.

"Where were you earlier tonight, Mr. Shaw?" said Baldy.

"With me," I said. Granddad shot me a look. I closed my mouth.

"And where was that?" said Baldy.

"We were at the movies," Granddad said, "and then we came here."

"Which theater?" said Youngs.

"The Varsity," Granddad said.

Baldy smiled at me. "What'd you see?"

I didn't answer.

"Forgot already?" he said.

"Go ahead," Granddad said to me.

"*Independence Day*," I told Baldy.

"'Welcome to Earth,'" he quoted. "Is this a special occasion?"

Granddad turned away from him and pointed to where the woman cop was looking under the seats of the GMC. "What's your cause? Because if you're just pulling a random, I'll leave the truck with you and call a cab."

The smile disappeared from Baldy's face.

"The Washington Mutual branch on Fortieth was robbed tonight, just before closing," he said. "The robbers left the scene in a black pickup with a canopy." He nodded at our truck. "One of the men matches your description."

"Was the other robber a ten-year-old kid?" Granddad said.

"Did you see anybody you know at the theater?" Youngs said. "Anybody who can verify you were there?"

"I've still some popcorn kernels in my teeth, if you'd like to look."

I wanted to scream. *Don't be idiots! He was with me. He's not dumb enough to rob a stupid bank. And be seen, too, for Pete's sake.*

"I think the boy should go back inside," said Baldy.

"No," I said.

"Yes," Granddad said to me. "Go inside."

I didn't move. I couldn't leave him, out of my sight. Anything could happen.

Granddad's face darkened, and I could tell he was about to give me an order when the woman back at the truck said, "Hey," very clearly. She had finished with the glove box and was looking up at the top of the cab. I could see a flap of tan fabric hanging where she'd torn the ceiling cover open.

She stepped down from the cab. "Gun," she said, and held up a pistol, fingers pinched around the trigger guard. Strips of duct tape dangled off the barrel and grip. It was a silver short-barreled automatic. I hadn't seen it before. It wasn't one of the guns Granddad let me shoot at tin cans out in the woods.

Around us the cops tensed. The skinny cop standing next to Baldy slid his hand up to rest on his pistol.

"Yours?" Officer Youngs said to Granddad.

"Nope," Granddad said.

"It's in your truck," said another cop.

Granddad shrugged. "Don't know what to tell you."

"I bet," said the woman cop, who had come up to join the group. She had brown hair in a bun and a square body and jaw. Strong-looking. "What the hell are you thinking, driving around with a gun hanging a foot above your kid's head? It's loaded."

Youngs leaned over for a closer look. "Serial numbers are ground off, too." He drew his stun gun from his belt. Baldy had already taken a step back and was holding his riot baton by its side handle.

Baldy pointed at the concrete in front of Granddad. "Sir, I'm going to need you to get down on the ground. Now."

It was crazy. *They* were crazy. Granddad and I *were* at the movies, and we could prove it if the cops would just calm down for a minute. We could call the theater right now. Surely someone would remember us buying popcorn or tickets or . . .

The ticket stubs. Granddad had let me hang on to them. "Wait!" I said, and reached into my coat pocket.

"Don't move!" Youngs shouted. The skinny cop reached out and clutched me hard around the upper arm. Pain zapped all the way down to my fingertips. I hollered.

Then the skinny cop was falling backward, Granddad's fist rebounding off his face. Baldy stepped forward, and I cried out as his riot baton hit Granddad on the back of the knee. Granddad staggered sideways. Youngs's big arm wrapped around me.

Baldy swung again, the baton bouncing off the top of Granddad's shoulder. Granddad fell. I screamed. Granddad curled into a ball as Baldy and the fourth cop kicked at him. The woman was yelling something. The kicks sounded like falling sandbags as they hit Granddad's body.

I thrashed and tried to bite the arm that was crushing my chest. Youngs squeezed harder. My vision went white.

When the world came swimming back into focus, Granddad was facedown on the concrete. Not moving. Baldy was on top of him, one knee pressing between Granddad's shoulders. Yellow plastic strips bound his wrists behind his back.

We didn't do anything, I tried to say. The air just wheezed through my throat. I pushed again at Youngs. The skinny cop was still out cold on the ground, his partner bending over him.

"Don't help or nothing," Baldy said to the woman cop.

Her face was red. "Go to hell," she said. She stepped around Granddad and Baldy over to where Youngs was holding me up.

She leaned down to look in my face. I tried to twist away, to keep my eyes on Granddad. He was moving a little, turning his head.

"I'm over here," I said. My voice louder now.

"He'll be okay," the woman said to me. "Hey. Look at me."

I didn't, but I stopped wrestling against Youngs.

"He'll be okay," she repeated. "But he needs you to calm down. Can you do that?"

Fuck you, lady. Even if you're right, Fuck you.

I nodded.

"Good," she said. Youngs relaxed his arm a little. When I stayed upright and didn't bolt, he let me go, staying inches away.

"We have to take your dad in," the woman said. I didn't correct her. "And we have to call someone for you. Is your mom somewhere we can reach her?"

I shook my head. My face was wet, and I reached up quickly to wipe the tears off.

"How about aunts or uncles?"

"Just us," I said.

"Fuck it," said Youngs. He was angry, I suddenly realized. His arm was scratched and dripping blood. Had I done that? "I'm calling CPS."

The woman nodded slowly. She reached out and brushed a drop of Youngs's blood off my coat. "You hang with me," she said. "While we go to the station."

Baldy and the fourth cop lifted Granddad to his feet. His forehead and chin were cut, and one of his eyes was puffed closed. There were dark red splotches all down his shirt.

He tilted his head to the side, peering around until he found me.

"S'okay," Granddad said. Blood dribbled out of the side of his mouth. "S'nothin'." Baldy and his partner half dragged him toward one of the police cruisers.

As they loaded him into the back and started the car, the woman cop put her hand on my shoulder. I wanted to shrug it off. But instead I just watched as the cruiser pulled out of the lot. Granddad was a dark pillar in the backseat. The car went around the corner and out of sight, but I could still see the light of the red and blue flashers bouncing off the windows of the buildings on the block. I counted one, two, three, four, until the last glow faded.

CHAPTER ELEVEN

THE THUNDER HURT, SO I figured it must be close. Each time it rumbled, there was a golden flash of lightning that lit up the sky and slowly faded until the next time. Part of me knew that was wrong, that the booming sound should follow the electricity, and it bothered me. I could feel my eyes shut tight in frustration. Except *that* was wrong, too. If my eyes were closed, how could I see the lightning? I'd have to open them. But I didn't want to.

And then I was abruptly back, eyes open after all, staring up at the ceiling of the foyer. The front door was still ajar. I could feel a breeze across my face. The room was still dark, too, although the streetlamps outside gave the windows of the front room a yellowish glow.

I was lying about ten feet from where Dono had fallen, I realized. Some of his dried blood might be under me right now.

That thought was enough to get me moving. I sat up, very slowly.

The pain had an epicenter somewhere over my left ear. I didn't have to touch it to feel the knot already forming there. My hand bumped against something on the floor.

It was Dono's blackthorn shillelagh, which he kept in an umbrella stand by the door. I picked it up and looked at it.

It was typical of Dono's humor that he would keep an Irish stereotype like the club-shaped walking stick in the house. It was also typical of him that the knobbed end was filled with an extra half pound of lead shot, to create the kind of impact that had put out my lights so efficiently. A harder knock and it might have split my skull like a cantaloupe.

Even as spacey as I was, it wasn't difficult to piece together what had happened. Someone—a small man with a healthy amount of white curls, if I could trust what I'd only partially seen—had broken into the house. He had heard my drunken progress toward the door and availed himself of the shillelagh before hiding around the corner. When I walked in, the motherfucker had used my head for a piñata.

I tried to listen over the slight ringing in my ears. Was he still inside the house? I didn't think so. I was fairly certain he was hightailing it even as I was taking my first bounce off the floor. If he'd meant to hang around, he could've tied me up like a rodeo calf—or taken another swing with the stick to finish me off—and enjoyed all the time he wanted.

I got to my feet with a lot of help from the wall. Carefully, I tottered to the pantry and opened up Dono's hiding place at the back. I took out the nine-millimeter Browning. It was doubtful I could hit anything outside spitting distance right now, but the weight of it in my hand made me feel better.

Back in the foyer, I saw that someone had been poking at Dono's security system. The rectangular metal facing plate was lying on the floor, and the internal wires were pulled out and stripped in places.

I stared at the alarm. It hadn't been bypassed by being rewired. The intruder hadn't *needed* to bypass it, because the alarm had remained off since Dono's shooting. So why would he take it apart and strip the wires, just to leave it alone?

I walked through it. The intruder had picked the dead-bolt lock on the front door—no easy task—and immediately opened up the alarm box inside, expecting to have to bypass it. And then he'd realized that the alarm was turned off, saving him the trouble.

The wires were already stripped, because he'd stripped them before.

Tonight wasn't the first time the fucker had broken into the house.

I moved slowly through each room. No other door or window had been breached. And nothing obvious had been taken. Maybe I'd stumbled in before he could do whatever he'd been here to do.

In Dono's bathroom I foraged through a drawer full of under-the-counter meds, a rainbow collection of safety-cap bottles and foil packets. The alcohol still in my system was probably dulling the worst of the headache, but it wouldn't last. Codeine, Darvon, an unlabeled bottle of what looked like OxyContin. I chewed two tablets of codeine. Bitter taste, to match my mood. I grabbed a handful of packets and put them in my pocket for later.

I went back downstairs to look at the security panel again.

The guy had skills. Better than mine, maybe. Not just picking the front door lock. Whenever he'd first broken in and beaten Dono's alarm system, he'd opened the box and played a few notes of Chopin on the wires before the allotted thirty seconds elapsed. That was Ph.D.-level breaking and entering.

If the intruder had decided to pay a visit at two in the morning, then it was a good bet he also knew that Dono was out of commission. Sure as hell he had thought no one would be at home. I'd surprised him.

Okay. Put myself in his shoes. I'm a professional burglar. I'm prepped with the tools I need, and I'm not expecting trouble. The target is the home of an old thief. What the hell could be in the place to make it worth the effort?

Thieves attract thieves. Maybe the burglar knew about a score Dono had made, and he was looking for the take. Maybe he was even a partner of Dono's on the job. Fair enough.

But presumably he was also smart enough to guess that Dono wouldn't leave a pile of money just lying around his house. I'm not breaking in on spec. I'm not tearing the place apart. I know what I'm after and where to find it.

I turned all the lights on and took a harder look at each room. Nothing appeared out of place. The semi-organized clutter of an old bachelor's home.

I felt a little ridiculous. A half-drunk, half-concussed man looking for something unusual in a house he hadn't occupied in years. The burglar might have been after something scribbled on a Post-it note, for Christ's sake.

Easing my way back down the hall to the taped-off front room, I paused to rest the side of my head against the cool doorframe.

Keep at it, dummy, I thought of Dono saying. *Better to seek and come up empty than wonder what you might have found around the next corner.*

Sometimes fortune smiles. Sometimes fate gives you a painful kick in the right direction.

Without the leftover fingerprint dust, I wouldn't have noticed it—Dono's chair had been moved. There were darker square patches on the oak floor, clean of any white residue, where the front legs had been. Two inches from where they were now.

I stepped around the tape and into the room, walking over to look at that corner. There was a tiny screw on the floor, resting in a groove between the hardwood planks. The ventilation grille on the wall had an empty hole where the screw belonged. When I bent down, I could see fresh scratches on the screwheads of the grille.

Dono had always kept a small toolbox for light house jobs in the kitchen. I went into the kitchen and found it, came back and used a screwdriver to remove the ventilation grille.

I leaned down and craned my neck to peer inside. About a foot from the opening, there was something taped to the top of the ventilation duct. It was compact and rectangular, with a dark gray plastic cover over most of its parts. A green wire led from the plastic box through a hole that had been drilled in the side of the duct.

I pulled the little object out of the vent, tearing the wire and the tape loose. I sat on Dono's chair and removed the plastic cover to examine the gadget more closely. It had a SIM card and electronics and keypad taken from a basic cellular phone, all soldered to a plastic housing and connected to the tiny horn shape of an expensive-looking receiver.

It was a bug.

And a reasonably good one, from what I could tell. I had seen a few hidden listening devices in the military. Those were mass-manufactured gadgets. This one was handmade—and with care.

I could guess how it worked. The receiver allowed it to be voice-activated, so that if someone spoke in the room, the microphone would register the sound and the cell-phone bits and pieces would call another phone somewhere, which would probably start recording.

The attached battery wouldn't last long. But there had been the green wire through the hole in the duct. The wire was probably tapping into the house power at the electrical outlet a few feet from the vent.

Slick. By feeding off the house, the bug could operate 24/7. The voice activation might mean you'd lose a sentence or two at the other end, but that was the only real flaw. It might have been sitting in the vent for weeks, happily transmitting everything within its range.

How long had it been there? And how many more of the things were in the house?

Over the next half hour, I checked every outlet and vent in the house, from the basement to the bathrooms. I shoved furniture out of the way and nearly tore the vent grilles off the walls with my bare hands. I found two more of the bugs and evidence of others in the holes drilled in ventilation ducts in almost every room, including the basement.

Dono had one landline phone in the house, on the wall in the kitchen. There were shiny scratches on the minuscule screwheads on the underside of it. Nothing unusual inside the phone. Not anymore.

I sat down at the dining table and laid the three bugs out in a row. All the same parts. All handmade.

The burglar hadn't been here to take something of Dono's. He had been here to get his toys back. I'd come along just as he was getting to the last of them.

That fit with the lump on my skull. I'd spooked him, and after he'd dealt with me, he'd chosen a hasty retreat over finishing the job.

And he'd left me alive.

Dono had been left alive, too. Was that intentional?

The burglar had planted the bugs. He had listened in on whatever Dono had said in the house, and to Dono's phone calls, for some unknown number of days. When he'd heard enough, he had returned to retrieve his gadgets. And maybe he'd been surprised by Dono.

My thoughts flew back over the last few days. What had I said in the house? There was the first morning, of course, with the whole circus of cops and paramedics and Guerin. I'd had my conversation with Addy Proctor. I'd talked to Ganz, and Hollis, although I was pretty sure I hadn't said Hollis's name. I'd talked to the hospital, checking on Dono.

What the hell did Dono know that was worth the trouble of bugging his entire house?

Dono. It finally hit me then, and I stood up, headache be damned. His shooting. His shooting would have been recorded by the bugs.

And the guy who'd shot him.

CHAPTER TWELVE

DETECTIVE GUERIN KNOCKED BACK the last of his coffee. I sat across from him at the kitchen table, holding an ice pack behind my ear.

Guerin's people hurried in and out of the rooms around us. They were hunting for any bits of wire or other evidence that the burglar had left attached to the power outlets in the house. As the crime-scene crew found each bit, they bagged it as evidence and brought it back and laid it on the table in front of Guerin. Like timid cats offering dead mice to their owner.

They had screwed up. After Dono was shot, the CSU should have seen the same scratches on the vent covers that I'd found and uncovered the bugs.

Guerin didn't offer any excuses. Their mistake was his mistake.

He nodded at the ice pack in my hand. "You sure you shouldn't be at the hospital?"

"I've had concussions before. This is just a headache."

He inclined his head a fraction. "Maybe call a friend to stay with you instead."

"How many other cases are you carrying?" I said. "Besides Dono's?"

Guerin picked up a larger plastic evidence bag, which held one of the two bugs on the table. The third bug was rolled up in a sock in my coat hanging by the door, where I'd hidden it before the cops had arrived.

He looked at the bug through his bifocals. "Your grandfather has my full attention."

I got up and walked over to the window. Dawn hadn't touched the sky yet. Every light in the house was on. The cluster of cop cars and lab vans on the street in front of the house had their parking lights blinking, per regulation. A Christmas display.

"Did he have your attention before he was shot?" I said.

"If you're asking me whether Dono was under investigation, I can't answer that."

I pointed at the evidence bag. "The guy who planted those went to a lot of trouble. There's money somewhere in this."

"Which means crime, when your grandfather is involved. Weren't you the one telling me you didn't know anything about Dono's life nowadays?"

"I didn't. But I can make some guesses. So I'm going to guess that you're even more in the dark than I am."

Guerin started to say something and then closed his mouth.

They drill politeness into the Seattle cops with six-inch galvanized screws. It always amused Dono, and I was starting to get the joke.

When Guerin spoke again, his voice was level and hard enough to skate on. "If you go around looking for your grandfather's associates, firing off any question that comes into your head, then we could lose a chance to build a case against someone. He could walk."

I took his coffee mug and refilled it from the pot. I traded my ice pack for a fresh one from the freezer—Dono had at least a dozen in there—and sat at the table again and looked at the detective.

Guerin could park me in a cell for a while. Two days, if the law hadn't changed recently. Then he'd have to let me go. A harassment charge could keep him from doing it again. Ganz could set that up.

But I didn't want to lose two days. And I didn't want Guerin distracted, thinking he should keep half an eye on me.

"Okay," I said. "You handle it. I want Dono's shooter busted, same as you."

Guerin frowned. "Are you sure about that? The same as me?"

"Why does everyone assume I'm going to kill the guy?"

He took a long inhale. Then he looked at the bug again.

"We'll find him," Guerin said. "These are handmade. There can't be too many guys running around with that kind of expertise."

I knew of at least one. Jimmy Corcoran.

AFTER THE COPS WERE gone, I left a voice mail for Hollis, asking him to get in touch with Corcoran. I checked the doors and windows in every room of the house and settled in on the couch in the upstairs office to get some downtime.

An hour later I got up and checked all the entrances again.

Eventually I went back to the couch, where I lay and just stared at the textured white semigloss on the ceiling.

I didn't want to close my eyes. Every time I did, I saw the three flashes of light, just off at my two-o'clock.

It almost always started the same way. Three flashes, the night flares from an enemy's Kalashnikov. The shots that had kicked off the fight. Then came the blast of an IED somewhere to my left, a slap of wind and a keening buzz that filled my ears and made the rest of the fight nothing but more hot lights and sweat trickle stinging my eyes and slaps on my shoulder to tell me when it was my turn to move and cover the next man as we fell back, rock by rock, out of the village.

It wasn't a long exchange. It wasn't even especially bloody. Two casualties on our side, one serious enough to earn a ticket home. The bad guys had lost at least three times as many.

There had been worse nights. Much worse. But that action was one of the times that stuck with me. Maybe because the K fire had surprised us all. Maybe because it had been my first real heat since I'd rotated back with my face patched together. The scars had still been pink.

I fought the urge to get up and check the house once more.

Instead I stared hard at the whorls of paint on Dono's ceiling, breath whistling fast and shallow over my dry lips. I held it in for a count of five, a three count after the exhale. And again.

My heart beat faster. Nearly up to the pace my stress had set. Like paddling fast on a surfboard to catch a wave. I let my breathing settle down, and my pulse followed like an obedient dog.

The breathing trick was only one step. There were others that the shrinks had explained. Most of them had me focus on the reality of my situation. Telling myself that I was safe.

Those wouldn't help this time. Because it wasn't true.

My hometown was one big minefield, just waiting for me to wander back in.

CHAPTER THIRTEEN

WILLARD WAS STANDING JUST outside the entryway of Corcoran's apartment building. He was smoking. The orange dot at the end of his cigarette bobbed up and down in the early-morning shadows. Dressed in his long coat, he looked like one of the building's support columns.

"Willie," I said. The orange dot jumped a little.

"Fuck," Willard said in his buffalo voice. "You snuck up on me."

But I hadn't. I'd just been walking, having parked a couple of blocks away. If Willard was keeping watch, he'd lost a few steps.

"You got another?" I asked. My head still hurt. One part hangover, two parts the knot behind my ear that the burglar had given me.

Willard grunted. "Don't remember you smoking."

"Army," I said. I caught a flash of teeth as Willard smiled, quick and flat.

"Me, too," he said. "Different war but same deal." He reached into his coat pocket and brought out a crumpled pack of Camels—and he tapped a stick out and offered it to me. The pack was completely covered by his shovel-blade hand.

There was a lighter in the pocket of the barn jacket I'd taken off Dono's coatrack. I lit the cigarette with it. I hadn't smoked in six months, and the first long draw tasted horrible and perfect at the same time.

"Dono?" Willard said.

I shook my head. Nothing new. "Is Jimmy coming down or are we going up?" I asked. It had taken me a few extra minutes to find the right block. Hollis might have beaten me here and told Willard and Corcoran I was on the way.

"Up. Once we're done," Willard said. "Jimmy's wife don't like smoking in her place, not even on the balcony."

The ash fell off my cigarette. "Corcoran's married?"

"Oh, yeah. Kids, too. Not his."

"You're shitting me." The idea of Jimmy Corcoran raising stepkids was about the same level of smart as asking a guy who'd pounded a case of Red Bull to hold your nitroglycerin.

Willard took a last drag, down to the filter, and dropped the butt to step on it. He looked at the pack in his hand for a minute and then put it in his pocket.

"Screw it," he said. "We only got an hour till the wife comes back. Let's go upstairs."

I stubbed out my half-finished stick on the nearest column. Maybe I'd light it up again in another six months. But probably not.

Bad Man Willard, banished from the goddamn building just to have a smoke. And the wife wasn't even *home*.

Sharing an elevator with Willard was like being in a horse trailer with a Clydesdale. He pushed the button marked 8, and the doors closed. The elevator walls were green silk. Next to each numbered button on the panel was a tiny brass plaque inscribed with Asian characters.

"Is Corcoran's wife Thai?" I said, guessing at the characters.

Willard exhaled, just enough to be a sigh. "Cambodian. Whole block is Cambodian."

I wouldn't have thought Corcoran that open-minded. Last I remembered, he was still referring to everyone west of the Pacific Ocean as Chinamen.

Willard must have caught the vibe of my surprise, because he raised his eyebrows. "Better'n being alone, kid."

We stepped out of the elevator into a narrow pink hallway, and I let Willard lead us midway down to a pink door with the number 87 in brass under the peephole. Willard knocked and tried to open the door, but it was locked. There was a sound of fast movement from inside.

"It's me. And Van," said Willard, and the door opened a crack to show Corcoran's glaring eye and half his bald skull.

I smiled. "I'll have the Kung Pao chicken and two egg rolls."

"Asshole," he said. He stepped aside, and Willard and I walked in.

The place looked like a two-bedroom, tidy but tight. An eight-by-eight dining area with a small circular table was on our left and a counter on the right, partly separating the entryway from a compact kitchen. The living room had a lot of plants crammed into it and wide brown awning stripes on the wallpaper. The only thing in the whole place that looked like it might belong to Corcoran was an easy chair in cracked and stained brown leather.

"Sit down over there," he said, gesturing to a low couch next to the ancient chair.

An intercom on the wall beeped. Corcoran pressed a button on it.

"—me, Jimmy," said Hollis's voice under the static whine. Corcoran pressed another button and buzzed Hollis in.

I took out the surveillance bug that I'd pocketed before the cops arrived and tossed it on the dining-room table. It landed on its side, the little receiver pointed out toward us like a mouth ready to whistle. Corcoran and Willard looked at it.

I raised my finger to my lips—don't talk—and showed Corcoran the note I had written on a page torn from Dono's notebook before leaving the house:

"When was the last time you swept your home?"

Corcoran sneered, which was probably a reflex for him, but his fore-head wrinkled with uncertainty. He handed the note to Willard just as Hollis came hurriedly up to the still-open door.

Hollis peered around Willard's broad back, his face bright pink. "Got here fast as I could," he said, clipping the words to rush to the next breath. He shut the door behind him. "What's on?"

I mimed silence again and pointed to the bug on the table. Hollis looked at it quizzically. Corcoran stepped over to the table to pick it up. He turned it over, poking at the inner workings with a yellowed fingernail. I pulled out a chair from the table and sat.

After a moment Corcoran set the bug down and shuffled quickly to the back of the apartment, returning with a large gray plastic toolbox. He reached for a remote control and turned on the plasma television. Trumpets suddenly blared over a frenzied commercial for a Ford dealership. Corcoran opened the toolbox and took out what I recognized as an old-school cell-phone scanner. He began fiddling with it, untangling its wires from a mess of other junk.

While Corcoran worked, Hollis went to the kitchen and opened the refrigerator. He found a sixer of beer and brought it back to the table, handing a can to Willard as he passed. Corcoran ignored us, walking around the room, holding the scanner close to the electrical outlets and the walls.

"Check the air vents, too," I said under the noise of the TV. Corcoran frowned, but he made sure to pass the scanner near each grate before moving off into other rooms along the hall.

Hollis sat down next to me, offering a beer. I shook my head. Willard finally moved, into the living room. He eased his bulk into Corcoran's leather chair.

Hollis leaned in to whisper in my ear. "What the fuck's going on?"

"We might be wired," I murmured back. I tapped the bug with my finger.

"Christ Jesus," Hollis said, blanching. "Is it feds?"

I shook my head no. Hollis continued to stare at the bug. Corcoran reentered the room with a screwdriver and started removing one of the vent grates. He was totally focused on the task, and I saw a bit of sweat on the side of his bald head.

"Okay," said Corcoran finally, "enough." He sat on the back of the couch and dropped the screwdriver into the toolbox. He looked flushed, like he'd just run a mile.

Willard turned off the TV with the remote. "You all right?" he said to Corcoran.

Corcoran motioned, and Hollis tossed him a beer. Corcoran popped it and took a long pull. "Fuck it," he said after a breath. He stood and picked up the bug off the table again. "This was at Dono's place?"

I nodded. "One in almost every room."

He grunted. "Do you know how long they were there?"

"No," I said. "What can you tell me about it?"

"All kinds of shit about how it's made," he said. "But that's not what you care about. You understand how it works?"

"Yeah," I said.

Hollis shifted in his seat. "Well, I fucking sure don't," he said. "Someone catch me up here, damn it."

I pointed at the little black snout of the receiver in Corcoran's hand. "These were hidden behind the vents," I said. "They pick up any noise in the room and automatically call a preset number, which records everything."

Corcoran belched softly. "The guy on the other end can dial in from anywhere and listen to the recordings. Just like voice mail."

We all looked at the device on the table again. Like it was a dead scorpion, something that had once been dangerous.

"How did you find the damned thing?" Hollis said.

I told them how I'd been cold-cocked by the intruder the night before. The story cheered Corcoran right up.

"The guy who hit me left three bugs behind when he ran away," I said. "I held on to this one."

"If it was me," Corcoran said, "I'd have finished the job. Tied you up. Or just stomped on your head one more time."

Hollis scratched the side of his neck absentmindedly. "The guy who shot Dono didn't stick around to finish *him* off either. Do you think it's the same guy?"

"The guy who hit me was small, with white hair," I said.

Corcoran grinned. "An old midget threw soldier boy a beating."

"This guy was good enough to fastball Dono's alarm system. And he built these bugs by hand."

"These ain't exactly state-of-the-art shit," Corcoran said. He picked up the bug again. "It's decent work, I'll say that much. This receiver is about as good as you can buy. I'd have used a smart phone instead of these old clamshell parts."

"There can't be too many small old men in Seattle who specialize in B&E and bugging," I said. "You know anybody who matches that skill set?"

"I know a couple who work local, who might be up to this," Corcoran said. "One's Chinese or Jap or something like that—"

"The guy who hit me was white, from what little I saw of him."

"Then you're out of luck. 'Cause the second guy I know is black and too damn old to be jumping out of windows. Like fourscore and seven."

I tapped the bug in Corcoran's hands. "Can you trace the number it's calling?" I asked him.

He smirked. "If it's preset in the phone? Please."

"I want to know everything about the account the number is attached to. What's the number, who set it up, when they've used it. The whole history. Especially if you can get access to the voice-mail recordings."

Corcoran shrugged. "That's not tech. That's phone-company records."

"Out of your reach?" I asked.

"Who said that? I didn't fucking say that." Corcoran tossed the bug back onto the table and began rummaging in his toolbox. "Getting the number's nothing. I can have that in two minutes. The rest of it—" He shrugged. "Depends on which phone company holds the account. If it's one of the big American companies, I could maybe try to get in touch with people who work for them. Data engineers, people like that."

I understood what he meant. Hacking into phone accounts from the outside was tough. It was a lot easier if you knew a company employee with the right access who might be willing to enhance his hourly wage by taking five minutes to look up information on your behalf. Corcoran may not know those employees himself, but he could ask around. The power of networking.

"But if it's some rinky-dink private business, then I doubt we'll get very far," Corcoran finished. He had fished an older-model cell phone out from the toolbox and was disassembling it.

"I'll deal with that if I have to. But I need to learn whatever we can fast. Like tomorrow."

"I'll have to spread some money around," Corcoran said. He began attaching the circuit board of the bug to the screen components of the second cell phone with narrow-gauge wires.

"How much money?" I said.

He glared at me. "Did I put my hand out? Fuck you." He went back to concentrating on the phones. "Punk," he muttered.

I needed Corcoran. But I was angry and tired and close to slapping the wire cutters out of his hand.

Willard saw it on my face. "You're thinking about Spokane," he said to Corcoran.

"Course I am. Nobody has to fucking remind me," Corcoran said.

Hollis looked between them. "What's Spokane?"

Corcoran's lip curled. "You tell them," he said to Willard. "I'm fucking busy."

"Jimmy was in with a couple of guys on a grocery-store job," Willard said. "In Spokane."

"I got that much," Hollis said, taking a swig of beer.

Willard ignored him. "Dono knew one of the guys. I don't know if he'd worked with him or just by reputation. Either way it wasn't good. He told Jimmy that he should leave it alone."

"But . . ." said Hollis, letting the word trail off.

Willard nodded. We all knew the probability of Corcoran taking anyone's advice.

"So Jimmy and the two guys drive to Spokane and break into the store," Willard said.

"*I* broke in," said Corcoran. "*They* sat in the car with their thumbs in their asses."

"Jimmy breaks in," Willard said, "and the first thing the two idiots do is go straight to the safe and try opening it with a maul and sledge."

"Every motherfucking alarm on the block went off," Corcoran said.

Unable to keep quiet while reliving the memory. "And they were gone. Dead run, slammed right into me, scattered my shit everywhere. Out the door, into their car, fucking gone. And me still throwing my gear into my bag."

"What did you do?" I said to Corcoran.

"I was trying to figure out just how many levels of dead I was. And then here comes Dono. Roaring up in his car. He tells me to get in, and I wasn't so punchy that I didn't recognize the fucking hand of God reaching down when I saw it. I got in."

"He followed you," I said.

Corcoran snorted. "For three hundred miles, he followed us. Just shows what morons those two were. Your grandfather hauled my ass right out of the fire. We were back in Seattle before dawn."

Hollis crushed his beer can with one thick paw. "So you owe the man."

Corcoran shrugged and turned his attention back to the cell phone. "Nothing I can do about the bullet in Dono's head," he said. "But I'll help catch the fucker who put it there."

He pressed a couple of buttons on the cell phone, and the screen lit up with ten green digits. The phone number of the burglar's account. Somewhere in its digital web, there was a recording of Dono's last conscious moments.

Corcoran grinned at the phone, showing small yellow teeth. "The little shithead screwed the pooch this time."

For once Jimmy C. and I could agree.

CHAPTER FOURTEEN

I LEFT HOLLIS AND THE others and let myself out of Corcoran's building. Dono's truck was parked down the street at a meter. I'd had to take his truck. The headlights on my rental Charger were smashed after the collision with the Ryder van the day before.

It had turned into a clear morning, cold and sharp. Traffic on I-5 Northbound was just starting to ease out of the morning jam. To edge around a rusty hatchback, I changed lanes. A hundred yards behind me, a large burgundy-colored Ford SUV did the same.

Maybe my nerves were just keyed up after the story about Dono following Corcoran all the way across the state. Or maybe I was just paranoid.

I changed lanes again, as if I had suddenly decided to take the next exit. The burgundy SUV hastily did the same, cutting off a minivan. I heard the outraged blare of the van's horn in the distance.

It wasn't paranoia.

It wasn't the cops either, unless they'd sent rookies to tail me. Whoever was driving the SUV was clumsy on the brake. And he kept edging out to see around the cars in front of him. Either he was very bad at following people or he didn't give a damn if I knew he was there.

Was it the burglar from the house last night? Or maybe the three stooges who had tried to stomp my head when I'd met Hollis. I was making friends all over town.

Dono's little revolver was in the truck's center console. I took it out and put it in my coat pocket.

I took the next exit ramp. Its long upward slope ended in a stop sign. I stopped at the end of the line waiting to go through the intersection.

The SUV joined the line four cars behind me. Mud or something like it was spread over his license plate. By the time I'd reached the stop sign, there were more cars stacked up behind the SUV, blocking him in.

I set the parking brake of the truck and edged over to the passenger side and got out, keeping my head down. My hand was on the revolver in my pocket.

The BMW coupe behind me started leaning on the horn even as I moved quickly past him. The noise must have alerted the driver of the SUV. Its engine revved, and it lurched forward and to the left, smashing into the back of the Lexus hybrid in front of it with a hollow thump and the crash of taillight glass.

I started to run toward it. I couldn't see the driver through the glare off the windshield. The SUV lurched again and forced its way out of the line with a squeal of anguished metal.

And for the second time in less than ten hours, I caught a glimpse of curly white hair. The burglar.

He didn't hesitate, hauling ass straight down the steep grassy incline and onto the side of the freeway, tires spinning and throwing up big rooster-tail gouts of wet earth. I watched as he floored the accelerator and joined the northbound stream of traffic. Mud on the rear license plate, just like in the front.

As I walked back to the truck, half the people in the line got out of their cars to better hear the railings of the unlucky driver whose Lexus had taken the brunt of the SUV's sudden departure. Nobody paid much attention to me, except for the guy in the BMW behind my truck. He was still hollering obscenities at me from the safety of his car.

I considered shooting the asshole, just so the day wouldn't be a total loss. Instead I got into the truck and drove to the nearest gas station.

Whatever skills the burglar had, tailing people wasn't one of them. He'd just been stumbling along after the truck. I knew he hadn't been behind me earlier in the morning when I'd driven from the house to Corcoran's apartment.

So how had he found me now?

I parked the truck by the station's air and water pumps and opened the back of the canopy to take out the toolbox that Dono kept there. I lay down on the wet asphalt and shimmied under the truck with a flashlight.

It was easy to see. A plain black rectangle of plastic, about the size of a paperback book, bound with metal-reinforced tape to the cross brace of the chassis. I cut the tape away with a utility knife and edged myself back out to get a better look at it.

A GPS transmitter. Handmade from separate components, as the bugs had been. Judging by the dirt on the black box, it had been taped under Dono's truck for at least a few days. The power light shone green.

Why would the burglar follow me so closely if there was a tracking device already on the truck? Most transmitters allowed for online tracking. The burglar should be able to see anywhere I drove just by looking at a Web site.

Unless he couldn't afford the few minutes' delay while the Web site map caught up to my real location. There was more to the burglar's motive than just wanting his expensive toys back. He was acting desperate.

He'd broken into Dono's house to reclaim his bugs. Maybe he wanted this transmitter back, too. Wanted it enough to risk following me closely, hoping I'd stop somewhere long enough that he could steal it out from under the truck.

I kicked myself for not thinking earlier that there might be a tracker planted on Dono's truck. The old man had been under some serious surveillance—of course whoever was after him would want to follow his movements.

If I had found the transmitter immediately, I could have laid a trap. Now the fucker was spooked. He probably wouldn't try again.

I pried the plastic lid off the transmitter and popped its lithium battery out. The little green light went dark.

Before I drove away from the gas station, I checked every inch of the truck, over and under. I didn't put it past the clever white-haired bastard to have planted a backup somewhere.

AT HARBORVIEW THERE WAS no cop outside Dono's door. Or even a chair where a cop would sit. I called Guerin. He didn't answer, so I called Kanellis.

"Yes?" he said after I'd identified myself. Not trying to keep the impatience out of his voice.

"Where's the detail on my grandfather's room?" I said.

"We can't keep a uniform on his door around the clock. The sergeant at East said they've warned hospital security not to let anyone but family into his room."

The casing creaked on my phone as I gripped it. "Dono might be able to ID his shooter. A two-week wonder strolling by every twenty minutes isn't going to cut it."

"We could take him into protective custody."

"What would that mean? A prison hospital?"

"Or the infirmary in County. He'd be downtown."

"Forget it." Dono needed neurologists, not some intern working a triple shift to pay off his tuition load.

"Harborview will allow a private cop. Celebrities do it all the time, I hear."

I hung up. I'd already pissed off the detectives once today. If I stayed on the line with Kanellis, I was going to say something that would make it two for two.

Hire a rent-a-cop. Jesus.

With what was in my bank account, I might be able to swing a week of twenty-four-hour coverage from a reliable security firm. I didn't want to go cheap. Just like with most skilled jobs, you got what you paid for.

I turned my phone back on, pulled up local branches of national firms, and started calling. When I found one called Standard Security Services, which employed off-duty cops and would allow me to contact the guard on duty directly at any time, I gave them my credit-card number for the thousand-dollar deposit. They promised to have someone meet me at Harborview within two hours.

Dono hadn't twitched once during my conversation with Kanellis. I sat down by his bed to wait. The room smelled of astringent over the thicker, grassy scent of a wilting bouquet of daisies in a plastic vase by Dono's bed. No card, but the vase had a Harborview price sticker on it. Probably from Addy Proctor, on one of her frequent visits. I owed that old woman.

Dono looked about the same as yesterday, like his long body was half melted into the thin mattress. The lines around his eyes might have been a little deeper. I listened to the rasp of the ventilator, up and down, and closed my own eyes and tried to breathe in time with the sound.

CHAPTER FIFTEEN

IT HAD STARTED TO rain outside Harborview, an insistent drizzle borne on gusts of wind, the drops looping their way under awnings and around corners. Water painted the buildings as negative images. The concrete darkened, and the windows gleamed as the struggling sunlight reflected off the sheen.

I had left the guard from Standard Security by Dono's bedside with clear instructions to call me if anything changed and to pick up his phone if I called, no matter what the hospital said. I was halfway down the hill toward the parking garage and enjoying the cold trickle of rainwater on the back of my neck after the stuffy hospital room.

Davey and his brother, Mike, were near the end of the street, jogging through the downpour. Davey held his coat up over his head. Mike waved a hand. They took shelter in the entryway of an apartment block.

"My head's still killing me," Davey said in greeting when I caught up to them.

"I think I can see and raise you on that one. Was Juliet pissed?"

"Naw. Special circumstances."

"Were you with Dono?" asked Mike.

"Of course he saw Dono, you moron," Davey said. "Why else would he be here? How is he?"

"He's still unconscious," I said.

Davey nodded. "He's a tough fucker." He pulled his leather jacket's collar up against the wind. "We went by the house first and guessed you'd be here. You gotta come to dinner with us."

"I'm not up for family time, Davey," I said.

"Don't even fucking try that. If you're not there, I have to make excuses, and Ma will get bent out of shape because she already shopped. And Juliet will grill me about why. Don't make me sit between them on my own, man."

I smiled. "I'll stop by. Let me grab some rest and a shower first. Otherwise Evelyn's liable to toss me right back outside."

Mike nodded. "We'll sit with Dono for a while," he said.

"They won't let you in," I said, and explained about the guard.

"What about the cops?" Mike said.

Davey snorted.

"We could look after him," Mike persisted. "You don't need to go broke."

"Not 24/7," I said. "And that's the only way I'll be able to relax."

Davey grinned. "So relax a little. Be at our house by seven. Bring beer. Ma conveniently forgot to pick that up."

I WAS PULLING UP to the house when my phone rang.

"Shaw. It's me."

Nasal and nasty. Jimmy Corcoran.

"I traced the number that the bug was dialing," he said. "Nothing special about the account except unlimited capacity on the recorded messages. So the bugs could record for days and days without any problem. The account was opened two months ago. The name on it is George Lincoln. That mean anything to you?"

"No. Sounds fake."

"I figured. Might as well be Abraham Washington or Franklin Delano Jefferson."

"Can you get the recorded messages off the account?" Those recordings were what I really cared about. Hearing what had happened at Dono's house the night he was shot.

"No," said Corcoran. "That's the royal bitch of it. The account was closed the night before last. Actually around two in the morning. And the voice mails were erased."

I wanted to slam my fist through the windshield. That would have been only an hour or so after I'd been hit over the head by the burglar at Dono's house. The little fucker must have run home and started erasing his tracks right away.

"What about backup tapes?" I said through clenched teeth.

"Nah. My guy there says the company doesn't hang on to backups of personal voice mails. Too much trouble. But I got more." He sounded jazzed. The thrill of the hunt. "About a dozen different phone numbers have called that voice-mail account. You got a pen?"

"Go ahead." Corcoran read me the account number and then a list of phone numbers. Most of the numbers were sequential, ending in 7704, 7705, 7706, and so on.

"The numbers belong to the bugs," I said, thinking out loud. "He bought a dozen phones from one store, and he cannibalized the works to build the bugs."

"No shit," Corcoran said. "There's hundreds of calls from these numbers to the account during the two months it was active. Almost every call is long. Ten or twenty minutes."

Making up dozens and dozens of overlapping hours of recorded junk. Televisions playing, shower noises. Even Dono snoring in bed. It would have been a full-time job just to skim through it all.

I ran my eyes down the list. "There are thirteen numbers here. But there were only eight bugs at Dono's."

"You sure?"

"I searched. The cops searched. Only eight. So there are more bugs planted somewhere." I slapped my hand down on the porch railing. "Dono's not the only person this son of a bitch has been watching."

"Okay, I buy that. Let's see if you can spot the real clue, smart-ass," Corcoran said.

I looked at the list of numbers. Twelve were in the same sequence as the others. One was completely different.

"It's his personal number," I said. My pulse throbbed in my temples. "He called the voice-mail account to listen to what the bugs had recorded. Maybe even to download the recordings somewhere else."

"Not as stupid as you look. But don't get too excited, kid. It's probably just another burner phone."

"But if he's still using it, it's traceable."

Corcoran sighed. "You going to spend all day telling me shit I already know? *If* your boyfriend turns his personal phone back on *and* my guy at the company can catch it, then maybe we have a shot."

"What about the other four bugs? If they're still active . . ."

"They're active. Two calls from them, late last night."

Where were they planted? Who else was the burglar following?

"Can you zero in on the address the bugs are calling from?" I asked.

Corcoran hummed a moment to himself, thinking it over. "I can find the nearest cell site that caught the calls. It'll have the GPS coordinates of the calling phones. Within a hundred yards, give or take."

"Good enough."

"Unless it's somewhere in the city. At that point you're stuck with knocking on doors, looking for a short guy with white hair."

"Move fast. This asshole is going to ground."

"I know we have to move fast, you dumb fuck. You think I don't? Shit." Corcoran hung up. Right back to his old angry self. Which meant he was feeling good.

CHAPTER SIXTEEN

DAVEY HAD TOLD ME over our third or fourth drink at the Morgen that he and his wife, Juliet, had moved into the little Tolan house shortly after Frances was born. Evelyn had shifted herself to a rental condo somewhere closer to the restaurant where she worked. She had insisted. A shitty little Burien apartment—Davey's words—was no place for a granddaughter to bloom.

The change in ownership showed a bit. The lawn was shaggy. The white paint over the garage door had a few broad streaks of rust or mud, like a giant child's finger painting. Davey's beater of a Camaro rested in the driveway, next to a more practical Honda hatchback. But it was still the house where I'd spent countless hours with Davey, sitting in the middle of the living room, weaving elaborate tales of adventure around Hot Wheels and G.I. Joe figures.

As I walked from the truck toward the house, Juliet came into view at the far left window. Her back was to me, but there was no mistaking the white-blond plait of hair falling to the middle of her back. She'd worn it the same way in high school. She began laying out silverware or plates on a table just below the frame of the window.

I made it halfway up the walk before I was spotted. Juliet knocked on the dining-room window and waved an eager hello. I waved back, and she vanished. An instant later the front door opened.

Davey stepped out onto the concrete stoop. "I knew it. You forgot the beer."

"Is that Van?" Evelyn's voice, from somewhere within. "Hang on, hang on." Davey and I stepped inside, jostling for room. The house smelled of pot roast and spices.

The living room was crowded with furniture and knickknacks and framed photographs. I was afraid I'd knock something over each time I turned around. Dono's house had more than twice the square footage and less than half the belongings.

Evelyn Tolan hurried in, wiping her hand on a red dish towel and beaming.

In the three seconds before she hugged me, I was struck by how much she still looked like her elder boy. The delicate features and wide blue eyes that made Davey almost too pretty were mostly unchanged in Evelyn. Her black curls had been invaded by a few gray and white strands I could see up close, as she pressed her head to my chest.

Evelyn had been very young when Davey was born and was probably still south of fifty. She wore a blue silk blouse and a long charcoal-colored skirt, cut to fit her small frame. A turquoise necklace and earrings. She'd dressed for company.

I remembered Davey being mocked by our classmates for having a hot mom when we were kids. Maybe his coworkers still teased him about it.

"My Lord, look at you," she said, releasing me. "You're so tan!" Her eyes touched only momentarily on my scars. Davey must have given the family fair warning.

Evelyn smiled haltingly. "You'll come in and sit. Dinner's nearly on the table."

There was a child's angry wail from deep inside the house, and Juliet breezed through the living room toward the back, grinning. "Hi, Van!"

"You can meet Her Highness," Davey said.

Mike was filling the doorway to the dining area, waiting his turn. He stuck out a hand, almost formally. "Good to see you," he said.

We shook. Mike was also dressed up, in a light blue button-down and black trousers. Even Davey had on a clean T-shirt.

"Get Van something to drink, Michael," said Evelyn. "I need to see to the roast. Van, you make yourself at home here." She hurried out toward the kitchen.

"He should go thirsty," said Davey. "Seeing how he turned up empty-handed."

I raised my eyebrows. "A roast?"

"The prodigal," Davey said. "You don't rate the fatted calf."

"Shush." Juliet came back in, carrying a red-faced and huffing toddler. Frances saw Davey and reached for him.

"Daddy's girl," Davey said, taking her. Frances glared at me. Her hair was so blond it was nearly translucent, but she had her dad's blue eyes.

"She's beautiful," I said.

Juliet petted Frances's head. "Ninetieth percentile for her height."

"But still a chubmuffin," said Davey, and he buried his nose in her neck. Frances squealed delightedly.

"And she's overdue for jammies," said Juliet. "I wanted her to see her Uncle Van before bedtime." Frances recognized a word or two and started whimpering. "Now, it's all right." Juliet whisked her away from Davey. "I'll be back after *Pat the Bunny*. Don't wait on dinner, Davey."

Mike came back in holding two bottles of Blue Moon. Davey took one from him and looked at it sorrowfully.

"Only two in the fridge," he said, and held it out to me. "Call it a welcome-home present."

"I had enough at the Morgen," I said.

"Bullshit you did."

"Last night was the most booze I've had in months. Afghanistan's a dry zone. My head's still pounding." The headache was from taking Dono's shillelagh across my skull, but it counted just the same.

"Hell, you don't have to ask me twice," Davey said, and took a swig.

Juliet called from the kitchen. Davey set his bottle on the coffee table. "Relax," he said. "Don't touch my beer." They left the room.

Left to my own devices, I wandered into the hallway. The striped green wallpaper was mostly hidden under dozens of framed photos. I stepped carefully around piles of children's toys to look at them. Davey as a baby. Juliet and Davey on their wedding day, squinting into the sun. Mike's kindergarten class. A stiff-looking couple that I guessed were Evelyn's parents, the man wearing a suit that looked like burlap and the woman with hair piled into a black beehive.

There were no pictures of old Joe Tolan, Evelyn's estranged husband. Not that I was surprised. He'd cut and run even before Davey and I had met in second grade.

Mike came up the hall, lugging a basket of folded laundry. "Hey, you see this one?" he said. He leaned down to point to a color five-by-seven in a birchwood frame.

It was a photo of Davey and me and Mike as children. Davey and I must have been about twelve years old, Mike only six or so. We were all in swimsuits, standing ankle-deep in water. We looked pasty and as skinny as fence posts and had huge smiles on our faces. Davey was holding a hot dog.

"Lake Washington," I said.

Mike nodded. "For Seafair, I think. We went to somebody's house and walked down to watch the hydroplane races. I don't remember, but Mom's talked about it." He straightened up, an inch taller than I was. The six-year-old kid in the picture had become a big dude.

He glowered. "Are the cops going to catch this guy?" he said. "Because I read if they don't find a suspect in the first couple of days, the odds go way down."

"You and Dono seem to get along. That's pretty rare, for him."

"He's been a good boss. He and Luce." Mike leaned back against the stairway banister. "I just keep thinking about this time I was bitching about him for making me clean out the back room at the Morgen and paint it. I had tickets to some stupid show with my girlfriend, so I rushed it. He made me scrape the molding clean and do another coat. Took up the whole weekend. Man, was I pissed."

"Did you tell him?"

"You kidding? I just whined about it when I got home. But Mom shut me up immediately. She wouldn't hear a word against Dono."

"Maybe Evelyn's being too nice. Dono can be pigheaded."

Mike smiled softly. "Yeah, I guess." He looked again at the photograph of us as kids. "You coming back to town. Davey was so psyched when he found out."

"I should have kept in touch."

"Nah, it's okay. It was tough on him when you left, sure. But having Juliet around helped a lot. At least Davey was smart enough to figure that out."

I followed Mike's gaze to the wall of photos, to another of Davey and Juliet's wedding pictures.

"Women civilize you," I said.

Mike almost smiled again, before his broad face fell back into its usual thoughtful expression. "Is there something I can do? Anything's better than just waiting around."

"It's still a family thing right now. Look after his bar. That's what he'd want."

Evelyn came into the hallway and laid a hand on her son's shoulder. "Michael, would you please set the last of the table? I'd like to speak with Van for a moment."

When he'd left, she closed the sliding wooden door to the kitchen. The hall was quiet.

"I wanted to talk to you about Dono," Evelyn said, "about how he's really doing. Before we sit down to dinner and the children are around."

"What the doctors don't tell me is more than what they do. I have to guess the rest."

"Still. I need to know the truth." She looked up at me, her jaw set.

"They don't believe that Dono will wake up," I said. "Even if he does, he's not going to be anything like the same. The bullet did a lot of damage to his brain. There may not be much of him left at all. His surgeon didn't come right out and say it, but he thinks it would be a blessing if Dono slipped away."

Evelyn nodded twice, very slowly. Her eyes looked down and focused intently at about the level of my chest. I reached out and caught her just as her knees sagged a fraction.

"Michael," she said.

"I'll get him."

"Wait. No, I'm all right," she said, but I held on to her arm while she leaned against the wall of framed pictures. "I'm sorry. I thought I was ready, and then—" She inhaled and stood straighter. "Strange that you never know how you'll fare until you hear the news for yourself."

I swore at myself. Evelyn was such a rock with her own family that I'd stupidly blurted out the whole story without thinking how she might react to the kind of violence around mine.

"Do you agree with the surgeon?" she said.

"I know what Dono would prefer."

Evelyn nodded. Her eyes were red. "Then we'll hope for what's best."

"Guys!" Juliet called out from the dining room. "We're ready."

Evelyn slid the wooden door open again, and we walked through the narrow kitchen. A massive table of oiled pine took up most of the dining room. I edged sideways along the wall and bumped against a shelf, grabbing a small white leather Bible before it fell to the floor.

Davey carried the roast out in its pan and placed it on the table. The juices were still bubbling around the edges. My stomach did a half gainer in anticipation.

After we all took our places, Evelyn bowed her head. The rest of the family went immediately quiet. "Bless us, Lord, and this meal we receive from your bounty. Thank you for seeing us through the darkness that we may be returned home." From the corner of my eye, I could tell she nodded her head toward me. "And watch over Van's grandfather. Through Christ, your child, amen."

We nodded, and Mike said "Amen" and stood to pick up the carving tools by the roast. Juliet began dishing from a bowl of mashed potatoes. The potatoes had been whipped to the consistency of pudding and coated with enough butter to be more yellow than white. It took some restraint not to bury my face in them.

"How is Dono?" Juliet said to me. She'd changed into a floral-print dress for the meal, with a gold necklace. "Any better?"

"The same," I said.

Mike put a thick slab of roast on Juliet's plate. "Do they have any clues on who did it?"

Evelyn shook her head. "Later. Not at the table."

As the largest, Mike and I had been given the ends of the table. He was clumsy with the knife and made chunks of the meat, taking six or seven passes for each plate until he'd built a small cairn of beef on each.

Frances slapped her high chair. "No green bean."

"Eat a few and you'll get po-ta-to," said Davey, making faces on the syllables. Frances cackled and grabbed a bean but didn't put it in her mouth.

My plate returned to me, overflowing. Evelyn stood to reach a bottle of wine on the sideboard behind her. "Davey tells us you're only back on leave. How long can you stay?" she said. She had the cork popped in ten seconds, showing off thirty years of experience waiting tables.

"A few more days," I said. "I'm trying to learn more about Dono's life now. Have you seen him lately?"

She nodded. "At the bar. He was there when I came by to see Michael at work just a week or two ago. When was that, honey?"

Mike's ears went pink. "I don't know. It was a Sunday, before we opened."

"Yes. To bring you your study guide, I remember. Your grandfather was there, Van, working on something or other behind the bar."

Juliet looked at Mike. "Study guide?"

"Don't get revved up," said Mike. "I'm just taking the GRE, see how I do."

Evelyn beamed. "Michael's economics professor from Seattle State thinks he'd do well in the graduate program."

"It's a very highly ranked school," Juliet said to me. She smiled at her brother-in-law. "You know you can get in, Mike."

Davey chuckled. "Mike's never doubted that for a second."

"Davey's doing very well, too," Juliet said, like she might be accused of disloyalty. "They gave him a bonus." She touched her gold necklace and smiled at her husband.

Davey winked at her. "Hey, I like spoiling you. A little profit sharing is the least they can do."

"Van doesn't have anything to drink, David," said Evelyn.

"There's wine open," said Juliet.

Davey got up. "Van's gone all Methodist on us tonight."

"Water's good," I said.

"Château de Faucet it is," he said, and left. He was joking, but I tried to remember the last place I'd lived where you could drink the water straight from the tap.

"I'd love to know more about your life, Van. We've heard so little since you left." Evelyn was serving a bit of guilt along with the side dishes tonight. "Why the army?" she asked.

Because they could take me fastest, and I could stop sleeping in the backseats of cars in the Green Lake Park & Ride.

"They had the most options for new recruits," I said.

Juliet took a few quick bites from her plate while Davey distracted the baby. "It's worked out well for you, from what Davey tells us," she said.

Then she looked at the side of my face and flushed.

This, I had learned, was how it was with civilians. Sometimes you had to confront it for them. I tapped the white line running along my jaw with my fork and smiled at her. "It worked out just fine, Julie. Kind of a rough start, though."

"Can I ask . . . I mean, how?" said Mike.

I spooned some potatoes onto my plate. "I was about two months out of RIP—Ranger training—when I deployed to Iraq. Twenty years old. I was sent to a unit that cycled through these tiny outposts in central Tikrit. One of the hot spots. About every third or fourth night, our unit would catch a bird and go hunting, checking for possible insurgent camps."

Evelyn held her water glass with both small hands. "A bird?" she said.

"Helicopter. It doesn't land, just pauses while we fast-rope down from a few meters up."

"Fun," Mike said, grinning.

"You know it," I said. "Anyway, on that night we dropped half a mile from this narrow path that wound down into the valley. About the only way in or out. We figured the camp we were looking for couldn't be too far off the path, so we moved parallel to it for an hour or so. The plan was to find and evaluate the camp, hit it if it needed hitting, and take any prisoners or intel with us back to the extraction point."

"What happened?" said Juliet. Baby Frances was nodding off in her chair, her food forgotten.

"Ambush. Probably some goat herder saw the chopper come in for the drop and called his neighbor, who called someone else. Damn near every family has a cell phone, even out in the boonies. So they had about twenty minutes' head start to get every bad guy with a gun and a grudge out of bed. They opened up with RPGs—rocket-propelled grenades—and then they just sprayed the area. We were really lucky."

Everyone around the table had stopped eating.

"Lucky?" Evelyn said.

"The bad guys were too eager. RPGs are meant for vehicles and urban assault, not a few soldiers spread out across a hundred yards. They made a hell of a lot of noise, but that was about all. We ducked into the rocks and just kept our heads down."

The roasting pan was empty except for the bone. There was plenty of meat still on it. But I wasn't hungry anymore.

"I would have died right there," said Juliet. "Weren't you terrified?"

I had been. When the first grenade flashed, it felt as if a thunderbolt had reached out and slapped me on the head. I'd been scrambling on autopilot, doing what months of backbreaking practice had drilled into me. But I was keeping the story light tonight. Dinner chat.

"We made sure everyone was accounted for," I said, "and started hauling butt out of there. I was bringing up the rear with another Ranger, Scoves."

I winked at Juliet. "That's when I got my tribal marks." I traced a finger firmly along each of the three white creases on my left profile. Dividing the eyebrow. Where a bit of my cheekbone was missing. Following the jawline.

Seeing me touch the scars always seems to put people at ease. Reminds them that the wounds aren't raw and painful. Not anymore.

I washed down what was left of the roast with water and pushed away my plate. "Somebody told me later it was a rocket, the last one they fired. It hit a boulder near us, and a lot of shrapnel went flying." I shrugged. "I went down. Scoves went down. When I came to, my ears were ringing and Scoves was still out."

There had been more. The part that the Tolans didn't need to hear.

Still half gone, I had turned toward a movement in my peripheral vision. Two men holding AKs with full banana clips were walking toward me through the tall grass. One so close that three steps later his foot tripped over my leg. It freaked me right out of my daze. I reached up and grabbed his rifle, and he fell down on top of me.

My pistol was already in my hand. I put two rounds into his center mass. He collapsed next to me. His friend still hadn't figured out what was happening. Two more rounds for him. Another for each of them through the head, just like I'd been trained, after I'd staggered to my feet. So jacked on fear and focus I hadn't realized yet that the left side of my face was pulp.

"Where were the other guys?" said Mike.

I wiped my mouth with my napkin, to give me time for a long breath.

"Fighting their way back, trying to retrieve us," I said. "But I didn't know that. My headset radio was trashed. I did my best to break the record for the quarter-mile dash out of that valley."

"What about your friend?" Evelyn's eyes looked as if she were in pain. "Scoves?"

Scoves had been bleeding out. I risked staying in the grass for an extra minute to slap some QuikClot and gauze on his neck and arm to slow the red wash that had soaked his entire upper body. Then I'd thrown him over my shoulder and started running, grateful with every step that he was about the smallest guy in our unit.

"He made it out, too," I said. "He's back with his family in Texas." In his last e-mail, he'd said he was on his third generation of artificial shoulder joint.

"They shipped us out to a hospital in Baghdad, and then I went to Walter Reed to see doctors for this." I pointed at my face. "They did good. Part of my jaw and brow ridge are made of bioglass. The bone re-forms around it, mostly. A couple of my teeth on that side are better than new." They would be just as white and pretty a century from now, I'd been told.

There was a pause. "And you went back?" said Juliet. "They made you go back after that?"

I made me. I had to get back on the horse. Therapy hadn't been cutting it.

"I was ready." They sent me back to Iraq for a last rotation. Then Afghanistan, when that heated up.

Evelyn reached over and touched my hand. "Thank you."

Juliet pointed to my wrist, where the fresh surgical scars edged out of my sleeve. "But you've been hurt again."

"Not really," I said. "Less surgery than people get for carpal tunnel."

"Tell me they at least gave you cash or a medal or something," Davey said.

I had to grin. Davey was still predictable. Looking for the reward. Mine had been a shiny little Bronze Star, with combat "V."

"It's in a box somewhere in a storage facility in Georgia," I said. "Along with my tiara and evening gown."

Mike picked up the wine bottle and poured a slug into my empty glass.

"Hangover or not, Van," he said, "you deserve a drink."

My phone buzzed loudly, making us all jump. I fished it out of my pocket.

A text from Corcoran. I got up. "Sorry. I need to check this."

"Is it Dono?" said Evelyn. I shook my head and walked out, through the front door onto the tiny porch.

The first line of Corcoran's message was just the word FOUR. Then a string of GPS coordinates, along with an address outside of Covington, a suburb about midway between Seattle and Tacoma. The last line of the text said, STILL LOOKING FOR THE LAST ONE.

The address was Corcoran's best fix on the location of where the other four bugs were planted. Maybe it was the home of one of Dono's partners. Maybe even somebody who knew who'd shot Dono, and why.

Jimmy C. was an asshole, but he was also as good as he claimed to be.

There wasn't much I could do until morning. But suddenly I wasn't in the mood for family chitchat.

I opened the door and stepped back into the living room. Davey was there, waiting. "You taking off?" he said, seeing my face.

"Yeah," I said.

"You need help? 'Cause whatever it is, man, I'm there." He sounded more hopeful than determined.

"No. Thanks, Davey. It's nothing. You'd be bored."

He looked at me, unconvinced. "Huh. Okay."

I walked into the dining room. Frances was gone, probably tucked away by her mother. Evelyn was putting a pie onto the table. Blackberry, and homemade from the looks of it.

"Dinner was terrific," I said. "I'm sorry. I have to go."

Juliet made a protesting sound, but Evelyn just nodded. "I'll wrap some of this for you," she said, and took the pie into the kitchen.

Mike stepped up. "Sorry you couldn't stay longer."

I leaned over to kiss Juliet on the cheek. She tapped the side of my face shyly and gave me a little smile. "I know everyone probably says this, but you look just fine. Like a pirate."

Evelyn came back in and handed me a Tupperware box with about half the pie in it. "Now you'll have to come back, to return this," she said. "Don't forget."

Davey followed me out onto the porch steps. "You sure you don't want company?"

"I'll call you tomorrow."

As I popped the clutch and pulled away from the curb, he was still standing there, watching me go.

CHAPTER SEVENTEEN

I STOOD ON A CORNER by a Chevron gas station. The street address in Covington that Corcoran had texted me turned out to be an intersection off of Covington Sawyer Road, a two-lane blacktop that wound past grassy fields and industrial parks. The sun wasn't up far enough to push through the clouds yet. Commuters ignored the speed limit as they hustled to work.

Four bugs. That was how many the white-haired burglar had planted, and I knew they were somewhere within a stone's throw of this spot.

A long throw anyway. A hundred-yard radius covered a lot of ground. Over thirty-one thousand square yards. If the address had been downtown, with a ten-story building on every side, I would have been screwed. In this suburban wilderness, I had a fighting chance to figure out where the little white-haired bastard had hidden his toys.

An empty field and the Chevron took up my side of the intersection, with a block of condominiums and a construction site on the other two corners. On the fence around the construction site, a large sign announced a coming apartment block, aimed at modern living for young professionals.

Maybe this place was somewhere Dono came frequently. Or maybe it was where a partner of the old man's had lived or worked. If I could find that guy, he might be able to tell me everything I wanted to know about Dono's shooting.

I ruled out the gas station and the construction site. And while it was amusing to think of somebody bugging an empty field and listening to the crickets, I was pretty sure I could rule that out, too. The condominiums. Dono's large house had held eight bugs. Four seemed about the right number for a one- or two-bedroom space. I waited for a break in the traffic and jogged across the street to the small complex.

A sign made of brushed aluminum read HIGHLAND TERRACE HOMES, with arrows directing visitors to the office and the pool. It was a small place, only eighteen or twenty units. The dew-soaked grass was trimmed and the walks swept. The carports held a lot of newer models, some of them two-seaters. Mainly single residents or couples.

It was early. Most of the carports were full. The spaces were assigned, with white tacked-on letters above each space identifying the matching town house. I didn't know which unit I was looking for or even what the residents looked like.

But if the burglar had bugged their house, he might have done more.

I took the physical-therapy ball out of my pocket. I hadn't used it at all since I'd come to town. Twice in the last day, I'd noticed my left fingers going slightly numb, like they wanted to remind me that I was slacking. I walked farther into the complex, idly bouncing the ball. When I reached the line of parked cars, I kicked it with my foot, and it skittered away.

I leaned down between the first and second cars, a Mercedes and an older Toyota and looked underneath. Nothing. Nothing at the third or fourth cars either.

The ball had settled behind the wheel of a GMC truck. I fished it out and stood up just as a resident came out of his apartment, briefcase and travel coffee mug in hand. He looked at me.

I held up the ball and grinned stupidly. "Bad hop," I said, and walked away, bouncing it again. He got into his Infiniti and drove off. The Infiniti wasn't one of the cars I'd checked. I had to pick up the pace, before the morning rush emptied the complex. I kicked the ball and kept looking.

The ninth space held a red Nissan Altima. It was clean and freshly waxed. And taped inside the rear fender was a black plastic rectangle, just like the one I'd found on Dono's pickup.

The burglar had held to his MO. Bugs in the house. And a GPS tracker on the vehicle. I grinned. Gotcha.

I looked inside the car. It was as clean as the outside. There was a pink metal water bottle in the center cup holder and two modern-lit paperbacks by female authors on the passenger seat. A lavender gym bag was in the rear seat.

The pristine Altima sure as hell wasn't the car of an old crook like Hollis or Jimmy Corcoran. I couldn't remember Dono ever working with a woman on one of his jobs. But the car was here, which meant she was probably home.

The white letters above the carport read H14. Building G was to my left and H to my right. I put the rubber ball in my pocket and ambled toward it.

H14 was at the far corner, on the top floor. A premium spot. It looked like it would command an unobstructed view of the small forest behind the complex. I raised my hand to knock and drew it back.

The door was open. Not much, just off the lock about half an inch, as if the door had been slammed hard and had bounced back before the latch could fully engage.

I listened. Nothing but the chatter of the early-morning birds in the forest behind the building. I reached out a knuckle and pushed, lightly. The latch gave up the fight, and the door opened a finger's breadth.

Something was not right. Not at all. Every part of me was howling that truth, from the hairs on my scalp to my clenching toes. My hand was already on the .32 in my coat pocket.

I stepped aside and pushed the door all the way open.

The large living room inside was as arranged and tidy as a magazine shoot. A chocolate-colored leather couch and a matching chair. Elegant, sleek bronze lamps and tables. Everything looking spick-and-span.

With the door open, I caught the smell. A combination of hot copper pennies and human shit.

Death.

I followed the odor to the master bedroom, at the back of the apartment.

It was a woman. She was seated in a chair. She was fully clothed and tilted slightly forward as if she had just started to look for something lost in the lavender carpet in front of her. The room was very dim. Tall trees behind the building shaded the windows from the morning light. Her long, dark hair obscured most of her face.

I flicked the light switch. Nothing happened. There was a lamp by the door, and I reached for it before seeing that the lamp's cord was cut at the base. Two feet away a clock radio lay upside down on the floor. No electric cord on it either. And I knew what was keeping the woman from falling all the way forward.

She had been wired to the chair. Arms and ankles and one long piece for her torso, under her breasts. The chair had been tied with something like scarves or stockings to one of the oaken bedposts, to keep it from tipping over.

As my eyes adjusted, I could see stripes of blood on her bare forearms where the skin had rubbed completely away. She had strained, over and over, against the wires. Another scarf was around her throat, pulled so tight that the silk was torn. Her face was purple and swollen. Swollen so much that I could barely make out a dozen or more small cuts around her eyes. The cuts had bled enough that I guessed they were made before she died.

She'd been tortured. And strangled.

The blood was dry, but the scent of bodily waste was still strong enough that I'd caught it two rooms away. I bent down to see the underside of her forearms. In the half-light, the lividity looked gray. Same for her ankles and feet. The fact that she was barefoot was somehow as bad as anything else.

She'd died last night, or very early this morning. Who knew how long she was alive in the chair before that?

I walked out of the bedroom and back to the open front door. The air outside was fresh and cold. I took a few deep breaths of it before stepping back inside and shutting the door.

Who had she been? Dono's partner on a job? Her apartment didn't look like the home of a professional thief. Had she been a girlfriend?

I felt lousy for the woman, but my overriding thought was, *Van boy, you are fucked*. The first person at two murder scenes in almost as many days. My immediate future would be heavy on steel bars and cinder-block walls unless I could come up with a good reason for being here.

I found her purse on the counter of the small kitchen. The purse was in the same dark brown leather as her couch. I grabbed a paper towel to avoid leaving prints.

Her driver's license identified the dead woman as Cristiana Liotti, forty-three years old, living at this address. Business cards said she was an executive assistant at a firm called Talos Industrial Equipment, with offices in Ravensdale.

I turned on her cell phone and scanned her contacts. A hundred numbers or more, but no names that I recognized.

Dono's burner phone was still in my pocket. I pulled it out and looked at its number. It started with 206-851.

I checked the call log on Cristiana Liotti's phone. It held a few months' worth of calls, almost every one to somebody already in her contact list. But way back in early January, Cristiana had been called by a 206-851 number. Not the same phone I was holding. But close. She had been called twice. And they had talked for an hour or more each time.

It wasn't hard to reassemble the facts. Dono bought a couple of burner phones. He used one of them to call Cristiana, months ago. They had long conversations. And then he did what a crook does with a burner phone—he trashed it. Because it wasn't clean anymore.

Whatever else Cristiana Liotti might have done during her life, at least some of it had been mixed up with my grandfather's work.

Somebody knocked on the door.

"Cristiana?" A woman's voice.

Even though I wasn't moving, I still froze on the spot.

"I saw your car. Can I get a lift?" A pause, and then a louder knock. "Are you here?"

Another few seconds passed, and then I heard footsteps moving away.

I couldn't spend much more time in the dead woman's apartment. I couldn't just leave either. Security cameras at the entrance would have captured me walking onto the grounds.

I started to call 911 and then changed my mind and hit the button next to a recent number in my own call log.

Three rings before the detective answered. "John Guerin."

"It's Shaw. I'm at an apartment in Covington. There's a dead woman here. Murdered. Sometime last night, from the looks of things."

"Don't touch anything," he said reflexively. "Was she shot like your grandfather?"

"No. Worse." I gave him the address. "I'll call 911 after we hang up. Unless you want more lead time."

Guerin grunted. He could get here and see the crime scene for himself before anybody with weight groused about jurisdiction. "I'm already driving. I'll call them for you. Stay on the line."

"My battery's almost dead."

"Shaw—"

I hung up.

Somebody was going to a shitload of trouble. Bugs. Trackers. Now torture. I could imagine the killer holding a knife, touching the tip of it to Cristiana's face and eyelids, making little cuts and letting them bleed until the terror became too much. Until she'd talked. And when he had learned what he wanted, when he was sure of it, he had killed her.

What was it that her killer had wanted her to tell him? Where something was hidden? After Dono had been shot, his shooter had stayed in the house. Guerin and I both guessed that the shooter had been hunting through the place before I'd surprised him.

I had five or six minutes, maybe, before the first car showed. Nowhere near enough time for a real search of the apartment, but I didn't want to risk contaminating the scene anyway.

In a kitchen drawer, I found a slim brown flashlight. Jesus, everything in the woman's place was coordinated. I picked up the flashlight with the same paper towel and went back into the bedroom.

I started where most people hide things, in the closets. There were enough clothes to make the thick wooden railing sag with the weight. Shoes, neatly arranged in their original boxes. A couple of woven bamboo storage bins. Nothing looked disturbed or missing.

As I came back out of the closet, I noticed a vent cover near the ceiling of the bedroom wall. I shone the flashlight on it. The screwheads had fresh scratches.

I guessed that after the killer had tied up Cristiana, he'd gone through her apartment and removed all four of the listening devices. And then replaced the vent covers, so that the removal wouldn't attract attention. One less link between Dono and Cristiana.

Were Cristiana's killer and the burglar the same man? She'd died last night. Maybe he'd been here before driving up to Seattle and knocking me on the head at one in the morning.

I was four minutes into the search and had one ear listening for the police knock when I found it. In the bathroom, under the sink, all the bottles and lotions and little plastic bins had been shoved aside. One of the sections of the fiberboard at the back was torn loose. Behind it there was a gap between the cabinet and the wall. Big enough to have held something the size of a large photo album.

The rough stucco of the wall had tiny bits of bluish clear plastic stuck to it, abraded off something like a trash bag. Or the kind of shrink-wrapping that banks used to keep stacks of currency bundled together. A space that size could hold a serious amount of cash, if the bills were high denominations.

It wasn't a great hiding place. The killer could probably have found it in less time than it took him to tie Cristiana up and make her tell him where it was.

But maybe that had been fun for the motherfucker.

Before leaving I took one of Cristiana's business cards from her purse and scribbled *"Highland Terrace H14"* on it. I needed some reason for being here that didn't burn Jimmy Corcoran. And a weak reason was better than none at all.

I was closing the front door behind me and dialing Ephraim Ganz on my phone when the first sheriff's cruiser roared into the parking lot, sirens wailing.

CHAPTER EIGHTEEN

EPHRAIM GANZ AND I sat on one side of a long conference table in the King County Sheriff's Office in Covington. The other side of the table was full. Detectives Guerin and Kanellis occupied the seats nearest the door. In the middle chairs were the detectives from the sheriff's department. A wiry woman with black hair and hard features, named Marques, and her partner, an equally thin man with a sandy brown comb-over, named Thomasen.

In the last seat was an older guy with a bald head and chalk-stripe suit who had introduced himself to Ephraim as Lieutenant Burrowes of MCU. The county's major-crimes unit.

He was the wildcard in the room. Cristiana Liotti's murder had been brutal, but not something that I thought would rate direct involvement from MCU, much less its brass.

Burrowes had the rank, but Marques had the lead. She was the one who'd given Guerin and Kanellis permission to sit in. She had also led the first round of questioning, asking me about everything from the time I'd landed in Seattle to the moment that the first trooper arrived at Cristiana Liotti's apartment. Then, without any signal between them, Thomasen had started over, asking about the same events from different angles. Instead of *what* happened, it would be *how did I feel when* this happened. Sometimes he got the events wrong just a little bit, to see if my story changed to match.

Dono had done this with me when I was a boy. He made a game of it. Tell me about math class today, he'd say. Make up a lie. Let's see if I can figure out what it is.

"You found Ms. Liotti's business card in your grandfather's desk?" Thomasen said to me.

"*On* his desk," I said.

"He must have a lot of business cards. Being a successful contractor and bar owner and all that. Why did this one stand out?"

I shrugged. "It wasn't filed away. Her address on the back was way down in Covington, and Dono usually worked in Seattle. And her personal number was there, too. I thought she was a girlfriend."

"But you didn't call her, you said." Thomasen tilted his head, like he was trying to comprehend such odd behavior. "Not even to check if she was home."

"Dono's been shot. If she was his girlfriend, she should hear bad news in person."

"So early in the morning?" Thomasen said.

"Gentlemen," said Ephraim, "and lady. Mr. Shaw has explained all these points already. He has only a few days of his leave left. Of course he was eager to get an early start on the day, like all veterans of our armed forces."

Kanellis snorted. During the past two hours of Marques and Thomasen questioning me, his attention had wandered a little. Guerin's hadn't. He didn't seem bored hearing me tell the details about Dono's shooting all over again. He didn't seem anything. He just sat there, listening.

"So unless you have any new questions," Ephraim said, "I think everyone will agree that my client has fully cooperated."

Marques took Cristiana Liotti's business card from Thomasen and looked at it for a moment. She set it down on the table, at a precise right angle to the notepad. Her hawklike face was reflective. It was tough to guess her age. Somewhere from late thirties to early fifties. Native American blood, maybe.

"Mr. Shaw, you said that you hadn't heard of Ms. Liotti prior to today," she said. "What about her company? Talos Industrial Equipment. Had you heard of that?"

I could feel the attention from the other cops in the room sharpen, like dogs catching a scent.

Even Ephraim was startled. "She worked for Talos Industrial?" he said, looking at me. "You didn't tell me that."

"I didn't know it was important," I said. "What is it?"

Marques stared at me for another beat. "It's a tool-manufacturing firm. A conglomerate, really. Their Northwest plant is in Ravensdale."

I knew where that was, roughly. A small town somewhere east of where we were now.

"Okay," I said. "So why does everyone look like they're waiting for me to faint?"

"I want to point something out right now," Ephraim said to the room. "Mr. Shaw has not been in the United States for many months, much less the Seattle area. Nor has he had any contact with his grandfather other than a short letter, which the police have already seen." He gestured toward Guerin and Kanellis at the far end of the table. "If you're implying that Mr. Shaw—"

Lieutenant Burrowes cut him off. It was the first time he'd spoken during the interview. "No one's making accusations. Mr. Shaw's movements have already been confirmed." He looked down the table at Guerin and Kanellis. "Correct?"

Guerin nodded. "At least so far as the army is willing to confirm Special Operations assignments. But we've been assured that for the entire month of February, Sergeant Shaw was deployed in the Kandahar province of Afghanistan."

"Very well," Ephraim said. "Please proceed."

"Not until someone catches me up to the rest of the room," I said.

Marques looked at Burrowes. He raised a hand, acquiescing. "Fine. Nothing you couldn't learn from the news anyway."

"Cristiana Liotti was a senior administrative assistant for Talos Industrial." She tapped the business card. "On the morning of February nineteeth, Talos—or more accurately a chartered armored car that Talos had hired—was the target of an armed robbery by three men. The robbers succeeded, although two of them were later found dead."

I had a sudden hollow feeling in my center.

"What was taken?" I said.

Marques wouldn't be rushed. "Talos is an industry leader in high-grade tools and factory machinery. Everything from drill bits to huge saws used to cut steel plating. In order to cut things of that hardness—"

"Diamonds," I said.

She nodded. I heard Burrowes exhale heavily.

"Diamonds," Marques said. "Not gem quality, but still diamonds. Mined in China and flown in to Sea-Tac, which is where the armored car picked them up. They were nearly to the Talos plant in Ravensdale when the robbers intercepted the car."

I raised my eyebrows, asking without saying it.

"Eighty kilograms," Marques said. "Maybe six million dollars, market value."

Six *million*. Holy hell.

Christ knew that Dono had done things just as crazy in his younger days. But the careful, analytical bastard who'd raised me would have pissed on the very idea.

And yet. It made a dark, slithering kind of sense. His letter to me. Changing his will. The bugs, trying to find out something that Dono knew. And Dono himself left for dead.

What did you do, old man?

I looked at Marques. All the cops around the table had been waiting, like cops do, to see where the silence might lead.

"You think Cristiana Liotti was the inside source on the robbery," I said. "That she knew when the diamonds were being delivered."

"Or she managed to learn it," said Thomasen. "Officially, only three executives at the company had the details on the shipment. But . . ." He shrugged.

"Somebody wrote it down," I said, "or left their computer screen unlocked."

"Let's say that's right," said Marques. "How would she know the kind of men who would rob the armored car?"

"Because you're asking," I said, "I'm guessing there's nothing in her history that might indicate criminal friends."

"Or family," Marques said. Making sure I got the point.

"Do *you* think she was the person on the inside?" Thomasen said.

I did. Not only because she'd been tortured and killed. Those tiny bits of blue shrink-wrap, left from the stacks of cash I believed she'd hidden in her bathroom, were enough to convince me. But I didn't want to tell the cops I'd searched the place, although I was sure at least Guerin suspected.

"Who were the two dead men?" I asked Marques.

"This is not a swap meet," Burrowes said. He looked at Ephraim. "You know we can hold your client."

Ephraim started to answer, and I stopped him with a raised hand, because Marques was shaking her head at Burrowes. "It's nothing he can't learn from the Internet, Dan," she said.

Burrowes's mouth made a thin line. With his shaved head, he looked like a peeved snake. "Your choice," he said, and got up and walked out of the room.

Marques reached down and withdrew a thick file from her messenger bag. She took out two sheets and slid them toward me.

"Sal Orren," she said, "and Burt McGann."

The photos were mug shots, blown up to take the full page. Sal Orren was maybe thirty, with oily skin and hair and a mournful expression. Burt McGann was older, buzz-cut, with hostile, hoggish eyes. I was sure that the mug shot hadn't been his first.

"How did they die?" I said.

"They shot each other," Marques said, "at the site of what we think was a vehicle exchange after the robbery."

I looked up from the photos. "Each other?"

"Did you think your grandfather might have killed them?" said Thomasen.

I hadn't ruled it out. That was how unsure I was of Dono and his whole life right now. Maybe he was the third man, the only survivor of the robbery. Maybe he'd even killed his partners after the job. Or maybe he was tied into the crime some other way.

He might even be innocent, although I put that at the bottom of a long list of possible truths.

"You told me the third robber got away," I said. "Back in February. There are no leads in the two months since? Nobody's tried to sell the diamonds?"

Marques frowned. "If your grandfather left you something, where would it be?"

"At his house."

"You know what I mean," she said. "Somewhere nobody else would know, or look."

"He didn't expect to be shot," I said. "He didn't plan to leave me anything."

"Why do you think he had Cristiana Liotti's card?" said Thomasen.

I knew we'd come back to the card. By selling the cops a story about finding Cristiana Liotti's business card at Dono's house, I'd unwittingly tied my grandfather to the robbery.

"I still think Cristiana could have been a girlfriend," I said. "Were the diamonds laser-etched? Or don't they bother if they're going be ground down to powder?"

"Forget the damn diamonds," Marques said. "Tell us what you know about your grandfather."

"We've been through that. I haven't seen him in ten years."

"Then tell me about before. When you were growing up. He didn't make all his money fixing cabinets and pouring drinks, right?"

"You know his record."

"I see what's on paper. But I don't think Dono Shaw had been straight for the last twenty years and then one day he decided to pick up an assault rifle and take down an armored truck."

Sharing time was over. The cops wouldn't give up any more facts about the robbery. And I wasn't going to tell them about my life with Dono. Even if it might help them.

On top of the yawning cavern in my gut, there was a kind of elation. Finally I saw a reason for all the madness that had been swirling around my grandfather, and around me.

"What you really need to know," I said to Marques, "is if I had any contact with my grandfather, other than the letter I showed SPD. And do I know if he was involved in the robbery. And if so, do I know where the diamonds are."

Ephraim cut in. "If both Seattle and the Sheriff's Office—"

"The answer to all three is no," I said. I stood up. Ephraim quickly did the same. Thomasen got up, too, and blocked the door.

"We're not finished," Marques said.

"I'm saving you time," I said, walking around the table. "I'm a dead end."

Thomasen stayed put. "Right now you're staring at accessory after the fact, minimum."

"So arrest me. If I'm no longer a menace to society, maybe one of you will accidentally stumble across the guy who shot my grandfather."

Marques held up a hand. "Wait while we type your statement—"

Ephraim was ready with one of his cards. "My office can handle that. No need to take up any more of your time. If you'll e-mail me the statement, we'll get Mr. Shaw's signature back to you right away."

Thomasen looked at Marques. She kept staring at me.

"Let him go," she said.

Thomasen moved, and I opened the door. I caught sight of Guerin. He looked resigned, like the interview had gone as badly as he'd expected.

"You should have walked out an hour ago," Ephraim said as we made our way through the small station. It was brightly lit, with high, red-brown cubicle walls dividing up the floor space.

Lieutenant Burrowes was standing in the reception area, talking on the desk phone. As we passed, he grabbed me by the arm.

"It's for you," he said, thrusting the receiver my way. His face was smug.

"Yes?" I said into the phone.

"Sergeant Shaw? This is Captain Bob Unser, at Benning HQ."

"Sir." I knew Unser by name—and reputation. He was the right hand of our battalion's XO. He determined which Rangers went where and which didn't move at all.

It was a lot of weight, and Unser liked to swing it around.

"Lieutenant Burrowes has been filling me in on your activities during your leave," Unser said. "Give me your own report. Now."

Ephraim was looking at me quizzically. I waved him off. He shrugged and went outside.

I told Captain Unser the basic facts. He listened without comment. When I'd finished, there was a lengthy pause, and I could hear him writing something down on the opposite end.

"Do I have to tell you how this looks to me, Sergeant Shaw? One of our own, involved with two homicides?"

"No, sir."

"It doesn't matter what the circumstances are. It's bad. Bad for you. Bad for the regiment."

"Sir."

"You will call my office every day by 1400 Eastern and give me a full update on every event during the past twenty-four hours. If I'm not here, you will report to the officer in charge."

"Yes, sir."

"If I don't like what I'm hearing, Sergeant, you will be assigned to Fort Lewis until the Seattle police and the sheriff and whoever else you've managed to piss off are finished with you, and then you'll be on the first flight back here. Get it straight."

"Sir," I said, but Unser had already hung up.

Burrowes swooped in.

"Tell Marques everything," he said. "Everything you have, everything you might even guess. Cooperate and I'll make sure to give Captain Unser a solid impression of you. If you play games with us, I'll throw you under a mile-long train. Understand?"

I think he was hoping for a *Yes, sir*. Instead I turned and followed Ephraim through the building's exit and into the overcast day outside.

CHAPTER NINETEEN

CAPTAIN UNSER HADN'T ELABORATED on what would happen if I stepped out of line. He hadn't had to. One glance at my service record would tell him that I was up for promotion and that another stripe meant the difference between my staying with an active unit in Afghanistan and being assigned back to Fort Benning more or less permanently. I'd be an instructor at Ranger School, or if Unser was really out for me, placed on some sort of administrative duty. He was smart enough to know that a desk job would be worse than tossing me into the brig.

Ganz dropped me off at my truck, where I'd left it near Cristiana Liotti's apartment. It was midafternoon. The truck had a parking ticket on its windshield, and someone had run a key down the side of the paint.

I sat in the driver's seat with the window open to the cold air and took out my phone. I brought up Google and typed "TALOS ROBBERY."

Over eighty thousand hits. Mother of God.

It wasn't just news. It had been *national* news, if only for a short time. I was surprised that I hadn't heard about it, even half a world away. Although back in February the shit had been hitting every fan in sight in Kandahar. America could have been invaded by aliens and it would have been a week before we knew.

Still, it took me ten minutes just to scan through the first dozen pages of results and figure out what was relevant. Every blogger and news service had long articles on the topic. I went with the local papers first.

DIAMONDS STOLEN FROM ARMORED CAR IN RAVENSDALE

Posted: Feb 19 3:30 p.m.

An armored car was forcibly stopped and robbed by armed suspects on Wednesday morning in Ravensdale. According to officials, the Securiguard armored car had been hired by Talos Industrial Equipment to deliver a shipment of tool-grade diamonds from the U.S. Customs Air Cargo holding facility at Sea-Tac Airport Customs Depot. The car was driving along 281st SE Kent-Kangley Road when it was stopped, police said.

"The car braked to allow a school bus driven by suspects to pull out of a parking lot," said Sgt. Walter Hodgins. "Then a second truck came from behind the armored car and trapped it."

The driver and a second guard were confronted by robbers armed with what may have been automatic weapons. Neither guard exited the front of the armored car, and there were no injuries. The rear door to the armored car was forced open, possibly by use of explosives.

Investigators are still determining how many robbers were present and precisely how much was taken. Police stated that the suspects were described as wearing dark hooded sweatshirts and dark pants and were of average build.

"This robbery was in a spread-out suburban area, away from buildings and people," Sgt. Hodgins said. "We are seeking witnesses who may have seen the suspects leaving the area."

Anyone with information about the robbery can call King County CrimeStoppers at 206.555.2030 or text CRIMES. Tipsters remain anonymous and may qualify for a cash reward.

I could translate the last paragraph of the article easily enough: *The police have nothing solid to go on, and they are hoping for a miracle.*

And then they got one. Maybe not the kind they were imagining.

TWO MEN FOUND DEAD AT AUBURN MUNICIPAL AIRPORT

Posted: Feb 22 7:20 a.m.

Two men were found dead in an abandoned hangar near Auburn Municipal Airport, police announced Friday evening.

The bodies were discovered by an airport maintenance worker, who was driving through the area south of the airfield and noticed an open side door on the hangar. From evidence at the scene, police believe the bodies to be those of suspects in the February 19 armored car robbery in Ravensdale, sixteen miles away.

And later that same day, there was an update:

Police have identified the bodies as Nelson Orren, 32, of Seattle, and Burtram McGann, 40, of Joliet, Illinois. Both had suffered gunshot wounds to the chest and abdomen.

"At this point we have not determined if the suspects were shot by other individuals or whether they inflicted the wounds on one another," said Detective Paul Toomey of King County Sheriff Major Crimes Unit. "Assault rifles were found near the bodies. We do believe there was at least one other person at the scene." A Ford Taurus was also found in the hangar, and police are verifying if it was the same vehicle used in the robbery.

There was a lot more from the news services during the last part of February. Updates on where the school bus had been stolen from. Escalating offers of reward from Talos. A few outraged editorials, both conservative and liberal. And follow-up blurbs about the criminal records of Orren and McGann, the two dead robbers. Orren had done some minor county time in his youth, for car theft and burglary. He seemed to work exclusively around Seattle.

Burt McGann was more of a mystery. And more of a hard case. He'd done two years in Indiana for assault with intent and had been suspected of "other violent crimes," as the police spokesperson put it. Not the kind of cowboy that Dono would usually choose to work with.

The real meat on the Web was from private sources. Six million dollars of missing diamonds provoked a lot of interest. There were whole blogs devoted to the crime and scores of low-res pictures taken by passersby on the day of the robbery.

One Web page in particular, run by an elderly crime buff in southern Washington, had done an expert job of finding the best photos. I studied them carefully and then started the truck.

I wanted to see the scene for myself.

RAVENSDALE WAS ONLY A few miles from Covington, down Highway 516 which turned into Kent-Kangley Road as it went due east. I drove along its length until I spotted the church steeple that had been visible in the background of photographs I'd looked at.

The gray afternoon was edging into evening, and the tall trees surrounding the road hastened the sunset. A cold night wind had already started to kick up from the west, and it bit at my cheeks as I got out of the truck and looked at the road. I had maybe another thirty minutes of decent light. The school bus that had forced the armored car to stop had pulled out of the church's parking lot.

I walked back up the road toward the church entrance, thinking about the sequence of events during the robbery. The pictures showed multiple angles on the armored car, which had not been the big silver tank that I'd imagined but a white reinforced panel van. It made sense. Securiguard wasn't hired to deliver stacks of cash to dozens of ATMs. They were making a single drop of eighty kilos of industrial stones.

Fast and discreet, I'm sure they had thought. Until the school bus pulled out and they'd been forced to hit the brakes. Then the real fun had begun.

The armored van had been wedged solid between the bus and a flatbed truck in back. The flatbed had a bumper extension on the front of it, set low enough that it wouldn't block the rear doors on the van.

Force the armored van to stop cold. An instinctive reaction, when there might be kids on the school bus. Come up behind the van fast with the flatbed and its heavy bumper. On the asphalt of the road, there were thick, dark hash marks of abraded rubber. Bam.

Other photos had shown the back of the armored van. One of the doors was completely off, lying on the road. I had recognized the black scoring and almost clean punched holes where the door's hinges had been as the sign of shape charges, probably C-4 or Semtex. BAM again.

The score had been as slick as shit through a goose. At least until the three men had reached the abandoned hangar to trade one getaway car for another with less heat, and Orren and McGann had killed each other.

I stepped off the road to let a Volvo sedan go by. A boy in the backseat wearing a bright yellow cap made a face at me as it cruised past.

Okay. Think about the scene the way Dono might have.

A remote location, away from cameras and witnesses. Inside information, of course, to know about the diamonds and exactly when they were due. A lot of prep work, with multiple vehicles preset, and explosives to boot.

All of that felt like Dono. Careful and considered.

On the flip side, there was the human factor, which he'd always despised. Orren and McGann, maybe getting greedy, maybe just freaking out with the adrenaline high. One of them twitches wrong. A third and fourth BAM.

Incredibly good fortune for the third robber, if you wanted to look on the bright side. They might just as easily have aced him as well.

But there was something else bothering me about the score. I backed up and played the scene through my mind again. Not like a crook this time. Like a soldier.

The two points of view weren't dissimilar, at least when it came down to tactical choices. Adequate cover. Clear fields of fire. Methods of extraction.

Both lenses showed me the same picture.

It had been a weak plan.

Three men in the crew. One to drive the school bus and cover the guards in the cab of the armored car. One to drive the flatbed and cover the road behind. While the last man would need to drive up in the getaway car, set the charges, and unload more than one hundred and seventy pounds of diamonds.

There should have been at least one more man. Sitting at the wheel of the running getaway car, watching the road in front. At the first sign of any trouble, the three men could pile into the car and be out of sight in ten seconds.

Without that fourth set of eyes, a large part of their horizon was left unwatched. Very risky. Almost unthinkable, for a man like Dono.

Almost.

And that was the conclusion that my mind kept circling back to. Even without knowing that the bugs connected my grandfather to Cristiana Liotti, or her torture and murder, that pretty much clinched her as the inside source on the robbery. Even discounting all of Dono's odd behavior lately.

It just *felt* like the old man. Almost like I could catch the scent of his shaving cream, still at the scene.

Shit, Dono. What was it? Reliving your wild years? Why suddenly start gunslinging like liquor-store trash?

With six million in stones and three partners, you would have expected to clear at least a million if you were running the show. Was that kind of money simply worth rolling the dice?

The wind heightened in pitch but didn't give me any answers. I walked back to the truck, over the permanent black scars left on the road.

AGE FOURTEEN

The day after school let out for the summer, Granddad and I packed our suitcases and a few other bags into a rental car and drove to a motel twenty miles south of the Canadian border. When we checked in, the fat woman behind the reception desk asked how long we expected to stay. Granddad said we weren't sure. He told her we were visiting his sister, who was ill. The woman clucked in sympathy.

When Granddad went outside to move the car, she eagerly asked me what was wrong with the sister. I just shrugged. She frowned and didn't bother pressing for more details. Granddad told me later that he envied teenagers, being able to get away with shit like that.

We stayed in the motel for a week. A few times each day, at different hours, we drove north on I-5 toward the border. We varied our route but always wound up on the same access road off the freeway, cruising smoothly past the same large buildings.

In the early-summer heat, we could drive with the windows rolled down. The white-noise hum threatened to make me drowsy. But I stayed sharp.

It was my show this time out.

Every evening we stayed in the motel room and watched TV, or went out to a movie, or played cards. Granddad preferred canasta, while I liked poker. We'd switch games each time we played.

On one of the daytime drives, we turned down a different road, parked the car, and put on rubber boots to take a hike through the wide, marshy forest behind the buildings. The forest was thick. We stopped behind a large tangle of blackberry bushes, fifty yards out from one particular warehouse.

It was a larger structure than the others along the access road. Four stories tall, with walls made of silver corrugated steel between green I-beams. Around the front there was a blue sign with the warehouse name in script two feet high, but here by the back doors the name was painted in plain black right on the steel, the narrow letters waving with the ripples in the metal. I knew what it said, even though most of the words were obscured behind forest. A. J. CARLSON BONDED WAREHOUSE AND TRANSFER.

The blackberry branches had thorns half an inch long. Carefully, I pushed one aside with my fingertips to see more. I could make out stick-insect outlines of workers hurrying around on the warehouse loading dock. That far away through the brush, Granddad and I were probably the next thing to invisible, but we still kept our movements to a minimum.

I looked at the dock through Granddad's good set of 10×50 binoculars. The workers were busy wheeling hand trucks on and off a large panel van, filling it with boxes.

"How's the height of it?" Granddad said.

I sized the loading dock against the panel van and the workers. "Looks like a standard four feet. There's a ramp." I focused the lenses past the open loading-dock door into the warehouse. "And I see a forklift inside. A little Hyster three-wheeler."

I could hear the smile in his voice. "Good. The truck I've in mind for us has enough load capacity for an elephant and his lunch besides. We can drive the damned forklift right into the back."

I laughed and kept looking. Behind the forklift was the end of the first massive row of racks. Each rack in the warehouse was twenty feet tall, stacked with crates and pallets of merchandise waiting for processing. Some intended for export to Canada, others on their first leg of distribution within the States. Granddad had told me the warehouse handled everything from liquor to lumber. Almost every bit of it had passed or would pass through the Peace Arch crossing at the border in Blaine.

Like the biggest open bank vault in the world.

I suddenly noticed that my breath was coming really fast, and realizing it made me feel dizzy. I let the binoculars hang from my neck and closed my eyes, not opening them even when one of the thorns poked into the side of my hand. The sharp pain of it steadied me a little. I knew Granddad was watching me.

When I opened my eyes again, he was looking at the warehouse.

"When I was nineteen—this was when your grandmother, Fionnuala, and I were still in Belfast, mind, before your own mother was born—I needed some extra money for the holidays. So I put my eye on a pub owned by a man named Hargen. Nasty bastard. Which was part of the reason I picked his place, I suppose. Anyway, I was sure that Hargen kept his weekend earnings at least a day too long, and I thought I'd visit one Monday night and lighten his burden."

Granddad's accent came out when we worked. I liked it.

"So I thought on it for a week or so. When Monday came along, I waited all night in the alley across from the place. I mean *all* night. The sun came up, and there I was, standing like I was waiting for a bus to come along."

I was confused. Maybe Granddad was hinting at something I hadn't seen yet. I quickly raised the binoculars and trained them on the building.

"The pub didn't look right?" I said, hoping for a hint.

"It looked just fine. It was me that wasn't right. That's why I couldn't move a step from that alley."

"You were nervous."

"I was, sure. But I was always nervous. I'm nervous now. We've talked about that."

We had. Nerves were okay. Granddad had given me a whole speech before he'd taken me on my first run with him, right after my twelfth birthday. Just a simple house job, and I'd had nothing to do but keep an eye peeled. Even though the nearest neighbor was a hundred yards away and out for the night. I could've yodeled and not gotten us into trouble.

Still, my stomach had been as knotted as a kinked garden hose. I'd puked up my cheeseburger after we'd arrived safely back home.

Since then Granddad had brought me on another score at least once every other month. Businesses and houses alike. Sometimes not so much for the money as the practice. Different places had different rules and different tools. By my count we'd stolen a hundred or more cars as well, driving most of them eight or ten blocks and abandoning them again, just to get the feel of it.

Over time he had started having me case our targets and letting me grease the doors or the alarms, too.

Nothing as big as A. J. Carlson Bonded Warehouse and Transfer, though. Not nearly.

"So if it wasn't nerves," I said to him, eyes fixed firmly on the loading dock, "why didn't you go into Hargen's pub?"

"Well, I *believed* it was because I'd thought too much about it. I cursed myself for having feet of clay. Swore I'd come back the next week, strip that villain down to nothing."

I'd heard a lot of Granddad's lessons. Enough to know there was a twist coming. I tried to guess.

"You saw something," I said. "And you didn't even really *know* you saw it, right? But it still made you stay away."

He laughed, and I lowered the binoculars and looked at him. The evening sun was behind his head, and his dark hair stuck out like the bristles of the world's rangiest bear.

"I'd love to have *that* particular magic power," he said. "What is that thing that your man in the comic books has?"

I knew what he meant. But I hadn't read comics in like two years, since before that first house job, even. I'd tossed them all, not long after Granddad came back from County. "Spider sense," I said reluctantly.

"Spiders. Lovely." He was laughing hard now, but I realized it wasn't at me. "No, it wasn't any such thing. And I hadn't thought about Hargen's place too *much*. I hadn't thought about it *enough*."

He took the binoculars out of my hand, put them back in their case, and slung the case over his shoulder. "I hadn't done my schoolwork, you see. The place might have an alarm I didn't know about. Or some friend of Hargen's, bedded down in the back room after a fight with his wife. Or a fucking dog. I hadn't thought about *any* of those possibilities. And the fact I hadn't thought about them meant the whole thing was a bad idea, and my guts were telling me that."

He put his big hand on my shoulder. "Forget the money. What are your guts saying about the risk?"

I thought about it. We knew the place and its people. We knew its alarm system.

"We've done the homework," I said. "Almost."

I instantly felt better.

Later that night one of the businesses nearby had a rock thrown through its front window. The police response took four and a half minutes.

On the next day, we took it easy. We went to a matinee. Dono napped while I watched Jackie Chan beat up everybody in sight. Late in the afternoon, we took one more pass, just to make sure nothing around the warehouse had changed.

"Go?" Granddad said.

I looked at the parking lot, at the way the workers went about their day. "Yeah."

He smiled and nodded.

Seven hours later we were high on the roof of A. J. Carlson's. Revving up the circular saws.

Chain saws would have been faster, but their grinding howl would also carry a lot farther than the whine of the eighteen-volt cordless Makitas. We cut through the upper layers of roofing and insulation, gouging a shallow six-foot crater. Sweat trickled down my forearms into my cotton work gloves. We tossed aside scraps of asphalt shingle and felt, until piles of it littered the smooth white moonscape of the roof around us.

Soon only a thick sheet of plywood separated us from the interior of the warehouse below. We pried at one end of the sheet with crowbars until the screws popped. Granddad wedged it open, far enough for me to saw off a couple feet at the end. We tossed the wood on top of the rest of the scraps.

Light boomed out from the new hole in the roof, stretching toward the sky like a weak searchlight for a movie premiere. The light attracted bugs. A mosquito whined in my ear, and I slapped at it. One big-ass moth flew into the gap, into the upper reaches of the warehouse. I had an instant's terror that the alarms would start ringing.

Dumb, sure. We knew the types of alarms inside. They were good, but not so delicate that an insect would set them off.

Still, it reminded me that the roof was only the first hurdle.

Granddad reached into one of the bags and took out a thin tarp, which he draped over the hole to block the light. There were four bags. Rope, power tools, hand tools, and a smaller one for Granddad's burglar kit. We'd had to make two trips up the ladders from the parking lot to get all the gear onto the roof.

"Go take another look around," he said.

I jogged to the nearest edge of the roof and gazed down at the wide expanse of parking lot in front of the warehouse. All the lampposts were dark. The automated timer turned them off at midnight, we'd learned. But the blue warehouse sign shone bright enough to let me see all the way to the access road at the far end of the lot.

Farther out I could see the ribbon of white and red lights on I-5. Traffic was steady going north, even at three o'clock in the morning. The last stretch before the border, six miles up the freeway.

A car was coming along the access road. I instinctively stepped back, even though it was probably impossible to see me from two hundred yards out. As I watched, it turned in to the parking lot of the warehouse. A white car, with a blue-and-red shield insignia on the door.

A security patrol.

I made myself breathe. This was *good* news. The security passes at the warehouse were infrequent, limited to a single driver making a slow roll through the parking lot of each business along the road. He'd take a look and then go on his way. We'd probably be clear for another two hours.

As I peered over the edge, the car made a wide circle, cruising past the entrance and continuing on to the opposite side of the lot. Where he stopped.

Oh, shit.

I turned and waved frantically at Granddad. My eyes adjusted, and I could tell he was standing, watching me. I spun back to the security car.

Still stopped. And now the door was opening and the driver was stepping out.

No reason to freak, I told myself. We hadn't touched a thing out front. Even if he came around back, our big moving truck would probably look like any other vehicle the warehouse might use. He'd think everything was all cool.

Unless he saw our ladder.

Or we'd already triggered an alarm somehow. Maybe the cops were on their way right now.

Oh, *shit.*

The security guard left the door of the car open and walked to the side of the parking lot.

Where he unzipped his pants.

Not taking a look. Taking a piss.

I made myself breathe—again—and by the time I'd stopped huffing like a buffalo, the guard was in the car again and driving out of the lot.

I walked back to Granddad.

"We're clear," I said, and told him about the security guard.

Granddad shook his head and sighed. Maybe at me, maybe at fate. He tossed the tarp aside.

Past the yawning hole was the huge interior of the warehouse. Silent and echoing all at once. The roof beneath my feet suddenly felt fragile, like it might collapse at any moment and send us both tumbling into the pit below.

Granddad had been unpacking the rest of our gear while I'd been busy with the guard. He picked up a small winch and used a power drill to secure it with bolts near the edge of the hole. He fed the end of the rope through the winch and handed the rope to me. I began tying the rope to a bosun's chair that Granddad had bought the week before at a marine salvage store. The chair was a simple rig, just thick blue canvas over a base of rigid plastic for the seat, forming a triangle shape with a few straps and D-rings attached.

It would let me sit in relative comfort while Granddad lowered me into the pit.

Within five minutes I was strapped into the chair while he cranked up the last foot of slack in the rope.

"Check the brake," I said. I'd seen him lock the winch. But I was about to be dangling a long fall away from a concrete floor.

He twisted the brake an extra millimeter. "It's set. Don't forget, now. If we have to meet later—"

"I know." If there was trouble, if I screwed it up and set off the alarms, Granddad would be gone. Down the ladders and through the forest, two miles away to where we'd left the rental car. If I couldn't find my own way out of the warehouse and back to the car, I'd be busted.

He was a convicted felon. I was a juvenile. No question.

"Let's go," I said. Granddad nodded.

I took a deep breath and knelt down to grip the edge of the hole with my gloved hands. I stepped backward off the roof into the hole, lowering myself slowly, like I was doing a pull-up in reverse, until the bosun's chair took my full weight. Its canvas creaked, and the safety straps tightened around my thighs.

I let go, and the chair swung lazily. My head was level with the cut edge of the plywood sheet. I could smell the singed wood and glue, still hot from the saw blade.

Only twenty feet from where I hung was the front of the warehouse. To my right I could see the top of the interior office space, and near that was the first gigantic row of storage racks.

We were here for something specific, but seeing those racks, loaded with huge wooden pallets of everything from food to furniture, made me feel like it was Christmas. I slapped a hand against the side of the chair. Giddyup.

Granddad passed me the bag of hand tools, and I clipped it to the D-ring at the side of the chair. He gave me the smaller bag, the one with his burglary kit. I cradled it in my arms.

Granddad tapped the kit. "You remember about the alarm?"

"The phone line first, then the battery," I said. I was sure I could get by with just doing the battery, but I'd told Granddad—after we'd argued about it for an hour—that I would take the precaution of bypassing the phone line beforehand.

He nodded. He reached over to ease off on the winch brake and turn the handle. Smooth as honey, I started sinking.

The clicks of the winch echoed in the gloom as I ratcheted down. It was like being on a trapeze. Without a net. Cool.

When I was halfway down, I held my hand up and Granddad stopped cranking. The chair spun, slowly. I had to keep turning my head to see the front of the warehouse.

On the wall above the office, there was a bank of passive infrared sensors, about twelve feet off the floor. The sensors were angled downward, covering a wide swath of floor near the office and front entrance. I knew the brand. Their effective range was fifty feet.

Knock the infrareds out and I would have clear passage to the office. And the main alarm box inside it.

I knew this because Granddad had bought inside knowledge about the warehouse's security from a guy I'd never met in person. One of Hollis's many buddies. Granddad must have trusted him, though, or at least believed Hollis when he vouched for the guy's creds. So far his information about the alarms was spot-on. I wondered if he was an employee of the warehouse. Maybe even the owner.

I frowned at myself. Better get my head in the game.

I unzipped the little burglary kit and looped its carrying strap around my neck.

"Okay," I said. My voice sounded loud in the big metal cavern.

Granddad reached down and yanked hard on the taut line. The tug started me swinging in a short arc that got wider as I leaned into it. Five feet. The heavy bag of hand tools bumped against my leg with each swing. Ten feet.

In one more pass, I was close enough to reach out and grab one of the wooden planks that made a broad reinforcing stripe every few feet on the corrugated metal wall. My weight tried to pull me back, and for a moment I hung by one arm like a gibbon. The corners of the raw wood bit into my palm, even through the glove.

Granddad gave me slack on the line until I could get a foot on one of the wooden planks and stand. Face-first against the wall, midway between the floor and the ceiling. The bank of infrared sensors was four feet below my shoe.

From the burglar kit, I took out a multifunction wrench and a set of wire cutters. I looked down at the infrareds and grinned.

Time for the fun part.

I took two deep breaths and heaved with my arms and legs to twist myself around until I was almost upside down on the wall. I shoved my sneakered feet into the gap between the wooden planks and the wall, jamming them painfully but immovably.

The chair tried mightily to pull me back upright. To stay where I was, I had to tense every muscle in my gut, like doing crunches in gym class. But doing them while blood rushed to my head and with my feet feeling like they were trapped in a vise. Then it got a little worse, when one of the straps started putting pressure on my balls.

I almost laughed. Granddad would have *hated* this. No wonder he let me take point.

But the infrareds—those were easy, even hanging head down like a bat. Pop the screws on the housing with the needle-nose pliers of the wrench and cut two wires. Dead meat.

"All set," I called to Granddad as I gratefully clambered right side up. He eased off on the brake, and I let go of the wall and swung like Spider-Man—no Spidey-sense necessary, now that the alarm was toast—down to the warehouse floor.

I unstrapped myself from the chair and let it fall.

"Take your time," Granddad said. His voice rebounded off the floor and walls of the huge interior. *Time- ime-ime.* The echo helping him get a few last reminders in.

From my new vantage point on the floor, the place was spooky, no question. The racks were like monoliths to some ancient pissed-off god. The warehouse behind them looked like it stretched on next to forever.

I took out my penlight and walked up the short flight of stairs to the door of the interior office. It was locked. I fished Granddad's snap gun out of the burglar's kit and had the lock picked in under a minute.

The alarm was right on the wall, directly across from the door, a box about the size and shape of a small medicine cabinet. Painted egg yellow, with the security company's logo in police blue. The padlock on the box was so tiny I used the wire cutters to snap it and reach the control panel.

Three minutes later I had the heavy twenty-four-volt brick battery connected to the alarm's power lines and I'd greased the phone line around the alarm connection. Just in case I screwed up somehow with the battery and the alarm tried to dial out. I knew it wouldn't.

But I still held my breath as I cut the alarm's power.

No blinking lights on the panel. No sirens. The alarm fed off the battery and never knew the difference.

We owned the place, right down to the coffeemakers in the break room.

I checked my watch—3:34 now. We had less than ninety minutes to take what we wanted and clear out, leaving a safety margin of a full hour between our exit and the first guys on the 6:00 A.M. shift straggling in. One more hour after that, we were scheduled to meet Hollis back in Seattle. We had to be on time. Granddad had been very clear on that point.

I jogged across the wide stretch of floor to the loading bay. Two Hyster electric forklifts sat against the wall, plugged in to their sockets like chained mastiffs. A rubber-coated button on the side of the door was obvious enough. I pressed it, and the heavy metal door began to rise with a loud hum.

Granddad was standing on the loading dock outside. Behind him was the dark forest of trees, with no lights in sight, except for stars, and no people for at least half a mile.

"So?" said Granddad.

"Cake," I said. I could see that he'd opened up the back of our moving truck and set the loading-bay ramp in place. It was a big truck, over a thousand cubic feet of capacity.

Granddad took the duffel bag from me and tapped the burglar's kit. "I'll find the goods. You get the forklift ready."

He meant disabling the warning light and beeping when the machine was in reverse. It only took a minute, and I was unplugging the forklift from the wall just as he came walking back.

"I found two," he said. "Follow me."

I pushed the button to start the forklift—the electric engine made a loud stutter—and I got used to the feel of steering it as I trailed Granddad slowly along the rows. We stopped at the end of a long row of large cargo on wooden pallets.

Granddad slapped the closest pallet with one gloved hand. "These."

Pall Mall cigarettes. They didn't look like I'd imagined. The cases were covered with a big sheet of protective plastic wrap that bound them to the pallet. The whole thing the size of a wide refrigerator.

The cases had been shipped straight from the manufacturer to the warehouse. Since the thousands of packs inside were intended as export products, they had not been stamped for Washington State taxes.

Unstamped packs were like gold. Any smuggler could slap on his own fake tax stamps, to match whatever country he wanted, and sell the cartons as if they were legit. The packs could even be sold under the table in the U.S., without any stamps at all. A lot of people were happy as clams to buy their smokes at almost half price.

Fifty cartons per master case. Forty master cases on each large pallet. Four pallets here in the warehouse, according to Granddad's source. At thirty bucks per carton retail in the States, that was almost a quarter of a million bucks here, a little less overseas.

Granddad would clear somewhere around a hundred grand for the four pallets, I guessed. Once I learned how much, I wanted to figure out what it came to per cigarette. Maybe it really *was* better than gold, if you compared the weight.

"Load 'em," Granddad said. "I'll find the other two."

Driving the forklift was a blast. It wasn't my first time, and I'd handled heavier equipment before, but these little machines hauled ass. After I unloaded the first pallet of master cases onto the truck, I took an extra loop around the rows, just to feel it corner.

I was dropping the second pallet in the truck when Granddad came out onto the loading dock.

"We've a problem," he said, turning and walking back inside.

I stopped the forklift and walked quickly after him. His long legs ate up the ground a lot faster than mine, even though I was only five inches shorter.

He stopped at a row not far from the warehouse office and pointed up at a higher level. "There they are," he said.

The two pallets rested on the third level of racks, maybe eighteen feet above the floor. Someone had cut off the thick plastic wrapping that protected the other pallets, but other than that they looked the same.

"Okay," I said. It made some sense that the warehouse might store the cigarettes up high. As cargo weight went, cigarettes were lighter than most things. Easier to put on a top shelf than lumber, at any rate. "I saw a hoist over on the other side. We can get them down."

Granddad shook his head. "That's not it."

"We've got enough time. Twenty minutes, I'll have them on the truck."

He shook his head again.

Whenever he went silent like this, I knew he was testing me. It really pissed me off.

I looked again at the pallets. And finally saw what Granddad saw. Not only was the plastic wrap gone, but the master cases had been moved and then restacked on the pallet. On the untouched pallets I'd loaded into the truck, the Pall Mall logos on every case lined up neatly in the same direction. These cases were jumbled around, some backward, some not. And the only reason I could think of for unwrapping and shuffling forty cases was . . .

"They've been opened," I said.

"And look," said Granddad.

He led me over to an area to the far right of the first rack. A large blue machine was bolted to the floor near the wall. A short conveyor belt made the short part of the machine's L shape, while the long arm looked like some combination of a table saw and a printing press.

"A stamping machine?" I said.

"Yep," said Granddad. He sounded a little amused. "Every case opened and every damn pack inside marked with a Washington tax stamp. We don't even have to take them down to know that. These cases aren't going over the border. They'll be sold around the state."

"So why are they *here*? Why send them to this place if they aren't being exported?" I caught the whiny tone in my own voice and hated it.

"Convenience, I suspect. The tobacco company just sends one big shipment. Half for inside the state, half for export."

"And your guy didn't know that? Was the idiot guessing or what?"

"He knew the cigarettes were coming in. That was all."

"Shit. Shit." I fumed and glared up at the cases, twenty feet off the floor, wishing them with all my might to go back to their original state. "How much can we still get for them?"

"Twelve to twenty years."

"That's not what I mean."

"But that's what they're worth, boy. I don't know if our buyer will want them with the tax stamps. And we sure as sin don't want to keep eighty cases in our garage, now, do we?"

"Somebody will buy them."

He waved a hand, like brushing away a fly. "Somebody, somewhere, sometime. If you don't have a buyer you can trust for shit like this, you leave it alone."

I fumed. Looked at my watch—3:58. "Okay. No cigarettes. What else do we want? Half the stuff in here is valuable. There's televisions over there. And appliances."

"Same deal. Just stones hanging around your neck."

"You must know *somebody* who'll take them. Three weeks of work and you're good with making . . . what, maybe forty grand out of it?" Granddad could clear that on a decent house job.

"Some people work a year to make less."

"We've got a whole empty *truck*. We're just going to walk away? Fuck that."

Granddad's face darkened, and he took a step toward me. I flinched.

He wasn't a hitter. Not to me anyway. He'd never done more than swat me on the ear when he thought I was being especially dumb. Then again I'd never argued with his decisions right in the middle of a job before either.

But he didn't raise his hand. He took a long breath. Stared at me. I could feel the blood going out of my face. The stare was almost worse than getting hit.

"All right," he said. "I told you it was your job. Your call." He looked around at the warehouse. "So tell me. What's it to be?"

I looked around. The warehouse seemed even larger than before. We hadn't even glanced at ninety percent of the place. Which racks held the best stuff? Was there anything even more valuable than the cigarettes?

Screw it. There wasn't time to search every rack hoping for something better. "Maybe those laptops?" I said, pointing to a stack of two dozen slim boxes. Granddad shrugged. "I might be able to sell them. A hundred apiece, maybe." He sounded bored.

I scanned the racks nearby frantically. Spotting a familiar logo, I ran over for a closer look.

"Here!" I said. "Canadian Club. Cases of it!"

"You'll hide the bottles in your locker at school, I suppose?"

"We don't have to hide them. They can go straight to the back room at the bar, right?"

Granddad leaned against the forklift and folded his arms. "So let's say we're willing to risk losing the bar forever to save Albie spending a few dollars per bottle. The government can seize a business, you know, if they think it's involved in smuggling. But put that aside. How do we get the cases there?"

"Well, we've got the truck," I started to say. And then

stopped. We had to drop the two pallets of unstamped cig-arettes off with Hollis first. That was set for seven o'clock. Then we'd have to take the truck—the stolen truck—through downtown during the morning rush hour and park it right in back of the bar to unload every case—every stolen case, clearly marked NOT FOR RESALE—by hand ourselves. And then we'd still have to get rid of the damn truck.

"This sucks," I said.

"The hard choices usually do," said Granddad.

"I can't believe there's nothing in this whole fu— stupid place that's worth the trouble to take."

"Don't think of it like something you've lost. It's a suc-cessful job. We're in the black. Provided"—he nodded toward the open loading bay—"that we get our asses out of here."

So we did. I went outside, still steaming, and made three trips up and down the ladders to load all our gear off the roof and into the annoyingly large empty space in the back of the truck. Granddad secured the pallets and closed the loading-bay doors—but not before, I would bet, having a look at the office to double-check my handiwork on the alarm.

By the time I was done putting the ladder into the back and locking down the rolling door, my temper had cooled down. Granddad was in the driver's seat of the truck, warm-ing up the engine. He'd turned the fans up high to clear the fog off the windshield. The moving air felt cold, and I wiped the sweat from my forehead with the back of my work glove.

"Did you get the rope and chair?" he said.

I nodded. "Everything." I handed him his burglar kit. He set it on the box between our seats, and I noticed that the box was a case of the Canadian Club. I looked at him.

He smiled softly. "We may not sell it. That's not to say I can't enjoy some for myself."

I laughed. "What about me?"

"I'll buy you a soda."

"Can I have a cell phone instead, Granddad?"

In the bluish dashboard lights, his broad hands looked like a marble statue's as he put the truck in gear, each vein standing out in sharp relief.

"Call me Dono," he said.

CHAPTER TWENTY

HOLLIS SHIFTED HEAVILY IN the passenger seat as we drove along the shore of Lake Union. His discomfort might have come from the old springs of the pickup's seat. Or maybe it was from his suit. When I'd pulled up to his marina, he'd come off the dock wearing a reddish sport coat that hung oddly on his top-heavy frame, with gray trousers and a wide orange tie. He looked like a circus ape escaping in the middle of the show.

"Ondine didn't say anything else?" I asked. "Just that she was willing to meet me?"

"Her man did the talking."

I nodded. Of course Ondine Long wouldn't bother with setting appointments. She had people for that.

To our left, the rusted monoliths of Gas Works Park loomed in the evening dark. I had the window down, to feel the rush of air. Hollis and I had to raise our voices to hear each other above the low moan.

"When was the last time you saw her?" I said.

Hollis thought about it. "A couple of years at least. I had these items from a Lithuanian crew off a freighter—"

"Two years. And on Sunday she called you to ask what you might know about Dono's shooting."

"The woman herself." He sounded a little proud.

It didn't seem odd to me that Ondine knew Dono had been shot. She probably had information sources in Congress, much less the SPD. And Hollis would be a logical choice to call, if she wanted to know what trouble Dono might have been into. Hell, he'd been *my* first stop.

What I was really curious about was why Ondine cared.

Once I'd come to grips with reality—that my grandfather had, against almost every cautionary lesson he'd ever instilled in me, robbed the armored car—my next thought was where he might sell the diamonds. There weren't many fences in Seattle who could handle six million dollars' worth of anything, sticker price. Fewer still whom Dono would trust enough to share the necessary details in advance. Dono hadn't stolen the diamonds on spec. He'd known exactly where he was going to take them.

Maybe he'd taken his business to one of the bigger markets—Los Angeles or Dallas—but I didn't think so. Not when I remembered that Ondine Long had called Hollis the very day that Dono had been shot.

"D'you really think he managed it?" Hollis said. "That Dono stole all those pretty rocks?"

"A lot of evidence points that way."

Hollis sat for a moment. Not fidgeting. "And do you think he picked his own team?"

I wasn't sure. When Dono worked with others, which was rare enough, he wanted reliable guys that he knew personally. McGann and Orren hadn't exactly proven rock solid.

"I think if he had a choice, he'd have gone with you," I said.

Hollis nodded. "Course he would."

Another quarter mile along the shore and we saw the golden lights of the Emerald Crown Yacht Club over the water.

The *Crown* was a ferry. Or it had been, back in the 1940s. A fat boat, maybe a hundred twenty feet with a beam about a fourth of that, standing three decks above the waterline. It had been a crappy design. Too tall to stay steady, too many windows to stay cool in summer or warm in winter.

But the very things that forced the *Crown* into early retirement made it ideal for a clever developer's needs. It had high ceilings and enough room belowdecks for a proper kitchen, once you removed the huge diesel engines.

They picked a prime spot, overlooking the lake with the towers of the downtown skyline glinting far in the distance. Builders reinforced the hull and sunk some pilings and scuttled her, and there she sat, a bright and shiny icon, guaranteed never to rock and upset someone's gimlet.

We pulled in and stopped by the entrance, an awning-covered gangplank leading to the main deck. A valet opened the door for me, and I handed him the keys. He looked at the truck like I'd asked him to sit on a compost heap.

Hollis and I walked up the gangplank. A pretty girl in a white suit and matching sailor's cap came over and asked us whom we were meeting. At the mention of Ondine's name, she almost curtsied, and she whisked us aft, to the bottom of a narrow stairwell leading upward.

At the bottom of the stairs, there was a reception desk. The girl picked up the phone on the desk and announced our names.

When she hung up, she frowned at us apologetically. "May I have your cell phones, please?" I handed her mine.

"I don't have one," Hollis said.

She nodded and picked up a black plastic wand from the desk. She swept it over our torsos and thighs, like a TSA screener at an airport.

"Thank you," the girl said when she was done. Chipper as anything. "This way, please." She led us up the stairs.

"What the hell?" Hollis whispered to me.

I didn't think Ondine was concerned about guns. Just taking reasonable precautions against one of us wearing a wire.

We came out onto the weather deck. The club had tables and chairs set outside in the mild evening. Hurricane lamps shone on each table, and bulbs hung overhead like big strings of Christmas lights. It was after the dinner hour, and the deck was quiet. The only occupied table was at the farthest corner, where a man and a woman sat having drinks.

The man was large, blond, and dressed in a light gray suit. The woman was Ondine.

Good genes and artful surgery had crafted Ondine's face into a semblance of forty, though she was probably two decades past that. Somewhere in her heritage, there was a healthy mix of Asian, though from what nation or nations I couldn't guess, and maybe some West Indian blood as well.

Long wasn't her maiden name. She had married young, to the late Hiram Long. Hiram had been the preeminent fencer of stolen goods way back when Dono had first been tearing up the town. A Seattle legend.

Hiram had wed Ondine when he was just past his prime and she was just coming into hers. Dono had made a joke once about Hiram never eating a fortune cookie because it wasn't kosher. I'd been too young to get it.

Hiram remained on top for another twenty years, maybe because he was wise enough to listen to his trophy wife's whispered advice. He finally died in his sleep, older and richer than anyone could guess, and by that time Ondine had stopped requiring a figurehead.

Ondine and the blond man stood as we approached. She wore a calf-length black dress with an ivory wrap over it and a strand of pearls so large they had to be real. Her straight black hair was cut to form precise square bangs.

"Hollis," Ondine said. Her voice was low and pleasant. "Van."

"Ondine, darlin'. Thanks for the invitation," said Hollis, standing a little straighter.

"This is Alec," she said, indicating the blond man. Alec nodded. He did not move to shake hands. He was handsome in a slick way, with a gold tie clasp and a matching watch that must have weighed a pound. He stood with his weight evenly distributed and his hands relaxed.

"Hollis, dear, I'd like to speak to Van in private," Ondine said.

Hollis nodded, exhaling into his usual slouch. "I believe I saw a bar back there," he said, and ambled toward the cabin.

"You're certain?" Alec said to Ondine. She nodded. He turned and followed Hollis but kept his eyes on me for an extra second.

Ondine and I sat down. She removed a pair of slim silver eyeglasses from a leather case and put them on to study me. The glasses had oval lenses and magnified her stare a fraction, making it as unsettlingly direct as a falcon's.

"I expected you to look more like your grandfather," Ondine said. "But it's only your eyes. And the hands, I think."

"Did you two have any recent business?" I asked.

"Right to the point, I see. A man of action." She waved a hand, and a waiter hurried to our table. I ordered a scotch. Seemed like the right drink for the surroundings.

"I made inquiries," Ondine said, "after Hollis called me this afternoon. You've had a very busy vacation. Do the county police truly suspect that you killed that woman?"

"They're more interested in what I might know about Dono."

Ondine sipped at her crimson drink. "And about the diamonds. From the Talos armored-car robbery."

"Someone bugged the murdered woman's apartment. She worked for Talos Industrial. Dono's house was bugged by the same man."

One of Ondine's carefully shaped eyebrows went up. "So," she said, "someone knew, or believed, that Dono and this woman—"

"Cristiana Liotti."

"That the two of them were both connected to the robbery."

"And they aren't satisfied with just eavesdropping anymore."

"No," said Ondine.

The waiter brought my drink. Neither of us moved while he set it down. The candle in the center of the table guttered and snapped in the breeze.

"What is it you want?" she asked.

"For starters? I want to know if you were Dono's buyer."

"Is that what you told the police?" she said.

I took a sip of the scotch. It went down smoky and honeyed. I was Ondine's guest, and the bartender had served me the good stuff.

"Let's stop screwing around, Ondine," I said. "Either you give a shit about the old man getting shot and you're willing to level with me. Or you don't, in which case I might as well drink up and go home."

Ondine's lips had gone white around her sienna lipstick. "I was wrong. You're quite a lot like Dono."

"You *do* care." I smiled. "You agreed to meet me. So the same question to you: What do you want?"

She continued to look at me for a long moment before answering. "Peace. And quiet."

"Murders are loud," I said.

"Yes."

"It would be good if this guy is stopped before he goes after more people connected to the robbery."

A corner of Ondine's mouth went up a fraction. She nodded toward Alec, who I could see through the broad cabin window standing with Hollis at the bar. He was watching us.

"I'm not terribly concerned for my own safety," Ondine said. "Alec's service record is even more impressive than yours."

"He's probably housebroken, too. But even a failed run at you might draw attention from the cops."

Out across the lake, an air horn sounded from a commercial vessel somewhere in the dark. It echoed off the city and came back to us, lower and slower, a few seconds later.

"If I'm to share information with you," Ondine said, tapping a fingernail on the stem of her glass, "I want some assurances."

"Go ahead."

"My name stays out of it, completely. With police or anyone else. No using my influence to smooth your path."

"Okay. My turn. What was your deal with Dono?"

"He approached me with the plan. I agreed to be his buyer. But when the time came, he had changed his mind."

"He wanted more?"

"He wanted to keep the diamonds for himself instead of exchanging them for cash. After what happened, his partners killing one another, Dono could renegotiate our terms. He gave me a larger amount than I would have been owed otherwise, and he kept the rest. Perhaps four million."

I thought about it. It made sense. Diamonds were a hell of a lot easier to hide than cash, and industrial stones wouldn't have any identifiable laser engraving. Dono could sell a handful whenever he needed. They might even increase in value over time.

"How did Dono meet Cristiana Liotti?" I said.

"He simply told me he had information on the shipment. I never heard her name before today. I presume he paid her directly for her information."

Damn. That was a piece I couldn't get the shape of. How a corporate type like Cristiana Liotti had managed to find a career crook, to take advantage of her once-in-a-lifetime inside knowledge.

"Not a bad deal for you," I said. "More money and less work."

Ondine tilted her head. Too refined to shrug. "Should you happen to find the diamonds—" she said.

"I'll keep you in mind."

"It may be out of your hands by now. There's a police search team going through your grandfather's house right this moment."

Shit. Of course they were. They had enough circumstantial evidence to get a warrant, especially with Dono in the hospital. No chance of the home's owner making a stink about it.

I stood up. "Good to see you, Ondine."

"Van," she said as I started to walk away. Something in her tone was different.

"You are direct. But you didn't ask if I was behind Dono's shooting," she said.

Just once, when I was around nine years old, Dono had brought me along while he was collecting a payout from Hiram Long. We'd driven up north to the massive house where Hiram and Ondine lived. At the end of the meeting, Hiram had been called away to take a phone call.

Bored, I wandered out into a sunroom, where an expanse of windows looked out across a lawn big enough to host an NFL game to the waters of Possession Sound beyond. Dono had stayed behind.

After a few minutes, I came back, just in time to see Ondine walk through the room where Dono sat, her waist-length black hair swinging. She didn't pause but reached out as she passed and trailed one long finger from Dono's shoulder down to his broad hand where it rested on the arm of the leather club chair.

Neither of them had seen me, and I waited another minute before noisily making an entrance.

Dono never gave me any hint that he knew Ondine as more than Hiram's wife. And I never said anything to him about it.

Ondine looked at me across the table. The stress lines around her eyes were too deep for any amount of cosmetic surgery to hide.

"I'll tell Dono you send your regards," I said.

As I walked back to the stern, Alec passed me with long strides. Ondine reached out a hand, and he took it as she rose from her chair.

Hollis met me at the gangplank. His face was flushed, and he'd loosened his orange tie so much that the fat knot hung almost to his sternum.

"Let's go get a proper drink," Hollis said.

I shook my head. "I'll drop you off. There's someone I need to see."

"You've a girl in mind, then." He grinned and winked. "Calling on two ladies in one evening. Shocking."

I had to hand it to Hollis. Even shitfaced, he knew the truth when he saw it.

CHAPTER TWENTY-ONE

THE ALLEY LEADING TO the Morgen was empty. I could hear muffled music coming from inside, slow electric guitar with a bass shoving it roughly from behind. The bar had no windows that faced out onto the alley, and a single bright bulb illuminated the only door, so that the emerald rectangle almost leaped from the brick wall.

It was a smaller crowd inside than when I'd met Davey, and I quickly realized why. The music was even worse at close quarters. Two guys in black T-shirts stood shoulder to shoulder on the tiny stage, each trying to make his instrument the lead. Most of the prospective audience focused intently on their drinks and iPads.

A light crowd and fewer staff. I didn't see Davey's brother, Mike, anywhere in the room. A guy behind the stage was busy adjusting the amps, probably making sure that Lennon and McCartney didn't blow out the subwoofers with their noise.

Luce Boylan was behind the bar, slow-pouring a Guinness. She looked over and saw me, and a bemused smile touched her lips. I wound my way through the tables to the long, pale bar.

I was surprised at her height up close—the top of her head came almost up to the bridge of my nose. Then I remembered that when I'd seen her earlier in the week, I'd been sitting down the whole time. Ungentlemanly of me, Hollis would have said.

"Davey's not here," Luce said, raising her voice over the music. She wore a white bar apron over her blue jeans and a dark gray short-sleeved shirt with epaulets.

"I came to see you."

"Well." She set the two-thirds-full pint aside and started pouring another. "Give me half an hour. My latest favor-for-a-friend will be mercifully over." She grimaced at the musicians, who had begun mangling a Soundgarden tune.

"I'll sing along," I said.

Luce turned away to grab a bottle of wine off the shelves. "Don't suffer. You know where the office is." She tilted her head toward the back of the bar. Her hair was pinned up, showing the fine blond hairs at the nape of her neck.

I tore my eyes away and walked around the end of the bar and down the short hall into the back.

I remembered being disappointed the first time Dono had let me join his meetings in the back rooms. They hadn't come close to what my imagination had cooked up. No cavernous chamber shrouded in smoke. No arsenal of weapons. Just one small office, reeking of cigarettes and made even more cramped by cases of liquor that overflowed from the two storage rooms. And the only item of interest had been a badly stained pine table used for card games and, occasionally, careful plans.

But the office had changed since Albie had parked his narrow ass behind the desk. It was clean and cluttered at the same time, with stacks of papers and books piled on every surface and a wall completely covered in tacked-up photographs and band flyers and stickers and ads and artwork, making a mural of riotous color. Against the other wall was a couch covered in cracked black leather. A folded blanket and pillows were stacked neatly on the couch seat.

I sat down on the other side of the couch and closed my eyes.

The next thing I knew, Luce was tapping my shoulder.

"Hey," she said. "You were really out."

I inhaled deeply and stretched my shoulders until they popped.

"Rest when you can," I said. "That's what we always teach the boots."

"Why do you think I have pillows? You could crash here."

Luce had taken off her bar apron and put on a blue suede coat. She'd unpinned her hair and brushed it out, too.

"Let's take a walk," I said.

We went out the front and through the alley and down Lenora Street, toward Pike Place. The asphalt changed to rough brickwork, and we walked slowly over the uneven ground, taking our time. The big neon signs above the market washed the gray streets with pink and orange, a glow of false warmth on cold pavement.

Luce put the collar of her coat up and folded her arms. "What do you think of the place?" she said.

"The Morgen? Doing better than I ever remember."

"I've worked at it. This area doesn't draw the frat boys or sororities from the U-Dub or the bar crowd from Capitol Hill. Too many closer options. And nobody who can afford condos in Belltown comes to a place like the Morgen."

"Seattle State?"

She nodded. "Heavy advertising around campus. Plus hosting a few bands—better ones than tonight—just to get their asses to come a couple of miles south."

"I'm guessing Mike helped with that when he was a student."

Luce frowned. "He's worked hard, too."

"Or you wouldn't have him working there."

"Damn right." She turned to me and squared her shoulders, jaw lifted in challenge.

"I missed something," I said. "Are you and Mike . . . ?"

"What? No! No, nothing like that. I mean he deserves it."

"The job?"

"No, not the job." Her blue-gray eyes widened. "Oh, shit. Dono didn't tell you."

There was a hell of a lot Dono hadn't had the chance to tell me. I had the feeling Luce was about to add a new entry.

"*Shit.*" Luce turned away and stared down the street. I waited her out, just watching the wind catch her hair and twist it into ropes, letting it fall and picking it up again.

When she turned back, her face was tight. "I really don't want this. You shouldn't be hearing it from me."

"It's the bar," I said. "Dono's leaving it to Mike."

"You knew?"

I shrugged. "Dono's lawyer told me that Dono was looking to change the terms of his will. When you got all mama-grizzly about Mike, I put it together."

It felt right. After ten years Dono had asked me to come back, to break the news to me in person. I never wanted a dime from the old man. The bar would mean more to Mike.

"When did Dono tell you?" I said.

"Last Saturday night. He came to the bar to see me."

The night before he was shot.

Luce hugged herself tighter. "Dono told me he was going to sign over his half of the bar to Mike."

"Did he tell you why? And why now?"

"He just said that he'd gotten what he wanted out of the bar." She looked embarrassed, like she was telling me gossip. "That Mike and I had proven ourselves."

"It's okay," I said. "I'm glad Mike was around."

"You know what Dono was like. Smooth as glass on the surface ninety-eight percent of the time."

"It was the two percent that I couldn't live with. Go on. He told you that you'd proven yourself. What did he leave you?"

She took a breath. "Selling rights."

When Dono and Luce's Uncle Albie had bought the Morgen twenty-five years ago, the deal was that Albie would run the place and they'd split the profits—Albie earning a little extra juice from the cash that Dono laundered through the bar's registers.

But Dono had retained control over all major decisions, including first rights of refusal on Albie's share for the same amount that Albie had put into the place. Which was next to nothing.

So Albie got a decent living, and Dono got control. Which he was willing to pass on to Luce. She would run things and split whatever profits she could make with Mike.

"He really did trust you," I said.

Luce's eyes welled up, and she started to walk again. I stayed at her side as we made our way along the brick road that ran parallel to the market stalls. The stalls were empty, but the lights above them shone twenty-four hours a day. All the vendors had packed away their candles and paintings and wooden spoons at dusk.

"I've been working at the Morgen one way or another since I was fifteen. Legal or not," Luce said after we'd gone a hundred yards, out of the market and onto the smooth black surface of paved streets again. "I *made* that damn place. When Albie died, I got offers from every shitty little development company around. They didn't know that Dono held the controlling interest. I figured out that if they were offering a twenty-one-year-old kid what sounded like a good price for the business permits and licenses, then the *real* value had to be huge."

"Hard to get those."

"Damn right. The economy's crap right now, but the lease has another thirty years on it. If we waited and built it up—maybe eight or ten more years—we could clear seven figures. I saw that future, plain as day. Albie never did." She shook her head. "And I don't think Dono had either. But he agreed with me."

"He's not sentimental. Not about owning things."

"Me neither. I don't want to be still pulling drinks when I'm sixty, shackled to that place."

"Like Albie?"

"Exactly like Albie. You know how he died?"

"Heart attack, Mike said."

"Mike doesn't know the whole story. Albie had that heart attack in a county holding pen. He'd been arrested the night before, trying to run away—literally running from the cops—after breaking into a jewelry exchange."

She was crying now. Eyes fixed on the street ahead, she gritted her teeth against the old pain.

"Trying to earn an extra few bucks. Or relive past glories. Shit, I don't know what Albie was thinking. He never got the chance to tell me."

"I'm sorry."

"Me, too, damn it. And the bar is yours now, and all the joy that comes with it. If you want to sell out, I won't kick at it. I've had enough."

"Dono's not dead, Luce."

"But he's probably not signing papers anytime soon either. Oh, fuck." She wiped at her cheeks angrily. "I'm sorry. Shit, I am sorry, Van. That was cruel. I've been on a roller coaster these last few days. Saturday night after Dono told me, I was bouncing off the stars I was so happy. Now . . ."

"Shut up for a second," I said. Luce looked up, startled. A teardrop clung to her lower eyelash. I reached out and brushed it off with my thumb.

"I figured Dono had changed his will years ago," I said. "I didn't come home for the damn bar."

"I know, but now . . ."

"I never expected to inherit anything. If Dono wants to give Mike his share and hand you the steering wheel, I've got no problem."

"And you don't want anything in return." Her strong jaw lifted again, ready for the blow. Not a woman used to hearing good news.

"I do want something. I want a straight answer."

"About?"

"Has Dono been laundering money through the Morgen? I don't mean the usual spare change. I mean has he suddenly started pushing money through as fast as the books can stand?"

Luce looked as surprised as if I'd suddenly sprouted wings. "Through the Morgen? No. God, he hasn't done that in a couple of years."

"Not at all?"

"Not since I proved we could turn a profit without it. He knew I never liked the Morgen being a front, even if it had been Dono's deal with Albie. I didn't push it. But one day I realized he hadn't handed me the usual stack of cash to enter into the accounts in weeks. And he never did again. I didn't ask why. I guessed he was handling whatever money he needed through his contracting work."

"So the Morgen is legit?"

"As legit as I can make it."

If Dono wasn't floating cash through the Morgen, maybe he hadn't fenced any of the diamonds yet. He'd renegotiated his deal with Ondine to hold on to the stones. Maybe that was his long-term plan, squirrel them all away until the heat was off.

Luce and I went back to walking, turning onto Virginia, leaning into the steep slope. A slower pace, both of us lost in thought. The wind coming off the water was blunted by the office buildings around us, but we could hear it, rushing like rivers through the cross streets.

Luce took my arm. "Do you like it in the army?"

"Yes," I said. "I'm good at it. And I'm needed."

Her eyes moved over the left side of my face as we walked. Not the embarrassed flicker of most people's glances at the scars. She was taking a hard look.

"Are you in for life?" she asked.

"I haven't found anything better." My call with Unser came to mind, and I shoved the memory down. My career might be circling the drain, but it wasn't anything I could fix right this minute.

"I read that the war is winding down," Luce said. "What? What's that smile?"

"There's always a war somewhere," I said. "Not always a big one, and not all of them make the news. Some guys go into private contracting after they sign out."

"So there's always work for you."

"Pretty much. Though I can't see myself bodyguarding some oil prince."

Luce grinned. "You'd look good in a tuxedo and sunglasses. Talking into your sleeve."

"Ouch."

Her face suddenly became serious. "How much longer are you in town?"

"Five days."

"Then we shouldn't waste time," she said, turning to me.

I leaned in and kissed her. She was a tall girl, and neither of us had to strain to meet in the middle. For a long moment, it was only our lips touching, testing. Then she pressed against me, and I held on to her, and she held me just as tightly as we continued to kiss. She smelled like jasmine.

My cell phone rang. And vibrated. We both jumped a little at it, and there was nothing to do but answer the fucking thing.

"Yeah," I said.

"I got a name." Jimmy Corcoran. Just about the worst mood killer I could imagine.

"Go ahead."

"Julian Formes. A real pro with listening devices and that crap, not bad with B&E either."

"I already know that."

"I'm just saying, that's his rep. He just got up from his second fall at Walla Walla a few months ago, so he's in town. And icing on the fucking cake, he matches the description you gave me. Well, what little you saw after he clocked you." Corcoran chuckled. "Pint-size, white hair. He's our guy."

"How'd you find him?"

"'Cause I'm a certified genius, that's how. I figured Formes would be scanning through all those hours and hours of recordings sitting in a chair in his nice comfy home, wherever it was. I found the cell site that caught most of his calls and all the base stations passing the signal from apartment buildings nearby. His name jumped right out at me off the list of residents. Abracadabra."

"So where is he?"

"Pioneer Square, kid. Pendleton Court Apartments. He must know his shit, 'cause I wouldn't mind living at that address myself."

"I'll find it."

"You're fucking welcome. Give the little turd a kick in the ass from me."

I hung up.

"Who was that?" said Luce.

"Someone with good news."

"Your expression didn't say good news. It said, 'I'm thinking about crushing this phone.'"

"It might not be good news for other people."

"Uh-huh. Well, it's fair to say the tender moment has passed. You want to walk me back home?"

"Yeah. Sorry."

"It's all right," she said. "You get what you get, and you don't get upset."

I smiled. "That's one of Dono's."

"Yes it is," she said.

AGE SEVENTEEN

"You two screwed like weasels," Davey said around a mouthful of french fries. "Admit it."

I was laughing so hard I almost fell off of the rusty hood of Davey's Corolla. "We didn't," I said.

We were in the parking lot of Dick's Drive-In on Forty-fifth, leaning back against the windshield of the Corolla and eating cheeseburger combo meals. Or Davey was eating. I was trying to catch my breath.

Davey liked to fill his paper container of fries so full of ketchup that it drowned any hint of potatoes. He licked his fingers clean and grinned even wider. "You did. You snuck Eden Adler out of the dance and went into the equipment room and did it right on top of the rolled-up gym mats."

"Fuck you, Tolan." I swung a lazy fist at Davey's head, and he ducked it. Our clowning was attracting attention from the long line of UW students waiting to place their orders at the window. A couple of the girls had been looking at Davey even before he started needling me about Eden.

"I swear I can't figure out why she's so wet for you," he pressed. "Is it the lapsed-Catholic thing? Yeah. Eden knows you and your granddad never go to Mass. She's trying to lure you into renouncing the true faith and putting on a beanie."

I flicked one of my fries at him, and it bounced off the center of his treasured vintage Clash T-shirt.

"Hey!" he said.

I grinned. "I can't lapse if I never started."

"You'll be speaking Hebe by Saturday," Davey insisted.

We had beaten the dinner rush at Dick's. Sundown had brought a wave of students from across the freeway, nearer the campus. You could tell the difference between the ones from the dorms and those from the fraternities and sororities by how they arrived. The dorm rats were on foot, the Greeks piled into cars.

"What time is it?" I asked.

Davey checked his battered Timex. It had been his dad's watch, back when old Joe Tolan was still spending any time with the family. "Six-fifteen," he said. "What time's tip-off?"

"Seven-oh-five. Close enough. Let's go."

We got off the hood, and I tossed my bag of trash to Davey. He walked over to put it into one of the plastic garbage bins at the corner of the restaurant. I could tell that Davey was feeling full-on rock star tonight, in his favorite shirt and black jeans and battered Doc Martens. He took the long way around, so he could walk parallel to the customer line and get a closer look at the sorority girls. None of them were as hot as Eden Adler.

On the way back, Davey slowed and smiled with full wattage at a petite blonde. She pretended to ignore him while watching out of the corner of her eye as he loped back to the Corolla. A tall jock in a U-Dub volleyball sweatshirt was standing next to the girl, not quite close enough to claim ownership. He scowled at Davey.

"You drive," I said to Davey, and we got into the Corolla.

"You see that girl?" he said, his eyes still on her as he pulled out of the lot and turned east.

"I saw her boyfriend ready to kick your ass."

"Shit," he said. "You got my back. What's the planley, Stanley? You want to go around back?"

I shook my head. "Too much security right now. The valets will wonder why anyone's leaving the lot this early. Hit the main parking lot by the stadium."

Davey made a face. "Ain't much *there* there, man."

"We'll find something. This isn't a custom order, just Frankenstein."

"What the hell's that?"

"Parts work. We dig up what we can."

He grunted. "Dono call it that?"

"Dono doesn't call it anything."

"'Cause you don't tell him." Davey was fumbling in his jacket pocket for something. I reached over and steadied the wheel as we half drove, half coasted down the long viaduct toward Montlake Boulevard and the university parking lots.

"He doesn't tell me everything *he* does, either," I said.

Davey laughed. "I'm sure he'd see it that way. Real understanding." He pulled a joint and a plastic lighter out of a partly crumpled cigarette box.

"Save it," I said.

"It's cool. I'm just staying slick."

"You're greasy enough. Take the back entrance, here."

"You're the only one doing real work tonight," Davey said, but he put the joint back in the box.

We pulled in to the parking lot and stopped at the gate. I handed Davey ten bucks, and he handed it to a guy in a shiny orange safety vest. The gate guy waved us toward another guy standing eighty yards in, who was motioning with lighted flashlight wands toward the nearest open parking lane.

The gate was the far side of Husky Stadium, maybe a quarter mile from the Hec Edmundson Pavilion, where the women's basketball game was being held tonight. The Huskies were doing well this season. Better than the men's team by a wide margin, and the lot was crowded. Two, maybe two and a half thousand cars.

It was cold. One of the reasons that basketball games made for good targets. Nobody wanted to stand around outside. Fans hurried from their cars toward Hec Ed, toting seat cushions and backpacks. We cruised slowly along the lanes, toward the impatiently gesturing flashlight guy.

"See anything?" Davey said.

"The lights here suck," I said.

"Told you we should've gone for the valet lot."

He turned in where the flashlight guy was pointing and drove past the open parking spaces, across the middle lane, and into the next row. I kept scanning the cars.

"What are we looking for?" Davey said.

"German."

"*Ja, mein Führer.* There's a Beemer."

"Too old. Hit the next row."

We circled through two more rows before I spotted a Mercedes CL500. This year's model, I was pretty sure. "Make another pass," I said, reaching down into the toolbox on the passenger-side floor. I took out half a dozen plastic Mercedes key fobs hooked together on a loop of twine. None of them had keys attached.

As we circled past the car again, Davey let the Corolla roll. I pointed the first key fob at the 500 and clicked it, then the second.

"Shit. Are we gonna have to do this the hard way?" Davey said.

I tried the third one, and the parking lights on the Mercedes blinked once.

"Nice," Davey said. He accelerated, and we drove across the lot to park in the next row. We put the seats back and relaxed a fraction. The moon roof of the Corolla was a big light gray rectangle in the darker gray of the car.

"Where'd you get the new keys?" Davey said.

"From Luis. He said they should cover about half the cars coming off the line."

"Not bad. You get to keep 'em?"

"No."

"Doesn't seem fair," he said.

"Three hundred for one hour's work. That's fair."

"I still think we should hit something with a better profit margin."

I grinned at him, not that he could see it in the dark. "Profit margin? Didn't Missus Gramercy give you a D in econ?"

"Fuck you," he said cheerfully.

"Parts work is easy. And safer. On a custom job, Luis tells me what car he needs and I have to run all over town and find it and wait for my shot at it. I don't want to waste a whole week sneaking around country clubs."

"Sneaking around Dono, you mean. You still ticked off at him?"

"No."

Davey snorted. "You are too."

"No." Davey knew that Dono and I had fought. I'd told him Dono was making me work construction over the summer.

What I was really pissed about was Dono not taking me with him to Portland.

I had spent a lot of time during the past two weeks reading through news articles online. One story in particular, about a dot-com billionaire in Hillsboro who had his collection of sculpture stolen from right out of his massive garden. The billionaire had been quoted as saying he was trying to create a postmodern Luxembourg, whatever that meant. The papers called the theft "brazen," which was their way of saying it happened during the daytime and someone should have been watching.

Statues, for fuck's sake. It must have taken six or eight guys and a couple of front-loader machines to pull it off. I could drive a loader.

"Where's the gate guy?" I said to Davey.

He raised his head to look out the hatchback window. "Gone."

"Can't be gone. Keep looking."

"All right, stay calm. Maybe you need a hit more than I do." He craned his neck, squinting across the shadowed field of parked cars. "There's the shithead. Talking to his buddy with the glow-in-the-dark dildos. They're still too near the exit."

I reached up and clicked the overhead light to the OFF position. "Where'd you get the joint?" I said. "From Bobby Sessions?"

"Fuck me. Don't start in on that again, Grandma."

"Some of that ditch weed he claims he imports from BC?"

"Like you'd know. The fuck is wrong with you and him?"

"Not a thing. He can sell all the dandelion stems he wants. And you should let him."

"I know people he doesn't know," Davey said. "I can move it with no risk."

"What about the risk on Bobby's end? He tries too hard. Someday he'll try to sell to the wrong guy. He'll say your name before the cops even finish cuffing him."

"Bullshit."

"It's not *if.* It's *when.* He's a fuckup, Davey."

"I can handle Bobby Motherfucker Sessions."

We sat and stared out the moon roof. The edges of it were starting to blur as the overcast sky outside darkened.

"Let's go," I said, opening the car door and slipping out. I had the Mercedes key fob in one hand and the toolbox in the other. A handful of latecomers making their way from the parking lot toward Hec Ed, and no one down at this end. I kept my head low and walked quickly along the cars until I reached the Mercedes.

I knelt on the asphalt and looked back toward the entrance gate. No sign of the two attendants. I waited. After a minute I spotted them, midway along the lot, sharing a smoke.

I clicked the key fob and heard the clunk of the Mercedes unlocking behind me. The flash of parking lights didn't attract a look from the attendants. I opened the door and got in.

It was nice inside the car. Tan-colored leather, fake hardwood dash. The owner had removed the faceplate of the stereo and taken it with him, or more likely tucked it in the glove compartment. Didn't matter. The wheels and seats and engine components were worth a whole lot more than his Blaupunkt.

I took a cordless power drill and a flathead screwdriver out of the toolbox. I'd fixed a slim tungsten bit in the drill before Davey and I had left the house. I lined up the bit with the keyhole, just slightly off center, and pushed it hard as I drilled out the first lock pin. The whine of the drill was rock-concert loud in the car. The first time I'd drilled a lock, I'd been sure everyone from two miles away was going to come running. I drilled it again, and then once more, wiggling the drill a little to make sure the pins were toast. I put the metal end of the screwdriver in and turned it, and the engine rumbled politely to life.

I switched on the lights, and Davey immediately pulled out of his parking space, taking point. I followed him from the lot, each of us waiting for the long wooden arm to rise and let us pass.

When we were farther down Montlake, we stopped at a red light before the onramp to 520. I was already dialing Luis to let him know we were on the way. I looked up and saw Davey in the Corolla. He'd turned around and was grinning at me out of the hatchback window. The joint was between his teeth, glowing bright. I gave him the finger, and he laughed and turned around to face the green light and floored it, leaving a yard of Goodyear rubber on the boulevard.

CHAPTER TWENTY-TWO

THE ROUGH FEEL OF the cobblestones underfoot in Pioneer Square brought back a memory from my childhood. My mother had brought me along while she shopped or maybe visited friends who worked somewhere nearby. I didn't recall many details—I couldn't have been more than five years old.

It wasn't too many months after that when an evening commuter, in a hurry to get home at the end of a long day, hit the wrong pedal and jumped the curb and took her out of my life forever.

But the visit to the square had been a good day. I remembered my mother pointing out the intricate ironwork on the tall pergola that curved gently around the western side of the square. It may have been a weekend. There were a lot of people, or it seemed like it to me, and dogs on leashes, and the flocks of pigeons I chased without malice around the cobblestones.

At one point I think my mother picked me up—probably to get me to settle down a little—and through the long strands of her straight black hair I could see the exuberant colors of a dozen kinds of flowers, all set out for sale in big plastic buckets along the sidewalk.

That was the sum total of the memory, just people and birds and flowers. And my mother's hair, lifted on the breeze. I could remember the feeling of her nearness far better than I could recall her face, on that day or any other.

Julian Formes lived in a three-story brick building at one of the corners of the square. A nice address for a paroled felon. An art gallery took up most of the street level, with the upper floors given over to loft apartments. The building retained some vestige of style from a century ago, with arched porticoes and ornamental carved stone between each story. But the modern Plexiglas-and-steel entrance spoiled the look, like welding a Caterpillar tractor grille onto a Rolls-Royce.

The day was overcast and drizzling. Regular folk rushed along the edges of the little piazza with its ironclad benches and massive black totem poles. The interior of the park was surrendered to the homeless. Most of them sat quietly and stared into space or muttered to themselves as they slumped low against the insistent damp mist. The more energetic ones tried prospecting spare change from the stream of citizens walking past.

If Formes had been the man who'd clocked me with the shillelagh at Dono's house, then he would know me by sight. I risked walking past the building to get a closer look. The door required a key card for entry. Past it was a foyer with old-fashioned brass mailboxes on the wall. *Pendleton Court* was painted in old-timey script across the leaded glass of the inner door.

A young guy in a conservative blue suit and striped tie under his Burberry raincoat came out of the building in a rush. He stopped suddenly and checked for something in the messenger bag he had slung over his shoulder and pivoted around to go back in. He took his wallet out of his coat pocket, swiped it on the key-card reader, and disappeared inside.

I kept walking to the end of the block and turned around to walk back. When Burberry came out again, running even faster, he slammed right into me.

"Sorry, dude," I said.

"Jesus," he said, and raced off.

When he was out of sight, I took his wallet from under my jacket and removed the key card from it. The card worked just as well for me as it had for Burberry. I dropped the wallet into the mail slot next to the brass mailboxes. A glance at the boxes showed one near the top: FORMES—309.

The lobby of the building was heavy on the historic ambience. The stairs were marble and the banister thick oak, maybe even original from a century ago.

I took the stairs to the third floor. Number 309 was just off the elevator. It had better locks than its neighbors, heavy Schlage bolts. I knocked softly. No answer.

Even with Dono's excellent set of picks and a little snap gun to force the lock, it took me five minutes of careful work before the second bolt gave up the fight. I was out of practice. Rangers use less subtle methods to deal with stubborn doors, like shotguns loaded with breaching rounds.

It was an open and airy space, with broad windows getting the most out of the overcast day's sunlight. Sparse. There was only one chair in the living room, a low-backed green thing that had seen better decades. A large table with a dust cover thrown over it was against the wall. The built-in shelves in the room were bare, as were the kitchen counters.

I closed the door behind me and locked it again. I went into the kitchen and checked the trash. Easiest way to guess if anyone was in residence. The plastic can was two-thirds full, mostly with take-out food containers from different restaurants.

I gave the bedroom a quick toss. Formes lived like an especially poor but tidy college student. One heavy coat in the closet. A few pairs of pants and shirts, each neatly folded and tucked away in the single dresser. A small TV, angled so it could be watched from the meticulously made bed.

I was starting to think Formes did all his work somewhere else until I tried the hallway closet. The only thing in it was a large red metal tool cabinet on wheels, three feet tall. The kind mechanics use to keep every wrench close at hand. I tried the top drawer and found wires in multiple gauges and soldering gear. In the large bottom drawer, a dozen new off-the-shelf cell phones, still in their packaging. The brand was the same as the ones used in the bugs at Dono's house.

Bingo. Julian Formes, you are about to have a very bad day.

A glance under the dust cover on the table in the living room yielded even more. A large Mac laptop, closed and sleeping. A disassembled transmitter, with delicate tools laid out in orderly rows next to it. And a thick black leather carrying case.

I unzipped the case to find rows of thumb drives, each tucked into its own little pocket. Some of the small metal rectangles had a letter or two written on them in blue permanent ink.

Three of the drives were labeled DS. Two others CL.

Dono Shaw. Cristiana Liotti.

I powered up the computer and plugged one of the DS drives into its port on the side. The computer pinged happily, and a window popped up, asking me for a password to the drive.

Encrypted. Son of a bitch. My sudden fantasy of listening to the audio recording of Dono's shooting, of finding the shooter and maybe the diamonds, too, in one swoop, vanished as quickly as it had come.

I thought about my options. The smart thing to do was turn around, pretend I hadn't been there, and tell Guerin to unleash his hounds on Formes. The police had plenty of computer-forensics wizards. They could break Formes's encryption. And Guerin could probably break Formes, too, getting him to spill on who'd hired him.

Then again, maybe not. The warrants and computer work would eat up a day or two at minimum. Formes could hide behind his lawyer at every step. And maybe destroy the evidence. The whole process could take weeks and might be a dead end. I had four days.

I didn't care too much about whether Julian Formes ended up back at Walla Walla State Pen. I wanted the man who'd put a bullet in Dono's brain, and the more I learned about Formes, the more he looked like just a hired hand. He didn't even seem to own a gun.

Guerin could eventually paint Formes into a corner, but I could do it faster.

I found an empty duffel bag in the bedroom closet and filled it with

Formes's laptop, the thumb drives, and the more expensive tools from the rolling cabinet. I replaced the dust cover on the table. With a black marker from the cabinet, I wrote *"TRADE YOU"* in big letters across the fabric, with the cell number of Dono's burner phone below it.

I was about to leave when another idea popped into my head. Formes's bug was still in my jacket pocket. I took it out and glanced at it.

The bug's battery had a full charge. It could work.

I dialed my own number into the keypad on the bug. My phone beeped, and when I answered it, I could hear the ghostly echo of my own movements in the room. In Formes's tool cabinet, I found duct tape. I taped the phone to the underside of the table.

It wasn't nearly as slick as Formes's work in Dono's house—I could listen only so long as I didn't hang up or until the battery on the bug gave out. But until then I could hear everything in the room.

See how you like it, you little fucker.

I locked the door behind me and left the building out of the alleyway door.

Keeping a close watch on Formes's building was going to be a problem. There were no restaurants or bars or other handy places to hang around within spitting distance. If I stayed in a single place on the street, I'd stick out like one of the totem poles.

Unless I could blend in.

I jogged back to the pickup truck in the parking garage across from the square to drop off the duffel bag loaded with Formes's laptop and other gear. I took off my barn jacket and grabbed a paint-stained hoodie out of the bins in the backseat.

There was a trash bin in the alley, its lid left unlocked. I spent two minutes grinding the hoodie into the muck and slime of the bin's interior. The garbage smelled like rotten cabbage and spoiled meat. So did the half-shredded Mariners cap I found in it. With the cap on and my hood pulled up, I was ready for the red carpet, Pioneer Square style.

Only one bench had a view of both the front and alley doors of Formes's building. It was occupied by a semiconscious Chinese man with spittle at one corner of his mouth. I stood ten feet from the bench and stared at him until something in his slack mind recognized the signals of potential danger and he slowly got up and moved away, closer to the others.

Van Shaw, tough guy. Just another tiny debt I could mark on the tally, waiting until I got my hands on whoever'd shot Dono. Maybe I would have the chance to tune the bastard up a little before I served him to Guerin.

And I *was* going to turn him in. I'd worked too hard to create a life away from all this crap with guys like Hollis and Corcoran and Willard. No matter how much I might like to see the shooter fry, killing him myself would just be stupid.

Might feel good, though. No harm in thinking about that.

I had an earpiece plugged into the phone. If anyone passing by noticed and thought it strange that the smelly homeless guy had cell-phone service, they didn't remark on it. The white noise of the empty apartment on the open line threatened to become hypnotic. I kept alert by scanning the face of every person who walked past the apartment building.

After about twenty more minutes, I spotted Formes. My burglar, no question. The curly white hair was distinctive and longish, like a little cape over his ears. He was short and stooped, and wore a red Puma football jacket over jeans with high-top sneakers. His skin had an unhealthy-looking yellow undercoat, his lined face resembling crumpled parchment. Too much time hidden from the sun.

I watched as Formes went into his building. Soon I heard the clunks and clicks of him opening his locks.

I had made sure Formes would see my writing on the table cover from the doorway. Through the bug I heard footsteps, and then a high, clear voice said "Fuck" very distinctly. That sentiment was repeated many times, with increasing force.

Welcome home, Julian.

A lot more footsteps. Pacing and fast. He was figuring out what to do. Call me at the number I'd left? Get help? Flee town?

After a few moments, silence fell. I heard something like water running, maybe from the kitchen. A creak. Then a bump of furniture, very close. Maybe he was sitting down in the chair at the table, looking at all the nothing I'd left him.

"It's me," Formes said, and I nearly jumped. His high voice sounded like it was right next to me. I had to hand it to him—the man could build a hell of a bug.

"Yeah, I know, I know," Formes said. He'd called someone, and I was only hearing his side of the conversation. "Look. Look. We got problems, damn it," he said.

"We shouldn't talk like this. But it's bad. I need some help here." There was a lengthy pause before Formes spoke again. "No, in person. You should see this shit. Uh-huh. No, no way. You're my first call, I swear. You think I'm stupid? Customer is king, you know it. I'm your guy. Yeah. I'll be here."

I heard movement and then Formes swearing a few more times. Indistinctly in the background, another voice, then another, and I realized he'd turned on the television in the bedroom.

So Julian had called one of his clients, and help was on its way. Beautiful.

Guerin should be in on this. He had a chance to at least see the players involved, even if there wasn't enough evidence to arrest them yet. I sent him a text message: OUTSIDE FORMES HOME PIONEER SQ. SHOOTER SUSPECT EN ROUTE. GET HERE NOW.

I went back to scanning faces, trying to place the client. The lunch hour was in full swing, and the crowd streaming and jostling along the sidewalk made it hard to get a good look at every person who entered the building before his or her back was turned. A FedEx delivery guy, in and out in three minutes. A good-looking brunette in a dress too light for the weather. She held the door to let a tall man in a dark suit into the building behind her. Two banker types, looking grim and purposeful and athletic enough to be muscle. Somebody inside buzzed them in. A portly guy with an umbrella and a fedora hat swiped his own card to enter.

I heard the doorbell buzz in Formes's place. No one was standing outside at the intercom. The client must already be inside, one of the people I'd seen enter.

Footsteps, then the sound of the door opening.

"I told your boy he needed to come." Formes's high octave.

"He's busy, Julian." A man's voice, rasping and amused. "What goes on?"

"You got eyes, man. All my shit's gone. My computer, the back-ups, everything here. The motherfucker was probably waiting on me to leave. I wasn't gone more than an hour or so."

The other man grunted. " 'Trade you,' " he said, reading what I'd written on the dust cover. "What do you suppose he wants to trade for?" The touch of a Midwest accent. Chicago or maybe farther south. I remembered the news articles after the robbery. The dead robber Burt McGann had been from Illinois.

"Hell if I know," said Julian. "I don't really give a damn. I never plan to see the sucker again. The other night was too close."

Boom. The last of my doubts that Formes was talking to the right client vanished. I glanced at my watch. Twelve minutes since I'd texted Guerin. Come on, damn it.

"So how much hurt are we in, Julian?"

Formes snorted. "You-all? Nothing. I know my shit, okay? My stuff's locked up tight. Anonymous voice accounts, and A-one encryption on the backups. But that doesn't mean I'm happy having all of it in some-body else's pocket. I'm out of town, as of now."

"And you gave us everything?"

"Shit, Boone. You got everything I got. I delivered, right? It's not my fault the mark wound up in a fucking coma."

Boone. I had a name to match the voice.

"But you did go back to his house to get your little toys," Boone said to Formes.

A cold wash went down my scalp that had nothing to do with the drizzle. I was up and moving across the park at a fast walk.

"Hey, I'm sorry about that," said Formes. "I just didn't want to leave any trail behind me. It's done."

"Pack what you need," Boone said in his sandpaper rasp. "We'll give you a car."

"Okay," said Julian. "I just want—"

Then there was a loud thump and a grunt of effort. My fast walk became a run, weaving through street traffic and pounding up and across the hood of a stopped car, hearing underneath the angry honks and shouts from the drivers a horrible coughing sound through the earpiece, over and over.

The sound of Julian Formes being strangled.

CHAPTER TWENTY-THREE

I BARRELED THROUGH THE SIDEWALK crowd like a running back. A mail carrier hesitated an instant too long in the open entryway, and I crashed into him, knocking him down and sending his packages flying. He hurled insults at my back as I took the marble stairs three at a time.

My heart was hammering too loud for me to hear anything through the bug. Was Formes still alive?

I came off the stairs at a crouching run, down the long hallway, boot soles as quiet as I could make them on the marble. Number 309 was at the far end. The door was closed.

I stood to one side and slowly tested the doorknob. Unlocked.

The rustle of soft movement inside, heard through the bug. The choking sounds had stopped. If Formes wasn't dead already, he didn't have long. Where the fuck was Guerin?

I eased the door open half an inch, on blessedly silent hinges. Maybe Boone was distracted enough with Julian that I could take him.

Another inch. Peering through the crack, I could see part of the living area and part of the kitchen. A fleeting shadow on the floor as someone moved.

The doorjamb by my shoulder exploded.

I flinched, stumbling back into the hallway. A second shot tore a fist-size chunk out of the door's edge, just about where my head had been.

I had the little .32 out of my pocket and leveled at the door. Come on, you son of a bitch. Come after me.

Instead there was a bang and the sound of shattering glass from far inside. Boone was breaking a window. Trying to reach the fire escape.

I kicked the door wide. The crunching of glass continued down the hall in the bedroom. I went in low and fast, ducking behind the kitchen counters.

Julian Formes was lying on the floor beside his worktable, twisted in a final backbend of agony. His face was mottled crimson, the pale bruises of finger marks still on his throat.

I heard the clatter of feet on metal. I aimed the .32 at the open bedroom door and went up the hall. Boone was gone, banging down the steps on the fire escape below. A flash look out the window. He was already two floors down, the tall man in the black suit I'd seen entering the building. Between the metal slats, I glimpsed brown hair, clipped to a stubble.

I slid over the sill, feeling a hot jab of pain as the broken glass sliced my jeans and leg. The rusted steel of the fire escape shook threateningly under my weight. Its stairs were too tight and too steep, and my steps felt maddeningly slow.

Below me Boone jumped from the last level to the alley, black coat flapping behind him. I kept scrambling until I reached the second-floor platform. Boone was ten yards out and running hard, heading for daylight on Second Avenue, away from the square and its sudden crowd of onlookers.

I pocketed the .32, climbed over the railing, and dropped, fifteen feet to the asphalt. I didn't roll with the impact so much as bounce, hitting feetfirst and hard onto my side. My newly repaired forearm twanged like a guitar string wound too tight. I forced myself up and after Boone.

Too slow. He had a big lead. I frantically scanned the street. Clumps of people going about their day, in and out of the stores and restaurants in the lunch rush. Nobody staring or pointing as if Boone had just run past them. The cars and trucks flowed sluggishly along.

Where would he go? The opposite side of the street and down another alley. I lurched through the traffic. A Subaru slammed on its brakes as the driver stress-tested his horn.

The first alley I checked was empty. So was the second. Doors off the alleys, some of them propped open. A seafood restaurant on this side of the road, with back entrances. Too many possible routes.

Boone was gone. Fuck. Double fuck.

That was two leads blown, him and Formes. And I hadn't even gotten a look at the bastard's face.

Sirens now, howling down James Street toward the front of the building that Boone and I had just fled.

As if on cue, my phone buzzed. A text from the detective: WHERE ARE YOU?

A good goddamned question. I wasn't about to limp back to Formes's apartment and submit myself for another visit to a police interview room. Even if Guerin cleared me as a suspect in Formes's death, Captain Unser would have a couple of warrant-officer MPs waiting in the precinct lobby, eager to provide me mandatory room and board at Lewis.

In a different alley two blocks down, I ditched my baseball cap. The .32 went under my flannel shirt, and I jammed Dono's lockpick set into the pockets of my jeans. There were holes torn in the knee and shin of my jeans. My leg was oozing blood into my sock.

I checked my cell phone. Still on. Give the maker points for durability. I'd lost the earpiece in the chase. I put the phone to my ear.

"—not the neighbors on this floor. Downstairs." A male voice. The bug in Formes's apartment was still working.

"Bang on the doors, see if anyone else is home and awake." It was Guerin. Even through the bug, he sounded pissed off and tamping it down. "How many cars did you reach?"

"Three."

"Get two more. I want cruising in a ten-block radius. Start from the outer edge and work in. And find me a witness who can tell us what they were wearing."

"I'll wrap this place up for CSU after we go." Kanellis's voice, farther away and faint. "Eddie?"

"There's blood here, on the windowsill," said a third voice. "One of the perps cut himself."

"Good. Maybe we pull a print, too," Guerin said.

"Where's your guy Shaw?" said Kanellis.

"Not answering his phone."

"Think he got impatient?"

Guerin didn't answer him. I'd heard enough anyway. I hung up on the bug and called Guerin directly.

"Where are you?" he said immediately.

"Forget me. The guy you want is named Boone. Six-two or -three. Lanky. Brown hair, cut so short he's almost bald. I don't know about facial hair, I didn't get a look. Wearing a black suit, ten minutes ago."

"Come in and we'll do a full workup," Guerin said.

"I feel like I'm telling you shit you already know."

There was a pause. "Boone McGann is Burt McGann's brother."

That explained Boone's Midwest accent. I thought of the robbery scene. The tactical choice I couldn't figure out. Three men instead of four.

"Where was Boone on the day of the robbery?" I said.

"In jail. In California. A probation violation."

"But he's out now."

"Yes."

"And probably pissed off about his dead brother."

"Come in and we'll talk about it."

"I can do better. I've got Formes's computer and thumb drives. And what I think is the recording from the bugs he planted at Dono's house."

Another pause. "Including the shooting?"

"I sure as shit hope so. It's encrypted."

"You can't stay out on the street, Van." First name. Never a good sign. He'd probably have a lock on my cell signal within a few minutes if Kanellis was already talking to the phone company.

"I'll drop Formes's gear where you'll find it."

"Shaw."

"And forget about the blood on the window. That's mine." I hung up and took the battery out of my phone.

Would Guerin put an all-points out on me? I had to assume he would. Dono's house was blown. With half of the West Precinct combing the area, I couldn't even risk returning to where I'd parked the truck, not yet.

And in all the action of the afternoon, I'd missed my daily deadline to report in to Captain Unser.

Fugitive from justice and AWOL, too. Lucky damn me.

AGE EIGHTEEN

I came up out of a sleep so solid and blank it was like a gray concrete wall. I was facedown on my bed. It was dark. My mouth tasted bad.

Something had woken me. A noise. I shifted a little, and the muscles in my neck creaked painfully. I was lying in the same position since I'd collapsed on the bed . . . when? After the party. The latest party.

The digital numbers of my alarm clock glowed blurry red in the black room. Four in the morning, almost. I was gingerly turning my head to rest on the other side, even out the twist in my neck, when the noise happened again. My new cell phone ringing. My graduation present to myself. The ringtone still sounded weird.

The phone was somewhere in the pile of clothes on my floor. I used my arms to pull my body off the bed—getting vertical was way too much effort—and fumbled around for the little hard rectangle in the pile. The ringing had stopped and started again by the time I found the phone.

I didn't know the number. I hit the green ANSWER button and grunted into the phone.

"Van? Fuck, man. Oh, fuck. Is that you?" Davey. His voice was hushed and even more hyper than usual.

"Yeah," I said. My tongue was thick. The days since graduation had been one long rolling kegger. Davey and I and a handful of other Emmett Watson High grads crashed one party after another for different cliques and different schools. There'd been a couple of girls and at least one fight. Last I remembered, Davey was going home to sleep off some of the fun.

"Van. Oh Jesus. I need you to come here, Van. Please."

"Davey, what the fuck?"

"Right, right. Okay. I'm . . . I'm near Broadway. In a store. Oh, Jesus."

"Slow down. Are you busted? Is this your phone call?"

"No, no. God, I wish. It's Bobby, Van. Bobby Sessions. He's dead."

Bobby Sessions. Davey's connection for selling weed—and maybe more crap besides. Dead.

"Van?" Davey's voice cracked. "Please, man. They're coming."

"*Who* is?" I was pulling on clothes with one hand. My hangover was gone, a miracle cure.

Davey exhaled a slow, shuddering breath. "I don't know. We went to meet some guys Bobby said he knew. At the reservoir. Bobby had some shit to sell, he had it in the trunk of his car, and we went to meet them. He said he'd give me a discount if I'd help load the stuff, but I think maybe he just didn't want to go alone." Davey laughed, a brittle cough.

The reservoir was only a couple of miles away. I pulled my boots on over bare feet. "What happened?"

"Fuck, Van. They didn't even *talk* to us. They were older guys. Badass. One of them, he just looked at the second one and said 'Okay,' and the other guy shot Bobby. Then they shot at me, but fuck, I wasn't waiting around. I've never run so hard. I'm still shaking. Oh, fuck, Van."

Told you. You colossal retard, I *so* fucking told you.

I found the keys to Dono's Chevy Cavalier on the floor in the hallway, where I'd dropped them the night before. "I'm coming to get you. Tell me what store."

"That place for Christmas, with the fake plastic trees and dolls and shit. They chased me across Broadway, and I cut through a yard, and I was in an alley—"

"Slow down. I know the store. Did you break in?" Maybe an alarm would bring cops. Not great for Davey, but better than getting dead. The Cavalier started up with an outraged roar, and I eased off the gas.

"Yeah. I was going to go right out the front, but I think they're already there. On the street outside. *I don't know what to do, Van.*"

"Stay tight."

Maybe I should just call 911 myself. No, that was the fear talking. *Don't ever involve the cops, not ever*—I could almost hear Dono growling in my head. No good ever came from those assholes.

Dono was out of town. He'd put up with sitting in the crowd for Watson High's graduation ceremony in the Seattle Central Community College gymnasium. After we'd finally thrown our caps in the air, he clapped me on the back and told me he'd be on the road until Monday and not to burn the house down.

I turned onto 14th Avenue almost on two tires, overcorrecting with my free hand and nearly sideswiping a parked station wagon. Two minutes away, if I caught some air going over the hills.

I could hear Davey hyperventilating through the phone, even above the grind of the transmission. "Jesus, Van. I can't be part of Bobby and all this shit. I can't." He was crying, I was pretty sure.

"I'll be there." I dropped the phone just in time to yank the wheel with both hands and sail through the red light on Thomas Street. The phone clattered to the floor, out of reach.

I raced past the black void of the reservoir, a half-acre expanse of water with no lights inside the high fences and very few outside. Good place for a murder. None of the homeless camped around the grassy edges of the facility would bother much about gunshots in the dark, so long as the danger didn't come their way.

Davey had said the men had killed Bobby immediately.

What the fuck had Bobby been selling? It must be coke or hash, something worth more than a trunkful of bad weed. Fucking Bobby Sessions. Dumb on so many levels, he needed a map to find his way to stupid.

The only thing Bobby's killers hadn't counted on was how fast Davey Tolan could run. Like a cat with battery acid sprinkled on its tail.

The Christmas store was near Harvard Avenue, not far from Broadway, Capitol Hill's main artery. I saw only a couple of cars moving on Broadway. There was no movement at all two blocks west, where the business district started giving way to cheap studio apartments.

The sun hadn't touched the sky in the east yet. It was starting to rain. I flipped the wipers on and forced myself to slow the car. To think. I wished Dono were in the passenger seat next to me. I tried to picture him there. What he might say.

Two men, Davey had told me. Would they both have chased him on foot? One might have gone back to their car, trying to get out in front of Davey and cut him off. They'd probably have cell phones, staying in touch with each other. Checking every doorway and trash bin until they flushed Davey out.

They sure as shit wouldn't give up. Davey had seen them shoot Bobby. They'd risk a lot to make sure he didn't get away.

So what, then? They probably knew that Davey was still in the area, but no more than that. If they'd been close enough on his heels to know he was hiding inside the Christmas store, he'd never have had a chance to call me.

I slowed as I neared the next block and took a right off of Harvard. Letting the Cavalier glide, like I was looking for an open space. The Hill never has street parking, but everybody tries.

The car caught up to a lean guy with a black cap walking parallel. He turned and stepped closer, bending to try to peer in my window. A sharp, goateed face. Wet and angry. He wore a stiff-looking leather coat. I kept pretending to search for parking as I cruised past.

Three doors farther down was the Christmas store. Holiday Haus, it was called. Not that anyone was calling it much in early summer. The place was shuttered. Dead season.

I drove around the corner. A service alley ran the length of the long block, between the row of shops and the looming apartment buildings behind it. The alley was wide enough for trash trucks to drive through and empty the bins.

When the Cavalier was level with the alley, I stopped and turned off the headlights. The alley was well lit. I could see all the way down, maybe seventy-five yards to the other end. Nothing moved. The rain was a little harder now. Another minute passed.

Then someone leaned out of one of the doorways, three steps up from the pavement of the alley. Just a dark torso and head, like a silhouette target. The figure stayed there for a few seconds, looking at my idling Cavalier. Then it faded back into the doorway.

It could be somebody waiting to catch his ride to the early shift. Or grabbing a smoke in the alley because his girlfriend won't let him light up in the apartment.

But I caught the same vibe from him as I had from the rat-faced guy out front. *Way* too edgy to be a citizen. Badasses, Davey had called them. Stone killers, for a few kilos of junk.

Fuck, this was not how I was supposed to be spending my graduation week.

It wasn't too late to get the cops here. The precinct was barely ten blocks away.

But if the cops grilled Davey—and me—they might want

to talk to Dono, too. Maybe even start wondering why he was out of town. Would the attention be a problem for him right now? What was he into?

I could handle it myself. Had to.

Okay. So look at it the way he would.

The first need, always, is an exit route. At least one open path that will stay clear. The Holiday Haus was only a third of the way down this side of the alley. It wasn't too far to make a run for the car, if I could get Davey out of there.

Too many moving parts, Dono would say. One man whose location you know, another on the move. And maybe they had even called for help. Too many gears that might grind me up.

So improve the odds, boy. If you can't simplify the situation for you, make it more complicated for them.

I put the Cavalier next to a fire hydrant and left the doors unlocked.

There was a small pile of broken cinder blocks against the apartment building wall by the alley. I leaned down and picked out a piece about half the size of a thick paperback. It had a good heft.

In the alley I jingled my keys and put the chunk of cinder block up to my ear, like it was my phone.

"Hey," I said into the chunk, "it's me. Just getting home."

The silhouette was still standing in the apartment building's doorway. I went up the stairs, sluggishly, fumbling at the keys.

"Fuck no," I said, chuckling, "I'm not that drunk. Not yet."

Up close the silhouette became a man, a jowly white guy around thirty with a blue parka and hair cut so short that most of his head was scalp. He leaned against a wall covered with a hundred flyers for bands and shows and furniture for sale. I nodded to him as I approached.

"Hang on," I said into the chunk. I looked up at the guy. "Locked out?" I said.

He shook his head once, cheeks wagging, and turned his attention back up the alley.

I nodded understanding and went past him, still jingling the keys, and as I came to his blind spot, I spun and smacked him hard on the back of his bristly skull with the flat of the cinder-block chunk. He fell forward onto his knees. I hit him again, in the same spot, and he collapsed completely, face-first onto the landing. Blood spattered off the chunk onto his parka.

Oh, shit. I'd panicked and hit him way too hard. The hood of the parka had fallen over the side of his face like a shroud. I tugged it back to look at him.

Breathing. Maybe. I felt the side of his neck. Yeah. Definitely a pulse there, or maybe that hammering was all me. Then he exhaled, and his warm breath made a wisp of vapor in the night air.

My fingers on his neck were an inch above a thick line of ink. I pulled the parka back farther. The tattoo went down past his collar, some messed-up design of arrows and swastikas and the top half a couple of letters in Gothic script—*NF*.

I'd seen the art before. Nation's Fist. A white-power bunch, mostly rural and definitely small-time, compared to the bigger supremacist gangs that made their trailer payments running drugs or guns in the Northwest. None of the Hitler lovers could push any real weight, not compared to the Mexicans or the newer Russian families.

But they were sure a shitload tougher than just Davey and me.

It wouldn't be long before Rat-Face finished checking the front of the block. Would he stay out there? Or come back here to meet his buddy?

I quickly rummaged through the skinhead's pockets.

Not easily. He was two hundred pounds of deadweight lying facedown and wearing a thick parka. He had a cell phone, more like a walkie-talkie, and a bunch of random crap like candy and half-chewed toothpicks.

Stuffed into his waistband was a target pistol, a Ruger Standard. I could smell burned powder under the bite of the cold air. Probably the same gun that had shot Bobby Sessions. I'd never liked Bobby, but the sight of that gun made me feel a little better about hitting the skinhead with a brick.

I stuffed his walkie-talkie in my pocket. The gun was a tougher choice. I didn't want to carry around a murder weapon. But I really didn't want this asshole to wake up and come after Davey and me with it. I tore one of the flyers from the wall and wrapped the pistol's grip to take it with me.

I glanced around. No movement up or down the alley. I took a deep breath and flew off the landing steps, running all the way to what I prayed was the right door for the Holiday Haus. It had no window and no knob on this side, just a spring lock. I had to peer closely to see that the door had been jimmied. I stuck my fingernails in the gap and pulled it open a few inches.

"Davey?" I said into the darkness inside.

A sudden rustle of movement. "Van?" His voice was so soft that I hardly heard it.

"Let's go, damn it. Come on."

"I *can't.*" A whispered wail.

I swore to myself and slipped through the door, into the void. With the front windows shuttered, the shop had the devouring blackness of an underground cave. I didn't dare move, in case I knocked over something large and noisy.

"What the fuck, man?" I said.

"Wait." More rustling, and I realized that Davey was crawling closer to me. I knelt to meet him. The Ruger in its paper wrapping banged on the floor tiles, and I put it down. Fucking thing was cursed.

"We have to go, Davey. Now, while he's still on the street."

"*Wait,* goddamn it." I could hear his palms slapping the floor as he crawled, but I still couldn't see a thing.

I smelled something sharp. Piss. Davey had hosed down his pants.

"We have to run for it, D. Right *now.*"

"I *can't*—" he said, and I reached out blindly and grabbed him. One of my hands caught him by his long hair. I clamped my other hand over his moaning mouth and shook him like a dog on a rat.

"You move, you moron, or I will leave you here. You understand? You want my help, you do what I fucking say."

He stopped making noise and nodded, over and over, until I let him go.

I felt for the knob of the door behind us. "We're going right. Dono's car is just up the street. Don't look around, just run." If Rat-Face was anywhere nearby, at least we'd be a moving target.

I swung the door open, and we exploded out into the alley. The electric lights were blinding after the pitch black of the shop. I squinted and kept going, hell-bent for the end of the alley. Davey's footsteps behind me, fast and light. We sailed past the high landing where I'd conked the skinhead. I couldn't see his body through the glare of lights and the blur of our run. We ran. Around the corner, sneakers skidding on the wet pavement, the Cavalier ten yards up by the fire hydrant and shining like dawn.

Then I was slammed sideways by a bullet train. I bounced hard off a parked car, reeling. Something smashed my ribs, and all the air was gone from the city, just like that. I was on my knees. Davey's voice, then a cry of pain. Hands pulled me up, and I saw a big fist curled and ready, way up over my head. Bad. I ducked. The fist hit me on top of my skull, making a light that put all other lights to shame, and I heard another yelp. I fell back against the car and stayed there.

I saw Davey. He was on the ground, scrambling like a bug. The skinhead was lurching toward him, clutching his hand. I pushed at the car, seeing if I could stand. Yes.

The skinhead saw the movement and turned back to face me, slowly. The side of his head was dark with blood. Right. Because I'd hit him. No brick in my hand now. He lurched my way. I tried to get my fists up where they might do some good.

A wasp flew past my head with a snap. The skinhead and I both turned to see where it had come from. Rat-Face was running toward us, up the wet slope of the hill, twenty yards away. Another snap and flame spouted from the gun in his outstretched hand.

I threw myself toward the skinhead. We crashed together like exhausted linebackers and collapsed to the sidewalk as Rat-Face fired again. He was much closer now. I tensed. The next bullet would tear through my guts.

A shot sounded, then another. I looked up and saw Davey, still on the ground, sitting up with the skinhead's Ruger in his hand. He fired over and over into Rat-Face, who was already sagging to the pavement. *Somebody converted the Ruger for auto,* Dono's voice said. *It'll keep shooting as long as he holds the trigger down.* Davey had a stranglehold on it.

The skinhead wasn't moving. Hadn't moved since we'd hit the ground together. Out cold again? In the flashes from Davey's shots, I saw a little black hole in the skinhead's face, just under his right eye. His other eye was open, unseeing. The tip of his tongue showed between his teeth.

I had to move. Up.

Davey's hands were still around the Ruger and still

pointing at Rat-Face's limp form on the ground. The gun was empty, its breach locked open. I swatted it out of Davey's hands. He had his driving gloves on. No fingerprints. I'd teased him about those dumb-ass things before, but right now they were better than money.

I hauled Davey to his feet and got us staggering toward the Cavalier. We leaned into each other.

I got the driver's door open somehow and shoved Davey across the seats. He didn't make a sound. A woman's voice yelled from up on the apartment block, asking what the fuck was going on. I fell into the car, started the engine, and hit the gas so hard it took the tires two seconds of spinning and spraying rainwater to grab the road and launch us up the hill and away.

Leave the headlights off. I opened the windows to listen. No sirens that I could hear. Okay. We had a few minutes, maybe. Think. Two bodies on the ground behind us. We were seen. The Cavalier was seen. Somebody could have called in the license plate.

"Van," Davey said.

"Shut up." The Cavalier wasn't in Dono's name. If the plates were run they would match another owner of a Chevy in the same color or maybe even a false identity of Dono's. Either way it was a dead end. If we could ditch it.

I could still get us out.

Davey had one hand on the dashboard, his forehead resting against his arm. "Holy shit. We made it. We're alive."

I rolled the windows back up and made myself ease off on the gas. We rolled up Pike. A block to our left, police cruisers flashing red and blue at the reservoir. They'd found Bobby.

"I shot that dude," Davey said. "I thought he shot you, and I just— Oh, fuck me. I can't believe it. Did you see?"

Although I really wanted Davey to shut up, maybe it was better that he talked. Vomit out all the words now. Because

I was sure as shit counting on him to keep his mouth shut after tonight.

The best thing right now was to get off the streets. The Cavalier could stay hidden in the garage until Dono got back into town. Safest place. I'd calm Davey down and drop him at home. We could talk through this whole freaking night later.

"You want to hear something funny?" Davey said. He made a noise that was half whine, half laugh. "In the shop back there. When you grabbed me?"

"Yeah?"

"I thought you were Dono. I thought that you'd brought him along and I just hadn't realized it before that moment. I would've sworn it was him. You scared me so much I forgot to be scared. You know?"

"Yeah." I knew. I knew exactly how scary my grandfather could be.

CHAPTER TWENTY-FOUR

THE SEATTLE CENTRAL LIBRARY was a busy place in late afternoon. I stood at the railing watching the crowd below streaming in and out of the doors off Fifth Avenue.

Above me a massive tidal wave of glass loomed. It started at the floor of the lobby and launched upward in a dizzying slope four stories high. The weight of it was oppressive, translucent or not. If it had all been made of concrete, people might have turned and fled back to the street, overwhelmed by claustrophobia.

I looked at my watch—16:45. I'd been waiting and checking out the crowd for two hours, fading back every time a patrol cop walked through the lobby.

Davey walked through the security scanners twenty minutes later, carrying a blue nylon duffel bag. Like most of the tourists, he did a double take at the menacing wall of glass. He wore a couple of layered T-shirts over the same tattered black jeans I'd seen the other night, and no coat.

He looked around and found the escalators I'd told him about—glowing lemon yellow neon—and then saw me standing above at the railing. At least he didn't wave.

I scanned the crowd again. High-school and college students with laptops, mostly, and a few older folks reading magazines. Almost everyone, young or old, had on earbuds or headphones. It was a good place for a private conversation.

"You look like shit," Davey said once he'd joined me at the top.

"Did you get into the house?"

He nodded, so jazzed he was almost bouncing. "I can't believe that spare key is still there. It was so rusty I was afraid it was going to break off in the lock. Didn't Dono ever notice the loose brick in the backyard?"

"Focus, Davey. Were the cops watching the place?"

"Oh, yeah. That's why it took me so long. I had to go in through the back door." He frowned. "But I got bad news, too. The truck is gone."

"Gone how?"

"I looked where you told me. An empty space. I even checked the other levels in the garage, to make sure. It's gone, man."

The cops had been all over Pioneer Square. Guerin could have had them looking for Dono's truck as well as for me.

If they had the truck, then they had Formes's laptop and thumb drives already. I'd lost my wheels—and the Browning—but the silver lining was that SPD might already be trying to break Formes's encryption. Guerin might be listening to the recording of Dono's shooting within hours.

Davey handed me the blue duffel bag. I led him away from the balcony and the lounging patrons to a tunnel connecting the third floor with stairs leading up and down. The tunnel and stairs were painted a vibrant scarlet, walls and floor and ceiling. It was like being inside an artery.

I unzipped the duffel and looked in. Dono's cell phones from his hidden compartment were on top of a pile of the old man's clothes, along with his large ring of keys. The box of shells for the .32 was wedged against the side, along with my passport and papers.

"I always loved that little squirrel hole of your granddad's," Davey said. "So cool."

"Thanks for this, Davey. You took a big chance."

Davey fingered one of Dono's shirts. "I hope these fit. I tried to find the largest stuff he had. So are you going to keep this up?"

"What?"

"The need-to-know crap. Come on, you ask me to put together what looks like an emergency-vacation kit for you. I don't ask why. And I deliver. At least tell me what kind of shit you stepped in. I know you found a dead body—"

"Two bodies."

His smile disappeared. "Somebody else? After that woman?"

I told him about the bugs and Julian Formes. And why I couldn't let the police take me in, because after they were done, they'd hand me off to Captain Unser like a relay baton.

When I finished, Davey was staring at me as if I'd lit my hair on fire. "Fuck. I mean, god*damn*, Van."

"That's why I want to keep you out of it. Too much heat."

"Screw that."

"What are you so pissed off about?" We were starting to attract curious glances from the people walking through the bloodred passageway. A couple of them were library personnel.

"I'm pissed because while all this is happening, I should have your back. *While* it's happening, not just when you're ready to skip town again."

"I'm not skipping town."

"I owe you. And fuck you, you owe *me* a chance to make it right."

"You owe your family to stay out of jail."

"Ten years, Van. You left and didn't say a word. At least have the balls to admit you're mad at me. I deserve that."

Five minutes with Davey and we were arguing like we were teenagers again. I hefted the duffel. "You already helped with this."

"And Juliet's car. It's a green Honda, parked downstairs, on Level Two. Here." He handed me the keys. "You can't go to the hospital to check on Dono anymore, can you?"

"No. But I've got that covered."

"Those security guards you hired?"

"And a neighbor of Dono's, armed with knitting needles. I'll let her know how to reach me if anything changes. You, too."

"Uh-huh," he said. Davey's fingers beat a hard-rock rhythm on his pant leg. His eyes had the happy-maniac look that they used to have when we were teenagers, waiting to boost a car or bust into a business. Ready for the fun.

A class of junior-high-schoolers flowed around us like breaking shore waves around dock pilings, noisy and jostling. I waited until they were down the stairs.

"I'm not holding a grudge, Davey. But I don't want to have to tell Juliet that her husband and Frances's dad is dead body number three."

His face was rigid. "I can take care of myself now."

"I'll call you if things get too tight." I walked away, through the gleaming scarlet tunnel.

He didn't believe me. I wasn't even sure why I'd bothered to say it.

CHAPTER TWENTY-FIVE

LUCE HAD UNLOCKED THE loading door to the Morgen for me. I slipped in and through the bar's back room with its uneven towers of booze, then up the stairs to the second-floor hallway. I was still in the torn and bloodstained jeans and dirty shirt, though I'd ditched the reeking hoodie at the library. She opened her apartment door at the first knock.

"You dressed up," she said.

Luce wore a silver button-down shirt over black jeans, with black ballet slippers. No jewelry. Light makeup. Her pale hair was brushed straight back from her forehead.

"How long have you lived above the bar?" I said.

"Just another thing that used to belong to Uncle Albie. What is that smell?"

"I should have brought flowers," I said.

"You know the police came by right after you called me?" she said. "They asked Mike downstairs if you'd been around today. Very casual, he said, like they needed help with a trivia question that was bugging them."

"What'd Mike tell them?"

"What could he? He didn't even know that you and I had talked. But

Mike's not dumb. When I asked him to run the bar on his own tonight, he must have caught a clue."

"Once I reach Hollis, I'm out of your hair," I said. "The cops won't be a problem for you."

"Don't be dumb. The police might poke around at the bar, but no one's going to come up here looking for you. Sit down and stop looming, for God's sake. I'm going to make coffee."

I sat, on a fat green velvet sofa. I felt a little of the tension go out of my shoulders. Guerin wanted Boone a lot more than he wanted me. The net would close, and that murdering son of a bitch and whoever might be helping him would go down. After that, I'd take Captain Unser's shit and keep smiling every minute.

Luce's place was a one-bedroom, barely larger than a studio. It was stuffed full. Dark green curtains were open to let the evening light stream in through big wood-trimmed windows. She had hung two dozen or more photographs in small silver frames on the main wall, until the volume of glass in the frames made a kind of mirror.

Every shelf in the room was groaning under the weight of books. I looked at the stacks. Lots of nonfiction, lots of literature. Addy Proctor the Librarian would approve.

Luce brought two cups of black coffee back from the kitchen. "I was a wreck after you called," she said. "I jumped every time I heard a siren. Which is a lot. Have I just gotten used to hearing those the whole day? Or did you do something to get all the cops in the city acting like angry wasps?"

I told her about finding Cristiana Liotti, and about Julian Formes, and the complete clusterfuck that had followed. Luce listened with growing frustration.

"But why are the police after you?" she said. "You didn't kill anyone."

"And I think the cops believe that. But they don't know for sure. I fled the scene at Formes's place. There was gunfire. They have to take me into custody and get a formal statement."

"Which you can't let happen."

"Not yet. Boone might slip past them. Could I borrow your cell phone?"

I called Addy Proctor. She picked up the phone just as I thought it was finally going to go to voice mail.

"Addy, it's Van. Are you in a place you can talk?"

"Van, oh, thank goodness. Yes. I'm fine. A little flustered, is all. I thought for sure it would be the hospital about your grandfather. I'm just on my way out of the house to see him now."

"Before you go, write this down." I gave her the number of my new burner phone. "That's where you can reach me now."

"Does this have something to do with the unmarked police car on our street? Two officers have been sitting right outside in a brown car since early this afternoon, looking up the block toward your house."

"It might."

"And may I assume that there's another two of Seattle's finest at the hospital?"

"You may. So I need—"

"I'll call you immediately if there's any news about your grandfather."

"Thanks, Addy. How are you holding up?"

"I'd do much better if I didn't feel like I was being watched. It's unnerving."

"Call 911 and tell them there's a pervert parked outside. They'll be gone in ten minutes."

"I might just do that."

We hung up.

Luce held her coffee mug with two hands, not drinking it.

"This ticks me off," she said. "If you'd sat back and done nothing, the cops wouldn't have the first clue as to who had killed those people."

"Neither of them was innocent," I said, "but I don't think they deserved what happened either."

"You're putting your whole career at risk. Can't the police department or the prosecutor's office or somebody get the army off your back?"

I amused myself for a second, picturing Captain Unser's reaction if some assistant D.A. tried to tell him what to do.

"Ultimately it'll be up to a JAG hearing to decide whether I really get busted. But I don't give a damn about the army right now. I need to see this through."

"What you need right now is a shower," she said. "Go. There are fresh towels behind the door."

The hot water felt like nirvana. Even across the cut and abraded skin on my legs, it was more pleasure than pain. I wanted to stay in it for a week. I got out of the shower and toweled off in the thick steam clouds.

Luce knocked and opened the door. She looked me up and down.

"Just checking if you had everything you need," she said.

I smiled. "Not everything."

We kissed once, in the doorway, then again in the hall. I'm not sure which of us directed the other into the bedroom. Her jeans fell to the floor with a whisper, and she kept her lips on mine as my fingers worked the buttons on her shirt. She had to turn away to throw a pile of pillows off the iron-posted bed. Her body was pale and improbably long, an icicle flecked with cinnamon.

She watched my face, her pupils as dark as the centers of whirlpools, while she removed the last of her clothing, proudly, knowing the effect she had. I caught up to her. We met in the middle of the bed. I reached out and found that her body wasn't ice at all, but the white flame of acetylene.

LATER HER BEDROOM WAS dark blue, matching the evening sky outside the window. Luce lay across my chest. I felt her lips and teeth resting softly against the heavy pulse in my throat.

"You don't have any tattoos," she said. Her breath was still a little fast, and warm against my skin.

"Neither do you, I noticed."

"I always thought soldiers got blind drunk and wandered into tattoo parlors together. Like team spirit for your unit."

I looked at her and cocked an eyebrow. She blushed.

"You know what I mean," she said.

"A lot of guys have ink," I said.

"You scared of the needle?" She nipped me on the shoulder with her teeth.

I laughed. "Somehow I grew up thinking that getting a picture drawn on your skin was a dumb thing to do. Too identifiable."

"Albie had one," Luce said. "An eagle."

"Well, Dono always said Albie was an idiot."

She punched me lightly in the ribs. "He did not. Did you know that Albie was the only person who visited Dono every week when your grandfather was in jail? He told me once. It was years before I went to live with him."

"How was that?" I said. "Living with Albie?"

"He came to my high-school basketball games with a flask," she said. "But he came."

"Dono and I would go on road trips. Or out on the water sometimes." In the half-light, I saw my forearm, brown against the alabaster sleekness of Luce's back. There was one thin white line that never tanned, just below my elbow.

"Was it fun?"

"The best was when I was about twelve," I said. "In the San Juan Islands. Dono and I were motoring around on this runabout he'd borrowed from Hollis. Hollis was anchored off Sucia, partying with some girlfriend. Dono took me fishing, mostly to give them some privacy, I think."

Luce chuckled, low and soft. "I'd love to have heard that conversation."

I grinned. "We took the boat to the outer islands, just to see what they looked like. When we got close to one, we dropped the lines. Something hit the bait right away."

"Tell me it was a mermaid."

"Might as well have been, I was so excited. I brought the tip of the rod across the bow a bit too close and snagged the fishing line on the bow cleat."

"Uh-oh."

"Not a big deal. But without thinking I reached across to free the line, and the tough little bastard of a fish picked that moment to make his run. The line whipped right over my arm and sliced the meat, right here."

Luce grimaced theatrically and took my arm and kissed it where I was pointing.

"Dono already had his knife out, and he cut the line," I said, "but by then I was bleeding all over the boat. I remember spots on the tackle boxes, our lunch, and my shoes, and thinking I was in big trouble."

"Was he mad?"

"No. No, not at all."

I remembered even more, with the telling of it.

Dono had taken off his T-shirt and slapped the folded cloth over my arm, ordering me to grip down hard. He tried to reach Hollis on the handheld VHF but got no reply, and after a moment's hard cursing he took the boat into shore.

"Too bumpy out here, boy," he had said, "for what we have to do." I hadn't replied. I might have been in shock, not from real injury but just from the suddenness of it all. The center of the floor was a watery pink stream, with flowers of red blooming around it. Dono's T-shirt looked tie-dyed.

He beached the runabout on the rock without much regard for its bottom and hauled me and a tackle box out and over to the nearest place to sit down. It was the broken trunk of what had once been a huge madrona tree. The top surface of the trunk was worn smooth by decades of weather, making a broad wooden throne at the very edge of the small island.

Dono had washed a slim fishing hook in salt water and threaded a fifty-pound-test line through it.

"This will hurt," he said, and it did. My grandfather was no great shakes at field medicine. Every time he pushed the hook through my skin, it was like he'd stuck me with a tiny branding iron. He had me bite down on a stick. But I held still, watching the dry wood of the tree trunk greedily soak up each red drop.

Dono's crude stitching held the gash closed, and before very long the blood flow abated. Hollis answered the VHF on the next try, and he and Dono had a low thunderstorm of a conversation.

While we waited for the cruiser to return, Dono sat next to me on the stained throne of wood. He handed me the thermos of coffee, which he'd been using like a huge mug.

"A good day," Dono had said. And I took a first cautious sip and wheezed a little, and nodded, and he laughed. I'd laughed, too.

"Hollis turned up an hour later," I said to Luce. "Red in the face and quiet, which isn't like Hollis at all. I barely noticed. I was so wired after the excitement."

"Scary," Luce said.

"Yeah. But after that, Dono and I were closer."

"Because you'd been brave?"

"Maybe. Or maybe because Dono knew that I trusted him again. He'd only been out of jail a few months. Looking back, I realize we were both taking things day by day. I wasn't so certain anymore that he would be around."

"Because he'd left you."

"He hadn't wanted to. But he screwed up and got nailed. And I went into foster homes for a year and a half."

"Tough little guy," Luce said.

I pressed my lips against her forehead. "But still scared of the needle."

"You don't have to get a tattoo on your arm, you know. You could put it anywhere."

"Like where?" I said. "Here?"

"On you, not me. Oh. Never mind. Keep doing that."

I kissed her. She kissed back, harder.

WE WOKE TO A cell phone ringing. It had started raining hard, and the trill of the ring melded with the sound of tires outside, hissing over wet pavement. It was the new burner phone. I rolled out of bed and went into the other room to find it.

"Oh, Van." Addy Proctor. "He's slipping. Dono. You need to come right away. Hurry," she said, her voice breaking. "Please hurry."

CHAPTER TWENTY-SIX

Rain hit me like a swarm of hornets the instant I stepped out of the Honda. The wind was flinging the drops almost sideways. I ran up the middle of the street, toward the eastern side of Harborview. Was I too late? Again?

The ambulance dock was the closest entrance. I followed a group of paramedics and drivers as they race-walked their gurneys through the automatic doors. One of the patients fought violently against his restraints, screaming. Nobody looked at me. Inside, I broke off from the medics and headed for the hallway.

It could be a trap. I didn't doubt that Addy's message was legit, but Guerin might still be counting on the news to draw me in. He could have a couple of cops watching the critical ward right now.

I had to risk it. Had to. Even if Guerin handcuffed me right next to the damn hospital bed, at least I'd be there.

And I had to be there, for Dono, if this was the end.

The elevator doors opened on the fourth floor. No cops in sight on the ward. No guards from Standard Security posted at Dono's door either. The hair on my scalp rose.

I ran, drops of water flying off me, down the hall. I was halfway there when Addy Proctor stepped out of Dono's room, followed by Dr. Singh and one of the uniformed men from Standard.

Addy spotted me first. "Van, thank God," she said. "He's still with us."

"You should go in," said Singh.

I did. They stayed outside. The door shut behind me.

He looked very thin. The day before, I might've believed he was only sleeping. Now his head didn't seem to dent the pillow quite enough, and his steel-colored hair was disheveled. They had more wires attached to him now, a new monitoring machine next to the bed.

I stepped forward and took his hand. It was cool to the touch.

"Dono," I said, "it's Van."

A nurse had tucked the sheets and the sky blue blanket very neatly around him. The top of the sheet made a crisp white stripe across his chest. It rose and lowered a fraction as the air was forced into his lungs and sucked back out again.

Rain beat against the windows, the wind behind it calling. Loud enough to mask the erratic tap of the EKG. A downbeat of Dono's heart every two seconds, then three, then holding back at two again.

"We'll get him," I said. "I've seen the son of a bitch. Boone McGann. He'll burn." I leaned in close. "You need to be there to see it. To watch his face when judgment day hits him. You need to see that, Dono."

His hand squeezed mine. Light as a spider's touch.

I squeezed back, willing it not to be a reflex.

"Dono," I said.

His back arched violently. He coughed and choked against the tube of the ventilator. I turned and yelled for help as his arm jerked weakly under my hand.

A nurse yanked the door open and pushed me away from the bed. She pinned his forehead down while her other hand began removing the ventilator. The heart monitor was shrieking. The nurse called for Singh. Addy's face at the edge of the doorway, pale and clenched.

Dono's eyes half opened. Black gun barrels in his long white face. The first I'd seen those eyes in ten years. His body was rigid, and his head, free of the ventilator mask, moved an inch one way, then the other.

I stepped forward, and his eyes found mine. Stayed there. His mouth twitched.

I leaned down and put my ear close to his face. Singh said something to me. There was an exhalation of breath from Dono against my cheek.

"I'm here, Granddad," I said.

Another breath. I was so close that the stubble on his chin grazed my face.

Somebody was pulling at my arm. The guard. I reached out without looking and shoved him, and he crashed over something and fell to the floor.

"*Van.*" I heard Dono say it. The *V* was only air, pushed out an extra fraction.

"Tell me," I said.

His big hand flailed suddenly and grabbed mine where it rested on the blanket, my fingers still looped around the ring of keys from Juliet's car. He gripped me with spasmodic strength until the metal teeth bit into my skin.

"*Here.*"

"I'm here," I said, my ear still an inch from his mouth. "Tell me."

Dono went limp. His clenched fist eased over my hand. I looked up in time to see his eyes lose the light.

Someone grabbed me again, pulling me back. I let them. Singh closed in and started checking Dono's pupils. A nurse gave him an injection. Another stood by a defibrillator cart, pads ready.

Addy was saying something to me, from outside the room. I looked at her.

"Come away, Van," she said. The orderlies at my back released their hold on me.

I went. My eyes were still on Dono.

Addy and I waited and watched the whirl of action try to match the storm outside. I already knew it was pointless. Three minutes. Five, until Singh called it. Then the air was still again, somehow, and everyone had left the room, hovering around my peripheral vision.

"There will be time later," a voice said.

It was Hollis, next to Addy. "We have to leave, lad," he said. The nurses and orderlies and Singh and Addy all stared at him, uncomprehending. "Police are coming. There'll be time for your man soon, but right now you and I have to get gone."

I wanted to stay with Dono, but there was no mistaking the tension lining Hollis's broad face. He was soaking wet, his dark shirt plastered across his barrel chest and belly. I nodded.

He turned and walked quickly down the hallway, and I trailed along. Hollis led me out of the ward and to the open stairwell by the elevators.

He grunted. "Pray God they haven't locked the fucking door," he said as we went down the stairs and into a side hallway. At the end of it was a security door. "I found this doctor's entrance." He pushed, and it swung open instantly.

"There." Hollis pointed, and I walked through the rain and stood at the passenger door of his big DeVille while he bustled around to get in the driver's side and hit the power locks. I opened the door and sat down next to him.

The wind wasn't as strong in the shadow of the building. With the starless night and the torrent of water washing over the car windows, we might have been on the ocean floor.

He started the engine and rubbed his hands together for warmth. "Christ Jesus. What a night." He looked at me. "I'm not meaning to be cruel, son, but did you make it here on time? For your granddad?"

Van, Dono had said. *Here.*

I nodded.

Hollis sighed. "Well, that's something at least." He reached out and gripped the steering wheel, pushing against it until it creaked to stretch his muscles.

"How'd you know?" I said.

"About Dono? That lovely old bat back there. Miz Proctor. She called and told me what was happening. She said she'd already sent you a message but you'd not replied. And that the cops were here, too." Hollis fidgeted in his seat, trying to face me square on. I hadn't moved since I'd gotten into the car. Hollis couldn't seem to stop.

"I knew you'd race here the second you heard," he continued. "So

I thought you could use a little help. I rang up Homicide. Your boy Guerin wasn't there, but his partner was."

"Kanellis."

"That's the name. I told him I was an old friend of your grandfather's and that you had turned up at my door pleading for shelter. I thought you were armed and desperate. Begged him to hurry."

I imagined Guerin out there in the rainstorm. "Where'd you send him?"

"Well, I might have told Kanellis I was Jimmy Corcoran. That little prick could use the excitement. Besides, Jimmy lives close enough to the hospital that I hoped they would send the cops on duty here. We got lucky."

He exhaled and sat back in his seat. "Listen to me run on. God, boyo. I'm sorry. You have to know that your granddad held on as long as he could. He must have known you were here."

I closed my eyes. Listened to the uneven drumroll of the rain on the roof. Twelve hours before, I'd listened to Julian Formes die. I'd chased after Boone. If I'd caught him then and been able to whisper the news in Dono's ear, would that have made a difference?

"There's something else I can do for you," Hollis said. "If you'll let me. Sometime back, your man was in one of his dark moods. He made arrangements for himself. A service, a wake, the whole deal. I know it's not something you want to think about—"

"Get it rolling. He'd want it to be soon."

"True enough." He looked at me. "You can't keep running like this, lad. Not for much longer."

"I won't have to. Thanks, Hollis." I opened the door and stepped out of the DeVille. The rain fell straight down now, from clouds to pavement with hardly a sound.

CHAPTER TWENTY-SEVEN

I WAS STANDING WHERE THE land met the water at the far edge of Seward Park. The park was closed. It had closed at dusk, a lifetime or two ago. Before I'd seen Luce. Before Dono had died. A sodden mass of clouds blocked any moonlight from above and refused to reflect the city lights from below. All I could see of the horizon was a flat, leaden gray.

Goddamn it, Dono.

I finally get it. Why you asked me to come back.

You hadn't planned on getting rich—that was your problem.

Sure, the Talos shipment was too good to pass up. How often does a chance at six million in untraceable rocks cross your path? Maybe you rushed the job, finding a crew you could get on short notice. Unstable assholes like the McGann brothers.

When Boone McGann was busted for violating his probation, did you see that as a good thing? One less guy who might betray you? With Boone and Burt together, it wasn't hard to imagine Dono and Sal Orren as the ones left to bleed out on the floor of that abandoned airplane hangar, instead of Burt and Sal killing each other.

I'd call you lucky, Dono. But that luck just kicked trouble down the road a little way.

You wound up with the whole shipment. Handed maybe a quarter of it to Ondine, and she was satisfied. Gave a few hundred grand in cash to Cristiana Liotti for the information. And you kept the rest.

So what then? You weren't going to buy a damn mansion. Sure as shit you didn't want to spend the rest of your life getting fat lying on some beach drinking umbrella drinks.

I thought I knew your way of thinking before I came back. But after the last few days of hell, I understand you a little better.

With a pile of diamonds suddenly in your hands, you started thinking about your legacy. Giving things away. You were handing over the reins of the bar to Luce and passing your share to Mike. And you wrote me a letter.

Because you had something to offer me, too. The diamonds.

I might not accept them, of course. You would have known that. It probably didn't matter. It wasn't just about offering me money. You'd be trusting me with the knowledge of what you'd done. A capital offense, with two men dead during the commission of a felony.

Just like the two dead skinheads ten years ago. So what if I hadn't pulled the trigger on those men? You hadn't killed Sal and Burt either.

Waves lapped softly against the low cement wall at my feet. I turned around and began walking through the forest trails of the park, back to where I'd left the car. The huge old trees blotted out the sky, until I made my way as much by feel as by sight.

The running had served a purpose while Dono had been alive. I'd wanted to tell him myself that we'd caught the man who'd shot him. See his face. My own olive branch to offer.

But Dono was dead now. And Detective Guerin would run Boone McGann to ground.

Staying at large was just kicking my trouble down the road, like Dono's luck.

I reached the start of the trail, where I'd left the Honda. My personal phone was in the duffel bag. I replaced its battery—so what if Guerin learned where I was now—and turned it on. I'd find a motel, crash for a few hours. And then turn myself in.

The phone brought up the last Internet search I'd done, on the Talos

robbery. There were fresh headlines: HOMICIDE VICTIM LINKED TO AR-
MORED CAR ROBBERY. Cristiana Liotti. The press had caught up to what
the police already knew.

It wouldn't be long before Dono's name was mentioned in articles
about the robbery, too. Maybe he was already news. I clicked on the
first link.

It was a full spread on Cristiana, with biography and a picture. The
biography was padded with details about her high school in New Jersey,
her volunteer work, anything that would make a short life seem richer.
The photo was from a formal party, Cristiana smiling broadly, cham-
pagne flute in hand. Her dress was dark blue, a good color to show off
her curled brown hair. People standing next to her were cropped out.

Behind her I could see part of a large banner, hanging on the wall.
The banner had a design on it in dark green and gold. The photo resolu-
tion wasn't great. Two thick gold lines on a green background. On top
of one of the lines was a notch.

Then the notch became a barb, like at the end of a fishing hook, and
the lines became two of the prongs of a trident.

And the design became the emblem of the Emerald Crown Yacht
Club.

Ondine's club.

CHAPTER TWENTY-EIGHT

ONDINE LONG'S APARTMENT TOWER was one of the tallest buildings in Belltown. From the roof I had an unobstructed view across a quarter of a mile, to the black waters of the sound.

It was three o'clock in the morning and almost pitch-dark on the roof. The wind moaned low and loud through the glass-and-steel canyon below. Every few moments a fresh dash of light rain slapped my back.

I looked over the edge. Fifteen feet down I could just make out the flagstone paving on Ondine's balcony. Her penthouse apartment was set back from the main exterior of the building, creating a private terrace. The terrace was about the same size as a volleyball court. A stone dropped from the wrought-iron railing of the terrace would fall twenty stories before cracking the asphalt on Battery Street.

I swung my legs over the roof edge. The wind whipped at my hair and tried to knock me sideways as I hung by my hands above the terrace. I let go and dropped the last seven feet.

No lights came on. I couldn't see anything inside the apartment through the reflective glass of the windows. I waited in the shadows.

Another minute passed. I tried the sliding glass door, lockpicks ready in my other hand, and was surprised to find it unlocked.

But not too surprised.

Ondine had been making a lot of bad mistakes lately.

I slipped inside and closed the glass door behind me. The sound of the wind was softer with the door closed.

Ondine's apartment had an open floor plan. As my eyes adjusted to the dark, I could see a broad expanse of living area, with low-slung furniture arranged to take advantage of the view. A dining room was on my right. Artwork on the walls and abstract statuary dividing the spaces in between. Everything was leached of color in the gloom.

At the very back, I could see a short entrance foyer and the front door. To the left of the living area was a hallway. Probably leading to the bedrooms.

I wanted to go that way. Get down to it. Instead I did the smart thing and moved across the room to check my exit route. The dead bolt on the front door was a top-of-the-line Schlage, with steel-reinforced plates. This one, unlike the back door, someone had remembered to lock.

"Alec? Are you home?" Ondine's voice, coming down the hall on the left. In a moment she appeared at the edge of the room, a ghostly blur in an ivory robe.

I turned on a reading lamp. Its silk shade was embroidered with dragonflies, and the outline of pale blue wings fell across Ondine's unnaturally smooth face.

"Have a seat," I said.

Her eyes flickered to the .32 in my hand.

"I'm expecting Alec back shortly," she said.

"Good."

Ondine gave a tight smile. Her lipstick was perfect. Maybe she really was expecting Alec.

"All business, like before," she said, crossing the room to perch on a chaise. I moved back toward the far wall, where I had a clear line of sight on the front door and the hallway. Just in case there was another entrance to the apartment.

She nodded at the gun. "That's hardly necessary."

"Tell me about Cristiana Liotti," I said.

Ondine removed a cigarette from a red lacquered box on a side table. She lit it with a match and took a small, unhurried draw.

"We've compared notes already," she said.

"You told me what happened after. The parts you thought I needed to know. I want the other half."

She brushed a hand through the long fall of her black hair. "How it started is common knowledge now. Cristiana Liotti learned of the diamond shipment while working at Talos."

"So she told the one person who might be able to help her profit from it."

"Dono."

"Not Dono. She brought it to you. Cristiana was a member of Emerald Crown."

Ondine raised an eyebrow.

"I'm guessing Cristiana had heard rumors about you," I continued, "and she had nothing to lose. Did she drop hints or come right out and ask if you could help her profit somehow?"

She exhaled a wisp of smoke. "The little secretary crept up to me at the New Year's banquet. Very, very nervous."

"And you could trust Dono to get what information he needed from her and not leave a trail back to either of you."

"Time was short."

"Who brought in the McGanns?"

"McGanns," Ondine said, stressing the plural. "You're positively bursting with new information tonight. I arranged for the personnel."

"When you say 'I,' you mean Alec."

"We'd used Sal Orren before. But yes, it was Alec who recruited the McGann brothers."

"Who were fuckups from the start," I said.

"Which is why I instructed Alec to make things right. He could handle Boone McGann."

"But he didn't."

Ondine tapped her cigarette ash into an oyster shell on the table. "Boone went into hiding after Dono. He'll surface eventually."

"Sure he will. Whose idea was it for Alec to go after Boone? Yours or his?"

Ondine opened her mouth to reply. Closed it again. We stared at each other.

"What is Alec to you?" I said.

"That's not at all relevant."

"Okay. What are you to him? The girl of his dreams? Or just a cash machine with benefits?"

Ondine's face flushed. "Get out of here."

"Dono made only one mistake, but it was a very big one. Taking the job and trusting that you could still hack it."

I tapped the unlocked glass door to the terrace with the barrel of the .32. "You're old, Ondine. And sloppy. Making a deal with Cristiana, who was way too close to home. Hiring psychos like the McGanns. Not to mention letting your piece of ass make a fool out of you."

"You son of a bitch."

"Dono's dead."

Ondine sat up rigid, like she'd leaned back against a needle hidden in the upholstery. She looked blankly at me.

"Dead?" she said.

"Earlier tonight. He came out of the coma for a minute or so. That was all."

She turned away. Her back hunched. Outside, the wind changed pitch as it gusted, like the inhale and exhale of the entire city. I listened, forcing my own breath to slow.

Ondine stood and walked over to a huge ebony sideboard, her silk robe whispering and swirling. Decanters were set in a precise row. She picked one with an amber liquid and poured it into a crystal tumbler, took the glass and drank.

When she spoke, her voice was approaching steady. "You're here to kill Alec."

"Where is he?"

"Why are you so certain he's helping Boone?" she said.

"Because Dono wouldn't have told Burt McGann a damn thing

he didn't need to know. There was no way for Brother Boone to track down Cristiana if she had just been Dono's source. Somebody else knew who she was. And only someone with your connections would know how to find a specialist to bug Dono's house."

I crossed the room to stand in front of her. She took a fractional step back, pressing up against the heavy sideboard.

"Somebody fed Cristiana to Boone McGann," I said. "It had to be you. Or someone very close to you."

We stood there for a moment, looking at each other.

"His eyes," said Ondine. She raised the glass but didn't drink, just inhaled the fumes of it. I was close enough to smell it, too: Pear brandy, thick and cloying.

"Alec was working with the McGanns all along, wasn't he?" she said. "If Boone had been part of the robbery—"

"Then the McGanns would have killed Dono at the hangar, along with Sal Orren. I think Burt tried to stick to the original plan and take both of them out on his own. But Sal was quicker than he expected. He took Burt with him." I shook my head. "You got lucky, Ondine. If it had gone down that way, Alec couldn't just skip town and leave you alive to figure it out. He would have killed you once they had the diamonds."

"Let me," Ondine said. Her hand gripped the carved edge of the sideboard. "Let me kill him."

Kill. Not "deal with" or "handle" or another euphemism.

"Just like that?" I said.

"I've loved two men," she said. "I lost the second tonight."

"So prove it," I said. "Alec and Boone want the diamonds. Which means they want me. No more bugs or tailing me around town. They'll have to grab me and torture me, like they did with Cristiana."

I pointed at the cordless phone on the wall. "I'll hold Dono's wake on Sunday morning. At the Morgen."

Ondine ran a fingernail along the edge of her glass. Then she set the glass down and picked up the phone. She tapped a button on speed dial.

"Darling?" she said into the phone. Her voice was faster and lighter. Almost happy. "I've just heard. Dono Shaw has died."

She listened for a moment. "I agree. The hospital is a dead end—Boone won't go there. And the police are still hunting for Dono's grandson. I think Dono's house is too risky for Boone to stake out, if he's determined to find Van."

I leaned in to catch Alec's next words through the receiver. "—to find him down in Stockton?"

"No," said Ondine. "I think your instincts were correct. Boone is still in Seattle. And Van Shaw will almost certainly appear at Dono's wake. The day after tomorrow, at his bar on Lenora Street."

Alec grunted. "If the police are hunting for Shaw, wouldn't he steer clear?"

"I know these people," Ondine said. "They are sentimental, even when that leads to making foolish decisions. Maybe especially then."

I glanced up in time to see one tear balance on the eye of her lower eyelash before she swiped it away, as deft as a magician.

"I'll find McGann," said Alec.

"Not tonight. Come home soon. I miss you," said Ondine.

"Yeah, you, too," he said, and hung up.

Ondine put the phone back on its hook. I put the .32 back into the pocket of my coat and picked up the same decanter Ondine had used. I poured a shot into a tumbler.

She walked back over to the chaise to sit down. She looked tired. And no longer fortyish. "I didn't think Dono would say yes to the robbery," Ondine said. "It truly surprised me."

"So why did you ask?"

"Six million in diamonds does not come along every day," she said. "And Dono had told me to call him if I saw an opportunity. He'd wanted to set some money aside, he said."

"For a rainy day."

"A hoard," Ondine said. "That was the word Dono used when he told me he'd decided to keep the diamonds instead of selling them."

"Hoard? Like treasure?" The word struck a note, high and far off in my memory. I was sure I'd heard it before.

Ondine smiled softly. "Later generations will marvel at it, he said. Your grandfather was exaggerating. I never understood half his humor."

Because it hadn't been a joke. The diamonds *were* for the future. Mine.

I downed the ounce of brandy in one swallow. It seared my throat and kept me from talking.

"You were right," I finally said to Ondine. "Love leads to bad decisions."

"Yes. Alec was a blind spot." She hugged her silk robe around her, like there was a chill in the wide room. "But I would never have taken his side. Not against Dono."

I looked out the glass door, at the terrace and the retreating storm clouds farther out over the sound.

"If I thought that you had, we'd be done talking by now," I said. "I'd have dangled you over that railing out there until you told me where Alec was hiding. Then I'd have dropped you anyway, just for your part in Dono's death."

Ondine was an ice sculpture. I set the empty glass back on the sideboard.

"Just so you know it crossed my mind," I said.

AGE EIGHTEEN, SAME NIGHT

By the time I pulled onto Davey's block, he was ass-deep into his talking jag again, laughing in shaky circles about how he couldn't believe we had actually gotten away, and fuck, weren't the gunshots louder than he'd ever imagined, and somehow he didn't think anyone had seen us. I was still thinking about the three dead guys and how to make sure nobody ever connected them to us.

I set the brake a few doors down from the Tolan house and just stared at Davey until he wound down a notch.

"Your mom's inside," I said once he could meet my eyes for more than half a second. "She's gonna ask where you were."

"Right. Okay. Well, I was with you, right? Just hanging out?"

I shook my head. "You weren't with me. You haven't seen me since we left the party last night. You were out alone. You were pumped up after the party, and you went out walking, and you've been walking for hours."

"That's it? Just walking? Shit, nobody's going to believe that."

It was still dark enough out that the streetlights were on. The beams cast deep shadows in the car. But I didn't need more light to tell that Davey's hands were twisting and pulling feverishly at his faded Slipknot T-shirt.

"Walking all alone means you don't need anybody to verify where you were, or when. You and I don't need to tell the same story, 'cause there is no story. You were out walking. Simple. You get me?"

"But Jesus, Van. My ma. She's gonna—"

My forearm cramped, I was squeezing the steering wheel

so hard. "Davey. Guys got *killed* tonight. You get it? I'm not worried about your ma. She's maybe just the warm-up, you know?"

"What do you mean? Cops?" Davey looked out the back window of the Cavalier.

"They could find out you knew Bobby Sessions and come around to ask about him."

"How would they know that?"

"I don't *know*, Davey. Maybe Bobby wrote a note for his girlfriend, telling her he was going to see you. Maybe the cops call every number in his cell phone."

Davey blinked at me. Not getting it. His brain was still redlining on adrenaline.

I stretched until my shoulder joints popped. Tried to relax so Davey could follow my lead. "It doesn't matter. What matters is that the cops might come around, so you pick a story and you stay with it. Keep it simple. Out walking. You don't know what time, really. If they push hard, then say you were drunk off your ass and you didn't want to get into trouble with your mom. But save it until they really push."

Davey shrugged. "Ma will think I was drunk anyway."

"Even better."

I'd have to think up a story to tell Dono. I couldn't let him go driving around town in a car that an eyewitness might be describing to cops right this minute. Preferably an excuse that didn't involve me being right in the middle of a triple homicide.

"You ready?" I said to Davey.

"Yeah. No problem. Fuck, what a wild night, huh? Can you believe—"

"Davey."

"Okay, yeah. It's cool. I got this."

I watched him lope up the sidewalk, a spring in his step. High on life. I'd have to keep close tabs on him during the next few days. In case he came crashing to earth. I could imagine another kind of talking jag, this one rocket-fueled by guilt. I should call him later, to check up on him.

Shit. My cell phone. Davey had called it from the Holiday Haus. It wasn't attached to my name. But could the cops track down where the phone was, somehow? I didn't know.

On the way home, I broke the phone into pieces and tossed the bits down a couple of different sewer grates. My graduation present had lasted five days.

Anything else I'd forgotten? The car, the phone. I'd been careful not to leave fingerprints at the Holiday Haus. But maybe Davey had. I couldn't be sure that he'd had his driving gloves on every minute. Or maybe we'd been caught on film by a security camera somewhere in the alley.

Nothing I could do about those things now. Just get the Cavalier tucked away in the garage before some alert citizen took any notice of it. And cross my fingers.

A light fog had drifted in with the dawn by the time I reached the house. I pulled in to the driveway, got out, and unlocked the garage door, pulled hard to roll it all the way up in one go.

And found myself staring at a familiar gray Silverado pickup.

Dono was home.

Shit.

He'd told me he'd be back on Monday, damn it. That whatever job it was he had going in the town of Gillette, Wyoming, would be on Sunday afternoon, and he'd be coming straight back. If it really had been Wyoming.

Focus. I had to get the car into the garage. I jumped back inside it and reversed out of the driveway. I didn't have keys for the pickup, but its doors were unlocked. It took me about two minutes to hot-wire the ignition and swap it for the Cavalier.

Once the garage door was closed again, I exhaled. And realized that the truck's engine had been cold. So Dono had been back for at least an hour, I guessed. Maybe he'd turned up right after I left. If he'd come direct from Gillette, he might have driven all night. He could be asleep right now, crashed out after fifteen hours at the wheel.

I unlocked the front door and slipped into the entryway. The security system was blinking red. I punched in the code, and the light went green.

"The graduate," Dono said, his voice floating in from the front room.

Damn it. I took a deep breath and came around the corner. He was sitting in his leather wing-back chair, a bottle of beer in his hand, long legs stretched out in front of him. He hadn't been watching TV. No book on the side table. Just sitting there, drinking and thinking. D&T, as he called it.

"You get your diploma?" he asked.

"They send those to us later," I said. "At the ceremony they just handed us pieces of rolled-up paper."

"Bait and switch." He waved at the window. "You want to tell me what the Christ that was all about?" He'd watched me swap the Cavalier for the pickup.

Dive on in. "I didn't want to leave the car on the street."

"No?"

"I got pulled over. Speeding. The cop ran the plates. I don't know how clean that car is—like, maybe it's okay for a traffic stop but it'll get flagged on somebody's report if the history's cloned from a car in another state. Figured I'd get it out of sight until I could ask." I was talking too fast.

Dono's dark eyes were flat, his brow smooth. "He didn't let you off with a warning." It wasn't a question.

"I offered to take care of it," I said.

"How much?"

"A hundred. What was left of the money you gave me last week."

"And the man took it?"

"Yeah. He thought a lot about it while he pretended to look over the car. But he took it."

Dono took a pull on his beer. Still regarding me. "He ran the plates, you said?"

"Yeah. At least I think he did. He sat in his car for five minutes before he got out and walked up to me."

"Not a cycle cop, then."

Shit. Almost all traffic enforcement in the city was on motorcycles. Cars were usually only on the freeways.

"No," I said.

"Seattle?"

"State trooper."

"Huh. I'd thought you said cop. Whereabouts?"

"Off the Stroud exit. He was behind the overpass."

Dono exhaled, a slow, whisper sound. He set the beer down and got up from the chair. His neck and chin had a five-day growth of black beard, and his blue chambray shirt and jeans were wrinkled and limp after the all-night drive, but he looked fresh. All loose muscle and long bone. He walked over to the front windows and glanced down at the roof of the garage with the Cavalier inside it.

"If I call a friend in SPD," Dono said, "and ask him to find out if anyone's looking for a car like our own there. What's he likely to tell me?"

"Probably nothing," I said.

Dono waited, still facing the window. Giving me a chance to confess my sins.

I needed to keep Davey out of this. All the way out.

If Dono learned the truth, he'd kill Davey. *Literally* kill him. Davey could link me with a heavy felony, manslaughter at least, even if he was the one who'd pulled the trigger.

I knew how my grandfather thought. Davey and I would hold that rap over each other for the rest of our lives. Unless Davey wasn't able to tell anyone.

I took a deep breath. "Cops might be trying to find a witness."

"To what?" said Dono.

"A shooting. Maybe more."

He turned to look at me. I managed not to glance away.

"I was setting up a job," I said, "on the other side of the hill."

Dono's face turned to stone.

"Planning a job," he said.

"Yeah."

"And then suddenly gunfire broke out. What store?"

I couldn't mention the Holiday Haus. What if Dono traded information with his cop contact while asking about the Cavalier? *Hey, tell me about this car, I'll tell you a way to look good with the local owners, point out where some lowlife has cut their alarm to come back later. Take a bite out of crime.* The police might sweep the shop, maybe find Davey's fingerprints in the place and connect them with the prints on the gun we'd dropped at the scene.

I rolled my neck, hoping Dono read my hesitation as fear of punishment. "It's a consignment place called Guinevere's, off of Summit." Two blocks away from where the shooting had been. "A lot of women's jewelry. I didn't get serious about it. Just checked out the cameras and figured out how to grease the rear alarm on the store. Later I could bring the right tools."

"And?"

"So two drunk guys came out of the alley across the street. Yelling at each other. Then one of them pulls a gun, starts waving it, and the other one takes off running up the street toward me. The first guy shoots—I don't know if he really wants to kill the other one or just scare him—but I tore ass out of there as fast as I could. Somebody might have seen them. Maybe the car, too."

"Fleeing the scene," Dono said.

"I was just trying not to get my head blown off. But then I started thinking about the car and wondering if somebody got the license, so—" I pointed in the direction of the garage.

"The right idea," said Dono, nodding slowly. "And all that bullshit about getting pulled over?"

"I know I fucked up," I said. "I shouldn't have gone looking for a score. I was pissed off about not going with you." I shrugged. "It was stupid."

"Yes it was." He took three steps and stood right in front of me. Eye to eye, except that his eyes were two inches higher.

"No jacket," he said.

"It wasn't so cold last night."

"Indestructible." He pressed a big finger to my forehead, on the puffy bruise where the skinhead's fist had connected. I winced. Dono reached out and tore open the snaps on the plaid flannel shirt, revealing my T-shirt underneath.

"Somebody's blood is decorating you," he said.

I didn't answer. No point.

"Tell them a story," Dono said quietly, studying the pattern of dried rust-colored dots on my T-shirt. "And keep that story close to what's real. Tell *me* a story." He might have been talking to himself, until he looked back up at me. There was something there I had never seen before.

An emptiness.

"What's real about you?" he said. "Did you pull the trigger?"

It was out. Almost.

Christ, Davey, you had better keep your mouth shut. You don't want to see what I'm seeing.

"Did you shoot somebody?" Dono said again.

"Yes," I said.

"You *kill* somebody?"

"Yes."

His fist caught me across the cheekbone, snapping my head back, sending me stumbling into the foyer wall. I knocked down the big framed picture of horses pulling a hay cart, and the glass shattered at my feet, a sharper sound than the burst inside my head as Dono hit me again.

I ducked and scrambled away, trying to cover up. Another punch caught me high on the ribs, an iron slap of pain that took the air from my lungs. I fell to my knees, rolled out of reach just as Dono's kick cracked the wainscoting.

"*Stupid. Ruinous. Fuck,*" Dono was saying, part of a torrent of words pouring forth with as much force behind them as the blows. He reached for the umbrella stand, and I knew what was coming. I scrabbled along the floor to the more open ground of the kitchen, scattering chairs as I ducked under the broad dining table. I couldn't breathe.

Dono's lead-packed walking stick smashed another chair aside like it was made of toothpicks.

"Come out!" he shouted. "Come out, you ungrateful filth!" He hammered the stick down on the table, and I heard the wood veneer splinter. "Take what's fucking coming to you!"

He was going to kill me. Dono was going to crush my skull and stuff me in the trunk of the Cavalier, letting us both sink to the bottom of the sound. He reared back and slammed the sole of his boot into the edge of the heavy table, sending it skidding a yard across the linoleum.

I got my feet under me and shoved up beneath the table as hard as I could. It was too heavy to lift completely, but I got it moving, tilting toward Dono like a wave. The thick oak slab crashed over onto him, pinning him back against the wall.

"Run, then," he said. "Run away from it."

I *was* running. I was clumsily scrambling over the table legs and toppled chairs toward the back door of the house.

Dono threw the shillelagh at me and heaved the table off himself. The door was bolted. I turned and grabbed the first thing I saw with any weight to it—an ashtray pinning down a stack of newspapers on the counter—and flung it at Dono's head. He ducked, and it bounced off his shoulder, shattering some dishes on the counter behind him.

He was on me. I swung frantic haymaker punches. Dono took the first on his neck and slipped the second, and then gave back a straight pop to my nose that might have ended it, except that I was already jumping aside to kick wildly at his groin. The kick smacked into his kneecap, and he hissed with pain, his next punch going wide, and I saw the opening, saw it like a good shortstop sees the easy double, and I threw a whipping left hook to his temple that landed so hard my hand and forearm went numb.

Dono fell, thudding against the overturned dining table. He was still conscious. His hand reached around, almost lazily, toward the small of his back.

I ran over to the sink, stretching to reach the top of the cabinet above it. Felt the steel grip of the Beretta that Dono kept hidden there. I pulled it down, my thumb flipping the safety without being asked, and pointed it at him. Center mass. Just like he'd taught me.

Dono lay there, one hand curled behind him. His eyes focused on mine.

"Filth," he said.

His eyebrow was bleeding, dripping down the side of his face. He didn't blink. "Do it. You've proved you can, haven't you? Murderous little shit." His hand relaxed away from his back.

I had to leave. Now. I walked to the other side of the kitchen, to the pantry, keeping the Beretta on Dono. I swept the canned goods off the pantry shelf onto the floor. It was hard to open the hiding place with one hand while keeping an eye on Dono. But I managed it. There was a roll of what looked like fifties there. Maybe a couple grand. I stuffed the roll in my back pocket.

"Lose your taste for killing now? Not so much *fun* anymore?"

I thought about my things upstairs. Nothing I couldn't replace. Or at least remember.

Dono's lips curled from his teeth. "Go on, then. Run."

There was a thick woolen coat hanging on the kitchen door that Dono used when he went out to smoke and watch the crows in the early mornings. I grabbed it. Threw open the dead bolt. Went out the door into the mist.

"Don't you ever fucking come back."

I was already gone.

CHAPTER TWENTY-NINE

I HADN'T CALLED TO TELL Hollis I was coming, but before I was halfway down the dock, he was out of the cabin of the *Francesca* and standing in the cockpit waiting. His was the only boat with lights on, like a lone candle in the quiet, dark cathedral of the marina.

When I got closer, I saw that Hollis wasn't looking at me. He was looking down at Dono's speedboat, still tied up at the *Francesca*'s stern. Hollis had tied it too close, and its bow rubbed up against the bigger boat like a pup nuzzling at its mother.

"His escape pod," said Hollis. "To a whole new life."

"Yeah," I said. The speedboat bobbed gently, little waves popping against its gray hull. Built and stowed for a long, fast run. One-way, if need be.

Hollis grunted. "Probably helped him sleep easier, having it at the ready."

I could empathize. I'd run away to make my own new life ten years ago. My army career, or what was left of it, had been on my mind all through the drive from Ondine's apartment to the marina.

"Don't just stand there," said Hollis, "Get your ass aboard."

He turned and shambled back into the *Francesca*'s big cabin. I grabbed a stanchion and hauled myself up into the cockpit.

The inside of the cabin was stale. The lights gave me a better look at Hollis. The usual pink of his face had concentrated into a rosy flush. His yellow polo shirt looked wrung out, wrinkled even where the fabric stretched tight across his belly. His thick paw was wrapped around a glass of whiskey. A strong waft of it came with him as he stepped past me to close the narrow wooden door at the back of the cabin.

I tossed the blue duffel full of clothes and Dono's stuff onto the settee, next to a pile of Hollis's own laundry. "Did you come straight here from the hospital?"

Hollis was having trouble throwing the bolts at the top and bottom of the door with just one hand. "Fucking things," he said. "No, I went by Willard's house first."

I tried to imagine Hollis waking up the huge man at two in the morning to tell him about Dono's death. Hopefully, Willard was an easy riser.

"I thought he'd want to know," Hollis said, "and besides, I need the big bastard to work with me on your man's funeral. Help yourself." He waved idly at the table, where a bottle of Old Ivory stood open. There was a Tupperware bowl next to it, filled with water and a few slivers of surviving ice.

"I want a wake," I said.

"Damn right you want a wake."

"At the Morgen. On Sunday morning."

He stared at me. "Well, that's positively fucking traditional. Good for you. He'd have liked being in the bar one last time. You're not drinking." He picked up the bottle and sloshed two fingers into a glass and thrust it at me. "Pay your respects."

"To Dono." I took a drink and let the whiskey ease its way down my throat.

"And the devil take his enemies."

"It's done."

Hollis almost dropped his drink. "It's done? You found the bastard who shot Dono?"

"Near enough. The brother of one of the dead men." I caught Hollis

up on recent events, at least where Boone McGann was concerned. I left
Alec out of it. Ondine could clean up her own corner.

"I hope they gas the pigfucker," Hollis said.

I couldn't improve on that. Part of me regretted serving Alec and
Boone up to the very different brands of justice that Ondine and Guerin
would mete out, even though I knew that was the smartest move—
much smarter than hunting them down myself.

Still, it might be worth something to see their faces at the end.

"Guerin will close the net on McGann," I said, "with a whole fucking SWAT team."

Hollis smiled grimly. "Never thought I'd be cheering for the cops."

"They have their uses. You're not drinking," I said.

He grinned and poured us another round. "You'll have one more,"
he said, "and then you'll sleep. No arguments. You look like steamrolled
shit."

"I was just thinking the same about you."

He spread his hands wide. "I'm in my own home. A man can be his
worst, and it's just him getting comfortable." He lifted his glass. "To
Moira."

My mother.

"I'd forgotten you knew her," I said.

"Oh, sure. At least as well as anyone knows the children of his
friends, which means I could wave hello and she might wave back."

"Why did she leave?" I said. "I know she was out of Dono's house
before I was born."

"Well." Hollis sat with a heavy exhale on the settee, squeezing in
next to the duffel bag. And suddenly he was smiling. "Moira was stubborn. As tough in mind as your grandfather. Or you." He took a drink.
"She wouldn't give up his name, you see."

"My father." It felt weird just saying the words.

"She told Dono that since the prick—sorry, boyo—since your father
had chosen not to be part of your lives, then he didn't fucking well exist.
And there was no point in telling Dono who he was."

Jesus. "I can picture Dono's reaction."

"He wanted to kill the boy. Didn't we all?" Hollis waved his arms. "But your mother wouldn't say a word. Not that I think she had much love for the tomcatting son of a bitch."

She wouldn't surrender him to Dono.

Just like I wouldn't give Davey up.

"Do you think Dono would have killed him?" I said.

Hollis's brow furrowed, making him look even more simian. "I think he *might* have, lad. Honestly, I'm glad it never came to a choice." He sighed. "Anyway, Moira left the house to let things cool off. And found she liked being out on her own, from what I understand."

For as long as it lasted. Six years, give or take.

The speedboat outside caught a wave wrong and thumped against the stern of the *Francesca*.

"I'll move that," I said.

"Here." Hollis reached into the open duffel for the big ring of Dono's keys. He tossed the loose ball of jangling metal at me, a fraction too hard. I snatched it out of the air a moment before it hit my head, my fingers catching the small chunk of wood tied to the center ring.

And right as the wood hit my palm, I knew. Before it even became a *thought*, I knew.

Here, Dono had said, his hand almost crushing mine with the intensity of it. My hand that held this ring of keys.

I looked at the piece of wood, the candy-bar-size hunk I'd assumed was just a float, in case the key ring was accidentally dropped into the water. Most of the piece was polished to a smooth grayish red by linseed oil and fingers and time. The deeper grooves of the grain, where fingers couldn't reach, were the original deep crimson. Blood-colored.

I recognized where the wood had come from. *When* it had come from.

I understood what Dono had been trying to tell me.

Hollis came closer to stare at me. "Are you crying?" he said.

"I'm laughing." That crazy old pirate.

"What did you figure out? Does one of those keys open something?"

I looked out the cabin window.

"It's the diamonds, isn't it?" said Hollis. "You lovely bastard, you know where they are."

Dawn was coming up strong, the slate-colored sky brushed clean by the earlier storm.

"I'm taking Dono's boat," I said.

CHAPTER THIRTY

THE ISLAND WAS NOTHING. A nameless half-mile square of trees and brush and rock and sand, one among dozens along the northern outskirts of the San Juans. It had no sheltered coves or smooth beaches to attract boaters from the main waterway, two miles to the east.

But it did have the throne. Right where I remembered it.

Madrona trees grew in bunches around the pitted shore. The orange-red trunks twisted and strangled one another for precious space. Some extended almost horizontally toward the water, straining to get their leaves out of the shade of the taller evergreens.

There was a big cleft in the shore. The bedrock of the island had cracked an eon ago and made a wide crevice running from the shore fifty feet inland. The high spring tide filled the gap to the top.

One old tree had forced its way through earth and sandstone to the sunlight over the crevice and grown to huge size, only to finally snap under its own weight in some long-ago windstorm. The thick stump of it still jutted out over the crevice, a few feet above the high tide. The top of the stump was worn almost smooth by the elements. It looked as if it had been hewn by some forest god, as a place to sit at the tip of the island and contemplate the vast sea.

I put the speedboat engine in neutral and let the little boat bob on the waves. It had taken me almost three hours of pushing through the big swells on the straits to reach the island. The morning sun was high and bright.

I shook out my limbs and ate one of the energy bars Dono had stored in the cockpit locker. It tasted like chocolate-flavored upholstery.

The speedboat floated near the spot where Dono and I had fished for rock cod back when I was a kid. When I'd told Luce the story of how my arm had been gashed by the fishing line, I'd remembered the island as being much larger. The stump of the ancient madrona tree that I'd sat on while Dono stitched me up had seemed monstrous. In life it was less than a yard across.

If I was right about my grandfather's scheming, he had made a good choice. The island was anonymous and only a short side hop from an escape path north into Canada.

If he had to collect the gems on the run, he'd want to get to them quickly, preferably without letting the boat out of his sight. That meant somewhere along the shoreline. It might be nighttime when he arrived, so the hiding place had to be distinctive enough to find in the dark or with only the small halogen spotlight to help him.

The thronelike madrona stump fit the bill on all counts.

I felt the chunk of red wood on Dono's ring of keys, rolled it between my fingers, and rubbed the grain. He must have carved the piece from the stub of madrona branch I'd been biting to fight the pain while the fishhook went in and out of my flesh. Whittled it down and polished it and kept it on his key chain. It meant something.

I guessed Dono's share of the diamonds at around sixty kilos. Even as heavy as diamonds were, that would still make a bundle at least the size of a suitcase. I looked at the stump for a few minutes, not seeing anywhere that a big package might be hidden around it.

And then I realized: That was the point. I couldn't see it at all. There was a whole bunch of shoreline that no one could see.

Because it was underwater.

Which was why the clever old thief had kept a full set of scuba equipment on his little boat. It wasn't for repairs. It was so that he could get to his treasure, no matter what the time or tide.

It took me three tries to set the anchor's flukes firmly on the sea floor, until I was satisfied that a shift in wind or current wouldn't blow the boat free while I was away from it. It would be a dark joke to come so far only to be marooned and die of exposure on this insignificant spit of land. I opened the cabin and began hauling out Dono's gear.

The scuba tank in the boat was full, and I could fit into his buoyancy-control vest. I couldn't say the same for his wet suit. The old man had been leaner than me, and there was no way I could squeeze myself into the neoprene. I'd have his bathing suit, gloves, boots, and fins. Skin diving in April.

Before putting on the gear, I collected a few tools and bungee cords from Dono's repair toolbox into the mesh bag that the mask and snorkel had been in. Ugly, but it would do for carrying the tools while I swam.

I sat on the edge of the cockpit, held the mask and regulator in place, and let myself fall backward into the water.

The cold squeezed my vitals as I sank. My teeth reflexively clenched the regulator, and I took a first hissing breath from the tank, the air cold and dry. I inflated the vest to keep me level and looked around.

The visibility was lousy. I could see the kelp-covered bottom and, vaguely, the sloping mass of the jagged shore twenty yards away, but that was about all.

In the center of the shore, there was a yawning vertical stripe of black water. The mouth of the crevice. I swam toward it, ten feet under the surface.

I had to grip the mesh bag of tools hard to make sure it was still in my hand. It wouldn't take long before my fingers would be unable to feel anything at all, gloves or not. Maybe twenty minutes before I started flirting with hypothermia.

At the mouth of the crevice, I stopped to turn on a flashlight. The crevice was about ten feet wide at its entrance, narrowing as it went farther inward. Crabs on the rock wall scuttled away from the light into the shelter of weeds. The waves pushed me forward into the murk.

I hooked the bag of tools to the tube of my air gauge so I could use my hands to edge along the crevice wall. Inside, it was nearly pitch-black. The flashlight showed just the wall in front of me. I couldn't see the bottom at all. Only by looking up at the surface could I get any sense of distance.

The crevice was growing tighter. Five feet wide, then four. The rolling waves kept trying to bash my head against the rock wall. I looked up again. It was hard to see clearly. My motion had stirred up mud and silt. Was that the tree stump above me now?

I was still peering up as I moved my hand to get better purchase. My hand missed the wall, and I had to kick hard to keep from toppling over.

There was a hole in the crevice wall. Not just a depression but a deep gash. Maybe two feet wide and four feet high.

I hung on to the rock outside the hole and shone the light in, scaring tiny fish into the shallows. Their frantic movements disturbed the muck. Clumps of slime swirled around my mask.

The hole was almost an arm's length deep. The back of it was filled with mud and algae and a pile of fist-size stones.

I brushed my gloved hand across them. For a moment the world was nothing but a tornado of evil-looking sludge. Then the current swept away the floating particles. Behind the stones I saw glimpses of flat gray where there should be mud.

Yanking at the stones, I let them fall into the depths below my fins. The flat gray was the top of a box. No, not a box, I saw as I shone the flashlight on it. A cooler. An aluminum cooler, just like the kind you might fill with ice and beer for a barbecue. The latch was on top and the hinges at the bottom, so that the lid would open toward me.

I braced myself and pulled as hard as I could on the sides of the cooler. It didn't give an inch. It might be bolted into the rock. I fumbled at the latch. My fingertips were numb, barely feeling the metal underneath them. I made my hand into a claw and tugged, and the lid fell open.

Part of me had expected a small flood of diamonds to come pouring out, like Spanish doubloons in an old movie.

But instead the cooler held a bunch of black rubber cylinders, each the size of a large thermos. I counted seven. They were hexagonal, for stacking, and secured in the cooler by a net of quarter-inch steel cable.

Dono hadn't taken any chances that the lid of the cooler might some-how come open during a violent storm.

I reached into the bag of tools. My fingers wouldn't cooperate. A wrench and a screwdriver fell, and I heard them clink off the rock wall as they sank. But I managed to keep a grip on the small pair of bolt cutters.

With the heels of my hands, I got the blades of the cutters around the cable and pushed. The blades oozed through the steel, and the cable snapped.

I freed the top cylinder from the netting. It was heavy, maybe twenty pounds. Like hefting an iron bar.

I started removing the black rubber cylinders and lashing them to-gether with the bungee cords from the bag. It was awkward. By the time I finished, the dead feeling had spread to my hands and feet. I sac-rificed more air to inflate my vest completely, trying to balance the hun-dred pounds or more of deadweight.

Bound together, the seven cylinders made a bundle the size of a big hatbox. I wound my arms around them and pushed off the wall.

The weight bore me down ten feet to the bottom of the crevice, fast. I kicked hard, fins almost tangling in the thick strands of kelp. I made it to open water and found the long diagonal of the anchor chain leading back up to the speedboat.

I was just leveling out to make a final push when I felt it. A regu-lar, ominous thrumming. Big propellers on big engines, churning the water.

Where? Sound in water echoed. There. Four o'clock and closing fast. I grabbed onto the anchor chain and floated, the heavy load of the diamonds in my other hand trying to pull me down.

A moment later I saw it. A fat, dark triangle on the surface, silhou-etted against the high sun, bearing down on the smaller triangle of the speedboat. A big powerboat. Maybe fifty feet in length, with twin props. It had come around the near edge of the island.

The rhythm of the props slowed as the big boat came alongside the speedboat. Bubbles rose to the surface from my breathing. Would they be visible on the soft surface waves?

I couldn't stay here. The cold was bad enough, but my air gauge was at zero. If I were lucky, I had two more minutes. I held tight to the black bundle of cylinders and followed the slope of the sea floor back toward the shelter of the crevice. Behind me there were hollow thumps. The two boats bumping against each other. Maybe someone jumping into the speedboat's cockpit.

My breath was coming fast, too fast to be just exertion. My lungs were trying to draw air where there was none. I was still twenty feet below and three times as far from shore. I wasn't going to make it to the crevice. Not with the cylinders slowing me down.

My breath stopped. The tank was dry.

I dropped the heavy bundle and fumbled to unsnap the vest clips, yanking myself free of the scuba gear and tank. They drifted slowly downward, chasing the bundle that had already disappeared into the darkness near the bottom. I surfaced as quickly as I dared, tearing off the mask and snorkel as I rose, until my head bobbed up out of the water like a seal's.

Floating a hundred feet away was the big powerboat. Not just any boat.

The *Francesca*.

For an instant I forgot all about the cold. What the hell was Hollis doing here? Had he somehow followed me? Or guessed that this was where I was headed? That sounded crazy.

I couldn't see Hollis anywhere aboard the *Francesca*. The speedboat was on the far side of the big cruiser, just out of my view. I heard voices. Two figures climbed up from the speedboat into the cockpit of the *Francesca*, and it felt for a moment like I was struggling for air from the empty tank once again.

Alec. And Boone McGann.

CHAPTER THIRTY-ONE

THE *FRANCESCA* BOBBED LAZILY on the gentle surface waves, its engines idling to keep it near to the anchored speedboat. It was sixty yards from where I was floating, about halfway down the long shallow cove of the island. I had a clear view of its port side.

The storm the night before had washed the big cruiser clean, and the bright noon sun gleamed off its metal stanchions and teak trim. It could have been a photo in an advertisement.

Alec climbed the ladder to the flying bridge at the very top of the boat. He was wearing a light blue hoodie and khaki pants, and his blond hair caught the sun. Alec took the helm, shifting the *Francesca* into slow reverse.

Boone came into view in the cockpit, a sliver of his tall frame just visible around the edge of the cabin. Salt in my eyes or not, I had no trouble recognizing what he was carrying: an M4 carbine. With a telescopic sight.

I ducked my head under the surface before either of them looked in my direction. Without the diving mask on, I swam almost blind back to the shore and felt my way into the shelter of the crevice. When I surfaced again, I was deep in the island's cleft, out of sight of the boat.

Alec was alive. Somehow he had escaped Ondine. Or she had set me up.

And he and Boone had hijacked the *Francesca*.

Which meant Hollis must be dead. Murdered. Probably only minutes after I'd seen him. I gripped the rock wall of the crevice, barnacles cutting into my palms through the gloves.

My chest was quivering. My body trying to force more circulation. Another ten minutes in the water and my limbs would be useless. I'd literally turn blue.

Think. I'd averaged about twenty knots in the speedboat getting to the island. The *Francesca* with its twin screws could manage a little more than half that over the ocean swells. Alec and Boone must have left the marina right on my ass for the big cruiser to catch up with me this quickly.

But there was no way they could have kept me in sight. So how the hell had they found the island?

The speedboat. Fuck. Of course it was the speedboat.

Alec must have tracked the old man's movements around town for weeks, using the GPS transmitter on his truck. So if Dono had visited his boat even once during that time, Alec would know about it. Of course he'd have put another transmitter on board.

I'd led them right to the diamonds. Like a goddamned bird dog.

I heard the *Francesca*'s engines roar once, then slow again to a steady thrum. Which way was it headed? I edged toward the mouth of the crevice to peer around the rocks.

The *Francesca* was making a wide arc, away from the island, and starting to circle back. The slow pounding of its props made a trail of white froth. Boone was climbing the ladder to join Alec up on the flying bridge. He was dressed in black trousers, black shirt, jungle boots. Carbine held almost lazily across his shoulder. Ready for hunting.

I was somewhere between very bad and truly fucked. I couldn't go ashore here. I'd be on the rocky beach with no shoes and no decent cover for thirty yards. Alec and Boone would spot me within seconds. And I sure as hell couldn't stay hidden where I was for much longer.

My .32 and Dono's weapons were aboard the speedboat. *Had been* aboard, I corrected myself. Boone and Alec would have taken them. They would also have taken the keys in the ignition, or disabled the outboard. Even if I could swim to the speedboat and board it without being spotted, it was a dead end.

I caught their voices on the light wind. Not words, just tones. Excited. Maybe angry. Alec was pointing toward the island.

It wasn't hard to guess their thinking. They assumed that I had anchored the speedboat and waded ashore. I must still be there, with the rest of Dono's treasure. I would have heard their boat approach. The best bet was that I was hiding somewhere in the three or four acres of fir trees and madrona and scrub that made up a haphazard forest in the center of the small island.

I realized I couldn't feel my feet in the fins. I clenched my arms and legs, hard, embracing the agony because it meant that the limbs were still responding.

Alec turned the wheel, and the *Francesca* straightened itself to point directly at the shore. Boone put a foot up on the dash and climbed right over the short windshield to jump down onto the roof of the cabin. Eager. He went up to the tip of the bow and waited as the boat edged closer to the island.

When it was about fifty feet from the beach, Boone stepped over the rail and dropped into the water. He began swimming ashore, an easy sidestroke that allowed him to hold the carbine over his head, same as I'd learned in the army.

Alec put the boat into reverse and began backing away. As I watched, he picked up another carbine and placed it on the dash in front of him.

Two M4s against my pair of swim fins. With the carbines' telescopic sights and time to aim, they could pick me off at a quarter mile. The island was barely twice that on the long side.

Of course, Boone and Alec didn't know I was unarmed. They thought I'd waded ashore, so logically I'd have at least a handgun with me. I'd have traded one of my thumbs for that to be true.

So the two hunters would take their time, reducing my chances of popping up and blowing Boone's head off. The smart approach would be for Boone to stay within sight of the boat and sweep the island slowly from one end to the other while Alec tracked him, watching for movement in the brush. They had hours of daylight left. If they carried handheld radios, all the easier for them. They could flush me like a pheasant, with the same result.

It was a solid plan. And it gave me a sliver of hope. Because so far they hadn't thought to look for me in the water.

I forced myself to take deep, full breaths, my chest fighting to expand against the crush of the cold. The *Francesca* was closer now, turning parallel to the shore, a hundred feet from the beach, backing slowly in my direction. They would start their sweep at this end of the island. Thirty-five yards from me. Thirty.

Now. The moment Alec put the *Francesca* into forward, even at a walking pace to keep up with Boone, my odds would go from slim to less than zero.

I dove. Or tried to. For a moment my limbs jerked clumsily before I got my legs kicking in rhythm, driving down.

The pressure even at five feet under felt like chisels jammed into my temples. The cruiser's big engines made a drumbeat I could feel all around me as the sound reverberated. It seemed to push me back as I fought against the current. My kicks were weaker.

I was out over the island shelf. Below me the bottom changed from the dull gray of the island's shore on my left to sudden black to my right as the shelf fell off toward the sea floor.

Then I finally saw her, the *Francesca*, all at once. A huge, dark mass, her shadow a black column. Her churning propellers painted circles of foam.

How close? Fifteen feet? Ten? I reached out toward her. There she was, right in front of me.

My hand banged against the stern swim platform. I grabbed at it, clutching my unfeeling fingers around one of the drainage slits.

As I did, the *Francesca* plowed forward. The propellers spun hungrily, six feet from my head. The wake bore me up to the surface. I gasped in a huge breath of air, hearing nothing at all over the engines and roiling water.

I tried to get an elbow up onto the platform. The push of the *Francesca's* wake was dragging me away from the boat. I got an arm up, grabbed the platform from the top this time, and heaved myself up and out of the water.

For a moment I lay on the teak platform staring dizzily at the foot-high letters spelling the boat's name in gold script across the white transom. Alec couldn't see me from up on the flybridge. But where was Boone? I craned my neck to see the beach. Boone's tall black figure was walking along the tree line, looking into the forest. If he turned around, there was no way he could miss me. I had to move.

I put a hand up on the transom and stood, tottering, and clambered into the cockpit. Ducked down below the rail, out of sight.

An eight-foot ladder led from the cockpit up to the flybridge. Maybe five more feet of open space to where Alec stood at the wheel. His carbine on the dash right in front of him. Could I reach him before he could grab it?

One breath. Another. The blood was returning to my limbs. My hands felt like I'd grabbed a stripped wire, but at least I could stand.

There was a fishing gaff strapped alongside the ladder, a sawed-off wooden shovel handle with a wicked steel hook bound to one end. I'd seen it on my previous visits to Hollis. My fingers didn't want to cooperate with one another. They tangled in the elastic cords as I pulled the gaff loose.

One more deep breath. And then I went up the ladder, as fast as I could move my feet, and took the last two rungs in a jump.

Alec's reflexes were excellent. He didn't turn toward the sudden noise, just lunged for a big Colt revolver hanging in its holster by the wheel. I swung the gaff wildly with my free hand. Its wooden haft came down like an ax onto his outstretched arm. The gun went off, the shot going skyward. The crack of it echoed off the island.

I dropped the gaff to grab Alec's shooting arm with both hands. He swung a haymaker, his fist glancing off the side of my head. I slammed his wrist onto the low windscreen, and the revolver fell, skittering across the cabin roof toward the foredeck.

Alec got a grip on my shoulder and head-butted me in the face. I felt something crack. Dazed, I bulled him backward. We slammed into the side of the bridge.

The cowling next to us exploded, sending splinters of fiberglass and teak into our faces. We both jerked back reflexively, breaking our clinch just as the high, supersonic *whap* caught up with the bullet. Boone. He was shooting at us from the beach. A second round tore a massive chunk out of the dashboard as my vision cleared.

Alec ducked away from the barrage, astonishment overwhelming the rage on his face. He scrambled for the M4 carbine on the dashboard. I launched myself off the wall and punched him with all my strength across one of his perfect cheekbones. The carbine skittered out of his hands and over the rail into the water. I clubbed him again, and he fell back onto the controls.

The *Francesca* leaped forward as if horsewhipped.

The sudden surge of the engines threw me backward. I hit the low canvas siding at the rear of the flybridge and crashed right over it, falling to land with a sledgehammer thud on my spine in the cockpit.

Everything slowed to the pace of drifting fog. I couldn't find the handrail to get up. I wasn't even sure I was reaching for it.

I saw the cabin window nearest me vaporize. Didn't hear it shatter or the crack of Boone's carbine. My ears were filled with nothing but a banshee keen.

In a sudden rush of clarity, I knew that Alec would go for the revolver. On the forward deck. The bow was that way. I should be moving.

A shuddering boom shook the boat, and I rolled across the cockpit. The *Francesca* was bouncing on the swells, big lunging leaps across each wave to crash down into the next. There was no one at the wheel. The boat was canted to starboard, the powerful engines carving a huge circle at full speed. Another shot whipped through the cabin windows.

Get up, boy. Dono's voice. *Kill the bastards.* Good idea. I got my legs under me.

I tried to focus. The *Francesca* was starting to draw parallel to shore again as she circled, the beach now a hundred yards off the starboard bow. I saw Boone, a miniature black stick figure, wading into the low surf. Swimming for the speedboat? No. Trying to get a better shooting angle around the rocks.

A noise behind me, port side. I fell to my left just as Alec came off the side deck and swung for my head with the gaff. The razor tip of the hook gouged my shoulder muscle. The boat hit a wave, and the impact flung us together. Alec tried to raise the gaff again, but we were too close. I got a hand under his chin and pushed. He dropped the gaff and clutched at my throat. I kept pushing. Trying to keep him from strangling me before my world went black. I was losing. Too tired.

Another wave smacked into the boat broadside. Alec and I were stumbling together like drunken dancers, down the slope of the tilted cockpit. The small of Alec's back hit the transom. The propellers carved a deep trough of thrashing water below us.

Both my hands pushed at Alec's chin now, my weight behind them. His head was over the stern, his body arched like a cliff diver's. He flailed crazily. I pushed harder. He made a long sandpaper sound as his nails tore at my scalp. Then red sprayed across us, a pretty fan shape.

Alec was two hundred pounds of wet cement, sagging to the teak floor of the cockpit, dragging me with him.

I was kneeling in a pool of blood. Mine? No. The inside of the transom was painted in crimson, where one of Boone's rounds had torn through his partner.

Boone. I needed the revolver. Anything. Where was the shore? I saw only ocean. Heard only the howl of the redlined engines.

To port, suddenly, there was a blur of stone and tree and surf. The boat was screaming past the tip of the crescent cove, past the huge wooden stump of the madrona tree. We were headed into the rocks.

Get to the helm. *Now, boy.*

Up the ladder, arms and legs grinding like rusted pistons. I flung myself at the wheel and spun it hard, knowing that it was too late, just as I saw Boone straight ahead. He was up to his thighs in the surf, teeth bared, his loose black shirt fluttering like wings. He raised the carbine to aim at me, his mouth forming a great O as the boat bore down on him.

Then a giant hand swatted me high into the air, a blow that spun me over and over like a guttering firework until its flame went black.

CHAPTER THIRTY-TWO

I WATCHED THE TINY CRAB, no bigger than a nickel, inch cautiously around the shape of a hand that was unfamiliar to both of us. I'd been watching the crab and the hand for a very long time, it seemed. The crab came closer to my nose. When I exhaled, it scuttled hastily away.

There was something behind me splashing, playing in the gentle waves. I wanted to look in that direction, but I wasn't sure how to do that. There was something important about the idea, though.

After a lot of thinking, I worked out how to stand up. Arm there, knee there. Easy as pie. I was twelve feet tall, and as thin as a drinking straw.

The world was very bright, except for the huge patch of shade a few yards away from where I tottered. The shadow of the beached *Francesca*.

She was completely out of the water, tilted pitifully on the rocks and sand. Looming above me like a church, thirty feet high. Behind her was the broad stripe she had gouged through the rock and sand, up from the sea.

My brain laboriously assembled the pieces. She'd been running nearly parallel to the shore when she'd hit. Another few degrees to starboard and she'd have missed the island completely. Instead the boat had beached itself at top speed. A fifty-foot-long, thirty-ton craft traveling at nearly twenty knots, crushing the brittle rock of the tidal pools in her path as efficiently as a diesel locomotive. She had massive holes in her fiberglass bottom, as if a gigantic mallet had splintered her sides.

I heard another splash. I staggered to my right, around the stern of the wounded cruiser. There was a big seal in the shallows, its black fins flapping, beating against the water.

I waded in shin-deep for a closer look. The sand moved treacherously under my feet.

The seal was Boone, lying on his belly in eighteen inches of water. He was half in and half out of the path that the boat had carved in the island. My brain vaguely warned me of danger, until I spotted his carbine. It was thirty feet from where Boone lay. The waves splashed around it, trying to push the weapon farther up onto the beach.

That was just about where the boat hit him, Dono's voice said, *and knocked his ass all the way to where you see him now.* The voice sounded joyous.

Boone ponderously raised his right arm and let it fall to slap the surface. His other arm was underneath him, pushing to keep his head just above the water. His legs were mostly buried in the shifting sand. They didn't move, even as his upper body twisted.

Again his arm rose and fell. A wave broke over him, and he coughed violently, flecks of something darker than salt water flying from his mouth.

I didn't think he knew I was there until his eyes rolled to meet mine. His mouth went wide in a horrible stained smile.

"Here," he said, so softly that the sound blended with the next wave. "Here. Burt. I'm here." He kept on saying it. "Here."

I walked forward and bent down, my mouth close to his ear.

"It's okay, brother," I said thickly. "I'm with you now."

He rasped something that sounded like relief. His supporting arm was trembling. Failing. The right arm rose once more, not even clearing the water this time. He sank a little lower, as another wave washed over the useless legs. His head dipped under, rose, dipped, and his long body gave a cruel, thrashing tremor that turned him halfway onto his side before it ended.

With Boone still, the only sound was the lulling wash of the surf. I was tired. I wanted to lie back down on the sand and sleep for days and days. I thought about lying next to Luce, and the memory made me turn and retrace my steps, following the gashed stripe of the *Francesca's* trail back out of the water.

Beached and tilted as the boat was, the swim platform at her stern was almost chest-high and canted like a playground slide for a small child. I crawled up onto it, on my hands and knees. My left hand wasn't right. Two of its fingers felt numb, and I couldn't make them squeeze the platform rungs very hard. Something under the fresh surgical scars on my forearm had twisted and broken again. The *Francesca's* transom had been unscathed by the disaster, and the gold paint of the boat's name sparkled cheerily in the sun. I carefully made my way over the transom into the cockpit.

I'd forgotten about Alec.

His pale body lay against the leeward side of the cockpit, face turned to the wall as if in shame. Most of the teakwood on the floor was stained a dark wine color that carried over into pink on the white fiberglass edges. The sandflies had already found the feast. They flew into a small, frenzied tornado as I stepped past the body.

Once I was inside the boat's main cabin, I closed the sliding glass door to the cockpit. The quiet was better. There was enough to think about without hearing the flies buzzing.

It looked like a bomb had gone off in the interior of the *Francesca*. The thirty-degree tilt to port gave the cabin the appearance of a place in a fever dream. Every object that was loose had been thrown around, repeatedly. Everything breakable was broken. There was a foot-wide hole punched right through a thick cabinet door, maybe by one of Boone's bullets.

I needed to concentrate, to find where Hollis kept his satellite phone.

Guerin. It would have to be the detective.

All at once I was laughing. I'd found a fortune in diamonds, left it on the ocean floor, and wound up with two corpses and a demolished hulk for my trouble. The *Francesca* was a pretty fair representation of my life.

I started rummaging through the drawers nearest the boat's interior controls. Then I heard it. A light scuffling sound, like pieces of paper rubbing together. As I listened, I heard it again. It was coming from the bow of the boat, past the short flight of stairs leading down to the forward staterooms.

There was an old diving knife with a red rubberized handle in one of the drawers. I unsheathed the knife and took it with me.

I walked very slowly down the tilted stairs. There was the noise again, and something else with it. A grunt. It was coming from behind the closed door of the head, the boat's single bathroom. I reached out and twisted the knob—unlocked—and let the door swing open.

Hollis was lying curled up on his side on the cramped floor of the head, bound almost rigid with silver duct tape. Loops of the tape were wound around his ankles and calves and thighs and upper arms. His forearms clasped the toilet, and his wrists and hands were completely mummified on the far side of the porcelain basin.

"Hollis?" I said.

The lower half of his face was swathed in tight loops as well. He could still turn his neck, however, and he craned it to try to look back toward the doorway. His skin above the bandit's mask of tape was a furious red, striped with maroon splotches of blood.

One of Hollis's bright blueberry eyes went wide as I stepped into the head and started sawing at the tape around his arms. His other eye was puffed shut. Even with the serrated back edge of the dive knife, it took me a few minutes to get his arms and encased hands loose from the toilet.

He pushed himself into a seated position and pointed angrily with one mittenlike hand at his face—do this first—and then sat very still as I unwound the tape from his head. When I peeled the last bit of tape from his mouth, it took strips of skin with it, and his lips gushed blood.

"Wher ah dey?" he said as thick dribbles of red fell down the front of his sweat-drenched shirt. The same yellow shirt he'd been wearing when he and I had shared drinks and toasted Dono.

"Hang on," I said. I gathered a wad of toilet paper from the roll on the wall and pressed it to Hollis's mouth. He held it in place with one wrapped hand while I worked on cutting the tape off his legs. Finally everything was free except his hands. He took the pink mass of tissue away from his mouth and said, "'M cramping like fugg. I have to moob."

He couldn't stand on his own. The muscles in his legs were shaking like leaves in a strong wind, and I wasn't strong enough at the moment to lift him. Together we got him onto his knees and then fully upright and leaning back against the sink counter of the head. I started unwrapping his hands.

"Oh, Jesus, Van," he said.

He started weeping. I let him. I handed him another wad of toilet paper, and he dabbed at his eyes and his lips until the shaking finally stopped and his breath was even again.

"Tell me," Hollis said.

"Alec and Boone are dead. So is your boat. Sorry."

"Yeah, I figured tha' part. I mean you. What happened to you?"

"You first."

"You lef' in the speedboat. About two minutes later, that fucker Boone came jumping over the side and pistol-whipped me. He and Alec must have been hiding out in one of the boats nearby on the dock. They didn't ask me shit. Boone just got his rocks off beating on me while his boyfriend played with some computer gadget."

"They were tracking the speedboat. My stupidity in action. I'm sorry, Hollis. They needed your boat to follow me."

He frowned at me, and the blood welled up on his lip again. "And if they hadn't? They'd have killed me outright. They told me as much. The only reason I'm still drawing breath is because the fuckers wanted a backup plan, in case you didn't lead them to Dono's score. They'd get in touch with you and offer to trade me for the diamonds. Not that you'd be that much of an idiot."

"I might have made that trade."

"Don't be daft," he said.

"I've already lost Dono. When I saw Alec and Boone on the *Francesca*, I thought you were dead, too. I didn't care for the feeling."

"Well, lad." Hollis gave me a broken smile. "We've no worries about it now. You said the two bastards are where they belong?"

I let him try his legs. He eased past me, both hands on the downslope wall as he worked his way up the stairs into the fun-house tilt of the main cabin.

Hollis took a long moment to survey the damage. He shrugged. "Not so bad as all that."

He made his slow way through the cabin. When he looked out the sliding glass door to the cockpit, he stopped short.

After a moment he turned back to me. "Alec?"

"Yeah," I said, nodding. I sat on a bench without bothering to clear the broken trash and papers off it.

He opened the door and looked down at Alec's corpse and the charnel mess of the cockpit floor. The swarm of flies sounded like it had doubled in number.

"Where's Boone?" Hollis said.

"Ten yards off the stern."

Hollis paused and then carefully circled the high edge of the cockpit, holding on to the rail to keep from stumbling into the worst of it. He looked over the transom and down to the beach. The tide was going out, I knew. I wondered how much of Boone would be covered in sand by now.

Finally Hollis turned around and came back into the cabin. He closed the door and managed to get himself into the captain's chair at the interior controls.

"And the day's not half over yet," he said.

"Maybe the island will sink." I was very thirsty. I got up and lurched back down the crooked steps to the galley. Some of the cabinets hadn't been latched and had swung open during the *Francesca*'s crash into the island. The sinks and counters and floor of the tiny alcove were dusted with a mixture of ground coffee and Quaker Oats.

In the icebox I found a six-pack of plastic water bottles and brought them back up to the cabin. Hollis was leaning forward in the chair, dabbing at his mouth.

"My tooth's fucking broken," he said.

I handed him one of the bottles. "Let this warm up before you take a swig, or you'll really feel it."

"I think the occasion calls for something stronger." He got up and went to the liquor cabinet. "Put something on your shoulder. You're making a butcher's block of the place."

He was right. Alec had torn a quarter-size chunk out of my deltoid with the fishing gaff. I had forgotten. The rest of my body was making enough thudding noise to drown the jangling sting of blood seeping out. There were little notes of it dotting the carpeted cabin floor.

I searched through the debris around the room and found two T-shirts, one dark blue and one bright orange with a faded stencil of a mermaid on it. Both shirts looked older than I was. I folded the orange one into a thick square and poured half of one of the bottles of water on it. I put the square on my shoulder. The trickles of water carved little canyons down my side through the layer of grime and sand. I put the blue T-shirt on over the makeshift bandage to hold it in place.

I downed the rest of the bottle of water and then another. A sugary cloud of liquor fumes wafted over from the cabinet that Hollis was gingerly poking through. "Anything survive?" I said.

"Not unless you have an unquenchable thirst for club soda. Jesus, why did I ever buy that?"

"Hollis, do you have a scuba tank? A full one."

"Hmm? Yeah, of course. I keep the gear on board, in case the anchor rope snags on something. It's been a while since I've checked it." He stopped and looked up at me. "You going after the diamonds?"

I nodded. He hurried back to the stern of the boat, toward the engine room.

The image of the black hexagonal tubes spiraling out of sight into the ocean clouded every other thought. I'd let the bundle go in thirty feet of water, not far from the drop-off that fell ten times that depth to the floor of the strait. One storm, one surging current, and they'd be gone forever.

And I wanted to *see* the diamonds for myself. See what Dono had risked so much for.

See what had made him call me home.

"At least he can rest now," I said out loud as Hollis came stumbling back to the stairs, treading uphill against the tilt of the cabin. A black rubber diving mask and a regulator set were draped around his neck. He dragged what looked like a stainless-steel tank up the steps toward me.

"You buy all that from Captain Nemo himself?" I said.

"What? Oh, funny man. It's old, but it fucking well works. What was that you were mumbling as I came in?"

"I was saying that Dono would have liked to see this."

"And do you imagine he's not? Your man is laughing his ass off right now—don't you doubt it." The sweat had finally dried from his hair, and his orange-white curls stood up like he'd touched an outlet.

I screwed the regulator set onto the tank with my good right hand. The tank showed about three-quarter pressure. Maybe twenty minutes' worth, if I could stay in the shallows.

Hollis sat down heavily in the captain's chair. "I'm as eager as anyone, boyo, but are you sure this is smart? You don't look exactly in top form."

"I'll be fine. And if I'm lucky, the diamonds will be right where I left them."

Hollis's face told me he thought I'd burned through enough good fortune today, but he just cracked the seal on his water bottle and drank from it like it was Bushmills.

"What's the plan?" he said.

"I'm going to swim out to the speedboat, see if I can get it started, and bring it in close to shore. You strong enough to wade out to it carrying the scuba tank?"

"Yeah, not a problem."

"We could get you a life vest," I said.

"Fuck you right back. Try not to run Dono's boat aground. One a day is enough."

Within twenty minutes Hollis was setting the anchor of the speedboat above where I'd dropped the diamonds. I was sitting on the bow, fitting the straps of the scuba tank around my shoulders. The wound in my shoulder had subsided to a dull throb.

"You get those diamonds," Hollis said, pointing at me, "and you could vanish. So far away that even the fucking army couldn't find you if they tried."

I put the mask on. "Maybe there's a way to have a taste and the bottle to spare."

He grinned. "That's one of your granddad's."

"I know." I put the regulator in my mouth and dropped into the water.

CHAPTER THIRTY-THREE

WITH NO BUOYANCY VEST, I was pulled down by the weight of the steel tank. I had to start kicking immediately to slow my descent. The cold clutched at me again.

I kicked over to the anchor chain, cupped a hand on it, and let myself sink. The pressure built, and every few yards I tightened my hold on the chain to stop and give my ears some time to adjust.

At thirty feet I felt the tension that thrummed through the chain slacken.

The chain's slant flattened out, curved, came to rest in one of the loose patches of kelp. Clumps of the thick seaweed waved gently in the current, all their strands pointing toward the open water of the strait.

I looked back up the long curve of the chain. Fifty feet to the surface. Not far, but already I couldn't see the boat. Just a wide cloud of bluish color in place of the sky.

Hollis and I had dropped anchor at the place where I remembered surfacing, after first seeing the *Francesca* and letting the bundle of cylinders sink to the bottom. If the bundle had sunk straight down from where I'd released it, it should be nearby.

I could see clearly for about eight feet, by the beam of the flashlight held in my weak left hand. Everything beyond fifteen feet might as well be a solid wall. I swam around the anchor in widening circles, through the storm of mud and silt that my fins stirred up, peering at every thicket of seaweed to see if the black cylinders were hiding within.

Five minutes passed as I traced that spiral path. Ten minutes.

A wave grabbed the flashlight beam, made it quiver. I realized that the wave was my own shivering, strong enough to make my whole arm shudder. I was running out of time.

The cylinders weren't here. They hadn't come to rest where I'd dropped them.

So where?

If the current had been strong enough to get the heavy bundle rolling, they would have fallen outward, away from the island, toward the deeper sea.

Toward the drop-off.

I'd seen the numbers on the depth sounder in Dono's speedboat when I'd first approached the island. The water had gone from near a thousand feet to five hundred to one hundred in the course of a minute. After that, the underwater slope of the island had become much more gradual, up onto the shore where the *Francesca* lay now, beached.

Nine minutes left on the gauge. Time enough for a quick look. I swam in that direction, the flashlight shining feebly into the dark.

Or at least what I'd thought was dark.

When I reached the edge of the drop, I learned what dark really was.

The land fell off at an angle steeper than a ski jump. The depths swallowed the tiny bit of light still present and gave away nothing.

Staring blankly into that void, I realized just how ridiculous my search was. If the bundle had fallen all the way down there, they might as well be on the moon. It would take an atmosphere suit and a lot more diving experience than I had to reach the bottom. I could sense the crushing weight of it from where I knelt, at the tipping point.

A muted flash of yellow. A fish, maybe, darting between the strands of seaweed. No, there it was. Ten feet away. I half swam, half climbed down the slope to it.

A bungee cord. Goddamn. A yellow bungee cord.

I looked around, almost frantic. Where were the rest? If one cord had come off, had they all? Were the black rubber cylinders scattered nearby?

The cord had probably been knocked off when the bundle touched bottom. It wouldn't have floated far before tangling in the kelp. So that point of impact must be near. If the bundle had stayed intact, it could be just below me.

I checked the gauge again. Three minutes. Less, if I went deeper. And that didn't count the time to surface.

I had to look.

I swam straight down the slope, sweeping the flashlight from side to side. The pressure increased, mercilessly. I equalized my ears and kept going.

The black was almost overwhelming. Ninety feet. One-twenty. It was too easy, falling down the underwater mountain.

My skull was in a vise. I hadn't felt a headache this bad since Ranger School, when they'd kept us awake for most of a week, with endless drills and tactical exercises. Droning. That's what we called it, dead on your feet, eyes wide open. My vision blurred.

Focus. I could go a little farther.

And a little farther still.

Something grabbed me and shook me, not outside but in my mind. *This is stupid, boy.*

Right. Absolutely right. I'd never make the surface from here, not if the air ran out. As it was, I'd be ascending so fast I'd risk the bends. Time to leave.

I turned, reaching out to touch the slope, stop my descent, and get myself oriented toward the surface. My hand was numb enough that I barely felt the mud force my fingers apart.

But I did feel the thump of something hard, tumbling in my clumsy wake, bumping against my knuckles.

I picked it up and stared at it hazily for a moment, the thick, hexagonal cylinder throwing off clumps of mud into the flashlight beam. I was dreaming, obviously. Nitrogen narcosis.

No. Here it was.

A treasure, right there in my hand.

And there was another cylinder, a couple of yards up the slope and to my left, standing almost vertical in the mud.

I swam to it. My deadened fingers didn't want to release the flashlight. I had to drop the light to pick up the cylinder and get it under my other arm, both of them cradled like footballs.

Enough.

Enough. I kicked hard, my legs reluctantly responding. The glow of the flashlight lying on the ocean floor retreated, became a dot, vanished below me. Nothing in the world but me now, and the black. I kept kicking, exhaling steadily to let the expanding air leak from my lungs. Rising alongside the bubbles, but no faster.

How far had I gone? With my hands full, I couldn't reach around to grab the gauge. I made myself stop before the sudden pressure change did very bad things to my joints. I couldn't feel the containers under my arms. Maybe I had dropped them. I looked down to check before I realized I couldn't see them either.

And then the air hose jerked once, my lungs grabbing at nothing. Hollis's tank was dry.

The bends would be better than drowning. I kicked again. Air in my lungs swelled and forced its way out of my mouth. The steel tank dragged at me, but there was no time to get myself free of it.

There. The cloud above me was definitely lighter now. Not as bright as the firecrackers exploding in my head. Almost.

I saw a flatness, the underside of the sky.

And then I saw nothing.

"JESUS GOD, KID. YOU scared the holy shit out of me."

I was in the water. Mostly. My head was out, and I took my first conscious breath, deep, before coughing it painfully back out. I looked up to see Hollis, leaning way down from the stern of the speedboat. He had a grip on the shoulder strap of the scuba tank and was holding me above water.

Hollis's voice was strangely high and fast. "You bobbed up next to the boat, went faceup, and then you started to drift back down. Thank Christ you were close enough for me to snag you with the boat hook." He shook me. "Are you all right? Say something, you mad son of a bitch."

Where were the cylinders? My arms were drifting aimlessly at my sides. I looked down dazedly. Maybe I could dive again, catch them before they got too far. . . .

"I've got the tubes here, lad. Don't worry. You were hanging on to them like they were your own babes."

"Get this damn thing off me," I said. We managed to undo the straps, and he heaved the tank up into the boat. I followed, with a lot more effort on both our parts. I lay against the side of the cockpit, too tired to even remove my fins. Hollis gave me a towel, and I rubbed at my limbs until they turned a raw pink while Hollis saw to the tank and gear. Before long I felt like I was past the danger of toppling over.

Hollis picked up one of the cylinders. He shook it gently, making a muffled rattle. "Are these what I pray they are?"

"All we'll get."

He handed the cylinder to me. The black rubber exterior was dirty and slightly pitted by the seawater. I twisted the end off, exposing a screw cap inside. I opened it and poured some of the contents into my hand.

They weren't cut or polished, but still unmistakable. Diamonds. Silver-white, the largest about the size of my thumbnail. Ice that would never melt away.

Here, Dono had said to me, his hand gripping mine.

Not only trying to tell me where the little hunk of madrona wood came from. But *here,* this place that only you and I know.

Here, this is yours.

After Ondine's cut I estimated that Dono had walked away with the market value of about four million dollars. Seven cylinders in the cooler. If each cylinder held the same amount of diamonds, that meant I had over half a million dollars in my hand.

Putting it another way, at my current pay grade I was holding about thirteen years' worth of salary. A quarter of a century, if you counted the other cylinder.

"The loveliest ugly rocks I've ever seen," Hollis said.

"Glad you approve."

He nudged me in the ribs with his foot. "Don't ever fucking do that to me again."

"Next time you go." I kicked the fins away and eased myself up to sit in the pilot's chair.

Hollis grunted. "And you said the rest are gone?"

"Not gone. Just way out of reach."

He thought about it, shrugged. "Still, a damn good day's work. Maybe if we come back with proper gear and some lights . . ."

Maybe. Or maybe the diamonds would be of more use to me if they stayed right where they were.

I was beyond tired. I wanted to curl up in the tiny cabin of the speedboat and sleep for a month.

"Let's take what we need off the *Francesca*," I said, "and go home."

We beached the speedboat and waded ashore to Hollis's boat. We went in the side door, to avoid stepping over Alec's body again. Hollis began packing up his personal effects, and I raided the *Francesca*'s rapidly warming refrigerator. I was ravenous. When Hollis came back to the main cabin, I was eating cold cuts straight from the plastic bag.

He looked past me to the main cabin. "That's not mine," he said.

It was a large brown leather satchel, half buried under one of the piles of clothes and other crap thrown around when the *Francesca* hit the shore.

I retrieved the satchel and opened it. Inside it was clothing, and a Glock pistol, and a canvas bag holding something large and squarish. A leather wallet and some papers—scattered receipts, a Seattle street map, a bus ticket—were tucked in an inside pocket.

"Boone's," I said, glancing at the dark, gaunt face on the Illinois driver's license.

"Shitheel," said Hollis, going back to forage for his belongings.

Maybe the Glock was the same gun that Boone had fired at me at Julian Formes's apartment. Any evidence would help. I took out the canvas bag and looked inside.

Bundles of cash. Still in their blue plastic wrap. The spoils that Boone had taken from Cristiana Liotti's apartment after killing her. I put the canvas bag back into the satchel. A dead woman's money, shrouded in a dead man's clothing.

"At least you can get your life in order again," Hollis called from the forward stateroom. "Get your truck back from the cops, see the house one more time before you have to leave."

I nodded without really thinking about it, looking around for anything I might take with us, still preoccupied with the cash. There was something bothering me about it, maybe not this money but a different stack of cash. And Hollis had said something too, about the truck. . . .

A cold snake writhed in my stomach.

I walked quickly back to the satchel, opened it again, and took out Boone's papers. Found his bus ticket. Leaving Stockton at 11:20 P.M. the past Saturday night. Arriving Seattle 7:40 P.M. Sunday night.

At least fourteen hours after Dono was shot.

I felt like I was back down in the black again, the pressure caving in my chest.

I'd been blind. Focused solely on Boone and Alec, the stone killers who were right in front of me. I had never questioned if there might be someone else.

But there had to be someone, the beast snarled inside me. *You just didn't see it.*

Maybe I just didn't want to.

CHAPTER THIRTY-FOUR

I STOOD IN THE STORAGE room of the Morgen, looking down at Dono's casket.

Somebody had cleared the room of all the cases of food and whiskey, but it was still a small space. The casket and the flower stand with its wreath of white roses took the lion's share. The mortuary attendant and I took most of the rest. Big Willard had to stand out in the hallway.

The lid of the box was closed. The attendant looked at me. I nodded, and he withdrew a hex key and unlocked and opened the top half of the casket lid. He and Willard walked silently back toward the main room of the bar.

Dono's skin had a slight sheen to it, like the casket's varnish. His gray hair was brushed back flat against his scalp. He didn't look peaceful. He didn't look angry. He had no expression at all.

The funeral home had dressed him in a navy blue suit with matching tie and white shirt. I didn't know if the clothes were his or bought by Willard for the occasion. Dono had been shot behind the left ear, but that side was turned to the back of the box.

Someone came up in the hallway behind me. It was one of the junior attendants, returning with the sash for the wreath.

"Get out," I said.

When I turned back to the casket, I saw that Dono had his wedding ring on. He must have mentioned it in the funeral instructions he'd left with Ganz. Even I wouldn't have thought to hunt through the house for the ring, much less put it on him.

For your grandmother. If I'm going to see her again, I'd better be wearing it.

"You should have sent for me earlier," I said. In the small room, my voice bounced around the walls, hollow. "You didn't need the goddamn diamonds."

There was no answer. I left him.

The main room was nearly empty. A couple of women in white shirts and black bow ties were setting up a buffet of food at the far side. The bar tables and chairs had been left in place for people to sit where they wanted. A microphone stand was in the center of the small stage.

The front door opened, and Willard and another girl in caterer's clothes came in from the alley. They were both carrying cases of wine. Willard wore a brown tweed suit made of enough fabric to cover a small car. He closed the door behind them, and they took the cases to the bar. The girl began opening them while Willard made a circuit of the room, checking everything.

"We're about set," he said as he lumbered past me. "You want me to open up?"

"Yeah."

He went back and unlocked the door and opened it wide. I stayed where I was, just out of the room.

There was a small crowd of people waiting outside. Jimmy Corcoran was first through the door, shouldering his way through the throng. He was followed by a couple of men I recognized, although they were a lot older than when I'd last seen them. Dono's associates, from back in the day. They filed in, shaking hands with Willard like he was a retired heavyweight champ greeting high rollers at a casino.

Luce came in next, leading Addy Proctor. Addy was wearing a black sweater and gray pants, with a black knit shawl draped over her shoulders. Her spiky white hair looked like it was freshly cut. Luce had on a black knee-length dress with two-inch heels, which made Addy look even shorter beside her.

Luce looked around the room and spotted me lurking in the side passageway. She gave me a sad smile. I smiled back. It made my face hurt.

Damn near all of me hurt. It had been only the previous afternoon when Hollis and I had left the island. We'd pounded the speedboat through the evening darkness down the straits as fast as we could stand it. When we finally reached Seattle, I'd dropped the exhausted Hollis off at a motel.

But I'd had one more stop to make before I could rest.

Finally I'd driven to Luce's to crash. I had called Detective Guerin on the way, to offer him a deal. I would hand him Dono's killer—and maybe more. And he wouldn't arrest me until he absolutely had to.

Another handful of people drifted in from the alley. Family types, maybe neighbors or some of Dono's old contracting clients. Ephraim Ganz came in, wearing a double-breasted suit in a dark purple-black. He looked a little lost. He peered around until he saw me and made a beeline.

"Hi, kid," he said, shaking hands. "How you doing?"

"Thanks for coming, Ephraim."

"I don't think I've been in this place in twenty years. I hardly recognize it. 'Cept for that thing." He pointed at the medieval tapestry.

I saw Hollis by the door, talking with Willard. Hollis had borrowed a dark blue corduroy suit from somewhere, and it actually fit him better than most of his own clothes. His face was still pink and swollen, but his cuts had scabbed over. He nodded toward the stage, and Willard patted him roughly on the arm and walked over. He ignored the microphone and let his rumbling mixer of a voice quiet the crowd.

"Okay," Willard said. "Thanks for coming. Dono Shaw was a hell of a friend to me. In a good way, I mean. To lots of you, too. Dono asked that Luce—Miss Boylan—start us off today."

He sat down. Luce walked to the stage. She looked good. Her blond hair was swept back from her forehead in sleek ribbons, held there by some mysterious product, and small silver earrings accented a thick chain around her neck. Someone, Corcoran maybe, whistled low.

Luce held up a sheet of paper. "This might not be what you'd hear at other services," she said. "But you all know that Dono was not your ordinary guy. He told me once that this song was one he and his late wife held dear."

She began to sing. She had a high voice, not perfect, but clear and strong.

> For to see Mad Tom of Bedlam,
> Ten thousand miles I've traveled.
> Mad Maudlin goes on dirty toes,
> For to save her shoes from gravel.
> Still I sing bonny boys, bonny mad boys,
> Bedlam boys are bonny,
> For they all go bare, and they live by the air,
> And they want no drink nor money.

There were surprised sounds from the crowd, and a brush of laughter from Dono's associates at the back.

I knew the song. Dono had an old long-playing record of it, sung by three women, with only a bodhran keeping a steady beat to back up the voices. An ancient poem of madness and defiance. Not your average dirge.

Luce waited until the noise had quieted.

> No gypsy, slut or doxy
> Shall win my mad Tom from me.
> I'll weep all night, with stars I'll fight,
> The fray shall well become me.
> So drink to Tom of Bedlam,
> Go fill the seas in barrels.
> I'll drink it all, well brewed with gall,
> And maudlin drunk I'll quarrel.
> Still I sing bonny boys, bonny mad boys,
> Bedlam boys are bonny,

For they all go bare, and they live by the air,
And they want no drink nor money.

Luce's last note died away. Her song had held everyone rapt, me included, and it was a moment before the applause started.

Over the sound of the clapping, there was a clunk from the back of the room. I turned to see Mike Tolan holding the door open for his mother, Evelyn, the family slipping in under the cover of the clapping. Davey let the door close itself. Luce walked across the room to greet them as Willard stood up again.

"So if anyone'd like to say anything, there's the mike," he said. "Whenever the mood strikes you. And if your mood needs some help, there's the bar."

Laughter from the crowd. Addy Proctor stepped up to the microphone and started telling a funny story about when she'd moved onto the block and finagled Dono into helping her fix her porch light. I joined Hollis by the door.

"You look like I feel," he said.

"It's almost over."

"Christ, it's just getting started. When word about the diam— about what happened at the island gets out, our lives are headed to hell in a bullet train. Every kind of cop you can name is going to want a piece of this."

One of Dono's legitimate clients was on the stage now, saying something about Dono's work on his home and how Dono was a true craftsman. Nobody paid much attention. The guys like Corcoran and Willard at the back of the room, the ones with the really interesting stories about Dono, would never tell them. At least not someplace where the tales might count as evidence.

Luce had taken a seat at a table against the back wall, with Davey. Mike wove his way toward them through the crowd from the bar, carrying a bottle of Redbreast whiskey and shot glasses. He caught my eye and waved me over.

As I crossed the room, people kept stopping me—all of them citizens, like the liquor distributor for the Morgen or the guy who fixed Dono's truck. Each shook my hand and gave his condolences. I nodded and said thanks and excused myself. I'd done all the mourning I could for one day.

At the table Mike was filling the three shot glasses. Davey already had a tumbler in front of him. Mike clapped a big mitt on my shoulder and passed me a glass. I sat down. Luce gave me a short but serious kiss. Davey downed the last of his whiskey and held it out to Mike for a refill. His eyes were on the stage, where another speaker had taken the microphone.

"You gonna get up and talk?" Mike said to him.

Davey snorted. "You're the one who always kissed Dono's ass. You go. It's your last chance."

"Davey," said Luce, glancing at me.

"It's nothing," Davey said. "Van knows it's nothing, don't you, Van?"

I sipped the whiskey. My throat was still raw from nearly drowning at the island, and the good liquor burned like acid. I set the glass back down.

"You and Dono never liked each other," I said.

"Never liked?"

"All right. You hated him."

Davey grinned. Now we were talking. "He hated me first."

"But not best. Dono didn't care enough about you to really hate you, Davey."

Mike looked back and forth between Davey and me as we stared at each other across the scarred wood of the table. My fingers were tight around the shot glass.

"The fucker kicked you out of town," Davey said.

"No. Leaving Seattle was my idea."

"You might have stayed with me and Mike. Ma would have let you."

"It was time for me to grow up. Take some responsibility."

"Bullshit," Davey said. "You're making excuses for him. Do you know why Dono asked you to come home? He wanted to twist the knife a little." Davey's voice was high. People glanced over from nearby tables. "Dono was giving the bar to Mikey. Yeah. The old fucker wanted to tell you to your face that you were disowned."

"What the hell are you talking about?" said Mike.

Davey toasted him. "Congrats, little bro. Free drinks for life."

Luce looked as puzzled as Mike. "No one else knew about that." Her expression changed as she stared at Davey. "You were here at the bar. The night Dono told me he was leaving his share of the place to Mike."

"Hey, it's not like I meant to listen in," Davey said. "I was headed out the back for a smoke, and I passed the office and heard Dono talking to you about Van. Of course I stopped." Davey looked at me. "Sorry, man."

"Must have been a shock," I said. "Your brother getting the Morgen."

Davey scowled. "It should have gone to family. To you."

Something tickled at my brain, but I set it aside. It wasn't important. Not yet.

I caught Jimmy Corcoran's eye and waved for him to come over. He grimaced. Willard and Hollis trailed after him. Mike and Luce looked at me questioningly.

When the three men reached the table, none of them took a chair.

"Hello, Lucille," Hollis said to Luce. "Thanks for hosting the party."

Corcoran nodded at me. "Sorry for your loss, kid."

"I need your expert opinion, Jimmy," I said. "How good are the white-collar cops here in Seattle? The computer-forensics unit."

Corcoran looked at me like I was nuts. "You wanna talk here?"

"Just the basics. If the cops had somebody's computer, what could they find out from it?"

"Okaaay," he said. "Well, unless the guy was some genius type, I'd say the cops could find everything. What's on the computer and every place that it had been on the Web, by stripping the internal drives and hunting around the net for traces of the machine's IP address. Stop me if I'm going too fast for you."

"I'll manage. So wherever the computer's owner hid something—"

"The cops would find it," said Corcoran. "Might take a while, but I'll give the pricks credit. They're good."

Willard nodded. "The cops even got some pet geeks on call. Those guys just love to hunt each other down, like some kind of pissing contest."

Luce looked at me. "You're talking about the laptop."

"What laptop?" said Mike.

"I found a computer," I said, "which belonged to a man who planted bugs in Dono's house. He recorded everything that happened in the house, for weeks."

"The night Dono was shot," Mike said. "Holy shit."

"I had the computer in my hand," I said. "But I had to stash it in the truck, and then the truck went missing."

Hollis nodded eagerly. "You told me the cops impounded it while you were avoiding their company. Don't they have the damned gadget?"

I shook my head. "The police never got the chance. They weren't the ones who took the truck. And they don't have the computer."

"So it's gone?" said Corcoran. "All that work for fucking nothing?"

Luce put her hand over mine.

"And you'll never know who did it?" said Davey.

"I already know who, Davey," I said. "You killed him."

CHAPTER THIRTY-FIVE

AROUND US THERE WAS still the buzz of conversation. But it retreated, shrank down until it felt like only Davey and I were at the table. Even Luce seemed miles away.

"If this is a joke, man," said Davey, "you lost me somewhere."

"I should've been clued by the money," I said. "Dono always kept a stack of cash in the house, for emergencies. But there was no money when I searched his hiding place the day he was shot. I knew that some cop hadn't found and pocketed the roll. Any cop would have also tagged the guns and other illegal shit hidden there as evidence."

Davey frowned. "So maybe Dono was broke."

"You knew that hiding place from when we were kids, Davey," I said. "And how to get into it."

"I didn't take any money when I got that bag of clothes and stuff for you, Van. I swear."

"You'd taken it already, and spent it. You were throwing fifties around, here at the bar when we first met last week. And you bought Juliet that expensive necklace the day after. I should have looked more closely at that, too. Back when we were teenagers, every time you had cash in your pocket, it never lasted more than a day."

"Van, you're not thinking right," said Davey. "I mean, you're wiped fucking out."

"But even with all that, I still didn't see you for Dono's killer. Until yesterday."

"Look at you, man. You're so spaced you can barely sit up straight."

"I found the truck, Davey."

I felt the crowd press in a little. It was hard to read Davey's face. His bright blue eyes held mine steadily.

"When you brought me the duffel bag from the house, you told me you'd looked for the truck where I'd left it in the garage. You said that it was gone when you got there. That was a lie."

"I never saw the damn truck," Davey said, loud enough to make Luce and Mike lean back in surprise. "That's why I lent you Julie's car, thanks very goddamn much."

"You went to the truck. You knew that the laptop was inside, that it might lead me to Dono's killer. You knew all that because I was dumb enough to tell you why the laptop was important, why you had to risk going to the truck with cops hunting through every inch of downtown for me. The laptop was there, and you had to get rid of it."

"Van, you're not hearing me. I didn't care about the fucking computer. Because I *didn't shoot Dono*."

"You had to get rid of the laptop. You couldn't just remove it from the truck. It would be obvious who'd taken it. So you stole the whole damn truck instead. Jumped the engine and drove it right out of the garage. Ballsy."

Davey was shaking his head no, over and over. But I thought I saw a flash of pride.

"You were in a hurry," I said. "You had to meet me at the library. But you had to hide the truck first. Not a lot of places to do that near downtown, not if the cops might be combing every garage."

Davey grabbed the bottle and poured himself another shot. Mike stared at his brother, looking as if someone had hit him in the back of the head with a plank.

"There's a gravel lot off Steinbrueck Park," I said to Mike, "under the viaduct. It's a pay lot where some of the cruise-line people leave their rides. Sometimes for weeks at a time. Just drop twenty bucks and your keys in the box, then pay the rest when you come back. A good place to stash a car."

I tried a second sip of the whiskey. It was warm from being in my hand, and it went down easier.

"It's the same place Davey and I would use when we were kids and we'd boost a car to go joyriding. Or to sell it."

Davey was staring at me. His mouth was set in a thin line. It wasn't pride I had seen. It was defiance.

"You drove the truck out of the garage," I said. "And you took it to the best place you knew to hide it. Trouble was, I knew it, too."

"You fucking punk," muttered Corcoran from where he stood. Davey shrank back.

While I'd been talking to Davey, a group had gathered around us. Maybe a dozen men or more. Luce had left the table. If there were any citizens left in the bar other than Mike, I didn't see them.

"Last night," I said, "I went looking. I found the truck in the lot off Steinbrueck. The cops have it now. And Julian Formes's laptop. You had to leave that in the truck. You couldn't be carrying it when you met me."

"Van," said Davey. He reached a hand across the table, placed it on my arm. "Van. The truck might have been where you say, all right? But I wasn't the one who put it there."

"You were," I said. "It'll be easy enough to prove. Fingerprints in the truck, maybe. You must have caught a cab back to the library, probably from in front of the Marriott or the Edgewater. The driver will remember you."

"Circumstantial," Davey said. If I hadn't been watching his face, I wouldn't have made out the word.

Willard was behind Davey, his shadow falling across Davey's shoulder.

Hollis nudged me on the shoulder. "No reason to talk about all this now," he said. His voice was almost a whisper. "We can take our time later."

I looked at Hollis and around the table at Corcoran and Willard and the others. Hard men. Angry.

"If anybody touches him," I said, "it'll be me."

Hollis stared at me for a moment. He nodded and eased off.

I turned back to Davey. "Yeah, all of that is circumstantial," I said. "But there's still the laptop. Before long the cops will be able to listen to each of the recordings. Including the conversation between you and Dono, right before you put the gun up against his head. That will be as good as a confession."

The bottle of Redbreast was almost empty. I poured the last of it into Davey's tumbler. "Unless you want to say it to my face."

He waited a long moment and then took the glass. His fingers were trembling. He wrapped his other hand around them.

"I told him," Davey said. "I told Dono about that night with Bobby Sessions and those two skinhead freaks. I told him you pulled my ass out of the fire and I saved you right back, before they could blow you away. If Dono had a soul, he should be fucking proud of you." Davey stared at his hands, holding the glass. "Instead you skipped town to get away from him, and now he leaves the bar to somebody else. He had to make it right."

"And you had a gun."

"I was wasted. I thought if Dono finally knew the whole story, he'd see that you deserved a fuck lot better from him." Davey shook his head no again. "When I told him, his eyes went dead. And then I thought, 'No, I'm dead. He's going to kill me.' He walked straight over to the side table, and I remembered that he kept a pistol in the drawer there. You showed it to me once."

I'd probably told Davey about the gun way back when I'd shown him Dono's hiding place. Just a kid, trying to seem cool.

Davey looked up finally, held my gaze. "I shot him. I didn't mean to." Somebody standing behind Willard cursed. Davey flinched at the sound. "I swear it."

"You should have told me what happened," I said. "Even if you couldn't turn yourself in, you should've told me."

"It was for you. I messed up, but I was trying to help. You know that, right?"

I didn't say anything. I didn't know what the answer was.

"Van," Willard said. "Clear out of here."

Jimmy Corcoran nodded. "We got this." Someone behind him laughed, one single humorless bark.

I looked across the table at the press of men.

"Davey's turning himself in," I said.

"Dono is our guy, too," said Corcoran. "Don't make this into something worse."

"Hey," Hollis said to him.

I stood up. "Nobody's stopped me yet, Jimmy."

Willard edged forward, half a step. Corcoran smiled.

"The police are coming." It was Luce. She elbowed her way through the circle. "I called them."

We all looked at her. Was she bluffing?

"Detective Guerin said they have a squad car on the block already," Luce said.

Hollis exhaled heavily. "Clever girl."

"Lucky," said Willard. I wasn't sure if he was talking to Davey or to me.

Luce glared at the men. "No more trouble over Davey Tolan. He isn't worth it."

I took Davey by the arm and got him up. He was nearly limp with fear. We could wait for Guerin outside.

The men blocking our way moved, just enough.

AGE ELEVEN

I'd been living in the Rolfssons' foster home for one hundred forty-two days. I knew the number exactly because I wrote it in the corner of each day on the Amazing Spider-Man calendar on my bedroom wall. I'd done the same thing every night at the Garbers' house before the Rolfssons—it had been a NASCAR calendar there—and at the foster home I'd been placed at before that one.

Added up, it was two hundred twelve days plus one hundred seventy-seven days plus the hundred forty-two at the Rolfssons' for a grand total of five hundred thirty-two. Five hundred thirty-three, really, counting the day that Granddad had been arrested at Farrelly's.

Twelve hundred and ninety-four days to go, in his five-year sentence. But I tried not to think about that.

Out in the living room, Aidan and little Roberta were shrieking at each other over whose turn it was to have the beanbag chair. Aidan was seven, and Roberta was six and much smaller, but she usually got her way.

It was the same every night. Carl and Loreen would let the little kids fight it out until *Wheel of Fortune* started, and then Carl would tell them to hush up. Everything Carl said sounded flat. He never looked at any of us when he talked.

He and Loreen weren't bad. Lazy, I guess. They liked to sit on the couch all the time. They took up most of it. But they never hit the little kids, and only Loreen would yell when things got too crazy. And they ordered pizza a lot.

There had been a fourth kid living with Carl and Loreen when I'd first arrived. A fourteen-year-old named Hunter. Hunter was fat—like Carl—but really strong and PO'd that he had to split his bedroom with a *turd* like me. He knew how to punch in the stomach, where it wouldn't show. The one time I'd tried to fight back, he'd hit me three hard smacks until I threw up on the lawn and had to clean up the mess with the garden hose before Loreen saw.

Carl and Loreen smoked pot a couple of times a week. Not in front of us. I knew because when I came home from school, the back patio would smell like old socks and burning wet leaves. Granddad used to cuss about the same smell wafting over from our neighbor's yard, back in the house.

One night I went into Loreen's purse and found the pot— I'd known what it looked like from cop shows—and took a few clumps of it out of her plastic bag. The clumps were sticky and smelled a lot stronger than the back patio did. I wrapped them up in a wad of paper towels to keep the smell down. Then I took a bunch of aluminum foil and wrapped it around the pot and one of Hunter's toy guns.

The toy looked pretty stupid, all covered in foil with lumps where the pot was. But I didn't know if the metal detectors at Ringdall High that Hunter was always bragging about—his new school was *"tough, turd,"* he said, it was *"hardcore"*—if the detectors would beep at anything metal or if they could actually see what stuff looked like inside kids' bags.

In the morning I shoved the toy way down to the bottom of Hunter's school backpack. About ten minutes later, he did his waddle-run out the door to catch the bus to Ringdall.

When I got home from school, Mr. Benbie was there. Mr. Benbie was the man from Social who shuffled me and other kids around homes. He was in the TV room talking to Aidan and Roberta, his thin body hunched forward and almost vibrating. He told me to have a seat—I plopped down in the beanbag chair—and Mr. Benbie went back to asking questions. Had they seen Mr. or Mrs. Rolfsson smoke anything, like a cigarette? The little kids kept shaking their heads no without saying a word. Roberta was trying not to cry. Carl and Loreen were in the kitchen, talking in quick whispers.

When Mr. Benbie let the kids go and talked to me, I said yes, I knew what marijuana was, and no, I hadn't seen any here. I told him I didn't think Mr. and Mrs. Rolfsson did anything like that. They'd told us drugs were very bad.

Mr. Benbie asked the same questions a couple of times, in different ways. It was easy.

Pretty soon Mr. Benbie nodded and went into the kitchen. I stayed in the living room and played with Roberta and Aidan until he left, pushing Hunter along in front of him. Hunter was carrying his suitcase. His fat face was white and sweaty. As he glanced at us, I mimed taking a drag off a joint. His eyes got wide and his mouth opened, but Mr. Benbie was already shoving him out the door.

After that day it was just Roberta and Aidan and me living at the Rolfssons'. Carl and Loreen let me stay in my room most of the time, except when I had to help with the kids. I always said I had homework, and after the first couple of weeks they never checked to see if I was doing it.

Tonight it was language arts. The book was open on my bed. The assignment was to write something about the theme of the story we'd read in class. Instead I was concentrating on tying and untying knots in a shoelace using only one hand. I had two square knots and one granny in it already, but untying was harder. I worked at it while listening to the TV. The audience clapping for every guess sounded like waves.

At the Garber foster house, I'd been able to see Davey once in a while—that was the only good thing about the place—but at the Rolfssons' I was farther away and Carl wouldn't drive me. Maybe after school was over for the year, I could take a bus.

The doorbell rang.

"Who is it?" Carl hollered. He wouldn't get off the couch for people selling stuff.

I just barely heard the answer over the blare of a commercial. Ron Benbie.

I was up and out of my room right away. Was it another kid? I'd have to give up half my bedroom. Carl heaved himself off the couch and trudged through the dining room to open the door. Aidan had snuck onto the beanbag next to Roberta. They were both focused on what was happening, just like me.

After a few moments, Carl stepped aside and Mr. Benbie came in.

My grandfather walked in right behind him.

He looked over Mr. Benbie's shoulder and saw me. My head was spinning a little. Granddad had a beard. A big one. It was like fireplace ash. And his hair was longer than I'd ever seen it, almost down to his shoulders.

Next to Carl and Mr. Benbie, he looked like a wolf. Big and lean and mean.

"What's wrong, Carl?" Loreen said over the TV.

"Nothing, Mrs. Rolfsson," said Mr. Benbie, "just checking in." Carl waved Mr. Benbie and my grandfather toward the kitchen. Roberta peeked at the men from behind me. I started toward Granddad, and he held up a hand to stop me.

"Pack up your things," he said to me, his voice just like I remembered it.

"Why's Mr. Benbie here, Van?" Aidan said.

"It's good," I said, and turned and ran down the hall toward my bedroom. I had a small canvas suitcase, given to me when I'd moved from the Social hall to my first foster home. I opened the suitcase and dumped out the old clothes inside and began stuffing it full of things I really needed. My Game Boy. A heavy leather coat, which was my grandfather's but which I'd told the counselors was mine before they whisked me out of our house to Social. A travel set of tools. And from under the bottom drawer of my dresser where I'd taped them, my set of lockpicks. I grabbed my school backpack and shoved the language-arts book into it and slung it over my shoulder and ran with it and the suitcase back down the hall.

The men were still in the kitchen. As I ran around the corner, Mr. Benbie kind of jumped a little. Carl turned around and put something he was holding into the freezer. A thick envelope, I saw before the freezer door shut. Mr. Benbie pushed something deeper into the pocket of his maroon jacket. The pocket bulged and crinkled.

"We're done," Granddad said to Mr. Benbie and Carl. They both said yes, quickly.

Granddad looked at me. "You're ready?" I nodded. "Okay, then," he said, and went to the front door and opened it. I followed him.

"Van?" Roberta called from the TV room. "Where are you going?"

"Bye, Berta. Bye, Aidan," I said. Behind them Loreen called to Carl, asking what on earth was going on.

Granddad and I went outside. His big black pickup truck was parked at the curb. It looked freshly washed and gleamed like oil under the streetlights.

"I haven't eaten," Granddad said. "Burgers?"

I nodded.

He paused before unlocking the truck door. "You all right?" he said.

I nodded again and stood there, uncertain. He stepped forward and wrapped his arms around me and squeezed the breath out of me.

"Good to see you, boy," he said.

He opened the door and got in. I wiped my eyes and face as I ran around the other side and jumped in, tossing the canvas suitcase into the backseat of the truck's cab.

Granddad drove us south on Aurora and parked at Beth's, a diner we'd been to a few times. It was open twenty-four hours, and I remembered that the last time we'd been there was for a breakfast before dawn, after he'd been casing a store most of the night.

The diner was busy. Granddad wore a brown leather coat, sort of like the one in my suitcase but new, and jeans and a T-shirt. His chest and arms looked bigger. I knew that weight lifting was something prisoners did. When he caught me staring, I pretended to be checking out the art that customers had drawn and taped to the walls.

"The beard look strange to you?" he said.

"It's weird."

"Well, enjoy the weird while you can. I'll be taking a razor to it tomorrow."

A booth in the back opened up, and we sat down. A waitress came and dropped off menus. Granddad ordered coffee for himself. "You still like milk shakes?" he asked me. I said yes. "Chocolate milk shake," he said, and she went away.

"I'm out," Granddad said to me. "Out out, not just parole. You know the difference?"

"Kind of."

"My sentence was short. Short time like that, they don't bother with jamming up the parole system. They just let you go when you've been in long enough, by their thinking." He rolled a straw between his fingers. "They treat you all right? That man Benbie, his people?"

"Yeah. I mean, yes, sir."

He nodded, still looking. I kept my eyes on the tabletop. There were little gold flecks under the clear plastic surface.

The waitress brought his coffee and my milk shake. We both ordered bacon cheeseburgers. I drank my shake, and Granddad blew on the steaming coffee.

"How's school?" he said. "You passing all your classes?"

"Yes, sir."

"Any sports? You'd been thinking about football."

"No. I've been practicing," I said. "I can do a Schlage lock now."

He raised his eyebrows. "Oh? How many pins?"

"Just five. But fast."

He grunted. He took a careful sip from his mug. "And where exactly do you practice this new talent?"

I let the straw fall back into the milk-shake glass. "Just around Carl and Loreen's place."

Granddad tilted his head, asking.

"Really," I said. "Nowhere else."

He poured some sugar into his coffee and stirred it. "You didn't take my set from the house," he said.

I shook my head. Granddad kept his lockpicks hidden in the pantry. I wasn't allowed to touch them without him around. "I made a set."

"How'd you manage that, now?"

"Out of some hacksaw blades. I bought them at Home Depot. And a file."

Granddad stared at me for a long moment. I wondered if I was in trouble already.

"Well," he said, "isn't that something."

A bunch of people came past us from the back entrance, talking loudly. One of the women in the group grinned at Granddad as she went by. Granddad turned a fraction to watch her as she walked away.

He turned back. "There's something else I've missed," he said under his breath.

"Did you have to fight people?" I asked. "In jail? On TV prisoners are always stabbing each other."

He waggled a hand in front of him. So-so. "It's never good, prison. But it wasn't hard."

"Not for you."

"It was different this time," he said. "Worrying about you being outside while I was in."

His eyes were so dark it was hard to tell sometimes if he was really looking right at you. People told me I had the same eyes.

Granddad pressed one hand flat on the table. "I'll be making some changes. Different ways of earning. No more face jobs."

I didn't know what he meant, but I nodded to let him know I was listening really hard.

He shrugged. "A face job is when someone sees you. Even if you've a mask on," he said.

Granddad reached across the table and tapped the plastic surface in front of me.

"I'm playing the safe hand from here out," he said. "I'll stick to quiet work. No more guns. Alone whenever I can manage it. And only with lads I trust when I can't."

"Like Hollis?"

He nodded. "It may not be as much money, but that's a fair trade." He leaned back and let out a big breath. "We'll not be apart again."

The waitress brought our cheeseburgers. Granddad cut his in half. I stared at mine, not really seeing it.

"Can I work with you, too?" I said finally. "I want to."

He looked at me. There might have been a smile behind the bristles of his beard.

"You keep up with your schooling," he said, "and we'll see."

I grinned and made my best effort to pick up the cheeseburger without it falling apart. Granddad started in on his fries.

"Granddad," I said after a few bites. "Do we get to live in the house again?"

My grandfather set down his food and wiped his mouth. Definitely smiling. "Nowhere else," he said.

CHAPTER THIRTY-SIX

WHEN I WALKED OUT of the King County Courthouse onto Jefferson Street, Evelyn Tolan was sitting on a concrete bench at the curb, her neat black curls pushed sideways by the wind. She saw me and stood, scooped up her handbag, and began covering the ten yards between us at a fast walk.

It was cold outside, a breeze coming sharp and purposeful off the water and into downtown. Evelyn had put on a beige cardigan over the demure blue dress she'd worn to Davey's preliminary hearing. It had been two hours since the hearing had ended. She had a tense and drawn look that made me suspect she'd spent every minute since watching the courthouse entrance until I showed.

"I want to talk to you," she said.

For the past three days, I'd done little except talk, or wait around until somebody official wanted me to talk some more. Most of it had been done in the building I'd just left. On the first day, right after Dono's wake, Guerin and Kanellis had taken me into custody, against the outstanding warrant for fleeing the scene at Formes's homicide. They didn't book me, and there was no need for me to make a phone call. Ephraim Ganz had been at the wake. I waited in a county cell until Guerin arranged for the warrant to be canceled, at which point he walked me across the Fifth Avenue skybridge between the jail and the courthouse and straight into an interview room.

Since then I'd been at the courthouse eight or ten hours each day, talking to SPD, state detectives, a handful of assistant prosecutors, a captain sent by the JAG office at Fort Lewis, and a suit from the Justice Department who wanted to determine if the line had been crossed on any federal laws. Everybody wanted to know about Formes and his bugs, and the diamonds, and about the bodies of Boone McGann and Alec that the state cops had recovered from the little unnamed island in the San Juans.

And I told them my story, over and over. McGann and Alec must have been in on the robbery. They'd hidden their share of the diamonds on that island in the San Juans. When the two thieves learned that the cops had picked up their trail after Formes's murder, they kidnapped Dono's old friend Hollis Brant in order to steal his boat as emergency transportation to the island. I'd arrived at Hollis's marina just in time to see McGann drive the boat away from the dock, but by the time I'd found a speedboat to follow them, they were already out of sight. Out on the island, the two men had killed each other over the fortune in stones. If Hollis hadn't managed to get free and call me on the boat's VHF radio, there's no telling what would have happened to him.

Guerin's people finally broke the encryption that Julian Formes had on his thumb drives. They found the recording of Davey shooting Dono.

I had asked Guerin if their final conversation had been as Davey had described it. He said yes, that Dono had become furious when Davey had told him about Bobby Sessions and the two skinheads and that Dono had threatened violence. The detective said that even if the recording was deemed admissible, it might do just as much to excuse Davey's actions as to convict him. And that the prosecutor considered the whole incident with the skinheads to be a wash, too far in the past and too complicated to bother trying to get any charges to stick. To Davey or to me.

Guerin also asked me if I wanted to listen to the recording. I had already decided I could live without that.

The various law-enforcement agencies all settled on the same conclusions. Davey had unknowingly set off a chain reaction. With Dono
in a coma, Alec had to abandon his original plan of tailing my grandfather to the diamonds. Alec told Formes to stop listening to the bugs,
and Formes went to retrieve his gadgets and ended up gifting me with
a two-day headache. When crazy Boone McGann got to town, he and
Alec settled on the direct approach—kill Cristiana Liotti for her share
and kill Formes because he was a loose end.

The cops and I agreed on one last thing: If Dono hadn't already
been shot, Boone and Alec would have killed him, too. After they'd
squeezed the location of the diamonds out of him.

Maybe that was the reason I couldn't summon any real hatred for
Davey. My grandfather had been a marked man, long before Davey
got shitfaced and stupidly confronted him. As bad as Dono's last days
had been, his passing had been easy compared to what Alec and Boone
might have done to him.

Ephraim was present at each interview, making sure everyone understood that I was fully cooperating. The cops didn't really believe me.
But what I was telling them did fit the evidence, and once scuba divers
working for the state police started finding black rubber cylinders full
of diamonds two hundred feet down, the atmosphere relaxed a little.

Evelyn Tolan followed me as I kept walking down Jefferson. My
body was stiff from sitting for too long. Evelyn hurried alongside as we
both wove through the early-evening sidewalk traffic.

"If this is about Davey, you should go home," I said.

"He made a mistake, a terrible one. But he meant to help you." Her
voice was tight.

We passed a newspaper stand. A city-council fight over a new stadium had pushed the police search for the remaining diamonds below
the fold since yesterday's edition. In another week everyone would have
moved on and the reporters would stop knocking on the door at Dono's
house. I started off again, downhill toward the water.

Evelyn kept up, the wooden heels of her flats slapping the concrete.
"Davey's not strong enough to survive in jail."

"He'll have to be." Though not for very long. Davey's public defender would probably plea-bargain the second-degree-murder charge down to manslaughter. With the overcrowded state prisons, Davey might be out in three years.

"You could at least ask the judge to set his bail at a sane amount at the arraignment tomorrow. Please."

"If I were Davey," I said, "I'd stay inside."

"Because of . . . of Dono's friends?"

"Yes."

"But you can talk to them. Ask them not to hurt Davey. They'll listen to you."

"Some of those guys knew Dono longer than I did. They'll do what they want."

"You won't even try," she said, catching my arm to stop me. She was so tight that she was almost vibrating. "Damn you."

"Go home, Evelyn."

"How can you do this? You owe Davey your life."

I looked at her. The same wide blue eyes as her eldest son. I felt the tiniest rush of anger, just at the resemblance. "What did he tell you?"

"Everything. He told me about those drug dealers you were mixed up with after high school. And how he went out to find you and get you to stop. He saw you panic and shoot one of those men." She glanced around quickly, lowering her voice to a harsh whisper. "For Lord's sake, Van, you murdered someone yourself. How can you judge Davey so harshly for his mistake?"

I started laughing. Evelyn stared at me like I'd just drop-kicked a kitten.

"I'm more worn out than I thought," I said. "Should have seen this coming." I steered Evelyn toward the park on the opposite side of the street. We jaywalked across. I sat on a stone bank that edged a section of elevated lawn, and after a moment she sat down next to me.

"Evelyn," I said, "Davey lied."

"I know what happened," she said. "I looked up the news story, from ten years ago."

"Yeah," I said. "But it wasn't my drug deal. And it wasn't me holding the gun. Davey called me, two nights after our graduation." I gave her a short rundown of that night's events. I mentioned Bobby Sessions and a few other details that Evelyn might have remembered from that long ago.

Her expression moved away from its taut anger to something like dread. "But you left town," she said. "Right after that."

"Dono caught me when I came home," I said. "I didn't tell him what Davey had done. I should have."

"I don't believe you."

"Believe what you like. Ask Davey someday how it felt, the first time he pulled the trigger."

She stared at me. "You think he shot your grandfather on purpose."

"Your son's a lost cause, Evelyn."

"Dono attacked Davey. It wasn't his fault."

"It never is. He killed that skinhead back when we were kids. It didn't shake him up much. He killed Dono. He has to pay for that."

"He's your friend."

I stood up. The sun was down behind even the lowest buildings, and the center of the city was rapidly growing dark.

"See you at the arraignment," I said.

"I know why you're giving your half of the bar to Michael," she said.

I turned back.

Evelyn nodded. "Your lawyer called us. He told Michael you had signed over the deed."

"That's what Dono wanted."

She shook her head, jaw clenched. "You know what you're doing to Davey is wrong. I think you're trying to make yourself feel less shameful."

"Mike's getting the bar," I said, "because Dono always took care of family."

Evelyn blanched. She opened her mouth and closed it again.

"When my mother fled Dono's house, he kept her in his will," I said. "When I left Seattle, he did the same for me. It didn't matter that he and I had almost torn each other apart. I was still blood."

"That's—" Evelyn said. "Michael was his employee."

"When Luce told me Dono was going to leave the bar to Mike, I thought the old man was cutting all ties with me. Hell, Davey overheard Dono talking to Luce, and even *he* jumped to that conclusion.

"But Davey had it wrong. Dono was planning to tell me about the diamonds he'd stolen. That could be his legacy to me, if I wanted to claim it. Which left Dono free to give the bar to Michael." Evelyn was looking down at her lap. I waited until she met my eyes. "Something for both of his boys."

"You know," she said.

I remembered Evelyn's reaction when I had leveled with her about Dono's chance for recovery. She was a strong woman, accustomed to hardship and loss. But the news had nearly floored her. She'd said Michael's name, because her first thought was for her younger boy. Who had lost his father.

"I guessed some of it," I said. "You and Dono, twenty-three years ago. Why don't you tell me the rest?"

She was very still. For a moment I thought that she wouldn't say anything, just stay there like a bird frozen in front of a snake, hoping it would go away.

"It was after Joe and I had parted," she said, "before he left town for good."

"Just after I came to live with Dono."

"You and Davey were so young." Evelyn's slim fingers worried at the strap of her purse. "I hadn't meant to get involved with your grandfather. He was trouble. But he was also strong, and I wasn't, not right then." She stopped, waiting until the shiver was out of her voice. "Dono and I had broken things off before I ever knew I was pregnant. Marriage was out of the question."

"You've never told Mike?"

"No."

"But Dono knew."

"I asked him to let us be." She stood up. "You'd been living in Dono's house less than a year, but already I could see his influence on you, Van. I didn't want Dono to have the same hold over Michael."

I smiled, without much in it besides the baring of teeth. "Not that it mattered. Mike turned out fine. So did I." I nodded up the street, toward the windowless block of the jail. "Davey's the rotten branch on the tree."

"Your grandfather was a criminal."

"Yeah. And I imagine he put some money in your pocket every few weeks. For Mike. You ever say no to that?"

Evelyn's face twisted. "You can't tell him. Michael is happier as things are."

Dono had wanted Mike to know the truth. Wanted what was left of his family provided for and brought together.

But the truth had turned poisonous. Mike's brother had killed his father. Who the hell would be richer for knowing that? Not Mike, and not Davey. Sure as hell not Juliet or their kid.

I looked at Evelyn. "You're right. Better to let it alone."

"He can't ever know," she said.

"Forever's a long time. For now you and I can carry the weight." I looked up Third Avenue. If I walked fast, I could be at Luce's apartment in time to have a quick dinner with her before she started her night at the Morgen.

"Tell Davey to stay where he is," I said.

I walked away. Evelyn stayed where she was, standing rigid in the cold wind.

THREE DAYS LATER THE city of Seattle, King County, and Washington State had all decided they'd seen enough of me. The county prosecutor signed off on sending me back to the army for local duty. The next morning I locked up Dono's house—my house—with the new police lock I'd installed and handed Addy Proctor the keys. She gave me a hug.

"I'll fight off the squatters," she said. "Just come back safe."

Luce was waiting at the curb in her old Audi, the engine idling. She had the top down, even though the day was too new to even hint at being warm.

"Nothing else?" she said after I'd squeezed myself into the passenger seat.

"Nope." I had my passport and papers and the clothes on my back. "Pretty much what I arrived with."

Luce grinned. "I'd say you've got a bit more than that."

I looked at her, then leaned across and kissed her. "Let's go."

She drove us up and over the hill to Madison and the I-5 Southbound exit.

"November twelfth," she said after a couple of miles. "Six months."

"Yeah," I said. The day my enlistment was due to end. Officially.

"Will you be in Afghanistan then? Or here?"

"I don't know. I'll be attached to the Second here at Lewis for a while, until Davey's case is settled. Then the cops will tell the army I'm all theirs."

"And you're sure the army won't punish you? For being AWOL?"

"Oh, they'll punish me. At least until they're free to rotate me somewhere more useful." By tonight I'd probably be baby-sitting a new class of boots on behalf of their drill sergeant, waking them every ninety minutes to do push-ups and yell cadence. But it beat a stint in Leavenworth.

Luce was quiet for a while. About the time we hit the S-curves through Renton, she said, "You won't re-up?"

She was picking up the jargon. I looked at her. She kept her hands at ten and two and her eyes fixed straight ahead. Her blond hair whipped behind her like a pennant.

"No," I said. "Once they stamp my papers, I'm done." I hoped they'd send me on one more rotation. I wanted to see my team one last time.

"Well," Luce said, and I could tell without looking at her that she was smiling. "At least you've earned a pension. Of sorts."

Talos had been pretty desperate to recover their diamonds. The reward had edged up steadily since the robbery in February, until it reached two hundred thousand. With the two rubber cylinders that I'd turned in to the cops and the others fished off the ocean floor by the state-police divers, Talos already had the lion's share back in their hands.

Ephraim was sure he could make their insurance company cough up. He had incentive, since the reward would be my only way of paying his legal fees, as well as Dono's astronomical hospital bill.

There was some money yet to be found. The cash from Cristiana Liotti's apartment. The police theorized that Boone had hidden it away somewhere. I knew that most of it was still in its plastic wrap, stashed in a locker near a temporarily empty slip at Shilshole marina. When I'd tossed the package to Hollis, I'd told him I thought the *Francesca II* should be bigger than her predecessor.

I couldn't keep Dono's diamonds for myself. I wasn't that boy anymore, the one who could turn a blind eye to the price paid for free money.

But I was okay with the gray areas.

I closed my eyes and leaned back, just to feel the wind rushing over me.

Even after all the debts, there should be a sizable nut remaining from the reward. Maybe enough to get a boat of my own. Take Luce out, point it south, and see where it takes us.

Pirate days.

ACKNOWLEDGMENTS

I would like to thank the following people for aiding and abetting *Past Crimes*:

My editor at William Morrow is Lyssa Keusch and at Faber and Faber it is Angus Cargill. Their perceptive insights have added spirit and depth to the book, and I am very grateful for their hard work and enthusiasm at every stage. The teams at each house have been as welcoming and focused as any new author could hope. Caspian Dennis of the Abner Stein Agency in London boldly represented the work on new shores. I also owe thanks to the sharp eyes of copy editors Maureen Sugden and Sarah Daniels, who removed the weeds from the garden.

This is a work of fiction. I have taken the occasional liberty with organizational structures, jurisdictions, geography, and anything else useful to help the story along. That said, I have aimed for accuracy wherever possible, and I am deeply indebted to the professionals who have lent their hard-won knowledge to the work. From the veterans of the United States Army, those are Chris Cooperider, 18E, Christian Hockman, Bco 1/75 Ranger Regiment, and Matt Holmes, 82nd Airborne, 1st Brigade combat team. From law enforcement, they include Officer John Skommesa from Seattle's East Precinct, and Sergeant Ed

Striedinger of the Major Crime Task Force. In each case, the cool stuff is theirs, and any mistakes are mine.

To my parents, Peter and Karen, thank you for raising me to believe that everything could be within reach, if eyes, mind, and heart all remain open. And to my wife and daughter: endlessly supportive, fiercely protective. I love you.

For mystery author and teacher extraordinaire Jerrilyn Farmer, and the rest of the Saturday Morning Gang, I value your opinions and friendship immensely, and I am honored to work with you.

I would also like to acknowledge International Thriller Writers. It was at their annual ThrillerFest conference where I first met my agent, as well a host of brilliant writers ranging from newcomers to the downright famous. All of them were friendly and generous with their advice at a time when it was most valuable.

My agent is Lisa Erbach Vance, at the Aaron Priest Literary Agency. She was the first in the publishing world to believe in this book, and by extension me, and support us both with her time, tremendous energy, and incomparable savvy. For an untested writer, that kind of validation goes beyond words. Thank you, Lisa.

And finally, my sincere thanks to you, the reader. At the end of the day, it is for you that this book exists.

Also by Glenn Erik Hamilton

Hard Cold Winter

The second Van Shaw novel, coming in spring 2016

Former Army Ranger and thief Van Shaw is thrust into a maelstrom of danger as lethal and unpredictable as the war he left behind in this emotionally powerful and gritty follow-up to Glen Erik Hamilton's acclaimed debut, *Past Crimes*.

When an old crony of Van Shaw's late grandfather calls in a favor, he embarks on a journey deep into the remote forest of the Olympic Mountains in search of a missing girl tied to his own criminal past.

Discovering a brutal murder scene, Van finds himself caught between a billionaire businessman on the one side and vicious gangsters on the other.

In an attempt to survive he will have to face some of the toughest questions of his life, not least over his relationship with his iron-willed girlfriend, Luce. But with the clock ticking, a desperate Van may just need every ally he can get, especially as someone prepares to unleash a firestorm on Seattle that could burn them all to ashes . . .

'Jack Reacher may just have a fresh rival in Hamilton's Van Shaw.'
Geoffrey Wansell, *Daily Mail*